D0066694

Praise for *She Lies Close*

"An explosive, darkly comedic thriller
that belongs on every to-read list.
Scrupulously plotted… a live wire of a debut."
MARY KUBICA

"I am gasping for breath–
what a terrific book. A masterclass
in voice, a psychological tour de force,
and one of the most original
stories I've ever read."
HANK PHILLIPPI RYAN

"Grabbed me from the first page and
wouldn't let go. A fast-paced, taut,
psychological mind-bender that
hits all the right notes."
D.J. PALMER

"The perfect blend of dark writing,
gripping characters and gasping twists
that will keep you reading late into the night.
Doering has knocked it out of the park."
SHERRI SMITH

"A psychological thriller unlike any
you've read before. A perfect mixture of
chilling suspense and twisting family secrets."
JAMIE FREVELETTI

"Doering's wordsmithing is the
absolute gold standard
and leads readers to a stunner
of an ending."
New York Journal of Books

CONFESS TO ME

Also by Sharon Doering

She Lies Close

CONFESS TO ME

SHARON DOERING

TITAN BOOKS

Confess to Me
Print edition ISBN: 9781789097191
E-book edition ISBN: 9781789097207

Published by Titan Books
A division of Titan Publishing Group Ltd
144 Southwark Street, London SE1 0UP
www.titanbooks.com

First Titan edition: June 2021
10 9 8 7 6 5 4 3 2 1

Printed and bound by CPI Group (UK) Ltd, Croydon CR0 4YY.

Did you enjoy this book?
We love to hear from our readers. Please email us at
readerfeedback@titanemail.com or write to us at
Reader Feedback at the above address.

TITAN BOOKS.COM

For my mom and mother-in-law,

Both kind and generous and
nothing like the characters in my novels

PROLOGUE

Rage spills like gasoline inside my head. I am volatile and combustible, igniting from the inside out. My breath comes fast.

What have I done?

I wipe my eyes with my palms, but that only makes my vision oilier.

I blink tears and blood away and hold out my hands, studying them as if they don't belong to me. My knuckles are raw and shiny with blood. Some of it mine.

Overhead lights are bright electric white. A faucet is leaking, and the drips plunk into a rust-stained basin. Each drip scratches at my brain. Air smells of iron and flesh.

The bathroom stall door is swinging, and the lock, hanging broken, clicks against the door. On the filthy linoleum floor, a body lies curled in a fetal position. A tangle of hair, blood-smeared skin and clothes, the faint rise and fall of a shoulder. A soft moan.

Rage lingers, clinging to my hot skin like beads of moisture after a shower.

My love. I did it for you.

"The people who say these cases aren't real, they're naïve. Oh, if they could be a fly on the wall in my office."

Doctor Clifford Paulson, PhD Psychology
Transcripts from the Sixth Annual Conference on
Adult Manifestations of Childhood Trauma
THE RADISSON PLAZA HOTEL, CINCINNATI, OHIO

1

HEATHER

I came back from the dead once in Hunther, Wisconsin.

Don't prime your mind for rotting zombies or cottony, lavender-scented serenity. I didn't watch the scene play out as I hovered, ghostly, above my dead body. And, strangely, there was no pain. Not that I remember anyway.

Because I died once, and it didn't seem to be all that big of a deal, most of my life I've felt comfortable with death, maybe a little too comfortable.

If death were a woman, I'd welcome her into my house, tell her she could keep her shoes on, and share cheap Moscato over ice in plastic cups on my back porch. *The best of friends.*

My memory was screwy, sporadically deviant, but I'd pieced together the details of my brief death from my older siblings' accounts—like taping together pieces of a letter that had been written and then torn.

We were an unlucky bunch, me and my siblings. Cursed, you might say. Only two out of five of us were alive now. Reaching adulthood for the Hornne kids was worse than a coin toss, a statistic that had fortified my intimacy with death.

Anyway, I was six, and it was an accident.

Six. That's how old Emily is now.

* * *

We were driving there now, to Hunther. The four of us in the old Toyota RAV packed with luggage, boxes, too many snacks, and a fishing pole peeking up from the way back as if it were our strange pet. Trevor was driving. Emily in the back, bouncing her feet and talking to Trevor. He handed a Starburst back behind his seat, and she took it, neither of them mentioning the transaction. Across from Emily, Sawyer slouched against the window, earbuds in, hoodie pulled up, face hidden.

Hunther was going to be our new, temporary home.

Trevor's mom was dying. Her oncologist had said, *three months*. Such a strange thing, a prognosis. An expiration date stamped on your forehead, everyone talking about you as if you were a tub of cottage cheese.

But that's not exactly why we were all in the car. Trevor had wanted to care for his mother on his own, make trips back and forth between his mother's house in Hunther, Wisconsin and our condo in Chicago. He hadn't wanted to disrupt the kids' school or my job at the clinic.

The reason we were all in the car was because I had insisted. "Let's just rent a house near your mom. You'll be close to her without all that driving back and forth." It was true enough, but I had my own reasons I needed to be here.

We passed a green rectangular sign. Hunther, pop. 8,553.

No welcome sign, only the facts: where you were, and how many were there with you.

Trevor and I were both born in this outworn town, clunky with its scattering of uninspiring shops, wide open with allergen-spewing prairies and failing dairy farms, and stunning with its clear rock-bed river, edged by old forest, meandering through the town proper.

Trevor stayed in town until high school graduation. I was only six years old when my family moved to a neighboring state. And now, at thirty-seven, I was back.

"We're getting close, guys," Trevor said, excitement in his voice, as if this were a vacation.

"Take Me To The River" played at low volume on the radio—Al Green's remastered version by Talking Heads, eerie and captivating. Trevor had magic radio fingers. Only good tunes when he drove.

We passed a strip of businesses. An auto shop called Doc Jerry's, a stretch of pastel-painted, stand-alone motels in a gravel lot, a monster truck tire leaning against a wire fence, a resale furniture shop called Auntie's Antiques, and a diner named Marjory's Greasy Spoon and Donuts. All those personal names gave off a conspiratorial, fraternity feel. They were in the club, and you weren't.

"I already put our sheets on the beds," Trevor said. "There's milk, coffee, and sandwich stuff in the fridge. Dishes in the cabinets. Your favorite mug too."

He was looking for props. No harm in giving them. "Aw, that was nice of you," I said, half sincere, half teasing. Which mug was he talking about? I didn't have a favorite.

He glanced at me and smiled.

First thing anyone notices about Trevor: his wavy blond hair. The man had damn good hair. He kept it short enough, but his hair gave off a vibe—artsy musician or tough-guy hockey player, depending on the clothes he wore. His eye color was hard to pin down. They could look green, gray, or brown depending on the lighting. His eye color said, *Hey, whatever you want, I can work with you, baby*. His eye color matched his personality.

Emily and Sawyer both resembled their father. Both blond and breezy with chameleon eyes. *His children*, in every sense of the phrase. I was the oddball.

"I can't wait to take you guys fishing," Trevor said. "In the summer, when I was a kid, I'd wake up early to fish and I'd grill bluegill for breakfast."

"Eww, Dad," Emily said. "I am *not* eating a fish."

"But you do eat fish," he said, his tone cheerful. "We literally ate fish a few nights ago."

"That's different," she said. "Wait, did you eat the eyeballs?"

With the sun warming the car, making me sleepy, I tuned out Emily's questions and Trevor's delightful answers.

Trevor was the high-voltage electric core of our family, the plasma ball with its brilliant neon light filaments, enchanting the kids, drawing them near, and rewarding their proximity with a pulsating, dancing light display.

He turned off Route 34 onto a hilly side road. I put my hand against my door and glanced back. Emily was wide-eyed and smiling out her window, still chatting about fish.

Sawyer didn't look up. Probably sleeping. Poor Sawyer. He was not looking forward to high school here. He was supposed to be staying in Chicago with his birth mom, but plans had changed abruptly three days ago. He loved time with his dad and didn't mind Emily and me, but still, as Sawyer had put it, "This was going to suck balls."

This was also going to be an interesting experiment. The four of us had never lived together full-time. We usually got Sawyer on Wednesdays and every other weekend. The three of us were used to Sawyer moving in and out of our space like a ghost. Sometimes he was rattling chains and putting us on edge and sometimes he slipped our minds because he mostly wasn't there and, when he was, he never left a mess. The kid was a minimalist. He didn't have enough clothes to fill a dresser. Didn't want them. All he needed was a toothbrush, deodorant, a pair of shoes, his phone, earbuds, and a charger.

"It's hilly," Emily said. "That's so cool, Dad." I hadn't remembered hills. Maybe this pocket of Hunther was anomalous. Were we anywhere near my childhood home? I couldn't recall the street name. It didn't matter. I had no plans to visit that house.

"Yeah, Em," Trevor said, tapping his fingers on the steering wheel. "We're not far from Chicago, but it feels far away."

"Like a different planet," I said, my sarcasm thick.

Trevor laughed. He liked my grumpy humor.

"Here we are, guys. This is our street," he said.

I read the street sign aloud. "Winding Way."

"Now, remember guys, this is temporary," he said, his voice rich and warm. "I didn't rent this place for the house. I rented it for the yard." He reached over and squeezed my knee. I laid my hand on his. "It backs up to the forest. We're gonna see deer back there," he said with the enthusiasm of a man who had "deer in the yard" on his bucket list. "There's a path back there too, just beyond the trees."

"Oh, no!" Emily's high-pitched shriek broke the calm. "No. No. We have to go back," she said, tears already swelling.

"What is it, Em?" I said.

"Quit it!" Sawyer screamed, yanking down his hood. "Don't be such a baby."

She cried harder, tears spilling fast.

"Sawyer, please," I snapped, reaching back and touching her leg. "What is it, Emily?"

"I-I-I—" she cried.

Christ, spit it out, Em.

"I forgot Lucky!"

Her bear.

Oh, good God, what a relief. This was a problem I could solve. "No, Em. I packed her. We've got her." I exhaled, my heart still hammering.

She calmed, still gulping air, her chest trembling and her cheeks shiny and wet.

"We are only a couple hours away from our condo," I said. "If we forgot anything, Daddy can grab it on the way home from work." Trevor worked an hour north of our condo in Chicago and an hour south of Hunther, Wisconsin.

"You can't let her just scream like that." Sawyer's words ratcheted up the stress. His knee bounced frantically. Sometimes he barely talked, barely moved; other times he was like a coiled spring.

I cranked my head and tried to give Sawyer a pleading half-smile. "We're all tired from the trip. Everyone needs to stretch their legs," I said. "Please."

He pulled his hood across his face, not interested in my bullshit. It was bullshit. We'd been in the car for two hours, not two days. Emily should be able to hold it together.

"There she blows, mateys. We're here," Trevor said, completely unfrazzled. He slowed and turned into the driveway, which was a long, asphalt incline up toward the house.

I gasped.

"You OK?" Trev said.

"Fine. I'm totally fine."

It was one of those houses that had a face, and this one was mean. Over the garage-mouth were two windows with upside-down "V" awnings painted black and shaped like symmetrical arched eyebrows. Wood siding, painted tan. Not flesh-colored, but, Christ, close enough.

He parked, pulled the keys out of the ignition, and turned to me. "Should I show you the yard first?"

I laughed. "Is the inside that bad?"

He smiled and shrugged.

I stepped out, stretched, and walked across the driveway to the edge of the garage. Lifted my hand as a visor against the late August sun. The house was modest, but the yard was huge. It was probably five hundred feet to each house that planked ours. None of our neighbors were out. The backyard went on for a long walk, ending abruptly at a wall of forest.

Emily ran past me, toward the backyard. "Look at all this grass!" she shouted, delighted.

Trevor came up behind me and put his hands on my shoulders. "What do you think?"

I smiled and reached back to hold his hand. "I think she's right. That's a lot of grass to mow." It was a good, wifely joke. Trevor gave my shoulders a loving squeeze. He liked it when I acted wifely. I peered over my shoulder. Sawyer leaned against the car, neck dropped, eyes on his phone.

My brow must have knitted because Trevor said, "Sixteen is a tricky age. He'll be fine. This is only temporary."

"If I had a quarter for every time you've said temporary," I said, turning to him, smiling. "I already know it's ugly in there, I don't care. You know why?"

"Why?" His eyes lit. He liked games.

"Temporary."

He smiled, but his eyes dimmed, no longer matching his smile. "You and the kids can go home at any time. Remember that. You guys don't need to be here."

I put my palm against his jaw and kissed him on the lips. He tasted like strawberry Starbursts. "Let's go inside," I said.

If I could go back, I would have gripped the backs of my arms tight enough to leave nail marks and warned myself, *This place is poison.*

If I could go back, I would have told myself, *Get. Out. Leave the bedding and that favorite coffee mug, grab your people, and get out. Hunther is a diseased tree, its rotten seeds riding the wind to sprout plague in the dirt below your doorstep.*

2

Trevor unlocked the door and we followed him in.

"Pew!" Emily laughed. "It smells funny in here."

No humor in his voice, all sixteen-year-old irritability, Sawyer said, "Yeah, smells like old lady, wet dog, and a cigarette." Was that old lady comment a dig about me? Sawyer could be sweet and cruel within the same conversation. *He didn't mean anything by it. Don't paint yourself as the hated stepmother.*

The foyer was tiny so we spilled into the parlor room. It was a vomit of warm colors. Three lemon-yellow walls. One hombre wall that faded from hot pink to orange to red. Ugly, disturbing, and brilliantly avant-garde. The couch was red, and the throw rug was orange and yellow with red bursting flowers. I felt energized and crazy and slightly nauseous. Maybe I would appreciate this room in the winter.

God help me, let us be back in Chicago by Christmas.

It was August, so that was likely.

A large vase sat on an end table. *Em's gonna break that by the week's end.* Where to put it? There were no high shelves or bookcases in here.

"So," I said, trying to make a good, fun memory of this. "A smoking granny with wet hair?"

"Yep, that's exactly what I was going for," Trevor said, winking at me. "I said to myself, what we really need is a dirty, *moist* grandma."

I smacked him playfully with the back of my hand.

"Let's name her Moldy Mildred," he said, scooping Emily up for a hug and a tickle. She beamed at him. Being swept into Trevor's creative, energetic mind was like being picked as the audience member who got to join the circus for a show.

"Mildred?" she giggled. "That's not even a name."

"Sure, it is," he said. "That's what we were gonna name you."

"Really?" she said, mind blown.

He touched her nose with his. "No." He laughed, spun her, and plopped her down.

Sawyer said, "You could stab someone in this room, drag the body out, and no one would notice."

"Mommy, did someone get killed in here?" Em asked, slipping her hand into mine.

"No, Emmy. Sawyer's only joking. Sawyer, please be more careful with your words."

Sawyer rolled his eyes and left the room.

"I'm going to grab some stuff from the car," Trevor said. "Sawyer, come help me." Trevor, bless his heart, was trying to redirect.

I moved through the first-floor rooms, Emily holding my hand. The house was dark. Lots of wood paneling. The family room had no windows. The windows in the living room and dining room were small, like they'd been put in as an afterthought. The kitchen wasn't bad. The cabinets and décor were fifty years old, oak, but the kitchen lighting was cheery, and a quaint chandelier hung above a cozy table. *You're stretching. To borrow Sawyer's phrase, this place "sucks balls."*

In Trevor's defense, there was not an abundance of houses to rent. People didn't pass through Hunther; they were born here and died here.

During our drive, Trevor had explained Hunther's layout. There was an apartment building on the south side of town, a screw factory and a trailer park to the east, a brushstroke of old mansions on the northern tip, a handful of dairy farms to the west, and sprinkles of businesses and houses all over town. Hunther had two cemeteries, two churches, and two high schools—Hunther North and South. Trevor went to North and played third base on their varsity baseball team. *Go Bobcats.*

I remembered so little about this place. When you're six years old, you have minimal interest in anything beyond the layout of your house and yard.

We'd visited Trevor's parents over the years, but our visits lasted no more than a few hours and we took the same door-to-door route. We never strayed from our route, never stopped at a grocery store to pick up a forgotten ingredient, never stopped for ice-cream cones at the general store before we drove back to Chicago, never stopped at a park or scenic lookout. Trevor knew I wasn't a fan of this place.

I opened the back door, and warm air seeped in. A faint low rumble simmered in the distance. Sounded like a train.

Trevor hustled into the room, carrying two boxes and holding the top one steady with his chin. As he set them down in the middle of the kitchen, Emily's hand slipped from mine, and she wandered away.

"Are there train tracks nearby?" I said.

"I don't think so," he said, gazing at the backyard, blissful. "Hey, you want to pick up pizza for dinner?"

"Pizza sounds good." My phone buzzed with a text. I pulled it out of my pocket, read the message, then deleted it.

"Who's that?"

"Just a friend from work," I lied.

"They miss you already?" he said, smiling. Damn handsome.

I smiled back. "I'll probably—"

Something crashed in the parlor room. I rushed toward the sound of Emily crying, already knowing. The vase.

Broken shards on the floor. Emily stood in the middle of the mess, crying. It hadn't taken her a week. Only fifteen minutes.

My reflex was to yell, but I squashed it. Trevor moved in and scooped her up. "It's OK, kiddo. Anything hurt?" She shook her head, no longer crying.

He kissed her on the forehead and looked at me. "Hey, I've got an idea. Remember that pool I was telling you about? It's supposed to be really nice. Why don't you two go dig up your suits and check it out. Sawyer and I can unpack."

I gave him a sincere smile. He was good to me. "Great idea. What do you think, Em?" I said, thinking our pool expedition might be an opportunity to hunt for information.

"At the first International meeting in Chicago, I listened to other doctors describe these cases. I remember thinking the cases were idiosyncratic and incredibly rare. It wasn't too long after that I found my own patient."

Doctor Clifford Paulson, PhD Psychology
Transcripts from the Sixth Annual Conference on
Adult Manifestations of Childhood Trauma
THE RADISSON PLAZA HOTEL, CINCINNATI, OHIO

3

The concrete edge of the pool snagged the ass of my swimsuit. It was two or three wears away from the garbage anyway, thinning to see-through. In the dim dressing room minutes ago, I had aimed my ass at the mirror and strained my neck over my shoulder. Could I see my butt crack? Faintly, yes.

I sat on the edge, circling my feet through bath-warm water near where Emily happily played. There were movable underwater structures to make the water shallower for young swimmers, and Emily splashed and paddled from platform to platform. This was definitely better than unpacking. And it was a good thing we'd left when we did. It was Open Swim now, but lessons would begin in thirty minutes. If we had driven all the way here and not been able to swim, Em would have melted down. And when she melted down, I occasionally did too.

The pool was encapsulated by a clear glass structure to keep the air in here warm and moist, and there were two doors, one at each end. To my left was a long bench backing up to a wall of glass. Behind that, eight showers in a row with low buttons, perfect for little kids. Guppy Swim was geared toward ages one to ten. A dozen kids splashed in the pool, most of them shouting joyfully, a couple of them whining. Parents were in the water or sitting along the edge like me.

I breathed in heavy, chlorine-saturated air, thinking about that text I deleted and what I should do about it.

The door opened, and a woman walked in wearing a red one-piece suit, holding a Pepsi bottle and looking at her phone. She was young, slender, and stunning. Dark hair tied in a loose bun on top of her head, her wrists covered in bangles. Eyeliner heavy. Obnoxiously heavy. Lips syrupy with gloss. Who wears a red one-piece? I felt like I was watching a Pepsi commercial. Her eyes still on her phone, she sat on the bench.

Chills ran up my thighs.

Becky. She looks like Becky.

Did she?

My oldest sister, Becky, died when she was fifteen, so who knew what Becky would look like if she lived to see her twenties?

This girl. She would look exactly like this girl right here.

No. It's just the loose brown hair, the beauty, the slender body. That's all.

My gaze drifted back to Emily. She was standing on a platform, belly-deep in water, talking to a rubber duck, teaching it how to jump through a ring. This place, Guppy Swim School, was going to be her favorite.

"Hey, you're new," the woman said, her voice scratchy.

I smiled. "Literally. We just moved in an hour ago."

She laughed, raspy and brazen, baring high, sharp canines. Her gravelly voice and the imperfection of those snaggleteeth made her more beautiful. She grabbed her soda and phone, brought them over, and sat on the concrete edge catty-corner to me. Her eyes were striking: an ultra-light fairy blue, rimmed with smudged black eyeliner. Becky had light blue eyes too, but I don't remember them this magical.

"I'm Desiree Moss. Welcome." She held out her hand, and a dozen bracelets jingled on her wrist. She wore rings on five fingers. Her hand was moist and warm when I took it.

"I'm Heather."

"You just arrived in town and came to the pool? That's kinda fucked up." Her rude words didn't match her warm smile.

"My husband let us off the hook with unpacking the car." Quieter, I added, "My daughter broke a vase within minutes of us being inside the house."

"Ha! It's hard for some of us to sit still. I get it, believe me." She spoke like an off-year Camaro. Crude, dated, yet flashy and packed with horsepower. "So, where you from and why the hell move to this dark armpit?"

"Chicago. My husband is taking care of his mother. She's got cancer in a bunch of places. She's got a few months left. So, it's temporary." Look at that. Now I was using the word *temporary*. Trevor would be so proud.

"I got ya. Hopefully she kicks the bucket soon, and you're home by Christmas."

I laughed because it was so inappropriate and it had been exactly what I was thinking. "This pool is really nice. It, well…" I hesitated.

"Does not fit with the rest of the town? I know. It's the newest building we got. One of our wealthy families built it. This couple, they have eighteen grandkids. Instead of building each of their five kids a pool, they built this." She pulled one bare leg up out from the water and wrapped her arms around it. As she moved, her breasts jiggled under thin nylon.

I relished the idea of having breasts like hers. Mine had always been small—*perky* was the kind, yet patronizing adjective—but since breastfeeding Emily, they'd lost the meager volume they'd had. Now they were tuberous, barely filled water balloons hanging onto my ribcage. Emily had drained my sexual appeal, literally sucked it right out through the nipple.

"The saltwater aquarium by the changing cabanas is the only aquarium in town," Desiree said. "This is literally the fanciest joint in Hunther. Maybe that's why I work here. I can fantasize that I've escaped."

"You can't?"

She shrugged. "My dad lives here. My boyfriend. This is what I know. These are my people. They may be scum of the earth, but they're mine." She smiled.

She had to know she could run a good hustle in the city. That she could have her pick of men and jobs. I bet she liked being the queen of this town—big fish in a small pond. Or maybe she truly couldn't see beyond the horizon.

Emily's fingers squeezed my big toe, then her face broke the water like a baby seal, her smile so wide, her eyes so bright. "I got your toe!" She laughed hard, and coughed a little.

"Hey, gorgeous," Desiree said to Emily. "Can you back-float?"

Emily stared at Desiree's eyes, mesmerized, and shook her head.

"Let me teach you. That way you can float with the mermaids

at Mermaid Lagoon." Desiree slipped into the pool without hesitating. The water hit her below her breasts. Her nipples were hard. "I'm Dezzy. What's your name?"

"Were you born with your eyes like that or did you color your eyes?"

Desiree smiled wide and her snaggleteeth slipped out. "You are such a doll. I painted it on. Doesn't your momma wear makeup?"

"No."

I did, but not like Desiree. Her smokey eye was obscene. On anyone else, it would look grotesque. On her, it was captivating. Me, I didn't like to draw attention. Same reason I never got a boob job. Once you have boobs, you are noticed. I would have liked to have boobs, but I liked being invisible more.

"It's pretty. I'm Emily."

"Emily, sweet pea, I'm gonna hold you like your momma held you when you were a baby, OK, hon? Fall backward into my arms." Desiree was fun, but bossy. Like a kid. Like a kid who'd like to drive a red, off-year Camaro.

Emmy did as she was told and Desiree held her, instructing, "Push your belly button up and tip your chin back." Desiree pushed Emily's chin up, and pulled her forehead back. Roughly, like she was positioning a mannequin. *If she got any rougher, you'd step in, right?*

"Good," she said. "Now make your hands and feet relaxed. Pretend they are Jell-o. Perfect. You're doing it. Let's sing our ABCs." Desiree sang while stealthily letting go of Emily. When Emily started sinking, Desiree caught her under the armpits and lifted her up in the air. "You made it all the way to G. Wow, are you sure you're not part mermaid?"

Emily liked that.

Desiree put her back on the platform and hopped out of the pool.

"She's amazing," she said to me. "I have a spot open in my next class if you want to wiggle her in. She could try today for free."

"I'll ask her. I'm sure she'll want to."

"So, where you guys renting?"

"Off Route 34. Near Marjory's restaurant. Our house is on Winding Way."

"Winding Way?" She slapped her thigh, thrilled. "You're neighbors with the lions?"

"Who?"

"There's a bunch of cages in your neighbor's backyard. They have mountain lions. I mean, cougars. They're the same thing, right?"

The skin on my thighs pricked and itched, suddenly irritated by the chlorine-charged air.

Pet cougars? She had to be messing with me.

I was opening my mouth to protest, *Come on, Desiree, that's against the law*, when she said, "Listen to this. I'm such a dope. Until I was, like, fourteen, I thought lions were boys and tigers were girls. I swear to God. How was I so stupid?"

My heart bloated. I couldn't hold back my smile. Shared idiocy is the best kind of connection between souls. "Me too," I said, my words actually coming out in a shiver.

"What's our problem?" she said, playful.

I laughed, then said, deadpan, "You're joking about the cougars."

"You'll see." Her smile was seductive, one snaggletooth slipping free. "So, your husband is from here? What's his last name?"

"Bishop, but you wouldn't know him. He's forty-seven. Twice your age, I'm sure."

"Yep. I'm twenty-four"

Here's an opportunity to dig. "I was actually born here too," I said. "But we moved away in 1991. I was little."

"1991, damn," she mused. "That year is famous around here. Carved into this town's memory. Dawn Young was murdered in '91. You remember that?"

"No. I mean, I was six when we moved away; I barely remember anything from back then." Most people couldn't recollect much of their early childhood, and my autobiographical memories were especially absent.

If a brainful of memories were a forest, trauma went in there with an axe and chopped memories down. For me, it cleared out most of the happy and mundane memories of my childhood, and it spared the most shocking ones. In the barren forest of my mind, these lonely trees were honey locusts, their branches spiked with long thorns, their trunks wrapped in treacherous barbs like shark teeth, warning: keep away.

"So, your hubby is," she said, tipping her chin up and closing her eyes, "ten years older than you. Damn, he made out well."

"Impressive math skills," I said. Seriously. "So, what happened to her? The girl who was murdered in '91?"

Desiree shrugged. "I wasn't even born then, but it's a juicy story. One of our only gruesome stories. My dad's a cop, and I was a bit of a true crime fanatic when I was in high school. The story goes, a couple of kids found the girl under the grate of a storm drain, her dress blood-stained down the middle."

I scanned for Emily. She was jumping from one platform to the next.

Even being this close, it was unlikely that Emily overheard Desiree. This pool-in-a-glass-box-room trapped the splashing noises, and the warm air venting in from big silver ducts overhead softened the shouts of kids and created the ultimate whooshing, white-noise machine.

"They said Dawn Young's body traveled from Crooked River to the pond through retention pipes and got stuck in that storm drain." I imagined a young girl's pond-bloated face under a storm grate. Eyes puffy and piscine. Hair splayed in the water. Blood soaked into her dress and diluted a pinkish brown.

"It was a woman who'd gutted the girl," she said. "But they could never pin it on her. The case went unsolved. Days before she killed Dawn, she'd killed her neighbor's pet opossums. Creepy, huh?"

A memory flickered, sharp and abrupt like a gun's safety clicked off. An image of a dead opossum in the grass, on its side, its fur matted, flies hovering in the heat. Under its back leg, something squirming. Oh God.

My stomach wrung itself.

"Lessons are going to start," she said, glancing at her watch. "Would you like me to tell the front desk that Em is going to try a free lesson?" That she called Emily "Em" caught me off guard. It was too familiar.

"Emmy," I said. "You want to try a lesson now with Miss Desiree?"

"Today?" Her whole face lit up.

"Yeah."

"Yes. Yes. Yes." She twirled on the platform, holding her arms out and splashing water.

I smiled at Desiree. "I guess it's a yes."

"You can sign the waiver when class starts. Should I sign her up as Emily Bishop?"

"Yes, we all use Bishop as our last name. Thanks."

"Got it. Hey, you were born here too. What's your maiden name?" Her eyes twinkling, her tone demanding—the Camaro's brake and gas pedals held down simultaneously, revving the engine.

I'd cut contact with my family when I was seventeen. Changed my last name because I hadn't wanted them to find me. I was used to keeping my birth name secret, but there was no point to it now. I was here to dig up the past.

This is why you insisted on coming.

"Hornne."

"Hornne?" she said, her lips parted, her jaw dropping. "Like a goat has horns? Extra N, silent E?" Her gorgeous moonstone eyes widened.

"Yes," I said, feeling like a spool of kite string unraveling quickly, the kite attached at the end taken by a sudden gust of wind. *This is why you came.*

32

The door opened, and a young guy shouted, "Hey, Dez. Kids are lining up." As the door whooshed closed, a gust of cool air hit my chest. I held my breath.

Desiree rubbed her nose. "Melinda Hornne was your mom?"

"Yeah."

"That's wild," she said.

"Why?"

"Why? I—You don't know?" she said, laughing.

"No. What?"

Her face fell solemn. "You don't know," she said, mostly to herself, and licked her syrupy upper lip. "Dawn Young's murder. Your mom was… Well. She did it."

4

Well, fuck, I wasn't expecting that.

I'd come to Hunther to learn what had happened to my mom while we lived here, but that she'd murdered a girl? Well, that one wasn't something I'd expected to draw out of the hat.

Part of me had suspected I would learn things fast. In towns like Hunther, word gets around. Everyone knew everybody's business.

The other part of me had suspected I wouldn't learn a thing. Secluded towns could be tight-lipped. Filled with people whose genealogies went way back, so that even if they didn't like each other, they covered each other's tracks. Places like Hunther didn't have outsiders, skeptics, *witnesses*, to offer alternative views. People wrote their own history, and in remote municipalities especially, everyone's narrative synchronized like a school of graceful anchovies, a flash of silver as they turned together.

I didn't believe Desiree of course. I didn't think she was lying—she was only repeating a rumor—but it couldn't be true. It just couldn't. My memories of my mom were shitty, but alcoholic-shitty, not violent. A few memories troubled me, but, I figured, if I dug deeper, their strangeness could be explained away.

My mother died four months ago. I found out on Facebook.

I wasn't Facebook "friends" with my sister Holly or Mom, but I occasionally checked in on them.

Holly had posted a photo when Mom died—both of them smiling, Holly's arms wrapped around Mom's neck. The photo was recent, both of them looking old, captioned, *I am sad to tell you my mother is no longer with us.*

I didn't reach out to Holly. I hadn't seen her post until weeks after the funeral—what was the point?

Mom's last Facebook post was five months ago: a photo she took of her legs stretched out in front of her on the couch, her bare feet crossed at the ankles, her cat's head resting on her shin. Her feet were pale, her toenails unpainted and yellowed. A patch of thin, wiry hairs sprouted from her right ankle. Missed by her razor. Her comment: *Plissken's a good boy.*

Her photo came across as either unselfconscious and honest and, therefore, likeable, or it came across as lazy and self-centered. I leaned toward the latter.

My online search for details regarding her death had uncovered a more gruesome story.

Burglary Gone Wrong: Local woman, Melinda Hornne, stabbed to death in her apartment.

When I'd read the headline, I'd inhaled sharply and held my breath, expecting tears or anger or regret because when you found out your mom had been violently murdered, you were supposed to *react.*

Except Mom had become abstract. We hadn't talked since I was seventeen. And I didn't remember much anyway. She had faded, becoming translucent, ghostly, scarcely more than an intimation of a real person.

No strong emotions had hit me, so I'd exhaled.

Stabbed? It sounded horrific. I sympathized with her on a human level, but her death hadn't hit me emotionally. I hadn't shed a tear or felt a pang of loss. Still hadn't.

You never feel much.

I'd told Trevor my mom had died, but that I didn't want to talk about it. Trevor didn't know the details of my childhood. He knew it was not a happy one, and he knew not to probe.

Fifteen days ago, I received a text message from an unknown number.

-Not robbery.

A day later, another text.

-Murder.

The next day.

-She was murdered.

Another text.

-Hunther.

I texted back. *Who are you? Why do you care? Who the fuck are you?* I never got a response.

The number changed every few days, but the texts kept coming. Whoever was texting me was using burner phones.

Again,

-Hunther.

And again,

-Hunther.

I dreaded these texts yet also looked forward to them. Like

blindly reaching into a dark basement crawlspace and rooting out old boxes, I wanted to discover what was in the boxes but I was scared to reach into the dark—would my hand meet a sticky spider's web or something that scurried?

My mom died four months ago, why were these texts coming now?

I received a text like this almost every day, including today.

5

TREVOR

Heather and I laid in bed, studying a satellite image of our neighbor's backyard on her phone.

"Do you see those? Cages," she said, both appalled and amused, tilting her phone toward me.

"Yeah, I see." From a bird's eye view, relative to the outline of this guy's roof and the old pine trees lining the back of his yard, it was clear the cages were massive. They were rectangular, each the size of a garage, and they connected to form an "L." Topping the structure was a lattice of what looked to be sturdy netting.

I squinted, searching the image on her phone for a dark, lurking shape. There were no obvious animal shapes, but overgrown bushes, young trees, and a jungle gym provided plenty of places to hide.

"Maybe they have koalas," I said, trying to ease her worry and draw a smile. "Did you know koala populations have raging chlamydia outbreaks? They are filthy sex-hounds."

She elbowed me jokingly, but didn't bite. "Cougars. She said cougars. What are the odds this guy would be six houses down from us?"

"Yeah, but with the yards as big as they are, that's a mile," I said.

"What's one mile to a mountain lion?"

I breathed deep. Our bedroom smelled like my dead grandparents' house, the wooden scaffolding steeped in nicotine and mildew. "True," I said. "You and the kids should go back to Chicago. For safety." It would make things easier.

"We're staying," she said, her tone easy but firm. "I'm just pissed. What's crazier is that there's no news article to be found on this guy. Nothing. Your neighbor keeps a pet cougar, and no one thinks it's a big enough deal to write a story on it. Who are these people?" Her voice teetered between being a mother terrified for her children and acting like an amused spectator at a circus who could leave at any time. And, she could. So why was she compelled to stay?

"I thought they outlawed exotic pets," I said. "You know, after that shitshow in Ohio where the guy let his lions onto the highway, then offed himself."

"Turns out they outlawed it in Ohio. Apparently, not in Wisconsin. The laws are loose here and change county by county."

"Strange that my mom never mentioned cougars," I said.

"This place seems tiny to us—I mean, it *is* compared to Chicago—but it's not so small that you're going to hear about everything," she said, her voice drifting. She sighed. "Any other wild stories about this place from when you were a kid? Ghost stories or gruesome murders?"

I turned on my side, propped my head with my hand, and searched her eyes. "That's what I love about you—your cheerful, optimistic soul," I teased, trying to get her to soften. "You are all bubble gum and kittens."

One corner of her mouth turned up, her tough shell cracking.

First thing anyone notices about Heather, her severe looks. Like Snow White. Dark hair, cut sharply above her shoulders, dark eyes, pale skin, and plum-colored lips. Snow White, or maybe a vampire.

She had this harsh, skeptical look to her face. Distrustful. Like she thought everyone was trying to fuck with her. They were. Well, at least when she was little. The youngest of five wild kids and growing up in that unpredictable household, she never knew what to expect. But, under that glare, at her gooey center, she was funny, easy, and gentle. She wanted to be a good mom so badly, it was occasionally painful to watch.

"Did you ever hear about Dawn Young's murder?" she said.

"It rings a bell, but I have to be honest with you about something. I hate to admit it," I said, exaggerating sincerity, "I was a bit of a self-absorbed asshole as a teenager." Selfish, really. Just thinking about what I was like in high school made me cringe. "If it didn't revolve around me, I barely paid attention."

"I can picture that," she said, smiling deviously.

I tickled her, and she laughed. Who had she talked to at the pool and what about? At the same time, I didn't want details. Between my mom's cancer and my job, I ached to keep things light. To focus on pleasurable things like Heather's smile, her laugh, sex. "So, the pool was a success?" I said.

"Emily liked it, yeah."

It had only been two hours in the car, but talking with Emily, entertaining her, keeping calm while her emotions fluttered, well, it was exhausting. What a relief to get rid of them. They could be needy, both of my girls. As Heather had backed out of the driveway with Emily, their swimsuits and towels in a bag, it felt like I'd dropped my heavy hiking rucksack. My shoulders lightened. I could breathe easy.

And I *knew* Heather. She hadn't wanted to hang around here, following Emily from room to room, searching for dangerous objects before Em found them. Heather wasn't keen on unpacking. She'd much rather sit poolside, steeped in her thoughts, while Em entertained herself in the water.

So, it had been a win-win.

"It was good here too," I said. "Sawyer and I talked a bit while we unpacked." It *had* been fun. Popping open a beer can, blasting classic rock, unpacking with Sawyer. The kid was so easy. Quiet. Every fifteen to twenty minutes one of us cracked a joke, but then we left each other alone. Our conversation wasn't incessant or cumbersome like it was with Emily or Heather.

It had been a good day. No, a great day. "And I feel good. The physical work of unpacking. All the green, the wide-open space, the random gust of cow manure."

"Oh, shut up." She laughed, tilting her head back and opening her mouth. I loved watching her shell crack.

"Dead serious," I said. "The smell of cow shit reminds me of being a kid." I rolled onto my back, tucked my hands behind my head. "It is the smell of no responsibilities. Of summer baseball. Of fishing. Of hanging out at the general store at dusk."

It was the truth. Today something nostalgic and ancient stirred inside me. Like a bear near the end of winter, rolling over in his dark cave, sensing it was almost time to get up and flex his muscles, to trap fish, to feed.

This town was umami to me, such a complex mix of flavor. Some of my best memories were here. Hunting with Dad, Mom ruffling my hair, making me cookies after school. She had taken care of me so completely—fed me, washed my clothes, put my shoes in the closet—it was embarrassing.

A feeling hit me. A reoccurring memory. Walking through the forest, the weight of my rifle in my hands, the sound of branches cracking under my boots, the cool air biting at my neck, the smell of gun oil and evergreen up my nose. I used to imagine I was hunting for survival, taking care of my girl. Such an arousing feeling.

Funny how when you're a kid, you're aching for responsibility. And when you find yourself saddled with a family, a job, a mortgage, and too many responsibilities, you fantasize about leaving it all.

"That's sweet," Heather said quietly. She meant it. Not an ounce of jealousy in her.

"Hey, while we're here we should get a dog," I said. "There's a Lab breeder in the next town."

"No dogs. Dogs are forever. That's too much pressure."

"Heather. You're married. With children. You're already tied down."

"People leave their spouses all the time. People let the grandmas raise the kids. But abandoning a dog? Unforgivable." There was truth to what she'd said, but she was just fucking with me. One of the effects of your older siblings constantly messing with you during your childhood, when you arrive at a place where you feel safe, you like to dish some of that shit out here and there. Heather loved to tease. "Besides," she said, "I already have a dog." She patted my head.

I grabbed her wrist and dragged it behind her back, gentle but forcefully, the way she liked, as I leaned over her. "I am not a dog."

"You are exactly like a dog." She fought me a little, her breathing heavier.

I slipped my other hand up her shirt, circled her nipple with my thumb, and leaned in for a kiss. Her lips opened, full and warm, and she kissed me slowly while pressing her hips up to meet me.

"I let you skip out on unpacking. Are you going to tell me what I earned?" I said, releasing her wrist and climbing her.

Her lips smiled as she kissed me and slid her hand down my pants. Her hand was cold, but it was her, and my body responded.

"You should lock the door," she said.

"It's locked. It doesn't matter though. Em is out cold, and Sawyer's locked himself in for the night, probably blocked his door with a chair."

"How are you so comfortable with his seclusion?" Her hand was still wrapped around my skin, but she was slipping from the moment.

"He's sixteen and wants nothing to do with his *parents*. Totally *normal*. He's *fine*. Stop talking."

"But he's not *normal*. And I am *not* his natural parent. And he *isn't* fine."

"Stop thinking so hard, Heather. Every word you say wilts my boner."

She laughed silently, small puffs of air from her smiling lips, as I slid my hand down her stomach. She closed her eyes and let her knees fall open. I moved to her side and explored her curves with my fingers. The skin at the top of her inner thigh drove me crazy. It was the most delicate, soft wrinkle of luxurious skin. Barely touching her, I cupped her with my palm and moved my fingers gently, rhythmically, until her breathing caught. "Tell me what I earned," I said.

She kicked the bedspread to the edge of the bed, pushed me down, and straddled me, giving the bedspread one final kick that sent it off the edge.

She lowered her lips to my ear and whispered exactly what I wanted to hear. She dropped her weight onto me, taking me inside. We were a perfect fit. This was how we connected. Not through words—we left so many things unsaid, and words could be useless or hurtful—but this. This was everything, the beginning and the end of us.

She moved slowly. Her pleasure came first, mine after. Her eyes closed, her chin tilted up, her fingers pressing on my chest, she moaned. As her body trembled, she bit her lip, trying to not be loud, and shut her eyes hard. Her fingernails dug into my skin, giving me a shiver.

We were as close as two people could get, flesh to flesh, but in some ways, we were so far away.

Where are you, Heather? Who are you pretending to be now?

"To those people who say these cases aren't real, they want recordings, they want access, well, first of all, there are patient confidentiality issues. Also, I don't like the idea of using these patients. I think this population has been used quite enough."

Doctor Clifford Paulson, PhD Psychology
Transcripts from the Sixth Annual Conference on
Adult Manifestations of Childhood Trauma
THE RADISSON PLAZA HOTEL, CINCINNATI, OHIO

6

HEATHER

We'd been in Hunther for seven days. The texts stopped the day after we arrived.

Someone was keeping track of me.

The thought should have terrified me, but the days had flown by with Emily constantly *right there* and the unpacking, the school shopping, Owen Elementary's "Meet Your Teacher" Day, and spending time at the pool. Any downtime I had, I spent looking into my mom's connection to Dawn Young. I'd made it to the library once, but the newspaper articles covering Dawn Young's murder were dry and nonspecific.

I had more questions for Desiree. She was either busy or avoiding me. I couldn't tell. The two times Emily and I had gone to Open Swim, Desiree hadn't been working. At Emily's second lesson, Desiree appeared seconds before the lesson and disappeared right after, so I didn't get a chance to talk to her.

Today was Emily's third lesson.

I walked Emily into the pool area and, with the chlorinated heat rushing into my pores, smothering me, I felt the urge to strip down.

Desiree was already in the water, eyes heavily rimmed in

black. Her trademark. Emily smiled brightly, let go of my hand, and sat on the ledge.

"Hey there, sweet pea," Desiree said, patting the water with her hands, then grabbing Emily's foot.

"Hi, Miss Dezzy."

"Desiree," I said, drawing her attention. "Can I talk to you after class?"

"Sure thing," she said.

She had a tattoo on the inside of her wrist. The outline of a bird in flight. It was navy blue, not filled in, and the lines weren't clean; it was probably inked in someone's garage. I noticed it only because she'd skipped jewelry today. No rings, no string bracelets or bangles.

"I never noticed your tattoo." It was a dumb thing to say. I blamed the sauna-baked air steam-cooking me to the temperature of slothfulness.

But Desiree was cool and unflappable. She smiled. "My mom liked birds. She died when I was a baby so I got this to remember her by."

I knew that though, didn't I? The way she spoke—carelessly, her words rough, her social cues off—she was the textbook description of a girl who grew up without a mom.

I left the glass room and its oppressive heat and sat in a chair aimed toward the pool. I shivered briefly, already longing for the heat.

As I watched the lesson, I hung on Desiree's every movement, every smile, every wink, every time she touched one of the kids. There were four in her class.

I couldn't take my eyes off her.

Girl crush.

You have a girl crush.

No. It's because she resembled Becky.

As I studied her face, her mannerisms, I tried to picture Becky. Had Becky thrown her chin back like that and opened her mouth when she laughed? Had Becky pinched her nose along the sides with both hands like that when she emerged from the water in the neighbors' pool? Had Becky had those sharp canines?

Quit it with this. Thinking about Becky takes you to bad places.

There were other parents like me, sitting in rows of fold-out chairs, watching their kids. Some were giving their full attention to their phone. The other half had snuck out to sit in their car or run an errand.

In the back row by the changing rooms, two women wearing flip-flops and spaghetti straps, one with no bra, drank from thermoses and laughed too loud. The woman far to my left wore rubber boots and loose work pants. A few seats away to my right, two women wearing sundresses discussed plans for a fish-fry fundraiser for their church.

These two reminded me of Trevor's mom. Judy Bishop set out doilies for tea and always wore stockings under her dresses and conservative heels inside her own home. Sunday, all day, was for church. She'd never liked me.

The first time I'd met her, when she'd opened the door to greet Trevor and I, she'd been wringing her hands, her eyes too wide. I'd thought it was sweet that she was nervous.

When I went to sit on the sofa, she rushed ahead of me

and grabbed the throw pillow, said, "I'll get this out of your way." She smiled too hard while she clutched it in her arms. "It's my mother's."

She hadn't been worried about making a good impression; she'd thought I was filthy.

It was puzzling, but I didn't cling to it. We only saw her four or five times a year for a few hours. She'd asked about my family occasionally. I'd shut her down each time, told her my parents were alcoholics, I cut ties with them, and I didn't like talking about my family. She stopped asking.

After I had Emily, she lightened up. When I fussed over Emily, I'd catch her smiling to herself. A real smile.

She let her guard down more each year. She'd be talking to Trevor on the phone and ask him to put me on. "Oh, Heather, dear. Could you make your potato casserole for Thanksgiving? I just love that."

I'd figured she'd been wound too tight, but she got used to me because what else was there to do?

But had I had it all wrong?

Had Judy believed the town gossip? Had she thought my mother murdered a girl like Desiree said?

"Parents," a young man in swim trunks called, his head peeking out of the glass pool room. "Come on in."

I made sure I was the last parent in line.

"Heya, sweet pea," Desiree said to Emily. "Your momma's here."

"Hey," I said, "I wanted to ask you a couple questions."

Emily took that as a cue to keep swimming. She hopped off

the edge, swam out a few feet, and paddled back.

"Shoot," Desiree said, one eye on Emily as she lowered herself and tipped her head back, moving her fingers through her wet hair. Desiree's authenticity was magnetic. She was comfortable in her skin. Of course it was easy to be comfortable in skin that happened to be gorgeous. "Be Yourself" was a mantra, a through line, of the physically attractive.

"I looked up Dawn Young's murder," I said. "Nothing came up online. Not a single thing."

"Duh," she said. "I mean, it happened what, like thirty years ago, before the internet. It's not like someone's gonna backtrack and write up a story for the internet just so it exists there. And you know," she said slowly, as if I were stupid, "when poor folks get murdered, it doesn't always draw lots of attention."

Her words were eerie, as if she were validating the insignificance of some murders. Like, if she didn't even care about it and she lived here, who else would give a shit?

"I wasn't expecting much from a Google search," I said. "But the library doesn't have much either." Three articles, short and bland. "You said your dad's a cop. Would you ask him for details?"

She laughed. "Oh, my gosh, I used to ask him about his cases when I was younger, and he would freeze. As an only parent, he needed to compartmentalize. Here I was, his daughter. And here was this violent stuff or these shady people he dealt with at work. He did not like the two to mix. I felt bad for him and stopped asking." She licked her wet upper lip and squeezed the water out of her hair. With her arms up and back, God, even her armpit skin was soft and flawless. "Why not ask your mom this stuff?"

As Em bobbed under water, I said quickly, "She was murdered four months ago. Robbed in her home and stabbed to death."

"Oh my God, Heather. I'm sorry." Her voice straddled sincere and flippant, like next she might ask where I got my shoes.

"Did your dad or anyone else ever mention a motive or a connection between my mom and this girl?"

She wiped under each eye, making sure her eyeliner didn't run, and said, "All I know is what everyone in town knows. Your mom was the last person seen with her. Dawn was at your mom's house for a painting class and she needed a ride to work. Your mom drove her."

This detail left me breathless.

I recalled splashes of paint—sunflower orange and seafoam blue—on the garage floor, softening the greasy car-oil stains. My mom taught oil painting classes out of our garage. The garage would be cluttered with card tables, easels, and metal folding chairs. She would fold and store them against the walls, dangerous booby traps for hyperactive clumsy kids.

The piney scent of turpentine lingered in our old garage in Hunther and then our next house. I'd find fine-tipped brushes hardened with paint that had fallen in the divots against the drywall. If I lingered along the side of the house during her evening art class, I'd hear Mom's sarcastic laughter, the tinkling of ice swirling vodka in her coffee mug, and women's sing-song chatter. They enjoyed her class; they enjoyed an excuse to leave their wifely house-bound duties. Basically, my mom ran a prototypical, garage version of *Paint and Sip.*

"Next class is starting," Desiree said, nodding at the kids beside me. "Alrighty, Emmy," she said and scooped Emily out of the pool by her armpits. "See you later, sugar baby. Love your suit. Wish they made one in my size." She motioned to the kids waiting near the pool's edge. "Hop on in, Alex. Heya, Mandy, how's it going, girlie?"

Emily drifted toward the showers. I followed, dodging children and their parents while trying to stay away from the pool's edge.

So, my mom drove Dawn Young to work, helped her out, and then Dawn's murdered. They simply blamed the last person Dawn was seen with.

Oh, look at you. Sticking up for a mother you walked out on decades ago.

7

When Em and I got home from the pool, Trevor was on the back deck, standing beside the grill. Misted in fatty smoke, he was holding a can of beer and wearing jeans. No shirt, no shoes.

"Hey, handsome," I said, stepping out. "What's for dinner, and where's my husband?"

He laughed.

"I thought you and Sawyer were supposed to be at your mom's all day," I said. "I had amazing mac and cheese plans for dinner."

He smiled, his eyelids heavy, blinking slowly. Relaxed. Buzzed. "It was a crazy day. Paulina's husband, Troy, stopped by to drop off a phone charger." Paulina was one of the nurses who took care of Judy Bishop. "Troy and I got to talking, and somehow, Paulina and Troy talked me and Sawyer into going hunting with him." Trev was smiling like a kid who'd climbed his first tree, standing up there on a branch, feeling like a king. "Paulina covered my shift, and we shot a duck."

I laughed. "What?"

"I know. I'm not even sure what the hell happened. I haven't gone hunting for nearly twenty years. It felt good. Teaching Sawyer, walking through the woods with him, it felt really good."

I stepped to him and laid my hand on his bare chest and

kissed his neck. There was a new smell to him, woodsy and musky. I took his beer and sipped it. It tasted cheap and watered down, but good, like the lazy end of summer. "Is that what's on the grill?"

"Yep."

I faked being horrified.

"You don't have to eat it," he said, stealing his drink back, and leaning in for a kiss. His lips were wet, his kiss slow and open.

Sawyer's voice cut through the moment. "There's a small monarch caterpillar under this leaf."

I hadn't seen the kids come out, but Emily and Sawyer were in the yard. Em was chasing a squirrel, and Sawyer was inspecting the milkweed patch that wrapped around the side of the house.

Trevor smiled at me, kissed me on the forehead, and said, "Can we see?" We walked over. I stepped beside Sawyer, so close my shoulder brushed his. He smelled of mint and deodorant.

He gently flipped a leaf, revealing its underside. The caterpillar was tiny, its beautiful striped pattern barely visible. "I never would have spotted that," I said. "You've got sharp eyes."

He didn't acknowledge my compliment. "It probably won't survive," he said, sounding fascinated. "Most get eaten by ants and garden spiders."

"My sister used to bring them inside," I said. "The funny thing is, you don't need a mesh cage because all they do is eat nonstop, so they stay on the milkweed."

"Which sister?" Emily said, suddenly under me.

"Becky, my oldest sister." I'd told Emily I had two brothers and two sisters, but they weren't alive anymore. It wasn't true. Holly was still around, but pretending they were all dead made things easier.

"How did Becky die?" Em said.

"She got sick," I said, heat washing over me. "I don't remember what was wrong with her, I was too little." It wasn't completely untrue.

I remembered Becky dying. That was one tree in my memory forest that hadn't been chopped. That tree had grown sharp barbs and taken on an eerie radioactive glow.

"Where you going, Momma?" Emily said.

"I'm going to get a water bottle and some scissors. We'll bring the caterpillar in."

In one short week, this house had brought about changes in each of us.

Emily no longer asked permission or told me when she was headed outside, she just went. Something inside her compelled her to wander out. She would creep along the edge of the woods, catch small white butterflies easily, and let daddy longlegs walk up her arm. Her knees were often brushed in dirt, and she didn't want me to wash her hair. She claimed the pool water was a sufficient cleanser.

Even Sawyer was spending time outside. Granted, he usually sat on the deck, his neck bent, eyes on his phone. But sometimes he wandered to the edge of the forest. He'd gone hunting today for the first time in his life.

As harried as Trevor was with responsibility, back and forth with work and his mom's house, as scarce as he'd been around here, he seemed younger, wilder. Even in sex. He was a bit rougher. Less inhibited. I liked the change.

That night in bed, as he parted me with his tongue, I closed my eyes and imagined Desiree's slender body was my own, that Trevor was her boyfriend even though I'd never seen him. I imagined her breath catching, her fleshy breasts, and her canines peeking out as she let her mouth fall open. I imagined her boyfriend sticking his fingers inside her, her moan matching my own. Her boyfriend's voice demanding, yet soaked in weakness and need.

His breath hot on my stomach, between my breasts, his voice gravelly, Trevor said, "What do I deserve?"

I was Desiree. Young, without regrets, fast-talking, utterly unselfconscious. I whispered exactly what he wanted to hear before he thrust into me.

8

I rolled off Trevor and said, "Hey, that reminds me. Have you seen the lunchbox I bought Emily?"

"What reminds you? Sex reminds you of a lunchbox?"

I smiled. "It's pink. Little owls. Totally sounds like your penis." I laughed. "I meant to ask you about her lunchbox before."

"Haven't seen it." He stood and shuffle-walked to the bathroom, half closed the door behind him. Peeing, he added, "I'm extremely surprised you can't find it." My unpacking was a joke that hadn't gotten old yet. I had been unpacking every day, but it was half-hearted and uncommitted. I unpacked the Q-tips and our first aid kit, but left them on the floor in the bathroom. I unpacked Em's clothes, but left them in a laundry basket in her room. I was moving us into this house at a snail's pace, one box a day.

I wasn't sure if it was the idea of putting down roots—albeit temporary, shallow roots you can shake loose from the dirt without causing damage—in this town or if it was just this house. Moldy Mildred was borderline creepy.

Trevor flushed the toilet and walked back to the bed. His eyelids heavy, he slipped under the covers.

"I'm gonna run to Walmart for a new lunchbox," I said.

"My car is low on gas," he said, his eyes closed, his voice velvety with sleep.

"I'm taking the rental." I'd rented an SUV a few days ago so we'd both have cars. I'd never needed a car in Chicago; my job and the kids' schools were both near "L" train stops.

"I don't know how I keep forgetting that," he said quietly, half asleep.

I grabbed my jeans and black T-shirt off the floor, dressed, grabbed my phone, and crept downstairs to the kitchen. I was pretty sure the Walmart twenty minutes away in Yellow Valley was open twenty-four hours, but wanted to check.

Leaning over the kitchen counter in the dark, I looked it up on my phone. Thankfully, Walmart was open.

Out of habit, I checked the news. It was a twice a day habit for me, slightly excessive, admittedly addictive, but not detrimental. I checked first thing in the morning to make sure the world hadn't blown up overnight and checked last thing at night to make sure the world wasn't in the midst of blowing up.

My news scroll was Local, US, World, and Entertainment. I skipped everything else.

A thumbnail photo of a woman that looked vaguely familiar topped my local news. Hairs prickled along my arms as I clicked on the headline. Words flashed onto the screen. Her photo, now tripled in size, landed beside the headline.

Desiree Moss, 24, of Hunther, arrested for home invasion and attempted burglary.

Same heavy eyeliner. Same tangle of voluminous wavy brown hair. Emily's Desiree. My Desiree. The woman I'd just pretended to be while I was fucking my husband. An inverted triangle of her red swimsuit peeked out of her gray zip-up jacket.

She must have gone straight from Guppy Swim School to her burglar gig.

She had bed head. Not of the sleepy sexy variety, but of the rough-night, resisted arrest and got wrestled to the ground kind.

Desiree's characteristic swim instructor face was bright eyes, wide-open smile, exposed snaggleteeth, and ready to say something wild or inappropriate. In her mugshot, her mouth was a thin line, her eyes hard apathy. She didn't give a fuck.

I grabbed my car keys and headed for the garage.

9

TREVOR

I woke suddenly in the night, my eyes flying open, not sure why I'd woken so abruptly. Had I heard something?

I didn't think so. I'd been overcaffeinated and overscheduled; even during sleep my brain was ready to slide into alertness. Eyes on the ceiling, I probed my mental calendar. Did I forget something?

No, you're good.

It was true. I was good. Even though Mom was dying, even though things were crazy right now and I was short on sleep, I felt good. Looser. More alive. That bear inside me was awake now, sitting up, eyes blinking, hunger coming online, sniffing the air to catch the scent of fish.

I reached for Heather, but the sheets were empty and cold. She was missing.

She was probably in bed with Emily. That one was needy during the night. Her head was full of boogeymen, and she didn't like this house. *Too many shadows here*, she had said. *All the rooms feel like night.* If the kid had a nightmare, it was easier for Heather to fall asleep in Emily's twin bed instead of waiting for Em to fall asleep and sneaking back into our bed.

I breathed in deep, trying to lull myself back to sleep. This room, more than any other room in the house, smelled like cigarette smoke. The wood floors and mattress were steeped in it. Someone could smoke in here and you could walk in five minutes later and not know. This crossed my mind not for the first time.

I had quit cigarettes when Trish divorced me.

No, that wasn't right. I'd smoked and drank to such an extreme after Trish divorced me that my lungs gasped for air while climbing the stairs. I'd smoked and drank so much that I could barely get out of bed on Saturday mornings when Sawyer was playing with the socks dangling off my feet and begging me for tickles. I had quit smoking to dig myself out of a hole. For Sawyer.

Fourteen years without smokes, and damn if I didn't want one every day.

Thinking about smoking reminded me of the three-day school suspension I got in eighth grade for smoking in the bathroom, which always made me think of Mom.

I pictured Mom showing up in the vice principal's office, her hair fresh out of curlers, her A-line dress buckled at her waist, stockings and sensible heels, looking proper and motherly, a severe look on her face that made me shrink in the uncomfortable vinyl chair. Anytime I had moved, the chair squeaked like I'd farted, which was both embarrassing and hilarious, so I'd tried to sit perfectly stiff and breathe shallowly. I'd assumed the cruel glare was meant for me until she opened her mouth.

Did Vice Principal McCrane think that pulling a child out of school for three days was going to help him get back on track, motivate him to study, and respect his teachers? Trevor, let's go. Mr. McCrane, your office smells like cigarettes, and this isn't the first time I've noticed. Does your wife suspend you?

Mom. Always on my side. Even when she shouldn't have been.

I hated her sometimes, really loathed her, and had good reason to, but tried to bury the hate because her sins were unintentional, borne of stupidity.

It hit me.

Heather's not in bed with Em. She's at Walmart, buying a lunchbox.

I sat up, reached under the bed for my shoes, dug inside the left one, and came out with a lighter and cigarettes.

I'd taken them from Troy's glove box today. After hunting, we'd packed his pickup truck with the rifles and game coolers. His cell rang, so I'd gotten in the passenger seat to give him privacy to take the call. Sawyer was in the seat behind me, his attention on his phone. Sitting there, waiting, I'd opened the glove box. Inside was a mostly empty soft pack, the cellophane like a sleek dress wrapped around irresistible flesh.

I'd held them to my nose and breathed them in as if they were Heather's skin. Five left. It was a reflex putting the pack in my pocket, I hadn't even thought about it. Then Troy opened the driver's side door, and it was too late to put them back.

Now I shuffled to the bedroom window on sleepy feet and opened it. Flicked the lighter, and the sturdiness inside me shifted.

My lips on the cigarette, I inhaled deeply. Oh, the crackling of paper, the singeing. The jolt to my soft tissue, the flood of dopamine in my brain. Oh, God. It had been so long. I blew smoke out the window, watched it curl and drift.

Outside my window was quiet. No crickets. No cicadas. A faint noise in the distance, a rising guttural vibration. Maybe a coyote. Hell, maybe a cougar.

Why had Heather insisted on coming here? I'd pressed her on it twice, but I wouldn't dare mention it again. The thing with Heather, you couldn't push too much. Like two tectonic plates slowly ramming into each other, she was riddled with hairline fractures. Push her too far, and you might end up with an earthquake.

I worried she was digging into her family history. Why now, after all these years?

You shouldn't have brought her back here. This place is no good for her.

10

HEATHER

Walmart was mostly empty. The bright blue-white ceiling lights confused my senses, and my skin buzzed.

The back-to-school aisles had been raided.

Snub-nosed scissors mixed in with glue sticks. Dozens of brightly colored folders sticking out under the bottom shelf. Lime green. Lemon yellow. Citrus orange. Someone must have dropped a box of them on the floor and swiped them under the shelf with the edge of their shoe. A shrink-wrapped toilet brush sat abandoned on a stack of notebooks.

When it came to school shopping, when it came to their own children, people were feral and not entirely themselves. Take me, for instance. I had always been comfortable with ugly things like death and homelessness. But give me a child, and I transform into a bobbing-ponytail sorority girl, anxious about committing a social faux pas.

No lunchboxes in this aisle.

No big deal. Emily could go to school with her lunch in a brown paper bag for a day or two. She'd survive.

A mother in her work clothes—pants and low heels—rolled her cart past the end of the aisle. A toddler sat quietly in the cart's child seat, sucking his pacifier, rubbing his eyes.

Mom and her baby and cart rolled out of sight.

I felt spoiled. Shopping alone was a luxury.

Headed for the next aisle, I let my mind go back to Desiree and the news story I'd read over and over.

Desiree Moss, 24, was charged with residential burglary and endangering the life or health of a child in connection with the 4:43 p.m. incident in the 600 block of Sheehan Road, the Hunther Police Department news release reported.

A juvenile was home alone in the residence and called police to report that a woman had entered her house through a window. The woman fled after encountering the girl. Investigators were able to identify the woman as Moss and arrest her.

The juvenile's grandfather, Marty Gerritson, said of his granddaughter, "She's a smart cookie, my granddaughter. Me and the missus have practically raised her since my daughter died. It's not cheap though, raising another one these days. I've been working at the Home Depot in Yellow Valley, and Cassie is a nurse at Warm Hearts nursing home."

According to a report by the Hunther police, there have been 18 residential burglaries since the start of the year. Hunther Commander Tom Stipes said there is nothing connecting this incident to the other break-ins, but they are not ruling out a connection.

Why would Desiree break into someone's house? She had a full-time job. Sure, she wasn't raking in cash as a swim instructor, but she didn't seem money-hungry. She wasn't the type who talked about designer handbags or shoes or what she had her eye on.

Drugs. That was the obvious answer. She needed money for drugs.

I turned the corner of the next aisle. Lunchboxes! Two dozen of them. And there, front and center on the shelf, like a platinum ring among fourteen carat gold, was a unicorn lunchbox.

Zipper had to be broke. Pessimist to my core.

But the zipper ran smoothly, without hesitation, right along the track. It was a clean, unbroken, lavender lunchbox with a white unicorn, its horn glittery silver, its mane and tail sky blue. Em would love it.

In addition to the lunchbox, I bought snacks for lunch, a pack of gummy bears for Em, and a Snickers bar for Sawyer. The parking lot was well-lit and mostly empty, moths fluttering near the yellow glow of overhead lampposts.

Inside my car, I locked the doors, tossed the lunchbox and bag of snacks into the backseat, and slid the candy into a mostly empty glove box. I'd put a Maglite in there.

I started my car and went to plug my phone into the charger but my charger was gone. *Damn it, Sawyer.* He had a habit of taking whatever he needed whenever he wanted without bothering to tell us. Quintessential teenager. My phone had 6 percent battery left.

That's OK. This will be quick.

I opened Google Maps and searched Hunther Police Department.

"If I'm being honest, some of my patients, well, their stories frighten me."

Doctor Clifford Paulson, PhD Psychology
Transcripts from the Sixth Annual Conference on
Adult Manifestations of Childhood Trauma
THE RADISSON PLAZA HOTEL, CINCINNATI, OHIO

11

Desiree wouldn't be there. Someone would have bailed her out by now.

Even if she hadn't been able to contact a friend or family member, and she remained in custody, she wouldn't be at the *local* police station. They would have brought her to the county jail. Life wasn't an old Sunday afternoon Western—a single officer eyeing a jail cell full of sleeping drunks and sly gunslingers, his single keyring hung on a thick rusty nail—was it?

Turned out, life *was* like a western in Hunther. Except for the keyring hung on a nail. I wasn't sure about the gunslingers. Also, bailing someone out was big business for the Hunther PD. They accepted Apple Pay, PayPal, Square Cash, credit card, Chase QuickPay, and certified bank checks.

But Desiree, she *was* here. Had been here for seven hours. What kind of asshole family did she have?

I put her bail on my credit card.

A door buzzed, and Desiree walked out with a smile up one cheek, as if this had been her plan all along. As if she hadn't been sitting in a holding cell, but had been drinking with friends.

Her hair and makeup contradicted her easy expression.

Her hair stuck out at odd angles, and her smokey eyes were smudged like sunrays.

"Heather," she said, drawing my name out, rolling it around her mouth like it was good whiskey.

"It's been real," she said to the woman behind the glass, pressing her hand to the window. Was Desiree going out of her way to be bitchy or did she know the woman? The woman nodded, giving the same ambiguous vibe.

I followed Desiree out, and pointed at my car.

The parking lot was well-lit. Seven cars parked far away from each other. The night shift consisted of smokers that needed space to enjoy their last cigarette before punching in.

I pressed my fob, it chirped, and my doors unlocked.

"Well, that sucked," Desiree said, her cool demeanor cracking as she slid into the passenger seat. "Smelled like sour ass in there. Piss flies everywhere. Can you imagine breathing in that nasty air all day?"

"I can't imagine. Which way?"

"Left." She flipped down the passenger side mirror and used her fingertips and spit to clean up her makeup.

I waited to take a left out of the police station onto New York Street. I checked both directions, glancing at Desiree for a beat. The sparkly trick was gone from her pixie-dust eyes.

She still wore her Guppy-logoed jacket and jeans over her Baywatch swimsuit.

Oh God, how uncomfortable. Even when I was a kid and mostly oblivious to discomfort, I wouldn't entertain wearing jeans over a swimsuit.

She's crazy.

Not that breaking into a house in late afternoon made her crazy, but wearing denim over a nylon/Lycra blend? Out of her damn mind.

Rolling down my window, I turned onto New York Street. Not much New York about it, but it was a main road, double lanes in both directions boxed in by small corner malls and fast food. Plenty of cars out even though it's a school night. We passed Taco Bell and KFC, both still open, deep-fried smells loose in the air. I should have asked if she was hungry—she was probably starving—but Taco Bell was already gone from my rearview mirror.

Everything else we passed was closed. Pancake Heaven, Something Borrowed, Mia's Dry Clean, Jerry's Bait and Liquor.

"I'll pay you back," she said nonchalantly. Noncommitted. "How much of a dent?"

"Seven hundred fifty."

She directed her entire body toward me. "You're kidding? Holy hell. That asshole. Well, alright. Shit, that's gonna take me a while."

"What asshole?"

"Don't even worry about it."

Seven hundred fifty was seriously low for bail. I was surprised she had no idea. The county judge who set her bail probably knew her. Small town perks.

It occurred to me then, I could have *called* the police station. *Should have*. Called, found out she was there, and pretended I'd never read about her arrest.

"You were there a long time. You didn't call anyone?"

"My dad would have killed me. Since he's retired, he doesn't know the new breed of cops and he doesn't read the news, so I think I can get by without him finding out. None of my friends have any cash." Her implying I had cash lying around irked me. We wouldn't have to move money around to cover her bail, but Trevor would notice. Well, if he weren't so busy, he would notice.

I opened my mouth to ask for details, what came next, when would she be arraigned, then closed it. I didn't want to know.

"My boyfriend was on shift," she said. "He was probably coming soon. Why'd you come anyway?"

It was an abrupt question with several possible implications, one being *Why'd you come here, we're not even friends?*

Why was I here?

Well, we connected. She reminded me of Becky, physically, that first time I saw her. And, honestly, she reminded me of myself at twenty-four. Rough around the edges, a lazy moral compass. A comfort with the ugly side of humanity. Maybe she hadn't felt the connection.

Also, my mom. Desiree had said she didn't know anything else about my mom, but I didn't believe that. Even if she wasn't lying outright, she might know more than she thought.

And, there was also Emily.

"Well, you've been nice to us," I said. "To Emily."

Truth was, Emily loved Desiree to a degree that was disturbing. Nights ago, Em and I had been snuggled under her plush blanket in her twin bed, reading a book, when

Emily said, "OK so, I don't want to say this."

"What is it?"

Emily had closed her eyes. "I can't."

"You can tell me anything, Em. I promise. I won't get mad or sad or anything." Keeping my voice calm while all my alarms were going off.

"OK. So I'll just say it. But don't get sad. Oh my gosh. I shouldn't say this."

"It's OK, Em. Go ahead, sweetie."

"OK. So. If you die, can Miss Dez be my mom?" Beside me, she shut her eyes hard, bit her lip, and made her tiny hands into fists.

Don't feel sad. She's a sweet, innocent kid. This had been a complex question, intricate like a knitted glove, but it was comprised of simple knots. One knot being: she had probably worried at some point about me dying because she loved me so much. Another simple knot being: she'd worried about keeping a family unit together. Her idea of a family necessitated a mother.

Or, she just likes Desiree more than you.

"If I died, you'd still have Dad and Sawyer."

"Well, could Dad marry Miss Dez and they could be my parents?"

"I'm healthy, Emily. I don't think I'll die until you're old. But if I did die," I said, "Daddy could remarry someone. If he wanted." Seeds of impatience and irritation inside me had been wetted and were beginning to swell. "Let's finish our book."

In the passenger seat, Desiree had her chin up, face against the breeze out her window.

"So, what's your trick with kids anyway? You're such a natural," I said. That I was seeking insight from a person who'd spent her evening in a holding cell was not lost on me. Still, I was curious.

The funny thing about memory loss was, it's not only memories you're missing; the nuances of social norms are slightly out of reach too. In this case, parenting norms. I didn't remember how my mom spoke to me, how she taught me, when she was strict, or when she was funny. She hadn't always been drunk and mean. But the thing was, there wasn't much there. I could count on one hand the conversations I remembered having with my mom. This lack of experience felt like I was going through life without a map, without a landmark, without references of how I should speak to my kids.

"I don't know," Desiree said, offhand, aiming her chin to her window as if she had nothing to say. But then she laughed at the wind and said, "I just treat them like adults. They're funny, the shit they say." She turned her shoulders toward me, suddenly amused and energized by a thought, her voice like a steamroller with no plans of slowing. "Like I could be working at a grocery store and hear the ladies talk weather and wrinkles, and customers complaining that I ripped their magazine. Or, for the same crummy wage I could throw kids around in the pool and teach them how to swim and hear the crazy shit they say about how they have a boy dog and you know it's a boy dog because you can see its wee-wee or they hate their sister because she picks her nose and wipes it on the wall by the toilet."

At the light there was a Mobil gas station and a KinderCare.

The daycare building was dark, but a light on in the back shined on a concrete slab with empty red tricycles and illuminated the chain-link fence in the backyard. The third corner at the intersection was under construction. A backhoe stood abandoned next to a pile of dirt.

She pointed and I turned left onto Crane Road, a two-way street, much darker than the last. More woods lining the road, the smell of pine and cypress in the air. The car behind me turned left as well.

Her words kept coming, rough like a roller coaster going up and down a wooden track. "And they tell you they can't put their head under, but you tell them, you can do it, really, I'm gonna push your head under for five seconds. Then you just do it, you just fucking push them under, and they let you because you're the grown-up. When you let their head out of the water, they're so happy they did it. It's nuts." She put one of her sneakers on my dashboard.

"But if I had to take one home with me," she said. "Man, that's another story. I would hate the kid. I mean I don't *want* them to *die*." As if this was something to brag about. "But you know that one guy, cute guy, young, washboard abs, orange trunks, his name's Matt or Mac and he wants you to feel sorry for him because he's got a baby *and* a toddler."

Even as I found her thoughts disquieting, her reckless honesty drew me in. She was a stunning turquoise rainforest frog, and even though she was poisonous, I wanted a closer look. I wanted to touch her skin.

"How could I not know that guy?" I said. "Huffing and

puffing, talking to his toddler really loud so everyone can hear, 'I'm sorry, Ryan. I can't throw you in the air. I'm holding Margaret. I only have two hands, and Mommy's at work because she needs to feel fulfilled and important too. If Mommy were here, I could throw you, but Mommy is *at work*.' That passive-aggressive douche is begging for a pity blowjob."

Desiree's laugh exploded in the car and her pleasure, brute and wild, pinged at my heart. "Oh my God, you nailed it," she said. "That's totally him."

"He doesn't seem like a fit for this town."

"You got that right. So the other day he asks me if I wouldn't mind holding his baby. Actually, it was my fault," she said sarcastically. "Because I said, 'Cute baby.' He said, 'Yeah, you want to hold her?' Like every human with a pussy loves babies. I didn't want to. I just said the baby was cute to be nice because I could tell he wanted me to say it. I said, 'Sure.' I held his baby. I held that baby for like fifteen minutes. And I loved it, that bald baby head, I actually kissed his baby's head, smelled it, which is weird, it's like I'm smelling his wife's residual pussy juice, it's so sweet, it's like beer and sugar, actual sugar, how the fuck does it get that way? But then, like in an instant, I can't stand holding the baby. I want to drop it in the water, get its skin off my skin. I had to tell myself, *Don't throw the baby in the water*. I told the dude I had to go to the bathroom so I could give him his baby back. I was working. Can you believe he asked me to hold his leech baby in the first place? Can you imagine if he asked one of the guy instructors?"

I understood her completely, but at the same time, I felt stupid.

Who tells a criminal they're a natural with kids and asks them for advice?

"Take a right here on Meridian, and a quick left onto Chokeberry. I'm kinda far for you. You regretting you picked me up?"

Hell, yes.

"No, it's fine."

"Dead skunk," she said. My headlights flashed over the dead animal on the gravel shoulder. Split open at the belly, its pink insides spilling out.

"Turn right here, River Road," she said.

No cars on this road except that car still behind me. Its headlights grew larger in my rearview. He was gunning it, actually, approaching my bumper fast. I checked my speedometer, and pressed down slightly on the gas because I was hovering around the limit.

"Bridge is coming up," she said. "Crooked River's literally right there." She pointed out her window. The darkness was soupy and revealed nothing but the sharp, broken shapes of leaves and branches. "After the bridge, you'll turn onto my street."

Behind me the car's headlights wobbled, then swerved across the opposite line. My pulse hitched, and I braked gently to let the unhinged driver pass.

Instead of passing, the car nosed ahead of mine and swerved back into my lane.

He's running you off the road.

I braked hard and swerved onto the shoulder, my skin lit with adrenaline and fear. Small rocks pinged the car's undercarriage.

Tall grass whipped at my windshield as my car bumped and jolted to a stop a few feet short of smashing into a cypress trunk.

In the wash of my headlights, the car that ran me off the road parked on the dirt shoulder fifty feet in front of me.

12

Desiree made a mewing sound, like she was going to cry.

"You OK?" I said.

She turned to me. Blood smeared across her forehead and snaked along the inside of her eye, down her nose. In her eyes, helplessness.

My heart fluttered. There it was again—our connection. It was stupid, of course. And false, but it felt real. She looked defenseless, and the urge to tell her my darkest secret rose up. "Desiree," I said, reaching out to touch her.

The weakness in her eyes vanished, and she swatted me away. "What. The. Fuck. Was. That?" she said and exploded into hysterical laughter, her head tipped back, her snaggleteeth bared, blood dripping into her mouth.

"It's not funny," I said. "And you're bleeding."

She stopped laughing like she had a switch for it. "If we were drunk, it would be funny. Seriously funny."

Ignoring her, I reached for my phone—I needed to call the police—but my phone wasn't in the cup holder.

Please let it not have jettisoned out the window.

I unbuckled my seatbelt and frantically moved my hands along the floor of my footwell.

Desiree's door opened, then closed. *Where the hell's she going?*

I glanced above the dashboard. One of my headlights illuminated disks of fungus growing on the side of the cypress tree. Five more feet, and I would have crashed into it.

Leaning into the passenger footwell, I ran my fingers along the floor. A wad of tissue. A pen. The rounded edges of my phone. Even before I pressed the button, I remembered.

Dead battery.

I sat up in my seat, my heart racing. *You've got to get out of here. That silver sedan ran you off the road. Who knows why? Get Desiree back in the car so you can peel out of here before—*

The guy had one of his hands on her breast.

I blinked to make sure that's what I was seeing.

Under the soft spray of my headlights, his triceps flexed in a short-sleeved T-shirt, and his fingers moved over her breast. Her hand clutched his wrist as if she were trying to loosen his grip.

What's he thinking? Doesn't he know there are two of us? If he was after Desiree, how would he know to follow my car?

His body pinned hers against the back of his car. His head blocked out her mouth. Blood lined the edge of her cheek, making her skin glisten. I imagined the look of horror tight on her face.

I fumbled with the glove box. It popped open with such force that Sawyer's Snickers and Emily's gummy bears landed on the floor. I grabbed the Maglite.

It was substantial, cold, and slick in my sweaty palm. It wasn't the long version, the one cops use, it was medium-sized but still hefty. I opened my door and marched toward them, tall grass scratching my ankles and wrists.

She wasn't screaming. Maybe she was trying to talk her way out of it.

"Quit it," Desiree said.

Adrenaline lit my nerves cold. *Don't freeze, don't just stand there. Help her.*

My senses hyper-alert, I breathed in the resinous smell of cypress, the mineral scent of river water, and his cologne, sharp and masculine.

Aggression thick on his tongue, he slid his hand down from her breasts to her crotch and said "… what I'm gonna do to—"

I raised the torch—he must have heard me and turned—and I brought the steel down on his head. I held back slightly, but I came down hard enough to throw my balance.

As I fell, I dropped the flashlight. Stiff grass scratched my neck.

He fell back onto Desiree, pivoted, and listed toward the trees. Put his hand out to grab a tree, but missed and lost his footing.

As darkness swallowed him, twigs snapped, first close, then farther. Dirt slipped, giving way, kicking loose and falling. Branches cracked. Then, a small splash.

13

"Get in the car." My voice sounded cold and certain—a different version of myself.

"Which one?" Desiree said, momentarily confused.

Under the spray of my headlights, she looked like she'd stepped out of a horror film. Pretty young girl, black eyeliner smudged down her cheeks, hair wild and wrestled, trail of blood down her nose and smeared on her ear, jacket open, flimsy red nylon accentuating hard nipples. *Maybe I'll just stand here and stare at the trees and wait for something to kill me.*

"My car."

I scanned the tall grass, searching for a spot of shiny blue. I found it quickly and picked up my Maglite, grass itching my wrist, the sticky wetness of his blood against my palm.

I looked down the road, one way, then the other. No headlights.

Crickets chirped rhythmically, the ribbing noise filling the space. I hadn't noticed them before.

My car door stood open. I reached in the backseat, grabbed the box of tissues, wiped my hand, wiped the Maglite. Tossed both into the car.

I sunk into the driver's seat, my neck itchy with sweat. "You OK?"

Desiree closed her door. It didn't catch, so she opened and slammed it again. "Yeah," she said, staring at the silver sedan. Her forehead wrinkled as if she were trying to solve a difficult math problem.

Ahead of my car, the sedan's lights were off and its doors were closed.

I started my car, praying I could get it back on the road. The slope was shallow, only a foot, but I have gotten stuck in less than that.

How did I want to approach this? Slow and easy or gun it?

It hadn't rained in days. The earth was hard and sturdy. I pushed the pedal down quickly, all the way. The Subaru jumped onto the road, and I almost drove right off the other shoulder. Another jolt of adrenaline before I swerved, straightened it out, slowed down. My breathing was heavy and wet in my ears. I smelled my panic, both dried and fresh.

My headlights caught the glare of copper ahead. The bridge was brown and rusty, the color of dried blood. I slowed the car to a roll on the bridge. With my window down, murmurs of the rushing river below drifted up.

Crooked River.

I was trying to process what the hell just happened when Desiree spoke.

"How'd you know?" she said quietly, staring out her window.

"What?"

"That I was arrested."

"It showed up on my local news." I sped up, leaving the bridge behind. "I saw your photo and read the story. I figured it had to be a misunderstanding." I didn't quite raise the end of my sentence into a question, but my cadence leaned that way.

"No, I meant to break in alright." She laughed softly. Her body was stiff and leaning against the door as if she were mentally preparing herself to open it and let herself drop out. Her voice sounded reflective, not at all herself. "I checked the windows, found an open one, pushed out the screen, and started to climb in. It was easy until I heard that girl scream. She looked so scared of me." She slipped back into her brash tone. "It's kind of thrilling, seeing a look of terror on someone's face. You ever see that on someone's face?"

Yes. But I said nothing.

"Oh well, she'll survive. She was a tween. A tweenie bopper," she said, barking a laugh, turning to me with a huge grin. Back to carefree. She hung her elbow on the edge of her door and brushed her fingers against the soft ceiling of my car.

"You were robbing someone's house?"

"Turn right here. I wasn't *robbing* someone. I was trying to get something back for someone."

As if she'd done a good deed.

"Who would ask you to break into someone's house to get something back? Why not do it themselves?"

She laughed again, like a punctuation mark, loud and brief. "Whoever would ask you to do something like that isn't your friend," she said, sing-song and teasing. "Your mother ever say stuff like that, Heather?" Her taunting tone caught me off guard.

"Not that I remember."

"So why did your family leave Hunther?"

"My sister died. We moved away soon after."

That's what I'd assumed. But maybe we left Hunther because of Dawn Young's murder. Maybe the accusations and rumors were too much for Mom to bear. Another thought bubbled up. Maybe Dawn Young's murder was related to Becky's death in some way. Becky died about a month after Dawn.

"She buried here? Your sister?"

"Cremated."

"My place is up ahead. First right after the Stop-N-Go."

We drove in silence for a minute. She pointed to an apartment building, and I pulled into the lot. Now that my pulse was calm, my mind shifted to logic.

"OK. Here's what we'll do. We'll go in and call the police. It's got to be now because—"

"Hell, no, we're not." She laughed. She opened the door and stepped out.

She'd spent her entire day at the police station and didn't want to go back for another chat. I understood her hesitancy.

"Listen, Desiree. We did nothing wrong. This was not your fault. He pushed you against his car, assaulted you, and I hit him with the Maglite. They'll find his car. If he's OK, they need to know there's this asshole out there. And if he's not, well, we don't want to get in trouble."

He's not OK. You heard the splash. You heard how fast that river picked up. Under the bridge, it was rushing.

"Is that what you think happened?"

She slammed the passenger door shut and peered in through the window. "No way are we calling the police." She held the window. Her fingernails, black paint chipped, still looked pretty.

"What do you mean, *no way*?"

She sighed like I was slowing her down, like it was obvious. "That guy you whacked? That was my boyfriend's brother."

"Wait, what? You *know* him?"

"Uh-huh."

"What? Why didn't you tell me? I thought some lunatic cut us off and assaulted you."

Had I misinterpreted the scene?

"Well, I mean, when he's high," she said, the one side of her mouth sliding up, her high canine exposed in a way reminiscent of a woman sliding up her dress to bare her thigh. "He likes to get rough."

"You shouted 'Quit it.'"

"I wasn't into it. Hello? I've got blood dripping down my face. I've been in a nasty cell for hours." As if I were the crazy one.

"Oh God, Desiree. We have to call the police. Now."

"I gotta pee so bad. And I still can't believe you whacked him," she said and laughed, but it was hollow. "He's gonna be pissed." Her liquid eyes flashed awe and a glimmer of fear.

Why didn't she tell me this as his body was snapping twigs and tumbling down the embankment?

But I guess I knew why. *Abusive relationship*. He'd run us off the road and pinned her against the car—neither were normal behaviors. Unhealthy relationships came in thirty-two flavors, and, no matter the flavor, the recipe called for equal parts need and revulsion. Equal parts adoration and fear. Love and hate.

Half of her might have wanted him dead. Maybe he'd

threatened to tell his brother that she was the one who'd come on to him first.

And who knew what the other half of her wanted? Maybe he was the wild brother, the dangerous brother, the hotter brother, the one who she'd secretly wanted for years, only to settle for his kinder, gentler sibling.

And what kind of disloyal asshole stabbed his own brother in the back?

"Now you really regret picking me up," she said, tapping the roof of my car. Behind her, the building was dark. Three stories. Brown siding. A dog barked from somewhere inside.

Yes, indeed.

"Oh, and I didn't kill your mom," she said softly. "In case that's what you're thinking."

"What? *What?* Of course you didn't. God."

"I'm not violent. I've never killed anyone," she said. She turned away and walked to the door of her apartment building. Seconds later, she disappeared inside.

Maybe that thought should have crossed my mind. My mom was murdered during a home invasion. Desiree broke into someone's house today. I missed things sometimes.

An image of my mother came to mind. My mother leaning over, elbows on the kitchen counter, her leopard print bathrobe revealing sloppy, blotchy-skinned cleavage. Long fingers, one ringed with a purple crystal, and raggedy unpainted nails wrapping around the handle of her coffee mug, the inner rim stained brown. The mug was usually filled with her signature drink—vodka and peach crystal light. The brownish-peach powder dusted the countertops and hung in the air. I'd bite a hangnail off my finger and taste sweet peach. My mom's smile was forced, and her eyes were empty. The image filled me with a kind of terror and hollowness.

My mother. My family.

I'd kept the hose kinked on my family memories for a long time. The pressure coming through was suddenly too much, and I let the hose slip away. It uncoiled wildly, thrashing, and my memories burst in a fast spray.

14

I left home eleven years after Becky died, five years after Rodney drove our station wagon into Tucker Pond and drowned, and six days after a roadside bomb blew Shane to pieces a world away.

I was in the throes of impulsive teenage fury, but what tormented me most was the imminence of Shane's funeral. Make me homeless, cut another child-shaped hole into my parents' atrophied hearts, never see my one remaining sibling again, but please, no, don't make me go to another funeral.

It was the *party* aspect of it that I couldn't bear, the forced sense of community that people so enjoyed.

Mrs. Trair brought her oatmeal scotchies. They're delish!

Brad Pike, I have never seen you look more handsome. That tie brings out the green in your eyes.

At all good parties, there were snacks. Funerals were no exception. Death whispered in mourners' ears, "You know what would be *perfect*? Cold cuts."

There was gatekeeping at parties, usually to the best alcohol or the coziest seats. At funerals, access to deli meats, cheese squares, cookies, and coffee in the back room was selective. You had to be tight with the deceased to garner a backstage pass.

By this point, I'd been to Death's party twice before. Fool me three times.

I'd left a note on the kitchen table the night before Shane's funeral. *I can't stand another funeral. I'm sorry. I'm leaving.* So they knew I didn't get kidnapped. It was cruel to leave, yes, but at least I'd left a note.

I stole the money my dad hid in his sock drawer ($145) and hitchhiked to Chicago.

I ran away in a fitful, childish rage, but I stayed away because, when my inner storm settled, from a distance, I was able to clearly see what had seemed blurry up close for years. I'd felt lonelier being near my family than being alone.

When most of them were around, before they started dying off, my older siblings occasionally reminisced about their own youth: that one time Becky fell on Rodney in the haunted house and peed on him; that one time Dad joined the kids in the kiddie pool, going for a running belly flop onto a tube, but ended up popping the pool; and that time Mom threw a Halloween party for the neighborhood, dressed like a cow, and served root beer smoking with dry ice, a separate cauldron filled with root beer and whiskey for the adults.

Trouble was, these fun Hornne memories didn't include me. I hadn't been born yet. The mother I remembered was hot-tempered, sarcastic, exhausted, or drunk.

Born too late, the party was already over before I was old enough to join in. My siblings laughed about these earlier, pre-Heather times. I wanted in on those pre-Heather days too, that family bonding, the silliness, my parents' good-natured smiles, except it seemed I marked the end of that particular party.

Rodney was the oldest. Becky came one year later. Shane came two years later. Holly, another year later. Everyone thought my parents were done, but five years later, they had another girl and named her Heather.

What had I done to crash the party?

Maybe I'd done something repugnant when I was three or four years old. Something like dropping one of our outdoor cats in the dryer, shutting the door, and pressing the "on" button.

I'd assumed they'd been waiting for the right time, when I was old enough, to tell me what had happened, and it would explain their distaste for me. It would explain why I'd catch my mom studying me, and when she was caught, she would squeeze out a strained smile. But when Becky died, the secret they'd been waiting to tell me shriveled under the weight of Becky's blue, bloated corpse.

After years on my own, I'd decided there'd been no secret.

They'd treated me strangely because I *was* somewhat strange. Quiet in a sulky way. Too loud at the wrong times. Too desperate for inclusion. Spacey. Missing something crucial related to social perception. OK, annoying.

I would steal Holly's senior high school yearbook when she was out with friends. I'd sneak it into the bathroom as if I were looking at porn. I'd flip the shiny, starchy-smelling pages and read all the things she'd *left* in her Dixon South High School Will and try to guess their meaning.

Brandy Candy: to you I leave my floody "mikes," forever froggies, toothpick undies, smarties in the stall, and iceberg in my teeth. Leann:

dog pee, lollipops behind your window, and cinnamon palm tree birthday.
Chrissy: your humping horn-rimmed glasses, and riding dragons.

I couldn't break a single code. *Cinnamon palm tree birthday* was a metaphor for my childhood confusion.

After I left, Mom and Dad never came looking for me. At the time, I had taken their lack of looking as a silent wink and a nod. Like letting a friendship suffocate under the weight of distance. Both parties knew it was a friendship of circumstance, so when one of you moved, it was a silent promise, a sigh of relief, that neither of you would reach out to each other.

In hindsight, Mom and Dad had probably only been too drunk, crippled with depression, and exhausted to look for me. When I'd left, Dad was fifty-six, Mom was forty-nine, but they'd both looked old. American Gothic weary, with a bottle of vodka instead of a pitchfork.

And with each passing year away and on my own, I'd felt more relaxed, less ashamed, and less of a moron. I'd realized, yes, I was sort of odd, but it was them, not me. My parents and Holly were all that was left, and Holly and I were never close. It wasn't a difficult decision. I no longer wanted to be found.

15

I pulled into the Stop-N-Go to call the police.

Desiree was either in shock or she was crazy. Her boyfriend's brother, whom she sometimes fucked, could be drowning, and she's laughing? She's crazy.

You, though, are not. You have to call the police. You have everything to lose.

Two topless skeletal guys loitering outside in front of the Stop-N-Go warded me off as if they weren't real people but skulls staked into dusty forbidden ground, an omen of warning. Americans who looked like they were starving scared me. Even when I was homeless, I ate the colors of the rainbow. If you're not afraid to get dirty, grocery store dumpsters hold treasures of unattractive produce and one-day expired yogurt, milk, and cheese.

I pulled out of the lot again, telling myself I'd call when I got closer to home.

I reworked my way back to the bridge, reminding myself, *River Road, Chokeberry, Meridian, Crane, New York.*

After the bridge, I slowed down.

Please let him not be dead. Please let him have climbed up the embankment and driven away.

No headlights behind me or in front of me, I eased along at

ten miles per hour so I wouldn't miss his sedan.

A rusty beater would have fit my narrative better. *When he gets high, he likes to get rough.* But her boyfriend's brother drove a silver Infiniti. New and shiny, like he'd run it through a car wash this week. Like he wanted his car to look nice for his respectable job at Hunther South Bank or Oak State Insurance.

Please let him not be dead.

My headlights washed over the Infiniti, and my heart pounded. I slowed to a crawl.

What if he's gasping for his last breath right now?

You're not going to stop and climb down that embankment. Don't even think about it.

I inched past his car.

A figure stood at the rear of the car, both hands on the trunk, head hung, clothes filthy and clinging.

My pulse pounded in my head.

It was him.

He lifted his head, and our eyes connected. I froze, unable to move fast enough. Oh, God. His eyes narrowed, and he clenched his jaw. He looked pissed. I pressed down on the gas pedal and sped down River Road, slowing only when I realized I was doing ninety miles per hour.

Well, at least you didn't kill him.

Yeah, but what if he holds grudges?

16

It was still dark out.

I grabbed my keys and was headed out the door when I spotted Heather's phone in the charger. If she didn't have her alarm set beside her, how did she expect she'd get Em to school on time?

I grabbed her phone and walked upstairs. Heather and Emily were nestled in Emily's twin bed, their legs tangled, Em's arm flung across Heather's chest.

Funny that Heather hadn't wanted kids. I mean, it made sense. She didn't like her parents; why would she want to become one? She had a bunch of rabid, dangerous siblings. She hadn't even liked kids when she *was* a kid.

I had to talk her into it. Beg a little.

And look at her now. She loved this kid so much. She was good to Sawyer too. Being a stepmom to a teenager was tricky, but Heather was managing it gracefully. She wasn't meddlesome or overbearing; she was hands-off. She was just *there*. Sometimes that was all a teen needed: the sturdiness of an unreactive, mellow, barely parenting parent. And maybe, just maybe, this twenty-four-seven time together would be good for Heather and Sawyer.

I placed her phone beside Emily's bed and crept out. Closed the door quietly behind me.

Driving away from our house in the cool dark with my window down, I swore I heard a deep, rumbling growl. It stirred something deep inside my brain, waking me up. It pissed me off too. On top of everything I was trying to manage, now I had to worry about the actual safety of my family because there were cougars down the street.

Hey, what do you say if you were to drive south, past work, past Chicago, and head for The Keys? Leave this headache behind.

I imagined a modest boat, a cooler of beer, and my fishing pole. Oh, God, fishing sounded good. Fishing all day long, all week long, was the polar opposite of my current situation.

You can't leave. You have loose ends to knot. If you can make it through this brief rough patch, life will settle back into place. This is temporary.

I stopped at a gas station on the south side of Hunther. Set up my pump, and leaned against my door while my car guzzled gas.

The sun peeked over the east horizon like the tip of a fingernail, bathing everything in soft bluish light. A semi idled at a pump nearby. I inhaled the morning air, the dirty smell of diesel and the cow manure that I did love, God's honest. It smelled of wide-open freedom and riding my ten-speed fast and, years later, driving my pickup truck with the windows down, tires kicking up dust, music so loud I couldn't think straight.

I'd always loved gas stations. Like airports, gas stations offered that strange transitory mingling of humans, so much possibility, a feeling of precipice. And I'd met Heather at a gas station.

On the way to an interview years ago, I'd been preoccupied,

hadn't checked the fuel gage and ran out of gas. Only a mile away from the station, I hadn't bothered calling a ride. I'd already messed up the interview. I'd never make it in time, so why waste money on a cab? It was summer, I was wearing a suit, and that one-mile walk under mid-day sun was sweatier than I'd expected. After I filled a plastic jug with gas, I bought a Slurpee, and sat at the picnic bench out front under shade. "Super Bass" by Nicki Minaj blared through the outdoor speakers.

Heather pulled up in a crappy car and got out to pump gas. She wore flip-flops and ugly sunglasses, her hair up in a messy bun. Since Trish had divorced me for that rich asshole and his Mercedes, nonmaterialistic women had become a serious turn-on.

I waved at her. She saw me, but ignored me completely. She was watching the gallons tick away as gas pumped.

I approached her, carrying my gasoline, my suit jacket, and my Slurpee. I stopped a dozen feet away. I wasn't the type that appeared intimidating, but still, I had manners. "My car broke down a mile north. If you're headed that way, would you give me a lift?"

She laughed. "Uh, no. That might be the craziest thing anyone's ever asked me with a straight face."

"Really?"

"Really," she said. "And sitting at a gas station around here, drinking that, that cherry Slurpee, wearing your fancy clothes, you're gonna get beat up." She gave off an easy vibe. She fell in that sweet spot between *kindness* and *didn't give a shit*. She couldn't have been more different from Trish.

"No one's gonna beat me up," I said, deadpan, "not with this song playing."

She laughed. "Yeah, you're probably right. But this song won't last forever." She'd glanced at my hair.

"Would you like to grab a coffee some time?"

She tilted her head and skewed her eyes. "I'm not a sex worker."

"No, I know. I'm not a creep."

She lifted her eyebrows and whistled. "Whatever you say." Her voice, her eyes, her expression: she was funny and no-nonsense.

I hadn't been looking for a relationship. Since Trish and I divorced, I was completely devoted to Sawyer. But, like a jolt of electricity, I was suddenly captivated. Infatuated. Ready to dive in.

I tossed the Slurpee in the garbage, set down my jug of gasoline, and grabbed the pen out of my shirt pocket. I propped my jacket against a gas pump, and wrote on it.

I laid my suit jacket on the ground as if I were a waiter setting a table, then I stepped back. "You're right, I seem sort of crazy. I'm not." I smiled. "Well, not in a bad way. My number is written inside my jacket. Call me or don't."

She studied me, judgmental, slightly annoyed. Her pump clicked off, and she pulled the nozzle from her car, rested it in the pump. "I'll think about it," she said casually but made no move to pick up my jacket.

"It's a good song though, isn't it?" I said. "Makes you feel like nothing is as serious as you think." I grabbed my jug of gasoline and walked to the highway.

She rang the next day.

"You called," I said, my heart fluttering.

"It's a nice jacket," she'd said. "I figured you wanted it back."

Heather. She made me laugh. She was wary and skeptical, but warm. And her nonmaterialistic approach to life had never wavered like Trish's had. Heather moved through life as if she didn't notice *things*, as if she was too busy with whatever was going on inside her head. She was an old soul who had already lived a few different lives.

I didn't want her to lose herself here. I didn't want to lose her.

"When people say, 'There's no evidence. They've never found a body,' that's baloney. They found a body in Detroit of a child just last month. In my own town, we had a case. There have been cases and there have been bodies."

Doctor Clifford Paulson, PhD Psychology
Transcripts from the Sixth Annual Conference on
Adult Manifestations of Childhood Trauma
THE RADISSON PLAZA HOTEL, CINCINNATI, OHIO

17

HEATHER

My phone alarm was going off, bell chimes on low volume, and before I opened my eyes, I had that *Where am I?* moment. It was exacerbated by the recent move to Hunther.

For a moment I was back sleeping on the rough carpet of the Holy Spirit Catholic Church's soundproof room for families. Churches, excessively vacant at night, made the best hiding places.

Then I was sleeping in my parents' hallway closet in our home in Hunther, the shelf bulging with bath towels three feet above my head. Dark brown shag carpet beneath my blanket and pillow. Walls closing me in on three sides, bifold doors protecting my vulnerable side. This bed was one I'd loved and hated, one that was both the coziest secret fort and a cruel joke.

Next, it's our king-size bed in our Chicago condo, white waves of billowing comforter and too many pillows. The overhead fan whirling fast, urging me to snuggle deeper under my comforter. The rumbling vibration of the train every twenty minutes, soothing, regular, rocking me to sleep.

I breathed in the sugary smell of my daughter, and felt hot skin against my bare stomach.

Emily's bed.

I opened my eyes. She'd turned herself perpendicular, and

her tiny, soft foot was flush against my stomach.

I reached down and felt the outline of my phone case on the floor and turned off my alarm. I didn't remember putting it there.

Trevor. I was already playing it out. He'd woken at the crack of dawn to beat rush hour.

When he'd been scurrying through the kitchen, gathering his briefcase and making his coffee for the road, he'd found my phone drowning in a puddle of cords at our charging station. So, he'd set my alarm, snuck in quietly, and placed it on the floor beside me. Thoughtful.

7:02 a.m. I had two hours to get Em to school.

Trevor was long gone. Sawyer's bus came at seven, so he was gone by now too, which I felt bad about. His first day of school, a junior at a new high school, and his stepmom didn't even get up to wish him luck, to make him a quick plate of scrambled eggs, or give him five bucks for lunch.

I could imagine him, pouring cornflakes into a big bowl, overpouring his milk as always, and scooping it into his mouth as he stared out at the wide green backyard and thought of his birth mom. She had been arrested for theft at Nordstrom, stealing a Louis Vuitton, and sentenced to three months in Cook County's Women's Correctional. It would have been hilarious had it not been so sad.

You have to do better by him.

My arms and ankles itched as if I'd rolled down a grassy hill. I hadn't bothered with a bath last night.

Sun burned softly through the curtains, easing Em's room into daylight, but she might sleep another half hour. I rolled out of her bed slowly, stealthy as a cat, and closed the door behind me.

Keeping the bathroom lights off, I turned the faucet to hot, peeled off my clothes, and lowered myself in.

I squirted Sawyer's body wash into the water, inhaling deeply—the masculine, spicy scent relaxed me. A faint smear of red-brown stained my palm. Blood. I scrubbed it away. I laid my head back on the ledge and closed my eyes.

Last night.

The warm, cushy comfort of lingering sleep fell away. My pulse quickened, and worry gnawed at me.

You hit a dangerous man with a steel flashlight. How much you wanna bet his head is throbbing right now and he's cursing you?

Last night.

Desiree's words played in my mind. *Oh, and I didn't kill your mom. In case that's what you're thinking. I'm not violent. I've never killed anyone.*

As if those last two statements were bound. Cause and effect. They weren't.

It would have been so much simpler to talk to my mom when she was alive. Ask her why she drank. I never asked. I never asked her about Becky's death. It had already been so painful. Part of me hadn't wanted to cause her pain, part of me was scared of her, and the remaining part of me was scared of her answers.

My mind searched for lost pieces to the puzzle of my mother. I didn't remember hearing of a girl's murder. I didn't remember police stopping by our Hunther home.

The dead opossums though, I remembered them. Desiree said my mom had killed the neighbor's opossums days before she killed Dawn.

I'd stood in the grass, flies hovering over their bodies in the heat, the smell of grass overpowering any animal smell. They had been laid in the grass, side by side, trinkets scattered about them. Playing cards. Eight of spades. Queen of hearts. A few rocks splashed with paint. A red crystal. A rabbit's foot.

Rodney had stood, bare-chested, beside me, wiry hair poking out from his armpit, meaty and sour smelling. There was a smattering of acne on his shoulder, and a drip of sweat rolling down his red cheek.

Mom wasn't in this memory though.

I searched for any memory of my mom with animals.

A stray cat used to come by. Long-haired and mangy, fleas jumping in his fur. My mom and sisters called him Barry Manilow. Mom used to scratch under his neck. We took in two stray dogs, later; this was later, after Becky died, after we left Hunther. The dogs stayed in the yard, but my mom filled their water bowls and tossed them chunks of raw, stinking hot dog.

My mom enjoyed our outdoor cats and dogs. She'd hike up her dress, sit crisscross and barefoot in the grass, and rub their mangy fur. She'd laugh if they snuck a lick of her cheek or neck. Tell them, "No licking me with that filthy mouth," but she was smiling and laughing all the while. I couldn't imagine her killing her neighbor's opossums.

A brushing noise beside the tub startled me.

Emily sat on the toilet, her eyes half-closed, her hair sticking up in a cartoonish way. Her underpants trapped at her knees, her little feet splayed apart, her toes flexed. She's holding herself up, had a hand on each side of the toilet seat. Her nightgown was bunched up at her waist, resting upon her thighs. She emptied her bladder, and the *tinkle* was so light, so scant, it's barely anything, wouldn't even fill a shot glass, before she's done.

I opened my mouth to say something, but stopped. I didn't want to wake her if she was sleepwalking.

Her eyes blank and staring at the wall, she said, "I had a bad dream that an animal was chasing me." She stood, pulled up her underwear. "Will you make me pancakes for breakfast, Momma?"

"Sure."

She pulled her nightgown over her head, dropped it on the bathroom floor, and walked back to her bedroom in her underwear.

I smiled at her nightgown. As a kid, I'd never slept in a nightgown. I slept in the same clothes I wore all day. Or the day before.

This small detail, putting Emily to bed in clean pajamas, was something to measure myself by. If my daughter slept in a clean nightgown, then I was a good parent. It wasn't true, of course, but it was the opposite of what my mother had done, and that reassured me.

I stepped out of the tub and reached for a towel. Today was going to be the day I got answers.

18

"Are there horses and cows at my school?" Emily said, smiling up at me, slipping her hand into mine as we walked through Owen Elementary parking lot.

"Nope, just kids and teachers, same as your last school."

"Hm." Disappointed.

"Did someone tell you there'd be horses?"

"No," she said. "I thought since it's *farm country*, there'd be horses."

Farm country had been my reference. *I can't believe we moved out to farm country*, I'd said more than a few times.

"There are farms around here. Wisconsin is known for cheese and milk, so there are lots of cows."

Lots of cows, and so many failed dairy farms. I'd had several mini lectures in the dairy section of Yellow Valley's Walmart since we'd been here. A guy with deep wrinkles in his face and wearing a Brewers cap had told me the governor screwed all the dairy farmers nearly a decade ago, gave them grants to increase their milk production, *think big, he'd told them*, and they'd listened. They'd exceeded their production targets. You know what they got for it? Less money. Everyone wins when farmers produce more milk except the farmers. "One of my buddy's farms went under," he'd said, reaching in the cooler for his third gallon of milk. "Guy was dumping milk down the drain and slaughtering calves cuz he couldn't support more livestock. He set his place on fire. Smoked himself along with the cows too stupid to leave through the open barn. Some were smart enough to escape the smoke, so now we got ourselves some roaming cows here. It wouldn't be too hard to catch 'em, but the funny thing is, no one wants them. Don't be surprised if you see a wandering cow," he'd said as he rolled his cart away.

On my next grocery visit, I was grabbing coconut milk, and a woman nearby said, "You know, the trendiness of almond and coconut milk is killing milk prices." She went on to tell me her father was a dairy farmer. "It's not milk by definition, you know," she'd said. "You can't milk a nut." Oh, the jokes Trevor and I shared over that one. Her small grumble fortified our marriage, each nut-milking fit of laughter was another slab of mortar to our relationship.

"We could probably visit a farm if you want, Emily." Her little hand was sweaty in mine. Only 8:45 a.m. and the September sun was already oppressive.

"I would love to milk a cow. Or ride a horse. Both! I would love both. Can we get a kitten?"

Had Trevor mentioned a pet to her too?

Approaching the front doors, I didn't want to give her a hard "No", and send her into her first day sobbing. "Um, let's talk about it later. Hey, I see your teacher. You remember her name?"

"Miss Baker."

Two teachers stood outside, lining up their students, ready

to whisk them away. I gave Emily a big hug and handed her off to Miss Baker. Charise Baker wore a pink sleeveless blouse, a floral chiffon skirt, and clean pink heels. A small heel, but still, *a heel*. Arms slender with long yoga muscles. She had a toothy smile and a personality you'd describe as *bubbly*.

I stood on the periphery, like the other moms, until the teachers led the kids, all wearing oversized backpacks printed with TV show characters and glitter glazed in shiny plastic, into the school. Once they were properly swallowed by the low-roofed building, I felt a surge of freedom and nerves, and my pace quickened toward my car.

Alone for the first time since we got here. It was time to get answers.

My hands sweaty and cold, I called the non-emergency number for the local police department. It was unlike me to be proactive, a go-getter, a take-charger, but this gruesome story about my mom was like a twitchy, unpredictable hand grasping my heart.

"Hunther Police Department," a woman said, tired. Maybe she was on the tail-end of her shift.

"Hi, um, I have an odd question. It's about the Dawn Young case. It happened in 1991."

"I've heard of the case, but I was in diapers then," she said, no humor.

"Well, I'm researching the story, but I can't find anything online or much in the library."

"You work for the *Beacon News* in Yellow Valley?" No suspicion in her voice.

"Yeah," I lied. "Are there police officers working in your department now who were working then?"

"Oh, gosh. Let's see. 1991," she said, letting out a hefty sigh. I was asking her to do math, and she was reluctant. "We got twenty-six officers. The police sergeant, he's the oldest at forty-eight. Let's see. He would have been what, seventeen or eighteen—just shy of working for the department. No, we got no one on the force that old."

"What about retired officers?"

"Let me think. Mikey Hooke retired a couple months ago, but he moved to Arizona, I'm not sure where. You got Ben Greer. He retired a year ago. He lives in the Dorcy Trailer Park in Yellow Valley. That's public information, by the way, I'm not giving out private, 'course."

"Oh, of course. Thank you."

"Ross Klepmeyer retired around then too. He had a massive stroke. He's in a nursing home out of town, not sure of the name. Before him, you got Asher Moss. He's in town, but I don't know his address."

Asher Moss. Desiree's dad.

19

The Dorcy Trailer Park was only fifteen minutes away. Going in blind was worth a shot.

This man was going to clear everything up and tell me how it had all been a misunderstanding. My mom hadn't been involved in Dawn Young's murder. It had been a case of town gossip spreading like a stomach bug. I would go back to Moldy Mildred with this nonsense behind me and take a nap.

I pulled into the trailer park and drove down a gravel road. I asked the first woman I came across.

"Yep, I know him," she said. Using a drinking glass, she was watering a pot of cherry tomatoes outside her trailer. "Greer's in the way back. Easy to find. Last trailer. It's white and it backs to the forest. Styrofoam cooler sitting in a tire tube out front."

Ben Greer's trailer wasn't white, but it used to be. Urine-yellow rust stains speckled his home. He sat on a lawn chair in front of a rusty grill, smoke drifting away from him and nestling in the green leaves of the sugar maple to his left.

It was the state tree of Wisconsin—the sugar maple.

We had a sugar maple in the backyard of my early

childhood home. It stood in the center of the yard like the star performer on a stage. In the autumn, its radiant colors—marigold, peach, and strawberry—glowed at dawn and dusk. When the leaves trembled in the breeze, they resembled flickering flames. I shook off the image. I still tried so hard to forget that tree and what I found there.

He eyed me hard as I stopped my car and got out. The air was oily with grilled fish.

"Are you Ben Greer?"

He nodded, didn't bother standing up. His skin was deeply tan, his face creased with wrinkles. He had a good head of hair, only beginning to gray, that made him look youthful.

He held a beer can in a red insulator, words written on it, some logo I couldn't make out. He wore jeans and a Brewers shirt. His fingers were stained red. So was the white T-shirt bunched up on the ground beside him.

"Sorry to bother you. I'm Heather Hornne." I paused, as if lightning might strike me down. *Keep saying that last name, it just might.* "I'm wondering if you can answer some questions about my mom… being… well." I shook my head. Even saying it, I felt like a traitor. I wasn't fond of my mom, but I had never accused her of violent crimes. I took a deep breath. "I heard my mother was a suspect in the murder—"

"Dawn Young," he cut in. "Yeah, I remember it."

Trailers away, a woman hollered. I couldn't make out the words, but it had that tone of an exhausted mother scolding her child for making a mess. Nearer, a screen opened, the spring creaking.

"We've had our share of murder over the years," he said. "Even if we can't prove it, even if we don't close a case, we usually have an idea about who might have done it. The Young case was different." He motioned to the picnic table a dozen feet away from him, shared with the neighboring trailer. "Have a seat." He didn't blink enough. It was unnerving.

I sat on the bench. "I never heard about it as a kid. Not a word. That's crazy, don't you think?"

He shrugged. "I never told my kids even half the stuff I did. Do you have kids?"

"Yes."

"If someone accused you of murder, whether you did it or not, would you tell your kid if you didn't have to?"

"No."

He raised his eyebrow, point made. He picked up a grill fork from the dirt, speared the fish, and flipped it. Fat splattered and sizzled. It smelled good. I was easing into the idea of fish and beer for breakfast.

Though I wondered if Crooked River was as clean as it looked, or if some local factory was dumping lead into the river while paying off a village councilman.

"Your mom was the last person who saw her. Your mom drove Dawn to her waitressing job at Marjory's Greasy Spoon. We were looking into everyone, lots of boys and young men visited Dawn at work, but, well, just weeks after it happened, your mom's doctor said she confessed to it. He recorded the conversation. It was damning."

We lived minutes from Marjory's restaurant. We'd passed

it on the way to our house the first day we'd moved in. The familiarity made the past feel accessible.

"Why wasn't she charged?"

He picked up a plate from the dirt. It held an open bun. He tossed the split bun, face open, onto the grill.

"Our town prosecutor decided not to. Your mom had a bunch of kids, she said she'd been medicated, she took back her confession, and the evidence didn't add up."

"What evidence did they have?"

"Dawn Young had sex before she was murdered. Could have been rough sex or could have been sexual assault."

His words didn't sit right, but I didn't want to interrupt.

"We collected evidence from the body, but this was the early '90s," he said with disdain. Based on his look, his early morning drinking, his rusting trailer, I had pegged him for old-school nostalgic. Maybe I was wrong. "It took a few weeks to do a DNA test. The evidence got contaminated or lost in forensics. That wasn't unusual."

He took his bun off the grill, speared the fish, and placed it in the bun. From the ground beside his chair, he picked up a glass container of something that looked like sauerkraut—wilted strands of iceberg soaked in milky dip—and dumped some on top of his sandwich. He set the jar in the dirt and waited with the plate on his lap. He wanted to eat. He didn't want to share his food or any more of his time.

"So, they didn't charge her, and then the investigation just stopped? Is that typical?"

He bit his lip, hesitating. "It fizzled, yeah. Dawn Young didn't have an advocate. No one demanding justice. Her only family was her mom, and her mom didn't have roots here. The mom was strange. Quiet. In that way, Dawn was a good target."

"Is her mom still in town?"

He shook his head. "Killed herself."

I inhaled deeply, pulling in smoke. "Do you think my mom did it?"

He glanced at his sandwich, and shifted in his seat. He sighed, annoyed, but trying to be patient. "The older I get, the less sure I am about my past opinions. But, at the time, I leaned toward no. Mainly because of the sex, but also because she came across as," he paused, searching for the right word, and gazed at his Styrofoam cooler, maybe considering another beer. "Tired. She seemed tired. This murder was meticulous. The killer had cut off Dawn Young's fingers."

20

TREVOR

Wren stood in front of the main entrance to J&B Graphic Design, vaping and scanning her phone. She was young, easygoing, and a master of small talk. *Heya, Trev. What is the one song you're still listening to? Which car on the highway pisses you off the most? Favorite late-night snack: sweet or salty?*

I didn't hate chatting, but my schedule was packed lately, I didn't have fifteen minutes of wiggle room.

This past week, I had avoided talking to my employees, which made me a terrible manager for the ones who needed constant hand-holding, *I'm talking to you, Yosef and Tiffany*, and a good manager for the independent ones, Wren and Niko. I didn't ride my employees, micro-anything them, as long as they got their work done.

If only my boss had the same mindset. In the Work Gospel According to Kevin, time spent in the office was all that mattered. Any day now, Kev and I would come head-to-head.

Sixty-two employees at J&B, a youngish company big on team-building. They held bi-monthly Fun Fridays, which were evenings of Whirlyball and laser tag. Seemed good-hearted, but it was pre-packaged corporate-adopted bullshit. Work your fifty-hour work week and just when you haven't seen your family enough, come play laser tag with your coworkers. It was a cruel trick designed to foster the idea that pay and flexibility shouldn't be important to your productivity, but that your coworkers were your team, your family, your fucking family; you owed it to them to work hard no matter the pay.

My company was located in the business and technology park in Elton, north of Chicago. When you turned into the tech park, you passed a large waterfall flowing over a shiny black obsidian stone—a value-building mirage. Black stone and waterfalls said: This place is classy and important.

J&B rented two floors in a tall building with large glass windows and a modern interior painted in white and shades of yellow, a productivity-boosting color.

I drove around back to avoid a time-eating conversation with Wren.

I didn't like parking back here. It wasn't that the back was seedier than the front. The back of the building was just as gorgeous. It was the pair of geese that had made a nest on the four-by-ten-foot curbed island of grass in the parking lot. They hissed and spat and chased anyone who parked near their goslings.

There were large ponds and grassy fields all over the place around here, why would they pick the parking lot?

Here they came now, from the far end of the lot with their brood following. The mother and father geese were like a pair of gun-slinging cowboys, chins up, ready for a fight.

My mom used to roast goose with obscene amounts of butter. It was moist and rich, so much better than turkey.

Which reminded me, I wanted to take Sawyer hunting again. Man, that had been a good day. My chest loosened.

I stuffed my keys in my pocket and grabbed my coffee out of the holder.

I stepped out, forced my muscles into a good-natured smile, and headed toward the back entrance.

My phone buzzed with a text. I knew the number.

It read:

-I'm worried about your wife.

21

HEATHER

Her fingers had been cut off.

My mom confessed, but took it back.

The last twenty-four hours had been too eventful. I wanted to lie down in Moldy Mildred's dark rooms and absorb the quiet.

But if I closed my eyes, I would see severed fingers. If I managed to keep those out of my mind, I would worry about Desiree's boyfriend's concussed brother showing up on my doorstep.

I could see myself pacing the house like an animal in a cage, which made me wonder exactly what animals were caged down the road. Were there really cougars a mile away in someone's backyard?

Before I could talk myself out of it, before I could open a bag of chips and flop onto the couch, I was fastening my sneakers. Going for a jog would clear my head.

Our backyard had a row of mangy pine trees lining the property. Planted twenty feet apart, they stood like exhausted soldiers, fat and tired, unkempt and whiskery.

Trevor had mowed two days ago and had let the clippings scatter. The thick scent of hot grass puffed up as I walked the length of our backyard.

As I cut through the trees to get to the path, wispy

threads of a spider's web caught my hair and arms, and I yelled out. I wiped a tangle of webbing from my hands onto my leggings and couldn't shake the feeling that bugs were crawling on my skin.

I broke into a run straight away, faster than my usual start. The forest to my right exhaled the cool dampness of a locker room. Backyards leading to houses on my left. The chalky path curved here and there and had mild hills.

I had never liked wilderness and wide-open skies. Too vast, too lonely, too many hiding places.

I was a city girl. I loved Chicago brick. The marble floor tiles of Union Station. The wide concrete walks winding along the lakefront. The steel lifting-bridges over the river.

You could count on these structures. They were sturdy and impervious. There were few hiding places in the heart of the city, places people could camp out, become feral, hatch mad hunting plans.

In the city, people were everywhere. They said crowds were dangerous, that when there were too many people around, no one took action, but I'd seen the opposite. I had seen people—a young black man, a middle-aged white woman, an old Asian man—step in between an escalating argument, ask a crying woman if she needed help, and chase down a thief.

And even when there'd been inaction, a dozen people with slack-jawed expressions, there was comfort in that because if something terrible happened to someone, *to me*, people would witness it, and when their brain fog cleared, the crime would eventually be reported.

No story scared me more than the story of a young girl *disappearing* in farm country. The girl who had been walking along a lonely road to the bus stop, but she'd never made it to her destination. She'd been swallowed up somewhere between the two points, and no one had a clue what happened.

I hadn't gone for a run since we'd gotten here, and my body had lost its rhythm. My calves burned with lactic acid, my forehead itched with sweat.

The path curved, I dodged an old, massive, dry pile of shit, had to be horse shit, and when the chalky path straightened out again, there was something big up ahead right in the middle of the path.

A lone male deer with huge, fractal antlers.

I stopped running. My pulse pounded in my throat.

I'd heard deer were skittish, but did they ever attack people?

Keeping still, I gazed to my right and singled out an evergreen tree with low, beefy branches. If the deer charged, this was the tree I would climb.

It lowered its head and sniffed the ground like a dog. I relaxed. If Trevor were here, he'd be so excited. He'd say this buck was some magical omen of good things to come. A spirit from the forest welcoming me, my very own Totoro.

It lifted its heavy head and gazed in my direction, looked me right in the eye. My heart twitched, a little fear but mostly thrill. The buck swooped its gaze toward the tall grass bursting with yellow wildflowers in someone's backyard. Golden ragwort. Picturesque, but its smell was weedy, warm, and dense.

He stepped across the gravel into the gorgeous spread of

golden flowers, and something cracked through the air, loud and sharp.

Instinctively, I dropped to my belly. Pain burst through my shoulder.

Thump.

The deer was on the ground, its body mostly in the grass. It stared at me with its black marble eyes wide open, its head on the gravel in a growing puddle of dark liquid.

Oh my God.

A golden retriever sprung out from the golden ragwort and stopped hard at the dead deer, sniffing at it, his fluffy tail wagging. He trotted to me with a stupid grin, droplets of blood clinging to his beard. He touched his wet nose to my cheek and licked me.

"Yuck. Go away." I shooed him and wiped my cheek.

"You're OK, miss. I saw ya there. Sorry to startle." The gravelly voice came from beyond the yellow weeds.

Don't tell me I'm OK, motherfucker.

Rifle in his hand, he stepped along the gravel path in his jeans and boots and walked right up to my face. It crossed my mind that he might kick me in the face and dump me in his trunk so I wouldn't report him.

"Come here, Rosy. Give her space." His dog obediently turned and fell in line beside her owner. The man bent over, some joint of his cracking, and held his hand open in front of my nose. He smelled like he'd been in the sun all day even though it was morning. There was an additional mystery smell oozing from his pores. Maybe last night's alcohol. His hair was due a cut, and his beard was patchy and starting to gray. He wore a Van Halen T-shirt with tiny holes at the collar and an apple-sized hole under the armpit.

His eyes were a beautiful light blue that reminded me of Desiree. This man had been a beautiful child. As a fifty-something, he was somewhere between repulsive and handsome. His eyes had that glassy dreaminess characteristic of alcoholics, the extremely religious, or the inexplicably kind.

I backed away from his hand and got to my feet, clutching my shoulder from the dull pain.

He let his hand fall to his side and smiled. "Scout's honor, I saw you there. I wouldn't have got you."

"What a huge relief to know you wouldn't have shot me on purpose."

He laughed heartily as if I'd been joking. He said, "You moved into the Conrad house."

"A week ago."

"Where'd you come from?"

"Chicago."

"So close, yet feels a world away, am I right?"

"Yes," I said, feeling my first moment of warm communion with this scary lumberjack.

"Cubs or Sox fan?"

"Fair weather," I said. "It's just a game, after all. Like mini golf." My favorite defiant statement, as it wiggled under people's skin and festered.

He laughed. "You might want to keep that opinion to yourself. People around here name their kids after their favorite Brewers and Packers athletes."

An image of Ben Greer in his Brewers' T-shirt came to mind. *The killer had cut off her fingers.*

The dog, her tail wagging, couldn't resist the stink of a stranger any longer. She came at me, sniffing my shoe, my knee, my crotch.

I'd never appreciated the incessant friendliness of dogs. I pushed the dog's nose away.

"Quit it, Rosy," he said. "Not everyone thinks you're as adorable as you do." The dog circled back past the man to the dead deer. Blood dripped from the buck's mouth onto the bright white gravel. "Being from the city, you probably think deer are pretty. Like spying a mermaid?"

I said nothing. I wasn't going to admit he was dead-on.

"But they're a real nuisance. Damage crops and vegetable gardens. Increase deer mice population, which spreads Lyme disease. A real bitch around here, Lyme disease. Gives you arthritis, depression, memory loss. You stay here long enough; you'll hate those deer. It's legal for us to shoot when they step on our property."

He'd probably been sitting with his rifle for hours.

"That's great that you're worried about Lyme disease and crops, but I have a small child. What if she was with me and you couldn't see her coming over the tall grass."

"Deer are skittish. That deer wouldn't have stood still if a kid was running at it."

"That doesn't give me the slightest bit of comfort."

He glanced down at his boot and said, "I'll make sure to be more careful." He rubbed his dog's head and said, "I'm Tracy Summers, by the way."

"Tracy?"

"Yep. My parents were kind, but they gave me a bit of a porn star name. My friends call me Summers."

"I know porn star names. My maiden name was Heather Hornne. Now it's Heather Bishop, which I like much better."

I hadn't said my maiden name in twenty years. That I'd said it three times since we'd been in Hunther was appalling.

"You're right, Bishop's better than the other." His dog was lying down behind the deer, panting, her tongue hanging out of her open mouth, waiting patiently for her next command. A circle of blood haloed the deer's head. There was a dark sticky hole in its neck. Was Tracy going to leave that puddle of blood on the gravel?

"Nice to meet you," he said, and walked toward the deer. He grabbed its antlers and yanked. It moved a few inches across the gravel. Rosy stood, ready and excited. Tracy tugged again, and the deer slid another inch.

"Hey," I said. "Someone said there's a house down this way with cougars. That true?"

He grunted as he yanked the deer's head. "Very. Two houses from mine. She has a four-cougar menagerie. Nice lady, but kind of weird, obviously."

Coming from a guy waiting in his yard for a deer to step over an imaginary line so he can blow its brains out.

"That's legal? You can *buy* a cougar?" I said, taking a few steps toward him, my eyes on the smear of bloody gravel.

"Yep. Pretty easy actually. Craigslist. Auctions. Exotic fairs in parking lots, warehouses. Couple hundred bucks for a baby mountain lion." Tracy Summers stood straight, put his palms on his lower back, and stretched. "They have started slapping some regulations on. I think you need a license now and a site inspection, but most of the folks here would be grandfathered in. It's probably less paperwork and headache for them to keep those cougars than I had adopting Rosy. Come on, Rosy Posy," he said, and his dog lifted her ears and wagged her tail hard. Tracy Summers turned back to his work of dragging the deer onto his property.

"You're gonna throw your back."

"Nah. I'll be fine." He wiped sweat off his forehead, leaving a bloody smear. "Two hundred pounds, max." His fingers were stained with the deer's blood.

The killer cut off her fingers.

When I pictured it, my mind imagined a stage prop hand with rubbery fingers painted red at their stumps. My brain had no real reference for what severed fingers might look like.

I weighed asking Tracy about Dawn. What did I have to lose? Also, he'd almost shot me, which was perversely intimate. I felt justified asking him anything.

"Hey, do you know anything about Dawn Young? She was murdered decades ago. They never found who did it."

He kept dragging the carcass, speaking in between huffs and grunts. "I moved here from Milwaukee. Five years ago. Don't know everything about this place. Heard about it though. Teenage girl."

He'd gotten the deer off the gravel, pulled it deeper into the patch of golden weed, bending and crushing the tall wildflowers and painting them in blood. "Someone slit her down the middle and dropped her in the river. They said this lady, I can't remember her name, they said she did, that it was devil worship. That was a thing back then, you know. The woman had teenage sons. I always thought one of her sons killed Dawn Young, and the mother took the blame. You think that's sexist of me, believing a woman couldn't do something so heinous?"

"I don't know," I said, not giving his question any thought, and walked away.

Shane would have been thirteen. Rodney, sixteen.

My head felt muggy with the stink of iron, of blood.

Desiree Moss telling me my mom murdered a girl seemed unreal; Ben Greer's mention of severed fingers felt foreign; but strangely, Tracy Summers mentioning devil worship and my brother hit home.

22

I pictured Rodney at sixteen, placing a dream catcher by the dead opossums' heads, and marbles, painted rocks, playing cards, and a rabbit's foot by their tails. I hated the feel of a rabbit's foot under my thumb. The fur was fake, the hardness underneath it was fake, but it felt real.

He'd stood beside me. My six-year-old head came up to his elbow. There wasn't much of a foul smell from the opossums. There were only the smells of hot grass and spicy body odor coming off Rodney.

Why had I been there with him? Had I been moping around in the backyard, dragging sticks and lifting rocks, and stumbled upon his ceremony? Had he called me over to bear witness? What or who had killed the opossums? I never asked these questions. I was used to going along with whatever the big kids were doing. I was usually happy to be passively included, a miniature ghost by their sides. Opening my mouth and asking questions would only remind them I was there, and they might decide they didn't want me.

I'd stared at the hovering flies, the opossum fur, patches of it matted with dried blood. One of the animal's mouths was wide open, its teeth pointy, its tongue swollen and purple.

Under the hind leg of that opossum, something squirmed, and I screamed. "Did you see that? Did you see, Rod? There's something wiggling by the leg."

Rodney, so comfortable with gross things, didn't hesitate. He pulled the leg back and revealed a gaping hole. As if I could feel my own thin tissue stretching, I winced.

"Eww," I yelled. "Worms. They're worms."

He elbowed me in the head, hard enough that I rubbed the spot with my hand. "Not worms," he said. "Opossums carry their babies in their pouch." He stuck one of his hands in the hole, ignoring the flies landing on his hand, his arm. One landed on his face. I backed up, disgusted. I didn't want those flies touching my skin.

He picked the babies out, placing them in the palm of his hand. They were tiny, hairless, some barely moving, some statue-still. Gross.

"They're like pink jelly beans," he said, his eyes lit with some fierce emotion. Desire? Delight? Fury? He walked around to the front of the house with those baby opossums.

I stood frozen, horrified. What was he going to do with them? Mother them? Use them as fish bait? I imagined him popping them into his mouth like jelly beans.

Later, maybe a month, maybe two. Grass was still green, but leaves littered the ground. It must have been early fall because the leaves were golden and edged in fiery pink, soft to the touch. If it were mid-fall, they would have been browning and dried out, their edges curled and crunchy.

I sat on the front porch after school, my sticker book spread open in my lap. I loved that sticker book, with its cellophane pages and treasures inside. Stickers puffy like marshmallow dreams and scratch 'n' sniff stickers that were more vibrant and delicious than real smells: pickle smells you kept going back to for another sniff, banana fragrance you wanted to lick, buttery popcorn scents you wanted to climb inside. Smelly stickers were a preview to the internet—more enticing than real life. I traced my finger over a scratch 'n' sniff sticker of pink jelly beans, hot pink and creamy pale pink, and thought of those baby opossums.

I had forgotten about those babies. What had Rodney done with them?

He'd probably carried them into the back garage. I was scared to go back there by myself. There was a single lightbulb dangling from a cord, so it was dark. I'd seen mice stuck in snap-traps back there, their necks broken, their bodies frozen in contortion.

He should be home from school soon. I'd wait here and ask him.

My nose in my sticker book, I almost missed him. He rushed past me, head down, into the garage. Where was his bookbag?

The garage was deep and sectioned off with metal shelves, their joints rusty, holding spray paint, hoses, and dented cardboard boxes. Opposite the tall rickety shelves was scrap wood of various sizes leaning against the wall, cottony balls of spider sacks clinging along their splintery edges. The shelves and scrap wood made a misshaped doorway of sorts, and I followed him back.

The dangling lightbulb cast a shadow of Rodney's profile against the stained drywall. He held his hands cradled just below his mouth, his hair sweaty and hanging over his cheek.

"Are the babies OK?" I said.

Startled, he looked over his shoulder at me.

Blood. His lips were shiny with blood. His teeth, outlined in red spit. I didn't meet his eyes because I couldn't look away from his mouth.

I couldn't help but think of him saying, *They're like pink jelly beans*.

"Get out," he said quietly, through clenched teeth. Trembling now, more furious, he said it louder, and his voice cracked. "Get out, Heather."

"You have to understand, this runs deep. Some of these people are bloodline, meaning, they were raised from birth in this cult. They don't know anything else."

Doctor Clifford Paulson, PhD Psychology
Transcripts from the Sixth Annual Conference on
Adult Manifestations of Childhood Trauma
THE RADISSON PLAZA HOTEL, CINCINNATI, OHIO

23

When I got home, my phone sat on the table where I'd left it, but it was lit with a text message.

A shiver raced up my spine. I hadn't received a text about my mom since the day we got here. I both dreaded another cryptic text and was desperate for one.

I should have told the police someone was harassing me. Even with burner phones, they might be able to figure out who it was. I should have told Trevor. I should *tell* Trevor.

No. You don't want anyone—stranger or husband—prying into your childhood.

I picked up my phone. The text was from Visha, my neighbor and good friend back home. I exhaled. I'd been holding my breath.

-You alive? I haven't heard from you since last week and worry the Children of the Corn tied you up on a cross.

I loved Visha for this: taking my distrust of remote towns dramatically further.

-I haven't seen any crosses, but I did almost get shot by a deer-hunter named Tracy.

-Serious?

-He missed me, but killed the deer.

-Gross. Hey, when are you coming to visit? You're only two hours away.

-We're still getting settled. School started today. Me and Em will visit soon. Miss you.

Walking upstairs, I called Guppy Swim School and asked for Desiree.

"Um, she doesn't work here anymore," the young man said.

I figured. Being trusted to keep small children safe in a pool didn't mix well with your mugshot in the crime section of the local news.

My best chance was bluntness. "I bailed her out last night and drove her home, but she left her jacket in my car. Do you have her number?"

"Yeah, sure." I'd assumed he wouldn't give it to me, so I had to scramble and grab a crayon and notebook from Emily's room.

I thanked him and typed a message to Desiree.

-I saw him standing by his car on my drive home. Is he OK? And please don't tell him my name.

I hit send and tossed my phone on my bed. Peeled off my sweaty clothes, walked naked to the bathroom, and turned the shower hot.

While I waited for hot water, I opened Sawyer's drawer below the sink. His shaver. His toothpaste. His deodorant. *Artic Plunge*. I opened it and inhaled.

I was a kid again, yearning for closeness. Stealing Shane's pillow so I could bury my nose in its slick, unwashed softness and inhale the scent of his dirty hair. Stealing Holly's jacket so I could smell her perfume.

I did the same with Trevor's stuff. I'd go into the bedroom after he'd left for work. His cologne and hairspray smells twirling under the fan, I'd stand there, breathing him in.

I never did it with Emily because she was always *right there*, touching me, never giving me space. I smelled Emily's stuff, of course, her sweaty socks or urine-tainted underwear, but that was only when I'd found an item on the floor and I needed to decide whether to drop it in her laundry basket or back in her drawer.

I capped Sawyer's deodorant and returned it to the drawer.

I showered, wondering if, deep down, Sawyer hated me just a little.

Sawyer and I, we played family. I loved him, but there was nothing bonding him to me, no hilarious shared joke that had knocked us off our chairs, left us breathless on the ground. No grumpy weekend of camping in the rain we could recall. We had shared space two or three days a week since he was nine years old—accidental roommates—but still we didn't have *history*.

He would not have picked me. What he wanted was for his parents to never have gotten divorced, to be living with both of them. That would always have been his first choice. His second choice was how he'd been living for the first nine years of his life, going between his mom's house and dad's house, having their full attention. Now that his mom was serving a short term in correctional, he couldn't have that either. His third choice was to have his father all to himself. Maybe that wasn't true. He loved Em. He had a bond with Em, and Emily and I were a package deal.

I had always told him he could call me whatever he was comfortable with. He called me Heather. We'd mostly gotten along, but I couldn't fully settle into mothering him because the big decisions—school stuff, electronic rules, punishment, the sex talk—had always defaulted to Trish and Trevor. I had grown accustomed to keeping my opinions to myself, especially now that he was pretty much an adult. If I pushed him too far or asked him for too much, I worried he would shut me out.

It was a bit pathetic. Here I was, nearly forty, but I was occasionally wooden and dull, keeping my mouth shut. In some ways I was stuck at seventeen—the age I walked out of my parents' house—still trying on different styles, different personalities.

I thought about Desiree. How was she so comfortable with herself, even with her shameful, criminal behavior? When I'd told her I'd assumed her arrest had been a misunderstanding, she'd said, "No, I'd meant to break in alright." She was just as comfortable telling me she was having sex with her boyfriend's brother. She had no shame. I wanted some of that.

I stepped out of the shower and wrapped myself in a towel. I let my hair drip onto my shoulders, down my back, and onto the floor. I stood in front of the bathroom mirror, the edges fogged.

I pulled my makeup bag out of the drawer and outlined my eyes in thick black eyeliner, smudged it with my finger to mimic Desiree's look.

I dabbed sticky gloss onto my lips and forced a smile, trying to show my canines. My teeth were too blunt, too seemingly harmless to match Desiree's seductive smile.

24

TREVOR

I sat at my desk, answering emails, this morning's text—*I'm worried about your wife*—like a fly buzzing in my brain. I'd swat it away, but a few minutes later it was back to distracting me. I knew who it was from, and they were anything but worried.

Coffee. I needed another coffee.

As I got up, Wren walked over.

"Hey," she said, "I'm headed to the break room for cake. You coming?"

"What's today's celebration?"

"Robin's birthday."

I could almost feel the icing residue, overly sweet and vibrantly dyed, on my teeth. The annoying questions: Why aren't you eating cake? You don't need to watch your weight? Are you having a hard day? Cake might be the solution!

"I don't think so," I said with a smile, annoyed that I couldn't grab a coffee. If I walked into the break room, there'd be no escaping the party. "I've got to finish up and put out fires at home."

"Party pooper," she said, pursing her lips. "If you change your mind and come for cake," she said, glancing in both directions, and whispering, "don't mention Robin's family. Her and Brooks just divorced."

"Got it," I said, shooting her with my finger gun and turning back to my desk. "See ya, Wren."

Poor Robin. Divorce sucked big-time. When Trish had divorced me, I almost hadn't made it to the other side. Those were dark days—alcohol-soaked days where I slept till 7 p.m. on the weekends I didn't have Sawyer, woke up to eat ice cream, and went back to bed.

Before I remarried Heather, she and I had an understanding. No divorce, no matter what. Heather and I, we'd come up with a game. *I wouldn't divorce you if.*

She'd once told me, "You could cheat on me with a young hot man—you'd better fucking not—but I wouldn't divorce you."

"You could shave your head and grow a full beard," I'd told her. "I would help you comb it out."

"You could crown all your teeth in gold," she'd told me. "That shit looks so nasty, but I wouldn't divorce you."

We would explore the most outlandish, far-fetched, marriage-straining scenarios. Heather would laugh so hard. She loved this game to such an extent it was almost disturbing.

But it was a game, we kept it silly, and we never brought real-life horror into it.

As I sat down at my desk, another text came through. Same number as this morning.

-Meet me in two hours. Same place as last time.

I exhaled. I closed my eyes, considering my day. Things I had to do. What time I needed to do them. My life had come down to a schedule. Like a fucking wedding planner.

25

HEATHER

Desiree hadn't texted me back yet. I'd put on jewelry, and lightened my makeup.

In the dining room, I kept six water bottles on the table. Each bottle held a thick stalk of milkweed. On each milkweed plant were one or two monarch caterpillars, several gorgeously fat. One had already formed a chrysalis, a brilliant creamy green teardrop, topped with a delicate metallic golden line like a crown of jewels.

My caterpillar nursery had expanded. The table was rustic and carved, so caterpillar crap lodged in the grooves. I should have put a tablecloth down. The room smelled like cut plants. Using the dust buster, I cleaned up after my pets.

The front door opened. "Hello? Anyone here?" Sawyer. He knew I was here, my car was outside, but we kept up these formalities.

"In here with your babies," I said. He had been the one to point out the caterpillars, so I joked that they were his.

He walked in and dropped his backpack on the floor beside the table. His presence always hit me sharply. His masculinity, his size. Broad shoulders, big kneecaps.

He had a good face like his father. Good hair like his father.

Clean yet vaguely wild. His short hair curled up like stiff icing peaks on a cake. His eyes were unreadable. He always smelled good and had clear skin.

I assumed his good hygiene had developed from his mother's unpredictability. I hadn't expected her to get arrested for shoplifting, but I hadn't exactly been surprised. He couldn't control his chaotic home life, but he could control how often he brushed his teeth. He wanted to appear clean because his insides didn't feel that way. But maybe I was projecting.

I rehearsed my words silently in my head before I said them. "Hey, would you mind transferring this lovely fatty to the new milkweed? I've been watching him bully his friend for the past fifteen minutes." I pointed to the caterpillar I was talking about. His stripes, crisp white, nuclear yellow, and pure black, were candy-vivid. Even now, as I put my finger in front of him, he reared his head up in irritation and bobbed it back and forth.

"Really?" Sawyer smiled, part child and part smug, amused villain.

"Yep. Everywhere this other one goes, Tough Guy follows. He keeps rearing up his head and dropping down on the other guy like he's John Cena."

"You're joking."

"Maybe a little."

"Where's Em?"

"School. I'll leave soon to get her. How was your first day?"

He shrugged. "Whatever."

We watched the caterpillars together for a full fifteen seconds, both of us silent. Their leaf-chomping was not audible, but the mind filled in the holes and it *seemed* audible.

Sawyer tried to pick the caterpillar off the leaf, but the caterpillar's feet were too sticky. The urge to direct Sawyer, to tell him how to do it was strong, but I bit my lip hard. *Let him figure it out. He's practically an adult.*

Sawyer's adult hand, broad and muscular, wisps of hair on the knuckles, moved in front of the caterpillar, waiting for the caterpillar's feet, pair by pair, to break suction with the leaf and move onto his hand. A single beam of harsh afternoon sun lit a shiny red smear along his thumb that he didn't seem to notice.

Blood. My mind immediately traveled to fights on the bus and nosebleeds from cocaine-abraded noses.

You're terrible. Why would you assume the worst?

"You're bleeding," I said.

"I'm fine," he said, impatience creeping into his voice. Caterpillar move complete, Sawyer's face changed. Stoney, dark eyes. Blank. As if moments before he had been faking being human.

This, this shadow moving across his face, across his soul, was his normal. He would be in a moment of childlike wonder, you'd blink, and he'd appear cold. I wavered between worrying about Sawyer's behavior and talking myself out of worry. I told myself, this is just teenage boys, or maybe teenagers in general. *Remember how temperamental you were as a teen.*

"Your dad thinks I'm nuts with this. Your fault, since you're the one who found them," I said, teasing, trying to make him smile. He ignored me, grabbed his backpack, and headed for the stairs, his movements smooth and athletic.

"You hungry?" I said, more out of politeness than practically. I hadn't made food. What was in the refrigerator? "Hey, we have guacamole and chips."

He said nothing. He was already stomping upstairs, his shoes hitting the carpet heavily. Sawyer's door banged shut.

I considered following him upstairs, trying to draw him out of his room, impress him with my story of almost getting shot by a deer-hunter today, but I didn't want to come across as desperate.

He spent so much time in his room. What did he do in there? Self-mutilation? Porn? Snapchat? Classical music? Read novels? Practice his cursive? Pray the rosary? There was so much innocence and malevolence a kid could get into with just a phone and earbuds.

The front doorbell rang, and I jumped. I clearly hadn't shaken this morning's gunshot.

26

Speak of the deer-slaughterer.

Tracy Summers stood on my doorstep. This man had bloodied the forest trail for me, and his devil worship comment had trawled up a strange memory. I didn't like him.

I peered through the glass panels, reluctant to open the door. Tracy made eye contact and, showing me something bright orange, mumbled something I couldn't quite hear.

Feeling lame that I'd hesitated, I opened the door.

"Heather Bishop with the great last name, I brought you something." In his hand was a limp piece of orange fabric, shiny and slick. My mind was grasping. Raincoat? Life jacket?

Seeing I was not getting it, he said, "It's a hunting vest. I felt bad that I scared ya and worried you wouldn't want to walk the trail anymore." *You got that right, Mister.*

"You *should* feel bad for shooting at joggers."

His cheeks burned red under his scruff and he glanced down at his hiking boots.

"I'm joking," I said, opening the screen and taking the vest. "Partially, at least. And, thanks." I let the screen fall closed and reached for the door.

"You kept the Conrads' red curtains." He nodded to his left, toward our front window. "Kind of hideous, kind of artistic." I got the feeling Tracy Summers was looking for a friend.

"I guess. My stepson calls it the murder room," I said, trying to stomp out any inkling he had about coming over for tea or a beer.

"Murder room?" he said, lifting his eyebrows, and shifting his gaze to the side. "It fits."

"I have to go get my daughter from school." I started to close the door. "Thanks again."

"Hey, there's something else. Do you happen to have a sister?"

I squeezed the doorknob to steady myself. "What?" I said, though it was obvious I'd heard him.

"I went to the hospital a month back for stitches. I, uh, cut my finger pretty deep. Anyway, I was talking to the nurse sewing me up. I made the porn star name joke. It's my go-to joke. My door breaker."

"Ice breaker."

"Yep. That's it. Ice breaker. She made the same joke about her last name. Same as you today. Déjà vu. Anyway, her name stood out because it reminded me of Christmas."

Sweat broke across my chest and forehead.

"Holly Hornne," he said. "I didn't think of it till after I saw you. I had a mini stroke a few years back and sometimes I'm not as sharp as I used to be." He tapped his forehead with his pointer finger. "Anyway, that your sister?"

"No. I'm sorry, I have to go. I'm gonna be late." I closed the door.

Fuck. When had Holly moved back here?

27

Whenever I thought of Holly, I thought of Roxy. She was the Barbie doll I got for Easter back when we lived in Hunther. Before Becky died.

I had loved Roxy. I liked brushing her sandy blond hair and taking off her dress and giving her a bath when I took a bath and tucking her in my bed at night. When my love for Roxy was still fresh, I'd eavesdropped on a doll-centric horror movie Rodney was watching. That ruined Roxy for me. I put her in the back of the closet in the room I shared with Holly and Becky.

Days later Roxy was in my bed, blond hair spread on my pillow, my blanket tucked under her chin. Her smile creeped me out. I stuck her in a drawer. Days later, again, in my bed. I cut her hair off, wrapped her in toilet paper, and put her in the bathroom garbage can. Days later, she was in my bed again. Her hair had grown back. A few more incidents of Roxy reappearing and I took her to the kitchen and tried to cut her into pieces with Mom's good scissors. I cut my finger and needed stitches.

I was hysterical at the hospital, panic-crying about the creepy doll, drawing suspicious, lingering looks from hospital staff, and it freaked my mom out. She conducted a brief investigation.

It turned out Holly was playing a joke on me. My sisters had gotten the same Barbie for Easter. There must have been a sale, and my mom bought three identical dolls. I was so young, I hadn't realized. Holly, Becky, Shane, and Rodney laughed about it at the kitchen table.

Roxy wasn't the only joke they played on me. That's why I always assumed they were fucking with me. What did it matter, right?

Most of the time it didn't matter—that I believed they were always screwing with me. But there was one time when it did, and I haven't forgiven myself since.

28

My phone, balanced in the cup holder, played the circus theme song—my ringtone for Trevor. I managed to push the speaker-phone button. "I'm driving to get Em. Can you hear me?"

"Yeah," he said. "Listen. DeeDee just called me. She's supposed to watch my mom tonight, but she's throwing up. Food poisoning or something."

"You think she's playing hooky?" I expected the worst of people.

"It doesn't matter." He never expected the worst, and he wasn't a gossip. "What matters is that I won't be able to come home tonight."

DeeDee kept night-watch for Trevor's dying mother at her home. Paulina kept day-watch. DeeDee was supposedly young, an LPN. Paulina was a retired nurse.

It crossed my mind, not for the first time, that maybe Trevor was having an affair. His *hair*, I'm telling you. You'd be crazy not to want to touch his hair.

I'd never seen DeeDee or Paulina. DeeDee could be a hot college grad. Paulina could be one of those trim, young-grandma hotties only five or ten years older than me.

I actually didn't care if he was cheating. I didn't want him to cheat, obviously, and I would be devastated if he fell in love with someone, but I love me a good hand and foot massage, and that's how I thought of it.

Hear me out.

I was twenty when I helped an elderly neighbor in my apartment building move. It wasn't backbreaking, but it was an hour of moving boxes. My neighbor had a massage-a-month membership, and she gifted me one. "Ask for Michael," she'd said. "He's a sweetheart."

When I laid there on my stomach, breasts smashed on the soft cotton-sheeted table, prewarmed sheet covering my back, low light, meditation music on, and Michael laid his strong, considerate hands on my back, pulling and probing, gently and harder, working out knots, I'd felt a swelling build behind my eyes, in my head, and in my chest. I felt a hot release rush through me. Not sexual. Emotional. I'd had some sort of strange emotional orgasm. I'd wept quietly.

If Michael heard me, if he felt a minor trembling in my shoulders, he said nothing. He'd probably seen it before and then some.

A penis was an appendage. Jerking one off seemed like the same thing as Michael or any other masseuse pulling and rubbing the knots and tension from my arms. Just a dick massage.

For me, with female parts, sex was more than a massage. It was an internal assault, even when it was loving and gentle, even when I was in ecstasy. If I were bloated, I didn't want sex. But if I were bloated and you offered to massage my arm, fuck away at it.

I had never told Trevor this, well, besides for our *I wouldn't divorce you if* game, which I adored.

"I wouldn't divorce you if you had sex with a young hot man," I'd said.

"I wouldn't divorce you if you stopped showering," he'd said. He screwed up his eyes. "Actually, that one might be a dealbreaker. Kidding!"

"What if my head got bashed in by a falling tree branch in a thunderstorm, and I acted like a dog, barking and crawling on all fours?"

"I'd scratch behind your ears and feed you gourmet dog treats." The sweet thing, the sad thing, was his seriousness.

Trevor had begged Trish to not divorce him. At the time, she'd been a secretary at a brokerage firm and had been sleeping with one of the bankers. Theo drove a Mercedes AMG, wore two gold rings and a Rolex, and had suggested she leave her husband. Trish couldn't resist shiny things, and she took Theo's advice. Even after she'd exposed herself as a cheater, Trevor begged. Offered to pay for couples' therapy, offered to take her to Hawaii, offered to take care of Sawyer evenings and weekends so she could go back to school. She nearly caved, it had been Hawaii that made her reconsider, but the banker had made a higher bid. Of course, the banker had only told her to divorce Trevor because he enjoyed the manipulation. Once she'd divorced Trevor, Theo's interest in her faded.

Who knew what I'd really do, though, if Trevor cheated? I liked to think I was easygoing and forgiving, but I had dark corners in me. Plenty of them.

I parked on the street near Emily's school. I took the phone off speaker and put it to my ear. "I can go sit with your mom. You could come home and relax."

"No, thanks," he said. "I like when you get your sleep and keep Em on schedule. I'm used to this random night shift."

"OK. Sounds good."

Which was true. My offer had been polite, but half-hearted. I did not want to sit with his mom all night. I got out of my car, catching a gentle waft of cow manure, and stepped through the freshly mowed grass toward Emily's school.

"Everything going smooth over there?" he said.

Well, I did crack a man's head last night and knock him into the river; I talked to a detective about my mom's possible involvement in a murder this morning; nearly got shot by a neighbor; and you know how I told you all my siblings were dead? Well, I lied! Holly lives nearby!

But I couldn't. I couldn't tell him about Holly. I couldn't tell him about digging up my mom's past. I wouldn't know how to be honest about some of my family history, but keep other parts secret. There were parts I needed to keep secret. Parts I couldn't even tell Trevor. And telling him about hitting a man over the head last night? Being drawn to Desiree? Bailing her out of jail? I didn't want to tell him those things. I didn't want to talk about my poor judgment. I didn't want him to worry about me as a wife, as a mother. I didn't want him to worry, period. He had enough on his plate.

A text came through. Desiree.

-He's got a nasty bump but he's fine. I didn't tell him, cross my heart, but he knows who you are. Not sure how.

My breath caught in my throat.

"Heather?" Trevor said over the phone. "Everything OK?"

"Everything's good," I said. "I'm walking up to Emmy's school."

He knows who you are.

29

TREVOR

DeeDee wasn't throwing up. I wasn't sure why I'd been compelled to tell that lie. That was a problem of mine. Taking things too far. DeeDee had asked if I could give her the night off. I'd told her I had to take care of something first, then I'd be there.

I parked in the gravel lot well-hidden by forest. This scenic lookout, Horseshoe Bend, was named for the way the river widened and then hooked sharply. Where the river widened, it deepened, and the shifting depths made for a gorgeous palate of color variations, turquoise blue to hunter green to deep black.

The person I was waiting for hadn't arrived yet, so I stepped down the broken cement stairs leading to the rocky beach. This is where I'd take the kids fishing. I should have taken them already. I'd meant to. I'd even bought a new pole, a good one with a baitcasting reel.

Soon. I'd take them soon.

It was stunning, Crooked River. Hunther's hidden treasure. I breathed in the rich, earthy, and mineral scents of the river. The gurgling of crystal water bubbling over rapids calmed my senses. I had the urge to take off my shoes and socks and walk carefully along the rock bed. I could almost feel the cold water numbing my skin, soothing my feet and calves.

My old girlfriend and I used to come to the river all the time. Bonfires, swimming, fishing. The day I'd met her, I'd cooked her a Bluegill from the river. I had just returned from fishing and was sitting on my parents' driveway, slicing open the Bluegill. Dad's small grill beside me, charcoals burning, glowing orange and fading to gray. Sixteen. I was sixteen. It was summertime, before sunrise. I did that in the summer, woke in the dark to go fishing. Brought a fish home and cooked it on my parents' driveway.

The early morning sky had been shot through with that electric magical blue. I loved that time of day when most people still slept, when anything seemed possible, the fresh-start cool and crisp feeling that you could be anyone.

"Whatcha doing?" she said from across the street. Her voice was like a fingernail tracing down my stomach. I almost slipped with the knife. My pulse was suddenly hammering, my skin was hot, and my dick was already hard.

As she crossed the road, her nightgown swaying at her knees, electric birdsong started in the trees as if she'd woken them.

She reached my driveway and tucked her wild morning hair behind an ear. Her fingernails were unpainted and chewed short. She wore rings on her fingers and a woven string bracelet on her wrist. Under her thin nightgown, her nipples were hard.

Instead of recoiling at the bloody guts on the asphalt beside me, the wide blade in my hand, she said, "Did you catch that in Crooked River?"

"Yeah." I wanted to tell her everything about me, about what I loved, about the light and dark in me, I wanted to rip my chest open and show her my insides. I took a deep breath. "I'm about to cook it. You want some?"

"Is it safe to eat?"

"I hope so. I've been eating from that river for years."

She smiled. "Um, sure." She slipped her foot free from her sandal, used her toenail to scratch the back of her calf. "Me and my mom just moved in."

"I noticed."

"We were in an apartment in Yellow Valley. My granddad died and left us the house, so here we are."

"I'm Trevor."

"I'm Dawn."

30

HEATHER

"Tell me about your first day of school, guys," I said.

Emily and Sawyer sat at the table, eating soup and grilled cheese.

"It was great," Emily said, without even giving it thought. I smiled at her perky enthusiasm, which she most definitely got from Trevor. "I like your bracelets, Momma. I've never seen those." I wore an armful of bangles on my right wrist.

"They're old. You want to wear one?"

"No thanks," she said, glancing at my eye makeup. "What about you, Sawyer?" Emily said. "What part did you hate the most?"

"Driver's Ed," he said and stuffed a square of grilled cheese in his mouth.

"How come?" she said.

"Everyone already knows how to drive, and they're all younger than me. I hit a curb. It sucked."

"You are driving on the first day of class?" I said, alarmed. "That doesn't seem logical."

He shrugged. "That's what I thought too, but everyone's been driving for years. Tractors, dirt bikes, three-wheelers, snowmobiles."

"What's a snowmobile?" Emily said.

"It's like a jet ski but for snow," he said.

"What's a jet ski? Throw me a bone here." Em was famous for pairing a rudimentary six-year-old's question with a sarcastic, overly mature remark.

"Like a one-person motorboat," Sawyer said. "I hate it here."

"Me too," Emily said. "Stupid wet shoes and bathroom puddles and Oliver saying girls can't play soccer."

I wanted to know more about this Oliver fellow, but they were slipping from me. "Let's go get donuts," I blurted.

Marjory's Greasy Spoon and Donuts had been on my mind since I'd spoken to Ben Greer this morning. I wanted to talk to someone who knew Dawn Young. The restaurant had probably been handed down to the next generation by now, but it was worth a shot.

"No thanks," Sawyer said, pushing his chair away from the table like it bit him.

"You have to go, Sawyer. You're driving." I grabbed the keys from the bowl on the counter and tossed them. "Catch."

He caught them. "I can't. I don't have my permit."

"The *school* let you drive without your permit. And if all the other kids have been driving for years, who cares? This is farm country."

"Literally?" he said.

I loved when he doubted me, when he didn't know if I was joking or serious. It reminded me; he was still a kid. Young man's body, young man's voice, young man's suave movements, teenager's silence, teenager's fury, but still a kid.

"Marjory's Greasy Spoon and Donuts. Let's go."

He smiled, and my heart skipped a beat. I could just see myself trying to lure this delicious smile from him in the future with other illicit ideas. *Sawyer, you want to smoke a joint? Sawyer, let's go tip some cows. Sawyer, let's go see the neighbor's cougars.*

31

Sawyer was a terrible driver. We almost made it to Marjory's unscathed, but while he was parking, he hit a cement cylinder holding a light post. First came the loud crunch of our headlight cracking, followed by plastic shards pinging like rain onto the pavement.

Hands in his lap in the driver's seat, staring straight ahead, he said, "I suck."

"You're right, you totally suck," Emily said. "Your phone fell under the seat, Mom."

"It's fine, Emily. I'll find it later," I said, irritation edging my voice. She always had something to say. It was my fault though. This was my bad idea. I touched his shoulder. "You're supposed to suck your first time. And, it's a headlight. A cheap fix. Put the car in Park."

He put it in Park. "Dad's gonna be pissed."

"First of all, Dad has several busted headlights under his belt. Second, when is Dad ever pissed? Don't worry about it. It's nothing. Seriously. Let's get donuts."

"Not hungry. I'll wait here," he said, his tone sharp, his fingers already tapping away at his phone.

I considered pushing, but bit my lip. It was probably better that he wasn't coming in since I wasn't here only for donuts. "OK, we'll bring you a donut. Let's go, Em."

Marjory's Greasy Spoon and Donuts stood between Auntie's Antiques and the Touchdown Bar on the corner.

Dawn had worked here.

I found myself wondering, how had Dawn Young moved through this town, through this building where she'd worked? Had this high school girl walked into work with a swing in her hip, or had she walked in as if her pockets were filled with rocks? Had she been the kind of young woman who didn't mind taking up space and some of your time, or had she tried to make herself as small and invisible as possible? Had my mom dropped off Dawn Young in this parking lot, and someone from the bar on the corner talked her into their car? That bar probably hadn't existed back then. What businesses had touched walls with Marjory's three decades ago?

The bell jingled as I opened the door, giving me a shiver of anticipation. I expected a cool wave of air conditioning, but it was hotter inside than outside. Nice. I never liked shivering in air conditioning in the summer anyway.

A ceiling fan spiraled slowly. Warm air wafted around the room, smelling of donut batter and refrigeration. My mind went to carnivals, the air sultry with the scent of funnel cakes. Crisp deep-fried dough, sizzling peanut oil, a huff of powdered sugar.

You could eat at the long counter. There were a dozen tall chairs. There were a dozen tables on the floor, five red pleather booths, and windows open along the walls. Cute. Four booths spilled over with teenage bodies. Maybe that's why Sawyer hadn't wanted to come in. Maybe he'd spotted the teenagers from our car. The teenage girl working the counter wore a T-shirt and tan uniform shorts, her long hair in a messy ponytail. I ordered Emily a sundae, me and Sawyer donuts, and I paid.

I got Emily situated in a chair at the far end of the counter. "I'll be right back, Em. I need to ask the waitress a question. Enjoy your sundae."

"Excuse me," I said to the waitress. Her back to me, she was making coffee. "I have a weird question for you."

She turned. Her expression dull, her movements slow.

"I am looking into an old crime, before your time, the murder of Dawn Young. She worked here. Have you heard of her?"

No recognition in her eyes, no change of expression on her face. "Hang on a sec," she said, and pushed through a swinging door to the kitchen.

Goosebumps popped on my neck. It was noisy in here with chatter. Good, Emily couldn't hear me. I waved at her, and she waved back.

A different woman came out of the swinging door. Older, salt and pepper hair down past her shoulders. Clumpy black mascara and red lipstick that bled beyond her lip line. Wrinkles around her lips like a starburst. She leaned forward on her elbows, and her cleavage thickened from her black T-shirt.

"I'm Marjory. Are you a reporter?" She was loud and unapologetic. This was what Desiree would be like at seventy-five.

Another wave of goosebumps raced along my skin. I actually shivered. I hadn't expected that I'd speak with the owner.

Marjory had probably seen a lot. Best to go with the truth. "No, I'm not a reporter. I found out last week that my mom was a suspect in Dawn Young's murder. I was—I am, shocked by the news. I was only six years old when it happened. I heard Dawn never made it to her shift that night. Can you tell me about it?"

"Dawn worked for me, yeah. She was a sweetheart," she said, but didn't smile.

"Did you know my mom?"

"Not well. I knew her, but she wasn't a lifer." She must have read the confusion on my face because she added, "Your mom didn't grow up here. Moved here after she had a kid or two. Once you keep having kids, well, you don't always get out much. Dawn talked about your mom though. She liked her." Marjory was the type of woman who didn't smile and still came across as warm. A nearly impossible feat. "They seemed to have a special relationship, Dawn and your mom, like an art-appreciation thing. I was surprised when I heard she confessed, your mom."

"Who did you suspect?"

"Oh, well, Dawn had lots of admirers. She brought me a lot of business, that girl. She wasn't sleazy or anything. She was, well, she was beautiful, but also a decent person. She wasn't loud, but she'd talk to people. I always told my cook to make sure he walked her out 'cause there were lots of young men interested in her. Older men too. Even the priests enjoyed talking to her. I always assumed the cops were covering for one of their own or your mom was covering for her boy. I got two daughters and I would serve time for either of them girls."

That image of Rodney again. Most of his face hidden by his hair, his mouth dripping in blood.

I glanced at Emily. She was lifting her shirt and wiping her mouth with it. Sundae bowl empty. My time was up. "Um, is there anything else you can tell me about Dawn's admirers?"

"She used to sketch on napkins for the customers. She sketched animals or she'd do their portrait on drink napkins. Ooh, they ate that up with a spoon."

The bell on the door jingled.

Marjory's eyes lit up as she glanced over my shoulder. "Hiya, Chrissy!" she said, smiling for the first time, a smear of red lipstick on her front tooth.

A woman was opening the door with her backside while cradling a baby in a blanket. Gray hairs fell loose from her floppy ponytail as she nuzzled the baby. Her wide, wrinkled face was made pretty by her happiness.

Marjory danced around the counter to greet the lady. "What'd you bring me, lady girl?" She did a hop and clap in place, then reached out for the baby. "Oh, looky look. Look at you. You are so, so, so precious. Gimme."

Marjory lifted the baby over her head, and the blanket dropped to the floor.

Not a baby. That's not a baby.

The paws were huge. There were black markings like exclamation points all over its body. It wore a diaper.

"Is that a tiger?" Emily said, dumbfounded and suddenly beside me, her hand slipping into mine.

Marjory, rubbing noses with the cat, making baby talk,

ignored us. Chrissy said to Emily, "This is Luna. She's a mountain lion. Look at those milky blue eyes. Ain't she just darling?"

The baby cougar opened its mouth, showing its tiny teeth, and made a chirping sound.

"She sounds just like a bird," Emily said, delighted. "Can we pet her, Momma?"

This was most likely my neighbor with cougars. She now had a *new* cougar. By Tracy Summers' account, that would bring her cougar total up to five.

"No, Em. I know she's a cute baby, but she's still a wild animal with sharp teeth and sharp claws."

"Oh, no, she's not even teething yet," Chrissy said. "She drinks from a baby bottle. You can come right over and pet her." Luna opened her small mouth and chirped again.

Without waiting for my approval, Emily pulled her hand away from mine. Walked up and pet her back leg.

The cougar *was* adorable. Chrissy was sweet. My heart was softening. I wanted to pet the baby too.

Which was the crux of the problem. Impulsiveness. Lack of foresight. This precious furry baby would quickly grow into a one-hundred-pound animal with sharp teeth, massive paws, and a hard-wired killer instinct.

Instead of hating this woman's ignorance, I was feeling for her.

Maybe she'd been one of those girls who answered "mother" when asked what they wanted to be when they grew up, even after that answer went out of style. All she ever wanted was a baby, a small curious helpless thing to care for. But she never got pregnant. So, she had a bunch of dogs and cats.

Like an addict plateauing on a stimulant, the vague emptiness solidified into an urge for more.

Or maybe she craved attention. Everyone had puppies. She wanted to stand out.

I glanced out the window at Sawyer. Still in the passenger seat and totally oblivious. Even though I didn't approve of pet cougars, I also wanted him to be here, experiencing this. *Sawyer, when will you ever see a cougar in a diaper? With your nose in your phone, you are missing the little things. You are missing spontaneity. You are missing everything. And, does it even cross your mind that I might need help?*

Emily still held onto the cougar's hind leg, baby-talking. "Aw, you are so sweet. Yes, you are. Yes, you are. Isn't she sweet, Momma?"

A trio of girls came up and cooed at Luna. Marjory was holding the cougar over her shoulder, rubbing its back. It was pawing at her hair.

The strangest feeling took hold of me. A ghost glided through me, turning my insides icy cold. I wished I would have seen it for the warning it was.

"One of the satanic lessons they follow is: if someone wrongs you or your family, do not turn the other cheek. Take vengeance."

Doctor Clifford Paulson, PhD Psychology
Transcripts from the Sixth Annual Conference on
Adult Manifestations of Childhood Trauma
THE RADISSON PLAZA HOTEL, CINCINNATI, OHIO

32

TREVOR

I pulled the lever, leaning back in Mom's La-Z-Boy. The sun was setting, and orange-tinted light snuck around the curtains.

Mom's living room had a gloomy, dusty, and outdated vibe. It had felt this way to me for a long time now. The smells though—sickness, dirty hair, a hint of coffee grinds (Paulina had placed in cups around the home as odor-absorbers)—those were new. When I lived here, the house smelled starchy and oven-warmed with a hint of rosemary. Mom liked to cook.

I should eat something, but my stomach felt sour.

The favor I had done today made me queasy. We'd met at Horseshoe Bend, the scenic lookout where I used to meet Dawn. Today, it had been spelled out for me that more favors would follow. I was already wrapped tightly around someone's finger.

I never should have let Heather insist on coming here. I should have pushed back. How had I thought we could move in and out of this town without it leaving its fingerprints on our skin?

Because it was just a few months, that's why. I figured everything would stay buried because we'd be here for such a short time.

I ran my fingers through my hair and stared at Mom. If she died soon, we could get out of here.

She kind of looked dead now with her eyelids closed and

thin as tissue paper, and her mouth wide open, lips dry, crust at the corners.

She wasn't dead though. Her chest rose. Her chest fell.

I imagined putting a pillow over her face. She would be gone fast and without much anguish.

I loved her. I hated her. My feelings were split down the center.

That's because you're two-faced.

I smiled to myself. I had been Two-Face once, quite literally. One Halloween, I must have been ten or eleven, still serious about candy and old enough to go with my friends (no parents), I went as Two-Face from the Batman comics.

Mom had a tray of creamy face-painting makeup. I liked the starchy, old lady smell of it, the tug of the cosmetic sponge pulling at my face, Mom talking to me, and not feeling like I had to participate in the conversation. I only had to keep my eyes and mouth closed and listen to her voice. I tuned out half of what she said, but the cadence of her voice was comforting. I had trusted her completely.

She'd said, "Oh, this is good, Trevor. Really good. I'm impressing myself. When you get home, give me two Snickers and two Kit Kats, and hide your candy so I can't eat it. There, you're all done. Go look in the bathroom mirror."

I did as she said. Half my face was untouched, all me. The other half was a sinister blue cartoon character with a sharply arched black brow, lid and under eye filled in stark white and outlined with black. Half my mouth was a ghoulish, painfully stretched scowl taking up most of my cheek, outlined in black and filled in creamy white, the lip stained red. I didn't even care if she used real lipstick, I looked so damn cool. She'd even spiked half of my hair with blue and gray paint.

It was exhilarating to be someone else. I'd felt unleashed. Buzzed. A little insane.

That's how I felt now. Two-Face. Two completely separate entities.

I loved Mom for her good intentions. I hated Mom for making me do those things.

She didn't make you.

OK, that's true. But if she wouldn't have filled my mind with that garbage, I never would have done it.

Mom made a choking sound. Gagging on her own spit woke her up. "Are you here, Trevor?" Her head laid heavy on her warm, damp pillow, and she gazed up at the ceiling. Her eyes fidgeted in their sockets.

"I'm here, Mom."

Her voice raspy, unoiled, she said, "I used to worry she would lace your coffee with—" She coughed a bit, cleared the phlegm rattling her throat, and continued, "with antifreeze. How could she not, being raised in that house?"

"Let's not talk about this, Mom. Can I get you something to eat?" Mom never used to talk about Heather like this. It had only started since we'd moved back.

"I waited, worrying, looking for clues, for years." She cleared her throat again.

"Would you like some water?"

She lifted her palm to him. *Stop.* She lowered her hand to her side, resting it on top of the thin sheet. *A cadaver's sheet.*

"I got tired of waiting. I got comfortable with her." Her mouth broke into a smile. "I saw in her eyes, she adored you. I started to eat her casseroles."

"I'm glad you let your guard down. She's a good person. Hey, do you feel like eating a bite of applesauce?"

"When I saw her with Emily, how she pecked at the girl with kisses, how much of a doting mother she was, I realized I'd been foolish." She turned her face toward me, locked eyes with me. "Now, Trevor, I am worried for her." Coughing gripped her. Tears leaked from her eyes.

I went to her and slipped my hand under her back. Her nightgown was damp against my palm. She smelled of skin and hair. All keratin.

"Better now?" I said.

She grabbed at my forearm and caught it, her nails scraping me. Her eyes were glazed and looked less human each day. She set those eyes on mine. "This town does not forget, Trevor. This town will tie her up to the cross on Dairy and 34 and set fire at her feet."

Panic stirred in my chest, a swarm of bees pulsing their wings, readying to take flight.

I broke eye contact, pulling gently away from her grip. I grabbed a pillow and propped it behind her back. "We're fine, Mom. Heather's fine." She *would* be fine. People here were just like people anywhere else. Some were small-minded, just like anywhere else, and maybe a touch lawless, but they weren't dangerous. "Will you eat some applesauce?"

Her intense gaze dissolved. Sleepy, she smiled. "OK. I'll try a bite." She patted my arm.

Heading to the kitchen, I pictured that cross. It was on some farmer's property. It was treated wood, had that green cast to it. It tilted east a bit, forced to bend by wind blowing in from the west. Sixteen feet tall and twelve feet wide. Everyone knew it was sixteen feet tall because that's the longest deck plank the Yellow Valley Home Depot carried.

I loved my mom. I really did.

But part of me wanted her to die. And soon. For her sake, to ease her suffering, and for mine. I did not want to knock fists with my past.

33

HEATHER

Sawyer flicked the glove compartment open. Closed. Open. Closed.

"Stop it, please. That's distracting. Can you imagine if I was snapping my fingers in your face while you were driving?"

"I'm not snapping."

I squeezed the steering wheel. "I'm making a comparison. You're making noise, and it's distracting. You crashed *without* distraction." I regretted it even as I said it. I puffed up my cheeks and exhaled. "Sorry. I don't mean to be a jerk. It's just distracting, and I'm already flustered. Those cougars down the street." I regretted this too, looking for sympathy, making excuses.

Sawyer said nothing. Emily said, "He was *so* cute, Sawyer. A *diaper*! Can you imagine a cougar in a diaper? Don't you wish you came in for ice cream?"

He said nothing.

I turned down Winding Way.

Sawyer flipped the glove box again.

"Um, Sawyer? That's just as distracting as it was sixty seconds ago."

"You can crash my car, it's cool," he said in a voice octaves higher than his own. It took me a second. Oh, he's mocking me. Then, in his own voice, angry and cold, he said, "You're not my mom."

Thank God. I opened my mouth to shout it, but bit my lip. *Breathe until you calm down.*

It stung. Sawyer hadn't said that for years, not since he was little and didn't know better. Back then, our relationship was easier because it's painless to forgive young kids, and they forget your sins as well. This teenage moodiness, I didn't know what to do with it.

Be kind. It had to be so hard and confusing for him with his mom in correctional. I pictured Trish wearing an orange jumpsuit, picking up trash on the side of a road.

Anytime I thought Trevor was amazing, near perfect, I had to remind myself, once upon a time, he had picked her. There was some part of him that clearly had terrible judgment. Anytime I felt superior to Sawyer's mom, I reminded myself that me and his ex must have something in common. *He picked you too.*

I'd asked Trevor what that commonality was. His answer was always the same. "Nothing. Before Sawyer, Trish was fun. Clean. No drugs, just money lust. After we had Sawyer, her money lust intensified, her selfishness sharpened. I wasn't enough for her."

I parked in our driveway. "I am not trying to replace your mom. I'm trying to help, that's all."

"Quit trying. I hate it." His feet hit the pavement and he slammed the door.

I threw my arm over Sawyer's empty seat and turned to Emily, ready to answer her questions about Sawyer's anger. "How you doing, Em?"

She stared out the window, watching Sawyer march into the house. She sighed, her chest lifting and falling. "How does that lady have a pet cougar?"

"Good question."

She turned to me with wild excitement in her eyes. "Imagine having a cougar in your bed." Emily unbelted herself, opened the door, and bolted out. "I'm going in the back."

"OK, Em. I'll be back there in a sec. I'm gonna look for my phone."

She stopped. "Oh, right. I can help you."

"It's OK. You go play. I'll find it." If it was cracked or if it wasn't in the car, I might lose my temper. I didn't want her to see that.

She darted to the side of the house.

I started in the back, with the doors open, in a lame push-up position, peering under the front passenger seat. The sun was still warm and golden, hanging low in the sky behind our house. The driveway was cast in shadows, making the car's interior dark. I felt around with my hand on the dirty carpet, found a few mummified French fries and sticky coins, but no phone. I went around to the other side and did the same thing. Nothing but broken crayons and gum wrappers under the driver's seat.

My knees on the back seat, my head resting on the scratchy carpet floor, I peered under the dark back seat.

I swiped my hand back and forth under the seat, crumbs and rough carpet sliding against my palm, a few pencils, crumpled soda straws. I came across a lighter.

Was this Sawyer's or from the previous renter of the car?

Good parents in this day and age did not let smoking cigarettes go unchecked. Then again, considering all the horrific things a sixteen-year-old boy could do, smoking cigarettes seemed to be a meditative, intelligent choice.

My phone buzzed with a text. Lucky timing.

The screen lit up, revealing its location further back. I grabbed it and laid across the backseat. Trevor.

-*What are you up to?*

-*Just got back from donuts and ice cream. Call me later.*

A horn honked three times, loud and close. I raised my head.

No car in my driveway, but a Ford pickup idled near our mailbox. Sawyer ran across the lawn and, in one graceful swoop, laid his right hand down on the edge of the truck bed and swung his legs to the left like a gymnast on the pommel horse.

Grace failed him on the landing. He tumbled into the back of the pickup, and the two kids in the front cab laughed, their voices free and masculine, reminding me of my brothers. A nervous butterfly flit in my stomach. Something about a deep, conspiratorial, masculine laugh was forever frightening.

Sawyer's head popped up, a sly grin on his face that I'd never seen.

The truck's tires squealed, and it shot down the street toward the main road. Behind the cab window, a gun rack, rifles mounted horizontally.

How had he made friends so quickly? It was the first day of school.

I grabbed the bag of donuts from the dashboard and

headed around the side of the house. "Emily?" I called, the neighbor's cougars coming to mind again.

"Back here," she said softly. Her voice was coming from beyond a cluster of overgrown lilac bushes.

I peeked around the lilacs. The late afternoon sun highlighted the back of her hair, setting it ablaze. She was sitting in the grass, gathering bouquets of dandelions.

The tangle of lilacs partially sheltered her head like a fort. The image stirred a strange sense of déjà vu, something from my childhood. A little girl, my age, just in front of me, pushing through an arcing tangle of mulberry bushes. Our fort. The passageway laden with juicy berries, and the dirt was dotted with blackish purple stains. The mulberry bush passage ended at a shallow creek where we'd laid a two-by-four as a bridge. Along the wet, rotting sides of the wood plank, tiny spirals of snails clung. A boy, two or three years old, sat in the dirt, putting a snail in his mouth.

"Yuck," I'd said, wiping at my own tongue as if I had something there. "Don't eat that. Yuck."

The boy mimicked me, wiping the snail away.

Such a strange memory because I couldn't recall these children's names. Were they old neighbors? I didn't know.

This memory was a scrawny tree in the slaughtered forest of my mind.

34

I was reading to Emily in her bed when the front door creaked open. Sawyer. He took the stairs two or three at a time, bolted past her room, and closed his door fast. The lock clicked.

"Are you thinking what I'm thinking?" Emily said. We laid in her bed under her cozy comforter, her teddy bear in between us.

"What?"

"We should take his door off."

I smiled at her, ready to explain about sixteen-year-olds needing privacy, but my phone rang—circus theme.

"Can I talk to Dad first?" Emily said.

"Sure. I'll be right back." I handed her my phone.

"Hi, Dad, it's Emily." As I walked downstairs, Emily said, "So you are not going to believe what we saw at the donut place."

Sawyer had left the front door open.

I locked it. I made a cup of tea, turned off the lights, and climbed the stairs with my drink.

A noise drew me back downstairs. It sounded like papers brushing together.

I checked each of the rooms. Everything looked in order. Had it come from outside?

I turned off the foyer light and peered outside into the night.

Movement caught my eye. Someone walked along the street, but—with no lampposts near our house—I couldn't make out any details. What if it's Desiree's boyfriend's brother? A chill ran down my spine, but I shook it off. Probably one of the neighbors on a late-night walk. Maybe Tracy Summers.

I walked upstairs. "My turn, Emily."

"Love you, Dad. Here's Mom now. Oh, and by the way, Sawyer crashed Mom's car."

I widened my eyes at Emily, she shrugged, and I said into the phone, "My car is fine. Just a cracked headlight. I let him drive to the restaurant three minutes away. How's your mom?"

"Mom is the same. Complaining about her feet tonight. For as crummy as she's doing, she has enough energy to complain," he said, his voice weary. "DeeDee needs tomorrow night off too."

"You sound exhausted. What about calling for backup?"

"They are short-staffed. It's not like the city where there are tons of nurses and CNAs just waiting for work." An edge crept into his voice. He's losing patience.

"Let me do it tomorrow. It's important that you see the kids."

"Let's take it one day at a time. Are you in your PJs?"

"Not yet."

"Do you have your tea?"

"Just took my first sip." I held up a finger to Emily, motioning that I'd be right back. "Listen," I said quietly, walking into my bedroom, "Sawyer left with some kids for a few hours today. He jumped in the back of a pickup truck loaded with a gun rack."

"That's fairly standard for these parts. I'm not too worried about it."

Trevor had two settings. *I'm not worried about it* or *I'm not* too *worried about it.*

"I know. I know you both went hunting, and you probably talked to him about gun safety. I'm OK with all that, but I need you to talk to him again. I don't know who these kids are or their firearm rules." *And he's acting rude*. I wanted to say it, but didn't want to come across as a tattle. "I'd like you to be home tomorrow. The kids need you," I said slowly so he would get it. "I'll sit with your mom."

The other day I'd been reflecting on the changes Hunther was bringing about in each of us. Trevor acting more rugged. The kids seeming more independent and carefree. I thought I liked those changes. Now I wasn't so sure.

And what of the changes in yourself?

35

TREVOR

I wasn't going to be able to keep Heather away from my mom. I didn't like the idea, but I'd have to suck it up.

I leaned back in Mom's recliner and let my eyes fall shut. I was physically exhausted and mentally wrung out. I'd been able to keep my memories of Dawn buried for years, but it was getting more difficult to do. As I laid back in the chair, another memory clawed its way out with fingernails caked in dirt and blood.

Dawn had doused the log pyramid in lighter fluid.

"That's *way* too much," I said, laughing.

She touched her chin to her shoulder, gave me the smallest smile, lit a match, and tossed it in. The wood ignited in a puff of fire. She laughed, grabbed my arm, and jogged me back. The rocky shore near Horseshoe Bend shifted and slipped beneath my boots and I tripped. She caught me, preventing my fall, and laughed harder. She delighted at my minor misfortunes.

Foggy mist moved in patches over the water. The rapids whispered in trickles and hushes. Frogs croaked.

When she unzipped her backpack, I unrolled my sleeping bag, catching a gust of fabric softener. Mom could be counted on to root out anything filthy in the house or garage and clean it.

Dawn pushed two marshmallows on her stick and held it in the fire. "Do you like your marshmallows burnt?" she said, her voice tilting playfully.

"Who doesn't?" I said. Just watching her silhouette against the flames, the light flickering against her face, her cheek blushing warm, made me hard. She was gorgeous. But it wasn't only that. She was comfortable with herself. She wasn't chatty, but if someone asked her a question, she didn't hesitate in her answer, she didn't mentally prepare an answer first. She was herself. It was the same with her drawing. She wasn't ashamed of it and she didn't brag; it was simply part of her.

We'd been spending time together. I gave her rides to school in my Chevy. I took her fishing twice. She drew a pencil sketch of my face after school in my truck. Both of us turned toward each other in the front seat. She'd taken off her shoes and slipped her bare foot under the hem of my jeans, rubbed the bottom of her bare toes against my calf, tickling me while she kept telling me to *sit still*. The sketch was good. I mean, really good. I put it in the bottom of my tackle box, somewhere Mom wouldn't snoop. The week before, we'd kissed for the first time. It had been wet with lots of tongue.

She pulled her stick out of the fire, marshmallows flaming, and she snuffed them with a few blows. She touched a crisp, blackened marshmallow with her fingers, yelped, and pulled her hand away. Too hot, but she went back again quickly to pull it off. I pulled my flaming marshmallows back and blew them out.

She ate her first marshmallow carefully. She pulled the

second marshmallow off her stick and slowly reached toward me. I opened my mouth. She shoved it in my mouth, abruptly, and spread sticky goo down my chin.

"What the hell," I said, my mouth full.

She laughed, took a marshmallow off my stick, and jammed another in my mouth before I'd finished the first. Laughing, she took the last one off my stick, smashed it in her hands, and rubbed it on both my cheeks.

Annoyance bubbled up, but I pushed it down. She was playing, and I was crazy about her.

"This isn't going to come off even in the shower," I said. "My face is so sticky."

She rubbed her palms against my forearms. "You're right. This is not coming off."

I grabbed her arm. "I know your trick. You want to get me in the river."

"No, I don't," she said, smiling.

I stood and pulled off my T-shirt. "Of course you do. Why else would you smash marshmallows on my face?"

She shrugged. "I don't know. Maybe to see if you'd get angry."

"Did I?" I pulled down my jeans, and walked backward toward the river in my boxers.

She shook her head. "I've never seen you get angry."

I stepped backward into the water, and sucked air through my teeth, pretended to cry a bit. "Cold. It's so fucking cold. This is your fault. Your turn. You owe me." The river water wasn't going to get the marshmallow off my face, but I wanted to be in the water with her.

She sighed, a smile sliding up her face, and pulled her T-shirt over her head. Kicked off her shoes and wiggled out of her jeans. Her bra and underwear were plain and white. Her body, backlit by the bonfire's flickering flames, looked like something otherworldly. Even with the cold water, I was hard again. She walked barefoot, carefully, watching where she stepped.

Her hair fell across her face, and she tucked it behind her ear. Her expression was masked and dark now because the bonfire was behind her, but my eyes weren't on her face anyway. She stepped in without hesitating.

"What the hell?" I said. "How are you not even cold? I feel like such a wuss."

She laughed, coming close. The moon reflected off the water, tinting her skin with a bluish radiance. The whites of her teeth, her eyes, her white bra; they were glowing. Her nipples were hard.

"Why would you want to see me get angry?" I said, my teeth chattering.

She bit the side of her bottom lip, then let go. "For fun."

"Victims of sadistic abuse often describe their trauma in a flat, unemotional way, and that might make those listening think the patient is lying. I'm here to tell you, if you've been brainwashed, if you have been chronically abused, this deadpan presentation is normal and necessary for self-preservation."

Doctor Clifford Paulson, PhD Psychology
Transcripts from the Sixth Annual Conference on
Adult Manifestations of Childhood Trauma
THE RADISSON PLAZA HOTEL, CINCINNATI, OHIO

36

HEATHER

I have held a grudge against casseroles for as long as I could remember. Casseroles reminded me of walking into my parents' house after school, a half dozen pairs of smelly sneakers kicked off at the door, and the oven timer beeping. Casseroles reminded me of after-dinner bloating and bickering, of alcohol-soaked evenings, dirty dishes left out for morning sobriety. Casseroles were the essence of life slopped together, a scoop of this trashy story, a dash of that tragedy, cover it in cheese, and shovel it down.

So, what do you know, I made a casserole!

A modern casserole, mind you. This one used two heaping cups of cauliflower rice, making it low-carb. Trevor's mom loved both cauliflower and casseroles. At least she used to.

I sent Trevor a text.

I made a casserole. We can eat dinner as a family, then I'll leave for your mom's house, and you can relax with the kids.

I didn't expect a return text. It was early. He'd only been at work a few hours.

Kitchen shears in hand, I walked barefoot out the back door to the side of the house where our milkweed patch spread. The sun was bright, the grass was dry and scratchy against my ankles. We were due for rain. I picked a stalk and before I made any cuts, I carefully checked each leaf on the stalk. Spiders, ants, and beetles easily killed the slothful caterpillars. I didn't want to bring any murderers into the house. I snipped the stalk in the middle, glue-white sap oozing from the cut and leaving a sticky drop on my shears.

"Hey," someone yelled.

In front of my house, a car idled against the curb, the driver staring at me. Silver Infiniti.

Oh my God. It's him.

Should I run, bolt my door, and call the police? Or should I apologize?

Shocked, I did neither. I stood still, milkweed stalk in one hand, shears in the other.

His engine switched off, his door slammed, and, in a few strides, he walked halfway up my lawn, his hand a visor against his forehead. A drip of sweat rolled down between my shoulder blades. My breath was stuck in my chest, thick like milkweed sap. He lowered his hand, revealing a square bandage fastened to his temple.

"You?" he said, smiling, serendipitously. As if he were as bewildered, as if he happened to be here delivering a package and just realized his assailant lived here. "It's you."

I gripped the scissors tighter so they wouldn't slip from my sweaty hand, and sap stuck to my palm. "I thought you were attacking her," I said, trying to sound sturdy. "I was driving to call the police, but then I saw you standing by your car. You were OK."

"How so very kind of you," he said, smiling, walking toward me. "Try to kill a man, leave him to drown, and plan to call the police later to check if he drowned." He kept coming, closing the distance. He had a familiar look to him. A moderately handsome face, good hair, loose casual curls. Like Trevor. This man wore jeans and a navy button-down shirt, untucked, but not sloppy. The only element that didn't match his car and outfit was his worker boots, which were brown and worn, laces loose and wide.

He did not look like someone who would recklessly run you off the road and sexually assault your friend. *When he's high, he likes to get rough.* Then again, some of the most dangerous men were handsome and professional in appearance, their good looks emboldening their bad behavior.

"What do you want?" I said, backing up slowly.

He glanced at the shears in my hand and smiled. He had a smile that a mother would interpret as sweet, but it was smug and superior. He stopped, dug his hands into his pockets, and rolled forward on his toes. "I'm guessing the husband isn't home, huh?" *He's messing with you.*

"Where's Desiree?"

He smiled and rubbed the back of his neck. "She's something, isn't she?" He laughed. "You've been in town a few weeks, and she's already put a spell on you too."

The wistful look in his eyes, it pretty much answered my question of why he would dare cheat with his brother's girlfriend.

"Where does she work now?" I said.

"Aldi's."

184

He took another step toward me.

"Does your brother know?" I said.

He laughed, then his smile flattened to a menacing line. "What? You're gonna tell my brother? You're threatening me? You have any idea what kind of guy my brother is?"

From the neighbor's lawn came a boisterous, "Hey there!"

Tracy Summers. Scrappy camo getup. His hand raised in a wave, the other hand holding a brown paper bag. In a few steps he was on my lawn. "Everything hunky-dory here, Chicago?"

"I'm not sure," I said.

"Hey, Brandon," Tracy said. "You might want to tell your big brother to check on our friendly neighborhood menagerie. We got five cougars now, I think. Someone ought to do an inspection, make sure we're all safe, don't you think?"

"'Course," he said to Tracy, his eyes on me. "Be seeing you, *Chicago*." He nodded slowly, his eyes squinted, and walked to his car.

Tracy and I silently watched the Infiniti drive away.

"You've been here barely two weeks; how do you know *him*?" Tracy said.

"He cut me off on the road."

"And you gave him your address?"

"I don't know how he knows my address. Who is he?"

"Corrupt contractor among other shady business ventures. His folks are from money. His mom's father built the hospital in Yellow Valley. He shouldn't be trouble, but he's got a Ho-Chunk thing."

"Ho-Chunk?" I'd heard that word before, but I couldn't put my finger on it.

"Ho-Chunk's a casino. Brandon gambles, gets himself into tight spots. Always seems to squirm out in one piece." He held up the bag. "I brought this for you."

My hands full, my palm sticky with sap, I took the bag awkwardly. "I don't know what's in here, but I'm sure glad you brought it over." I didn't want to think about what could have transpired between Desiree's side boyfriend and me had Tracy not brought over his brown sack.

"It's deer jerky."

My mouth must have dropped open because he laughed hard and slapped his thigh. "Don't knock it till you try it. Stay safe, Heather Bishop."

37

Aldi's sat in an oversized, sun-bleached, mostly empty parking lot beside Bert's Dollar Store. No trees, only cement. Bert had signs and ads taped to his front window and blue plastic kiddie pools nested and trapped under a brick in front of the door.

I was walking up to Aldi's when Desiree walked out. A young guy with a skater haircut, short in the back, long in the front, and sweeping over one eye, followed her.

She walked toes pointed out, ballerina-plié-style, which was the walk of only the coolest girls in my middle school, circa 1998. I hadn't seen an adult woman walk like that in years. Desiree leaned against the brick side of Aldi's and tilted her head back to sip from her soda can. The guy stood beside her, back to the wall, smoking.

She didn't notice me until I was in front of her. "Hey, you," she said, surprised, but sleepy and warm. Her eyes, pale-blue liquid crystal, squinted slightly from the sun's glare. There was a small scab high on her forehead. "You OK, hon?"

I wasn't expecting the love. It disarmed me. OK, charmed me. "Yeah, I'm fine. You?"

"I land on my feet, sister." Smiling, she took her time with her words. This was the kinder side of Desiree. Or maybe she was a little high. "Hey, I met your son last night at a party. Holy hell, he is a hottie." She said it like she wanted to slide her nails up his thigh. "The girls in this town will eat him alive. You'd better tell that boy to be careful." She smiled seductively, one of her canines slipping out. Like she knew that if I went and told my teenager to be careful, he'd do the opposite.

So that's where he went last night.

"He's too young for you," I said jokingly, and added a harsh touch, "even in Hunther."

"Good point." She didn't take my sarcasm to heart. She sipped her soda can slowly, smoothly, like a smoker inhaling. I was glad she didn't turn nasty. I wanted her to stay away from Sawyer, I wanted her to hear my threat, but I also wanted her sweet acceptance.

Christ, Heather.

Her fingernails were short, painted midnight blue. She wore three rings, and a dozen bracelets covered her bird tattoo. One of her rings caught my attention. Three silver clawed fingers grasping a purple crystal ball around her middle finger.

"Oh, hey," she said. "My fuck-buddy hasn't mentioned you again so I think you're good."

Her young friend didn't flinch at a single word. Maybe he was on something. Maybe he had a Desiree-crush too.

"Well, he stopped by my house. Brandon."

"No way." She laughed, then narrowed her eyes. "Really?"

"Really."

"Huh. What did he want?"

"I don't know. That's why I'm here. Well, partly. What do you think he wants?"

She thought about it, shook her head. "I honestly don't know." Heat blew through me, and my skin prickled. Would he come back to my house tonight? She motioned for her friend's cigarette. He passed it, and she inhaled, offering no further thoughts on her fuck-buddy's motivation.

"That's a pretty ring," I said. "Where'd you get it?"

She gave me a weird look, like who cares? "My pops gave it to me ages ago. When I was in high school, when I fantasized about being a witch." Softening, she said, "It was my mom's."

"My mom had one just like it." I pictured Mom in her leopard print robe, elbows on the counter, breasts leveraged against her forearms, wrinkled cleavage popping. Ragged fingernails. Cataract-purple crystal held by claws on her ringed middle finger. Her coffee mug of vodka and peach crystal light.

Desiree sucked on the cigarette again, exhaled, and handed it back to her friend. "I guess I'm not too surprised. They had a bunch Wicca shops in Yellow Valley when I was a kid. Beautiful jewelry. Most went out of business, but there's still one there. The Red Butterfly."

Desiree's mom was probably ten years younger than my mom, but they existed during the same grunge fashion of the nineties. Mood rings, slip dresses under flannel shirts, and fringe coats. "I guess," I said. "The reason I stopped by. I really need to ask your dad about the Dawn Young case."

"Hea-ther," she said, pausing between syllables, as if I were her baby sister. "Drop it. Seriously. It's just town gossip, but the

189

thing is, people in this town, they need to hold on to their version of history." To her friend, she said, "Break's over. Let's roll."

He held his cigarette like he was playing darts, tossed it as far as he could, and walked away.

She followed him, but stopped. "Heather. We're off work in an hour. We're going to the river, under the bridge. You should come."

"I can't. And I can't drop it," I said. "And how hard could it be for me to find out where he lives?"

She rolled her eyes and smiled. "The intersection of Route 34 and Salisbury. Red house with a cow out front."

38

I was looking for a cow statue by the mailbox.

Nope. Asher Moss had a real fucking cow. It stood out front, near the road, chewing the tall grass Asher hadn't mowed. It looked like a peaceful cow. A storybook Holstein dairy cow, white with black spots, but I wasn't familiar with bovine behavior. If it charged, I wanted to be up on that porch.

His house was set back from the road, and I drove all the way up his long driveway. It would be a bitch to back out, but at least I wouldn't get trampled by a cow.

Asher Moss answered his door. He had a tight body for late fifties, and his white T-shirt was tucked into his jeans. He seemed like one of those guys always working on a carpentry project or getting up early to go on a ten-mile bike ride. His face was weathered, creased, but his blue eyes were enthusiastic and pretty. Not as pretty as Desiree's, but the slate blue of a lake. Handsome.

"Hi. I'm friends with your daughter."

"She OK?" Calm, but concerned.

"She's fine."

"Oh, that's good." He smiled. He had an aw-shucks smile. "That girl raises my blood pressure." He must have had a heck of a time raising a daughter on his own. Desiree probably had him wrapped around her finger.

"I'm Heather Bishop. I'm in town with my husband. We're visiting his mom. Judy Bishop."

He nodded. "I know Judy. Sorry to hear about her diagnosis."

"Thanks," I said, remembering the cow. I glanced back. It remained near the road. "My maiden name is Hornne. My mom was Melinda Hornne." His gaze drifted over my shoulder. "I just found out my mom was a suspect in a murder case. Dawn Young."

He nodded, stepped out, and whistled with both pinkies in his mouth. "Come here, Ginger," he said, walking down the porch and sitting on the bottom step. I stayed where I was, standing on the porch, watching the cow mosey over.

"I didn't know people had pet cows," I said.

He laughed softly. "I don't know that they do. We've had a few dairy farms go under in the past decade. One fellow let his cows loose and burned down the barn, killed himself. Neighboring farms have collected the cows, the ones that didn't die, brought them into their stock. Ginger was a loner. You'd be driving by and see her eating grass. When people tried to catch her, she ran. Which is hilarious, because if you know anything about cows, they aren't typically hard to catch. How she got her name." He turned his head and winked at me. "Gingerbread Man," he said. In case I'd missed how she got her name, which I had.

"Oh, right," I said. "Cute."

"She started showing up in my lawn, I started feeding her apples and carrots, and we became friends." He held his hand out in a stop-gesture. She walked right up to him, put her nose against his palm, and licked him. He moved his palm along her skin and rubbed behind her ears. When he stopped, she nudged him for more attention. "I fill the shed with hay and leave the door open. She's a real polite lady too, even potty-trained herself. Only craps over by the trees." With his other hand, he motioned to a row of old trees lining the left side of his yard. "So we get along real well, don't we, girlie? Wanna pet her?"

"Oh, I'm OK. No, thanks." In this heat, her meaty smell was fetid. I wanted nothing to do with it. And, I worried she would sense my fear and bite me.

"I'm not sure I can help you with your mom though," he said. "What does she say about it?"

"I can't ask her. She's dead."

"I'm sorry to hear. I didn't know."

"How would you? She was living in Southern Illinois. I wasn't close with her."

"Well, that was a long time ago. I remember a little. Some boys found the dead girl under a storm drain." I walked to the end of his porch so I could get a better view of his face as he talked. "Your mom was barely a suspect at first, but several weeks later, she ended up confessing to her head doctor. The county attorney let it go because he was friends with your dad and your folks had a litter of kids. Sorry. No offense."

"None taken. What about signs of rape?"

He patted the cow on the head and said, "Alright, that's enough, old girl." He dropped his hands, and the cow turned away. "We weren't sure if it was rape. The coroner tried his best to collect evidence, but since she was in the water, I'm not sure if he woulda found much. What he collected came back contaminated. The DNA tests weren't great back then. This was the nineties."

"It was probably a rape though, right? I mean, weren't her fingers cut off to get rid of evidence of a struggle?"

He shrugged. "Seems like it, but why else would your mom confess?"

Maybe to cover for Rodney.

"What about my brother Rodney? Was he ever considered a suspect?"

"Hm," he said. "Nothing stands out in my memory about him. I'd have to pull the case out and go over my notes. What does he say about it?"

"Nothing. He died years ago. What about the dead opossums?"

He nodded slowly. "Right. That's right. When we started investigating Dawn's murder, your mom's neighbors said they found their opossums torn up in their yard days before. They suspected your mom."

My stomach twisted.

"Did you or your wife know my mom?"

"I knew who she was. I didn't know her well. She wasn't born in town. I don't think my wife would have known her. Too much of an age difference. Why?"

"Desiree was wearing a ring today. She said you gave it to her when she was a teenager. My mom had that same ring when I was young." I used to sneak into her jewelry box and try on her jewelry. That ring stood out because it was mysterious and a bit creepy. I never saw that ring after we moved away from here. "I was thinking maybe they knew each other and my mom gave it to your wife?"

He shook his head. "Most likely, they both got those rings from the same rinky-dink shop in town. There were a number of mystic shops in Yellow Valley. Dream catchers dangling in the front windows, tarot cards, fortune telling, jewelry. There's still one left."

"Yeah, Desiree mentioned that," I said. "Makes sense."

"I never believed in that spiritual, mystic stuff. What about you?"

"I don't know what I believe." Truest thing I'd said in a while.

39

Home from picking up Emily, I was dropping my keys in the bowl when Trevor called.

"What a relief you answered," he said. "I ran into traffic. I'll be home in forty minutes, but you have to go to my mom's now. Paulina's been with my mom all day but needs to leave as soon as she can. DeeDee's got the night off, and I can't afford to piss off Paulina."

"What about the casserole?"

"Forget the casserole," he said, annoyance edging into his voice. "Just leave it, and go."

"OK. Give me a minute to set Emily in front of the TV and tell Sawyer he's in charge."

Five minutes later, I was backing out of the driveway.

An image of Brandon walking up my lawn, a bandage on his head, came to mind. I should have told Sawyer to not open the door for anyone.

I popped in my earbuds and called Trevor, "On my way."

"Heather, there's something I have to tell you." His tone serious, so unlike Trevor.

My heart skipped a beat. "What?"

"My mom. I haven't updated you on my mom." He sighed,

and static buzzed my earbuds. "She's not herself."

"Of course she's not."

"No, I mean she says crazy things."

The car behind me was riding my bumper. I wanted to brake hard just to make him crash, match my shattered headlight in the front. But then I'd be late. "It'll be OK, Trevor. I saw her, what, four weeks ago." I hadn't seen her since we'd moved in. Trevor had brought Sawyer and Emily once, but I hadn't gone.

"No, no. Four weeks ago she was different. She's meaner now. Kind of, well, raunchy." As if I were a schoolgirl. As if I didn't just fuck him the other day and whisper nasty things in his ear.

"Even if she makes a move on me, I'm way stronger."

He didn't laugh, which made me feel both sleazy and cruel. "She's not going to touch you," he said. "She's weak. Just don't take anything she says seriously, OK?"

I turned left, and the car that had been riding my bumper made a U-turn.

The door opened before I reached the porch, and the smell of warmth and homemade food wafted out.

"Come in, come in," Paulina said, bossy but with love. In a single movement, this sturdy woman wearing green scrubs pulled me into a hug like a strong undertow. She grabbed my biceps, pushed me away to have a look at me as if I were twelve with newly budding breasts. She shoved a hot mug into my hands that smelled of medicine and said, "Nettle tea."

Paulina was beautiful, her gray and black wavy hair striking and exotic, her scent woodsy, her accent European. Polish, Czech, Lithuanian, or Russian. I imagined she'd experienced a bit of war, maybe followed her daughter to the States.

I was simultaneously in love with her and appalled by her. She treated me like close family, which stirred homesickness deep in my belly. At the same time, I didn't like her invading my space, expecting things from me, assuming things about me.

Speaking quickly, Paulina showed me Judy's prescription bottles, where to journal the medicine I administered, and how to empty Judy's urine jug. "Oh heavens, why am I even telling you this? Trevor said you're a phlebotomist, bless your heart, you're a pro."

"Not really. I just do blood draws."

"Oh, honey. You're an angel. Give yourself credit."

Honestly, I'd expected Paulina to be cold. *So, you're the wife. Why haven't I seen more of you?*

I'd expected to offer excuses, *I've offered. Trevor keeps telling me, he's got this.*

That Paulina was soft and motherly toward me made me well up.

"What's wrong?" she demanded. "You tell me. It's OK. You can tell me anything. Tell me."

"I'm good. Just a tickle in my throat." I sipped my tea and wiped a tear from the corner of my eye.

I could see how Trevor might want to bury his head into her bosom. This woman was a giver. Maybe she blew him in Judy's dusty, floral bedroom, and didn't expect anything in return. A blowjob for the sake of loving dick or not even loving dick, only wanting to make someone else happy. I couldn't blame him. I wanted her to take me into her arms too.

"I have to go," Paulina said. "My daughter is working the night shift at the hospital and I'm the chauffeur for her two sons." She rolled her eyes, but with a smile on her face. She liked *complaining* about being the chauffeur, but she loved *being* the chauffeur.

Of course Paulina's daughter was a nurse. Paulina was the type of mother that daughters wanted to imitate.

"There's pierogi in the oven. Judith loves it. Take it out in fifteen minutes. Call me if you have any questions. Anything. I left my number on the table. Love you, hon. I'm so glad to meet you."

And she was out the door.

Paulina and her type, cozy and too friendly, made me uncomfortable, but this type of motherly woman was also the reason I'd become a phlebotomist.

After we'd moved away from Hunther, Rodney had to go in regularly for blood tests. I couldn't remember exactly why; my kid brain assumed it had something to do with him being not quite right in the head.

Each time I tagged along, it was the same trio of woman phlebotomists. A Black woman with clumpy mascara on her lashes and short black hair dyed orange at the edge of her forehead. An Asian woman, smiley and chatty, who wore no makeup. And a white woman with her hair in a messy bun, four studs up each ear, sloppy tattoos on her fingers, and hanging on to a smattering of teenage acne.

These three women had joked sharply with each other, touched each other often, and laughed easily. They were competent, tough, and smooth with people and needles. In my young mind, they were goddesses. I'd wanted what they had. I craved their closeness and their confidence. I grew to love the smells of ethanol and apple juice. Sometimes picking a job is that simple. That stupid.

"Who's there?" A wobbly whisper of a voice from the next room.

"It's me, Judy. It's Heather." I walked out of the oven-warm kitchen, down the hall. "Trevor couldn't get here in time, so I'm here."

From her living room came soothing, melodic voices and the sizzle of butter on a frying pan—a cooking show.

Judy lay on a hospital bed, her head slightly inclined. Her eyes were fish gills, barely open and drug-dazed. Her body was covered with a flimsy sheet, and the blue absorbent pads layered underneath her hung off the mattress on both sides. Her feet stuck out from the sheet, toes gnarly and veiny. Very Wicked Witch of the West after the house fell.

Her hospital gown was open at the chest, and her pain patch stuck to the sunken skin beside her clavicle. "Paulina made you pierogi," I said. "It will be ready soon. Do you have an appetite?"

"God, no. Everything tastes like tree bark. Have you ever eaten tree bark?" She rubbed her fingers together like she had a booger between her fingers and was trying to brush it away.

"No," I said. "What are you watching?"

"Nothing. Just voices, happy voices. Good show for dying. That, and *The Price Is Right*. They must be actors these days, they act like such idiots. I don't remember them being idiots." She rubbed her fingers together again. "Go and get my smokes, would you? They're in the toilet."

"What?"

"Under the, under the, you know, the flap." She closed her eyes tight, frustrated, searching for a word. "Toilet top. Tank lid."

"How do you get them back there?"

"DeeDee hides them for me. Don't you dare tell Trevor or I will tell him all your dirty secrets," she hissed with such threat, my jaw dropped. "Don't be a prissy bitch," she said. "Go fetch them for me."

Trevor wasn't joking.

What if she died tonight because I gave her a cigarette?

She whined. "DeeDee! I want DeeDee. Trevor's a bully and Paulina's Stalin. I want a cigarette!"

She's dying. If she wanted a cigarette, she should get one.

"OK. OK. Settle down. I'll get them." I walked to the bathroom.

They wouldn't be under the lid. She was delusional. DeeDee wouldn't hide cigarettes in the tank.

I lifted the lid.

Unbelievable. A messy patch of silver duct tape, frayed at the edges, held the pack to the underside of the lid.

I set the lid on the sink countertop and freed the pack of smokes. The thin cardboard was soft and flexible in my hand. Half full. I went to the kitchen, opened her silverware drawer, and grabbed matches. I turned off the oven, but left the pierogi in to keep them warm.

I walked into the living room and said, "How many cigarettes do you have each day?"

"Two when DeeDee's here. DeeDee lets me have two." Her hands kneaded the sheet pulled up below her flat chest, her breasts fallen to the sides of her ribcage. "But DeeDee isn't here," she whined.

"She's sick," I said, slipping a cigarette in between my lips. I struck the match against the thin box, but the match cracked.

"Oh, come on. Come on," she snapped.

I had the urge to laugh, but held back. Struck another match, brought it to the cigarette, and breathed in.

"There you go," she crooned, her eyes open and staring at the cigarette between my lips. "Come here now, it'll be alright," she said, her tone riding the rail between sexual and maternal. When I brought the cigarette close to her mouth, she grabbed my wrist with her shaky hand, pulled it close, and sucked greedily.

The coughing fit that followed—violent hacks her body didn't have energy for, tears rolling down her papery cheeks—sent me into a panic. I dropped the cigarette into a barely eaten plastic cup of applesauce, the foil standing up like a sail. I slipped my hand behind her moist gauzy gown and pulled her to sitting. *Please don't die on my watch. This would be bad for my marriage.*

Her coughing calmed and she said, her voice wispy and brittle as a wasp's nest, "Put me down. Just put me down."

I eased her down.

"That was good," she said, easing her eyes closed, her dry lips stretched into a smile.

"Judy, that was anything but good."

Peaceful, she said, "Now, how is your mother?"

Which caught me off guard. Judy and I had known each other for seven years. We saw each other two to seven times a year depending on the year (the year Emily was born; it had been seven). We had an understanding. She knew I didn't like to talk about my family. When Trevor and I got engaged, I'd told her I was not inviting my parents to the wedding because they were alcoholics.

"I don't like to talk about her, you know that, Judy," I said gently, as if she were a child.

"I was worried about you," she said, her eyes remaining closed. "But you seemed to turn out fine." She smacked her lips together, rolled them against each other.

"Thank you for your worry. That's very sweet."

She exhaled so slowly and quietly, I thought she'd fallen asleep. Eyes closed, she said, "Poor woman. They say God only gives us what we can bear, but she sure did get a heaping."

"She's not alive anymore."

"Oh, that's right. You told me that." I hadn't. "Well, it's for the best, for the best," she said. Her breathing deepening, rattling. Her eyes rolled back and forth under the lids; a sliver of white sclera exposed. "The devil knows us. Oh, you may not know him, but he knows you, and sometimes, sometimes he squeezes in."

"Judy, what are you talking about?"

"He knew your mother."

"Judy?"

"He squeezed in." Her eyeballs twitched under the lids. "Judy?"

In response, she rattled out a snore.

She's out of her mind. Dying, and high as a kite.

Still. When I walked into the kitchen to throw the cigarette and applesauce cup into the garbage, my hands were trembling.

"Worshipping the devil is not necessarily crazier than worshipping God. Just like the love of God makes people feel special, so does the love of Satan."

Doctor Clifford Paulson, PhD Psychology
Transcripts from the Sixth Annual Conference on
Adult Manifestations of Childhood Trauma
THE RADISSON PLAZA HOTEL, CINCINNATI, OHIO

40

TREVOR

Vibration pulled me above the rippled surface of sleep. *Your phone is buzzing.* I reached under my pillow for my phone and forced my sleepy eyelids open. 1:15 a.m. *You have so much more time to sleep.* I let my eyelids fall, my bones feeling heavy like quicksand, but—

My phone continued buzzing. *Shit, that's your other phone.* I reached down to my briefcase beside the bed, into the leather folds and compartments, blind-feeling for it.

I'd missed the call, but there was a text waiting.

-Out front.

Cold adrenaline surged through me, yanking my body abruptly from sleep.

Had Heather heard my phone?

Before I rolled over to check, it sunk in. She was with my mom.

I laid back onto my pillow and typed, furious, but tired.

-You can't come to my house. We talked about this yesterday. Meet tomorrow.

-I need you now.

-My mom is DYIng. I started typing in caps, but didn't have the energy to follow through. *-I have my hands full. I'm sleeping.*

I closed my eyes, relishing the give of my pillow, and rubbed my toes against my warm tented comforter while I waited.

-I need to give you something right now. I guess I could always come back around for breakfast with the kids.

Fuck.

-Give me a few minutes to get dressed.

-No need to dress fancy for me, Trevor. I'm not interested in your clothes.

-I need to check on the kids first.

-And I need you to clear your schedule for tomorrow.

Fuck.

Stepping into yesterday's worn-in, softly creased work pants, I stumbled and stuck my hand out against the windowpane to catch my fall. I grabbed my shoes and shuffled out of my bedroom to check on the kids.

Emily was flat on her back, her blankets kicked onto the floor, sleeping in her underwear. That kid went to bed in fuzzy pants and a long-sleeved shirt because she was so cold, but as the night went on, she baked.

Sawyer slept with his door closed. That was fine. I'd lubricated the brackets with liquid silicone before we'd moved in, and we had a no-locking-your-door-at-night policy for the sake of fire safety.

I turned the handle. Locked. *Damn it, Sawyer.*

I fetched a flathead screwdriver.

Hours ago, I had stopped Sawyer in the hallway after his shower. Caught him at his most vulnerable, skin moist, towel around his naked waist.

Sawyer admitted that a couple of kids he'd met at school brought him to a party, then to the woods to shoot. I was fine with both. I'd done the same thing with friends when I was sixteen. Guns were the norm in this town. Both high schools gave kids three days off in November for hunting. I had walked into school on those mornings, wearing my knife, my rifle strapped around my neck, to grab homework. I told Sawyer I'd take him shooting a few more times, that it was safer to go with his dad.

He liked that. He was a good kid.

I pushed the flathead into Sawyer's door handle and turned. The handle gave.

Moonlight cast a blue glow on Sawyer's black bedspread, which was thrown back, revealing gray sheets and nothing else. Empty.

Seriously, Sawyer?

The blinds were up, the kid's window was wide open. So was the screen. So much for keeping mosquitoes and spiders out of the house. Man, Sawyer. Now I got to worry about being caught by you too. Where was he?

From the open window, I checked up and down the street. It was dark and vacant except for the glow of a phone in the driver's seat of the car—the one waiting for me.

There was a sturdy branch of a crab apple tree a couple feet from the window, but I bet the kid skipped the tree. If he hung from his fingertips at the window ledge, his feet would only have been six feet from the ground.

I felt a surge of love for the kid and his boldness, this teenage daredevil.

Bad timing though, Sawyer. I sighed. Bad fucking timing.

If Sawyer happened to see me get into the car down the street, I would have hell to pay with the kid. Would Sawyer rat me out to Heather? I didn't think so.

I stepped quietly down the stairs, my feet bare, my shoes in hand. I hated to leave Emily home alone.

41

HEATHER

While Judy slept, I watched an old movie and sketched a bird on my wrist with a blue pen—a sloppy imitation of Desiree's tattoo. Pathetic, really. I thought about Desiree, how her life had led her to become this person: bold, unapologetic, apathetic, dangerous. I thought about Becky, who was none of those things. I muted the volume on the television and drifted off to sleep.

I dreamed I was chasing butterflies with that little girl from my childhood. Her brother was there too. He was clumsy, all chubby knees and elbows, and kept tumbling in the grass.

A pair of tiny white butterflies flitted and swirled around each other, touching down on the grass for a brief rest, and off again.

We passed a tree with knotted roots breaking the ground, and there was Becky. I stopped running, letting the boy and girl go on ahead without me.

Becky wore her AC/DC T-shirt, her frayed jean shorts, and her dusty sneakers. She had Mom's clothesline in her hand and was working on a knot. I stepped up onto a tree stump beside her and balanced on one leg.

"How do you know how to make knots? There's no internet," I said.

"Rodney's Boy Scout book."

"You always were the smartest one."

She smiled and brushed a strand of hair behind her ear. "Thanks." Most beautiful too.

"What are you doing?" I said.

She regarded the girl and boy. Both holding sticks, they poked at a grated drain in the back corner of the yard. "I wish you wouldn't have asked that," she said.

"Why?"

"Because I don't want to make you sad."

"Just tell me."

She held up the rope, smiling and showing me what she made. She slipped the noose around my neck. "It's your fault." She reached out and pushed me off the stump.

I woke up startled, yanking my head upright, snapping a thread of drool. I was in Judy's recliner, my thighs and arms spread like a drunk.

Judy lay on her back in the metal bed with the rails up, her hands in a semi-clench of the white sheet near her chest. Like a scared kid. Her mouth was open, wide open, exposing her top row of teeth. Her chest lifted and dropped. Still alive. Thank you, Judy.

The room was bathed in the flickering glow of the television I'd left on mute. Dark outside, but it was too warm in here to fall back asleep. I had been instructed not to turn the AC below seventy-six. Judy liked it balmy.

I missed Emily. I missed her as if she were one of my limbs, and the phantom throb of her absence was deep, itchy, and maddening. I missed pressing my lips to her warm soft cheek, smelling her sweaty hair, holding her itty-bitty toes, listening to her random spoken thoughts.

I limped to the bathroom to pee, then to the kitchen to check the *Judy To-Do List*. My bones ached from sleeping in the recliner, my brain felt raw, hungover.

Taking care of the dying was exhausting. It should have been easy. They didn't want food and they slept more than an infant. But it *was* exhausting. All that piddling, checking their breathing, setting your alarm according to their medicine, pestering them to drink, knowing you couldn't leave.

I sat at Judy's kitchen table with my phone and pulled up the local news. My heart jumped at the first story. Another break-in. Yesterday afternoon, sometime between the hours of 8 a.m. and 3:50 p.m.

Audrey Burhn was the school nurse at Owen Elementary where Emily went to school. Audrey, who lived alone, told the reporter, "I always thought this was a safe, wonderful neighborhood, except for the dogs. Some people raise their dogs mean." Her husband had died five years ago of a heart attack, and her son lived in Michigan.

Mrs. Burhn said she came home after school to find her window screen ripped and the window pried up. The burglar(s) stole fifty dollars cash, tore apart her jewelry drawer, her drawer under the television, full of old videotapes, and some boxes in the basement. She hadn't found anything missing besides the cash and a bracelet and a few rings of her mother's, but, as she said, "When you get to be as old as me, it's hard to remember what you have."

No one witnessed the intruder, and Hunther police didn't have any suspects.

Desiree? Wouldn't they consider her a suspect?

A heavy thump from the other room. I ran toward it as Judy whined.

Please let her not to have fallen. Not on my watch. Let her fall for Paulina.

Judy was in her bed, thank God. She was moving her legs up, her knees tenting the blanket, and she was grasping for something.

No cigarettes for you, young lady. If she asked, I'd tell her she smoked the last one yesterday.

"What do you need? I'll help you, honey." I had never called Judy "honey." She would not have liked that. It both comforted me and made me feel a bit nasty.

A Bible lay face-down on the floor, pages smashed. It had been on her bedside table yesterday. Paulina probably read it to her for comfort.

Judy howled and reached for her feet, but couldn't catch them.

"Are your feet bothering you? Do you have pins and needles? Numbness?"

"Scratches."

"They're itchy?"

"Scratches."

I scratched her ankles, shins, calves, and the tops of her feet. I didn't mind. Her skin was cool and paper thin.

Her whiny howling shifted into cooing and purring. Her eyes closed, she stretched her thin lips into a smile, bringing a

213

scab on her lip to its breaking point. A bead of bright blood cut through the scab.

I scratched gently; I didn't want to leave her skin looking clawed. She had curvy lines of dirt and dead skin along her ankles, reminding me of soap scum buildup along the bathtub. Dead skin balled up under my nails, which didn't bother me because I planned to scrub every inch of my body when I got home anyway. Once you committed to a filthy job, you committed.

"You're a good girl," she purred. "Sad what happened to your family. After the, um, after the, uh." She tried to wet her lips, work them away from her gums, but they were stuck. I dipped the mouth swab in a cup of water and dabbed her lips. "Never quite the same after," she said. "I saw her once after. Looked like her soul was sucked out of her. He will do that though, yes, yes he will."

Not this again.

The skeptical adult in me had barely given Judy's evening sermon a second thought.

But the child in me had taken the dying woman's whispered, calloused words to heart last night. *The devil knows you.*

The child in me knew there were malice and horror in those words. The child in me believed in anything and everything. *The devil, he squeezes in.*

I ached for gossip about my mother. It was a dangerous ache, like wanting the Ouija board to spell out your name. "What happened to my mom, Judy?"

"We used to say it at baptisms when the baby cried." She dry-laughed and it died quickly. "Father Greg would smile and tell the parents, 'We're getting the devil out.'" She worked her dry lips up and down. I sponged more water on her lips, and she sucked at the sponge like a fiend. "Say what you want about this town, it's not fancy, but we get things done. He got the devil out."

My stomach grumbled. "Judy, are you saying my mother was possessed?" If anyone else heard me say that, I would have been embarrassed. But it was only me and Judy, who had a less-than-functioning mind at this point.

Her brain literally has holes in it, Heather. It's like the hungry caterpillar. On Friday he ate five apples. On Saturday he ate six bites of her brain.

"Like in horror movies?" I said. "Possessed by the devil?"

Judy smiled tightly, righteously, and opened her eyes halfway, drugged and hazy. "Mm-hmm. She cut that poor girl. Father Greg told me everything. I'm his favorite." Her gauzy eyes sparkled.

Of course you're not buying this. The woman literally has disease-reaching tendrils through her brain, strangling neurons, gobbling them up.

"What did Father Greg tell you?" I said, feeling like a yo-yo at the end of this dying, deranged woman's finger.

She closed her eyes and smiled. "Tired."

"Can you tell me about Father Greg, Judy?"

She sighed, already dozing.

From the other room, Paulina happily called, "Good morning, ladies!"

42

There was a package sitting there on our front porch.

Trevor was always ordering random things. Fun things. Glow sticks or sticker books for Emily, earbuds for Sawyer, more gardening gloves for himself. But it was early for a delivery. The sun hadn't cleared the horizon.

Parking my car in the driveway, I had a view of the front porch. The package's shape wasn't rectangular.

Before I shut my car door, it sunk in. It was a dead opossum.

It didn't make sense. Why would someone send me those texts, lure me here, then send me a nasty warning?

And that's what it was, a warning.

I donned gardening gloves—good thing Trevor was always buying more! Turned my face away as I grabbed it by the foot and scooted the corpse—it was heavy—into a black garbage bag, then threw the gloves away too. Tossed all of it in the trash and dumped soapy water on our front porch.

By the time I was done with my hot shower, everyone in the house was awake. I didn't mention the opossum.

* * *

After I walked Emily through the front doors of Owen Elementary, I grabbed a coffee at the McDonald's drive thru and parked in the lot. Holly's Facebook page said she lived in Dixon, Illinois, an eight-hour drive from Hunther, so I'd assumed she still lived there. On my phone I searched, "Holly Hornne and Hunther." God, it was a fucking alliteration. Holly and I, both. *Heather Hornne from Hunther hates her history.* What a joke.

She had purchased a house in Hunther three months ago. Shortly after Mom died. 5218 Cross Street. Once you bought a house in the US, your privacy went out the window. Seeing Holly's name in print gave me a wobbly feeling. The surname I had been so eager to bury, she'd kept when she married. Her husband, Bruce Chicone, was on the mortgage too.

Twenty minutes later, I was parked on the street in front of her house, my hands slick and my stomach sweaty.

This house looked similar to the scrappy ranch she'd had in Dixon, Illinois, which I'd known from her Facebook photos. She'd moved from one outworn town to another outworn town right into the same shitty yellow ranch. Dandelions, the nasty ones with needles, towered over the bushes bordering her door.

A red dog lead had been left on the front porch, along with a full and knotted bag of dog poop. Nothing more welcoming than a bag of crap on your front porch.

Drive away.

I couldn't. There's no way I'd be able to forget Judy telling me they "got the devil out" of my mom.

OK, maybe I could do this, but I needed to stop home first. Even with the air conditioning on, my forehead was prickly and my guts felt oily. I shifted gears and gazed in my rearview. I waited for the approaching car to pass, but it slowed and turned into Holly's driveway.

The Corolla was the color of a gloomy day and its bumper was tied on.

A woman stepped out, balancing two brown paper bags in one arm. She slammed her car door shut and squinted at my car, her hand going up as a visor against the sun. The skin under her arms was loose. Her brown hair had an inch of gray roots. She wore baggy jean shorts. Sneakers with crew socks. Large breasts tented out her baggy shirt.

She'd always hated that about boobs and said, "There's only two looks with big boobs—fat or sleazy. Wear fitted shirts, you picked sleazy. Wear loose shirts, now you're fat." She'd been the only girl in our family to get boobs, and she'd hated them. In high school, she played volleyball and basketball, and her boobs got in the way.

Holly.

She's only forty-two. Why does she look so old? She looked nothing like she used to. Then again, the last time I saw her, she was twenty-two

I wasn't expecting the emotional punch of seeing her. I thought I'd shaken free of them, of all of them, a lucky fly that had torn free of the spider's web, but I hadn't. My wing had been ripped, and the sticky webbing stuck to my limbs. I'd lost pieces of myself, and I couldn't shake the residue of being a Hornne.

Drive away.

My eyes stinging, I stepped out of my car and took a few steps toward her.

She saw me and dropped one of her bags, spilling it onto her driveway. "Shit. Shit," she muttered. She set her other bag down and scrambled to pick up what had rolled out of the bag as if it were irreplaceable. White liquid spilled down her driveway, following some invisible, curvy crack and picking up dirt.

She picked up a leaking carton of Half N Half, stopped mid-squat, and held her one hand out to me, palm out, as if I had a gun. "Don't go anywhere," she pleaded. "I need to get something. It's leaking."

"I won't," I said, though I hadn't decided.

"Stay right there." She set the Half N Half down slowly, again, as if I had a gun trained on her and she was setting down her own lesser weapon. She speed-walked to her front door and fumbled getting her keys out of her pocket. When she managed the door open, a big dog nosed at her, its tail wagging hard. "Scoot, Diesel. Move your big ass outta my way."

In my memory, Holly was stuck around fifteen. She was beautiful with her long dark hair and her big brown eyes, but she was also tough—athletic and strong. She was girly, gossipy, opinionated, bossy, and phone-obsessed. She had a Velcro wallet filled with dollar bills, and she'd shove it into her flea-market fringed purse along with her Carmex. I pictured her lying on her back, legs up, with the phone balanced on her feet, the spiral cord wrapping around her legs, the receiver held tight against her ear by crooking her shoulder. She'd hold a compact mirror in one hand and tweeze her eyebrows with the other.

After Becky died and my family moved, Holly and I shared a bedroom. In our room, she'd hung a poster with a shirtless male model, his chest shiny with oil, his jeans partially unzipped, his hand gripping a pull-up bar over his head, everything about the poster inappropriately *old* for a teenage girl. There was another poster of a famous bull terrier, Spuds the Budweiser Dog.

It was my room too, but I never hung a poster or made any of the decorative decisions. Holly was center of her world, and I was a tagalong, a pest, a snoop. She played TLC on her boom box and wore sweatpants with her name spelled on the butt. At one point, she divided our room, stapling a blanket to the ceiling so she wouldn't have to look at me.

This older, rundown version of Holly pushed the screen open and marched out with a Tupperware bowl in her hand. She set the Half N Half in the Tupperware on the asphalt. The neck of a liquor bottle peeked out of her other bag. Was it vodka? Like mother, like daughter?

Holly walked down the driveway with her hands on her hips.

"Jesus, Mary, Joseph, I thought I was seeing a ghost. You look *just* like Mom."

Jesus, Mary, Joseph. Mom used to say that.

I said nothing.

"Holy shit, Heather," she said, her expression caught between pissy and delighted. "I thought you were dead."

She lurched forward a step, then pulled herself back. Like I was a cute dog, and she instinctively wanted to pet me, to hug me, but reconsidered, reminding herself that even friendly-looking dogs can bite off your finger. She stood close, inspecting me like a strict grandmother inspects a child for dirt behind their ears. Hands on hips, looking at my skin, my clothes, and not being discreet.

Her eyes were bright and watery, warm and full of life, but the rest of her face was haggard, unplucked, and without makeup.

"I'm not dead."

"No shit." She smiled, not unwarmly. "I'd invite you in, but Bruce, my husband, well, guests make him nervous. He's recovering. It's a long story. But, listen, sit in the garage with me." She could see my hesitancy. "Just for a couple minutes."

She hadn't asked, she'd told me. Typical Holly. She was already walking toward her garage, expecting me to follow. She pulled the garage door up with one hand. I hadn't seen anyone do that since I was a kid.

Another small crummy car sat in the shade of the garage. Two chairs faced each other. She sat in one and said, "Mind if I smoke?"

"Go ahead." I dragged the empty chair a couple feet away from hers. It had been too close.

Holly brought her lighter to her cigarette, flicked it, and breathed in. "Next time you come over I'll make sure Bruce is settled," she said. "Next time you'll come in for coffee."

I felt like Gulliver, surrounded by teeny people swiftly wrapping strings around each of my limbs, shooting tiny darts into my pants and shoes.

Holly met my eyes. "Did you know Mom was murdered?"

I nodded. "I saw it on Facebook a few weeks after it happened."

She sucked on her bottom lip and thought about that, why

I hadn't contacted her. "You don't know how happy I am to see you, but I have so many questions. I'm angry too. You ditched us, and I haven't forgiven you for that." She was direct and said what's on her mind: that was Holly. She probably slept like a baby. "It tore them apart when you cut us out. Why did you do that?"

"I had to." I'd spent years digging up my resentment, and my well was dry. I couldn't come up with a succinct answer anymore.

"No, really. Why?" She really had no clue. It made me feel dizzy and lopsided, as if I'd made up my whole childhood. Was that possible? I mean, I had holes in my memory, acres of trees completely wiped out. I had that in me, that confusion. Was it possible I was one of those kids that made up a crummy childhood?

I reached for memories of my mother. In so many of them, she was passed out drunk in various unsavory positions. They say vodka has no smell on the breath, but metabolized vodka oozing out of a woman's pores hours after she's slushed, the smell is bitter. I was in middle school when she first asked me to make her a drink. She'd said, "Go ahead and make yourself one. We're all ruined, why the fuck not?" She glared at me, hate in her eyes.

No, you are not making it up.

She wasn't all bad of course. No one is. Some mornings, she'd make pancakes, the smell of burning butter infusing the air, and she'd hum commercial jingles. *Kiss a little longer with Big Red. I don't want to grow up, I'm a Toys "R" Us kid.*

On rare evenings when she wasn't drinking, she'd talk on the phone while she was chopping onions for dinner. If you wanted a snack, you'd have to maneuver around the telephone cord. Occasionally, she'd ruffle my hair as I passed her.

"I ran away, and they didn't even try to find me. They were both *drunks*." I spit the word with disdain. Coming here was a mistake.

She didn't take offense to *drunks*. "They were grieving. First Becky, then Rodney, then Shane. Can you imagine losing a kid every few years?" I couldn't imagine, which is probably why I didn't fight them, I just slinked out of their lives. "Yeah, they were drinkers," she said. "They weren't perfect, but they didn't hit us. They were good to us."

My insides burned. *They were good to us?* How could two siblings have such different views of their own childhood?

"Well, I'm glad your childhood felt safe." Mine had felt like a minefield. "I didn't come here to talk about us. You know people in this town think Mom murdered a teenage girl."

"She didn't," Holly said, firm and calm.

"How do you know that? You were only eleven when we moved away."

"She wouldn't. I don't have to even consider it."

"I've been here two weeks. It seems to be common knowledge in this town. My mother-in-law said Mom was not herself." *Just say it.* "That some priest, well," I said. *Say it.* "Some priest worked with her." *Fucking say it.* "Like, like an exorcism."

She looked down at her cigarette. "Come on, Heather," she said quietly. "Are you really that stupid?"

"Yes. Yes, I am that stupid. Enlighten me."

She tapped her cigarette, ash fluttered loose and drifted. "Mom was a *good* person," she said, but she said it slowly, like she was trying to convince herself.

"Bullshit she was."

"Why'd you even come here then?" Oh my God, she *assumed* I was in Hunther as some sort of tribute to my mother.

I wasn't about to tell her she was partly right. I wasn't about to tell her about the texts that had piqued my curiosity and lured me back. "Because my husband's mother is dying," I said. "His dad had a heart attack when he was a teenager. He's an only child. He's taking care of her." It was convenient to blame it on Trevor's mom. "Why are you here?"

"My youngest went to college and I, well, I needed to come back and look into something for Mom. But we moved in and right away Bruce had a stroke and I'm working overtime at the hospital and well, it's been overwhelming. I've barely made any progress. Listen, there's something I need you to do. I need to show you something." She said it like she'd organized our meeting a week ago.

I felt her needling her way into my life, asking me to do things for the family when the family had already emptied me out, shaking me so hard upside down like a piggy bank. I felt my cheeks flush.

"Holly," I said. "She confessed to murdering Dawn Young. You know that, right?"

Holly narrowed her eyes. "She didn't do it."

"Why would she confess?"

"I don't know." Maybe Holly's memory was as useless as

mine. She sighed, her body full of regret. "I never asked her. We never talked about it."

Holly knew? I couldn't believe she'd never told me. That wasn't true. I could believe it.

Holly went on, "I should have asked her, but you know how you put off saying things, and then years go by, and it's too late. It doesn't seem worth it."

Yes. I'd done the same thing with Trevor.

"Let me show you something," she said.

"Was Mom covering for Rodney? Did he kill Dawn?"

"What?" she said, appalled. "Are you kidding?"

Holly was like the mother who thought her children, her family, could do no wrong, even after they'd been convicted.

"This was a mistake. I'm sorry I came here." I stood. "I'm glad you're well." I walked down her driveway, and she didn't try to stop me.

43

TREVOR

Don't think about what's in the trunk. You're almost in the clear.

Was I though? Seemed like I'd told myself that a lot lately.

My palms were sweaty on the steering wheel, and I eased onto the brake because the red Mazda in front of me dipped outside its lane again.

A truck honked. Might have been the one behind, but it was hard to tell; semis were everywhere. Seemed like everyone was pissed off and honking today.

I took the pot-holed Dan Ryan Expressway into the city. As I watched my surroundings lose their fractal and wistful greens and sharpen to gray geometric edges and skyscrapers in the distance, I reviewed a checklist of things I needed to do in the next hour.

Once you empty your trunk, it will be alright.

I heard the sirens before I saw them. Glanced in my rearview. The semi was gone. In its place was a Ford Explorer, blue neon line of light spinning on its roof.

I couldn't be speeding. I was in the right-hand lane, and there was too much traffic. The cop had to be rushing to an accident.

Please let it be someone else. I counted to twenty slowly, but the cop stayed on my ass, sirens loud, cool blue light flashing.

Next exit was two miles away, so I signaled and pulled onto

the shoulder, which was always a bad feeling on the highway—a trapped, how the hell am I going to get back on—feeling. The cop would pass, I knew it.

No such luck.

The siren died, but the strobing lights stayed. The cop parked behind me.

I sat stiffly, my thoughts scrambling, sweat dripping down my sides under my stiff shirt. My mind straddled between it's going to be A-OK, cowboy, he won't look in your trunk, and that cop's going to read panic in your eyes and search your trunk for sure.

Poor Sawyer. What a crummy deal it would be to have two parents in prison. As if one wasn't bad enough.

Why was the cop staying in his car?

He's calling in your plate number. Next, he'll check your license.

Oh, right. License and registration. I opened my wallet.

Cops hated me. A cop would describe me as a hipster, a wuss. My hair fell in waves past my ears. I was a little pretty.

I should cut my hair. But Heather loved it, loved playing with it. So did Emily. So had Sawyer when he was young and cuddly.

I rolled down the window and peered at the slow-moving traffic. From the passing car, a middle-aged guy made a fish mouth at me. The next car passed, and a blank-faced teenage girl stared at me. From the next passing car, an old lady gave me the finger.

What did I do to deserve that?

Tan pants. A button-down tan shirt bearing insignia. The woman was petite, white, and young with shoulder-length hair. I felt worried for her. Oh, honey, this is the Dan Ryan, the most violent highway in the city with the most shootings. You don't have to do this.

I felt bad for stereotyping. She could be a decorated war veteran or an expert in knife combat. Or maybe she was a dick, a stickler who got off on giving tickets for minor infractions.

"I'm sorry," I said, "I'm not sure what I did." A drop of sweat slid down the side of my forehead.

"License and registration, please," she said plainly. There was none of that subservient lilt to her voice, the tone characteristic of many young women. Which did women have to practice: the appeasing voice that ended in a question mark, or the low-toned unapologetic voice?

I handed both over, and she walked back to her car.

A vein pulsed in my forehead, coming alive, and I sensed what was in my trunk pulsing too. Like it might call out to the officer.

What would I say to Heather when I got to make a phone call?

Heather, please believe me, I would give anything to take it all back.

God, that was like a bad movie line.

Heather, I'm a liar, right from the fucking start.

That. That was the truth.

"Sir," the police officer said, back at my door. I turned to her, feeling defeat envelope me like a cold wet towel.

"Yes?"

A truck rolled over metal. Boom. Boom. Highway noise never stopped.

"Sir, did you know both your brake lights are out?"

"What?" I'd barely heard her.

"Your brake lights are out. Did you know?"

"What? No. God. I'm sorry. I—oh God, it's been so hectic. My mom is dying and I've been driving in and out of state to work and…"

"Sir?"

"I'm sorry, I didn't mean to rant. I just had no idea." Probably why the truck was honking.

"I'd like you to put your hazards on, drive to the next exit, and get them fixed right away so you don't cause an accident. Take the next exit, head west a mile. There's a Jiffy Lube." She handed me my license and registration. "You have a clean record. I'm not giving you a ticket, just get them fixed right away. As in, right now. I'll follow you."

"Thank you, officer. I'm sorry. Thank you." I pushed my palm against my eye, wiping away the wetness. Crying? Shit. I puffed my cheeks out and exhaled with force. I jammed my license and registration under the visor clip.

Thank God I wouldn't have to tell Heather.

44

HEATHER

Holly wasn't willing to entertain the mystical aspect. Father Greg might.

Priests lived upstairs or around back. St. John's church was a squat building, so I walked around back. Beyond the dumpster, a small building budded from the back of the church like the freshly growing limb of a starfish—stubby and unattractive. One and a half stories tall, few windows, and no walkway leading to a door. An old metal table and chairs sat on a slab of cement porch overlooking three acres of grass, a glimpse of a pond in the distance.

I pressed the doorbell, counted to one hundred twenty, and pressed it again. Counted to sixty, rang it again.

Priests were stubborn. They had to be. Committed and steadfast was part of the gig.

I expected one of three things:

They would call the church receptionist and make her hobble back here to do their dirty work.

They would call the police. An officer would arrive in ten minutes to tell me I was trespassing.

One of these priests would either be pissy enough or relaxed enough to open the damn door.

I got lucky on my fifth ring. As the door opened, a breeze of cool air and aftershave whooshed out from the bat cave. The man who answered was old, tan, and athletic, his veins prominent on his slender hairy arms. He wore a wristwatch, white shorts, a white and blue polo, and white gym shoes. Maybe he had a game of tennis on his schedule.

"Holy moly, you know you have to go through the church." He was one of the good ones. His eyes were bright and green.

"I'm sorry to bother you, but I really need to talk to Father Gregory."

"Ho, girlie." He laughed. Like it would be a cold day in hell for Father Greg to walk outside. "Greg has the day off. He won't be in the atrium until tomorrow evening. I couldn't lure him to the door with a slice of pumpkin pie delivered by Cindy Crawford."

I took a deep breath, closed my eyes, and said, "It's about an exorcism he did in 1991." Closing my eyes made it easier to say.

I opened my eyes. He gave me his first serious consideration, enthusiasm creeping into his eyes. He loved horror stories. "OK, missy. Better follow me then."

He led me along a dark hallway with ugly tiled floors, smelling like the subway, and up a dark wooden staircase, to an open dining area attached to a kitchen, all of it dimly lit and somber. A long rectangular dining table. A few saggy couches. The bones of this large room had potential, but it had never been painted or decorated, and it was filthy.

Dishes piled high in the sink, the smell stagnant, grimy floor stains near the baseboard that had attracted and trapped hair. I could not even imagine the state of the bathrooms.

How did these old bachelors live like this? My question pretty much answered itself.

Never married, never *once* nagged at by a woman. Like college boys, except college boys cleaned and decorated their frat house to attract girls.

These men had no one to impress. Their maid probably came tomorrow. And being the good Christian she was, she wouldn't dare call them pigs. She would wash their dishes and scrub their floors, thinking she was doing God's work.

"Have a seat at the table," he said. "Wait here, please."

"Thank you. I will," I assured him as he headed down a hallway.

A hardened dime-sized circle of mint green with black flecks stuck to the table to my left. Chocolate mint ice cream?

A man emerged from the hallway, old and rosy-cheeked, a venti Starbucks in hand. He had wild, white eyebrows, and his belly bulged over his belt. He was put together in tan pants and shiny shoes. His T-shirt said, *Lord, Keep Your Arm on My Shoulder and Your Hand over My Mouth*. Another funny priest. Game night here was either a blast or passive-aggressive and bitchy.

"Hello there. I'm Father Greg. How can I help you?" he said, slightly annoyed.

"Hi. I'm Heather Hornne. My mom was Melinda Hornne, and I've heard from several people that you helped her?" My fingers were cold, and my teeth chattered briefly from nerves. "This would be about thirty years ago."

He smiled and warmed with recognition. He had the smile of a philosophical academic. Even if he believed in soul-sucking demons, I liked him. The other guy too. Their uncleanliness was simultaneously off-putting and relatable.

"I remember you, Heather," he said, his eyes wandering left, recalling something pleasant. "You and the kids used to run around in the yard, adding scraps of fabric and wood to your fort under the mulberry." He sat down across from me. "It was you, Claire, and Donnie."

I squeezed my hands into slippery, clammy fists. Nausea raced around in my belly like a trapped mouse.

Claire and Donnie.

I'd always wondered about my memories of these two.

"Who are Claire and Donnie?"

He smiled, his eyes liquid and kind. "You don't remember? Oh, of course you don't, you were so little. You and Claire were thick as thieves. Always giggling. Holding hands. Donnie was younger. My niece and nephew." My head was warm and my palms were cold. I felt sick, yet relieved to be filling in a puzzle piece. "You and your mother stayed with my brother's family. Cliff is a head doctor." He raised his eyebrows, dubious of the profession.

The athletic priest quietly emerged from the hallway. He fetched a mug from the kitchen and went to the faucet.

"I had four siblings," I said. "Did you know my oldest brother?"

"I don't think so, no."

"Why was I the only one living there?"

"You might not remember—you really were so young," he said gently. "But you witnessed Dawn Young's murder. My brother was helping you work through it."

Chills racked my body so fast and hard, I shivered. No, that couldn't be true. "I don't remember witnessing her murder."

"It's probably better that way," he said sadly.

"But—"

I had so many questions, but my mind was stuck, blanking. I should have written my questions down. It couldn't be true, but why would he lie? Mom's head doctor might have more answers. "Does your brother still live in town?"

"Cliff?" He leaned back and sighed like he had a bit of family baggage himself. "Yes, he's the last house on Harvest Road. No outlet. The only house that looks like an elementary school. You could talk to his wife, but there's hardly a point visiting him. Dementia, I think. He was fine this past Easter, but his symptoms came on quick. Getting old, as they say, sucks."

The athletic priest laughed once. He opened the microwave before it beeped, retrieved his mug, and dunked a tea bag into it.

"Why do you think my mom stayed with a psychiatrist instead of going into police custody?"

Father Greg shrugged. "I don't know that I have a good answer to that. Things were different. Police stayed out of people's business more often than not." Yeah, that was true. Trevor'd said he grew up down the street from a child molester, that everyone knew, but instead of police getting involved, his parents told him to not go inside the neighbor's house. "People went missing, and there wasn't always a big search," Father Greg said, his wistful tone suggesting nostalgia for the time when people went missing and that was the end of them. "Anyway, I don't affiliate with police officers. We exist in the same high rise, but on different floors." He raised his eyebrows, proud of his joke.

I was listening, but it was a struggle. *You witnessed Dawn Young's murder*. My mind carouselled around that statement. "Can you tell me about your visit with my mom?"

"Cliff called me in." He stiffened his posture, took a sip of his coffee. "He called me because your mother had signs pointing to satanic indoctrination."

"What signs?"

He gazed down at his coffee, smeared something on the lid, and nodded to himself. "Screaming strange things, hitting, threatening."

Sporty Priest remained at the counter, slowly bobbing his tea bag. He didn't want to miss the gossip.

"Well, what happened when you visited her? What did she do?"

His exhale was heavy, reaching. "It's frightening when evil finds a small hole, a fracture in our faith, and decides to burrow in. Melinda agonized. Nurses had to tie her down. I said a lot of prayers over her. When I..." He closed his eyes and shook his head as if he'd had a sour burp. "Have you ever heard a fox scream?"

"No."

"It's an awful sound. That's what she sounded like, your mother, when I crossed her forehead with holy water. She'd screamed like a fox in agony. She said," he paused and shook his head, closing his eyes, "the most awful things. I'll never forget."

"What did she say?"

"I can't... I can't repeat." He opened his eyes and forced a smile. "She got better so that's what's important."

235

"How did you know she got better?"

"She was, well, she was herself again. Confused and exhausted, but peaceful."

I was trying to picture it, but my mind painted a generic, glossy scene. I needed specifics. "I really need to know what she said."

He covered his eyes with his hand and shook his head.

That bad?

"Father Greg," Sporty Priest said, "maybe you could write it down?" He opened a drawer, pulled out a pad of paper and a pencil, and placed it on the desk. Walked back to the kitchen, sipped his tea.

Father Greg sighed, dropping his hand from his eyes. He didn't want to.

"Please," I said.

He nodded. He wrote with his thumb tucked under the pencil, and he shielded his paper with his other hand. It was such a childish gesture. He folded the paper twice, dropped his head against one of his palms, and pushed the note across the table. "Please don't read it here. And rip it up after you read it."

"OK," I said. My teeth might have chattered. "I really appreciate this."

Sporty Priest left the kitchen and walked down the hall. Time for him to disappear. He didn't want to get scolded when I left.

"One last question," I said, the note tight in my sweaty hand. "Did you know Dawn Young?"

The corners of his mouth drooped, and he looked down at his coffee. "I still have the picture she drew me. Deer, birds, trees—a beautiful scene, just beautiful." He shook his head.

"Perhaps she shouldn't have been so friendly with people." He sighed and lifted hooded eyes to me. "All this talking has me exhausted. Can you let yourself out?"

In my car I unfolded the paper, anticipation bloating in my chest. He had the handwriting of a child or a serial killer, all caps and messy. He'd even spelled out the bad words. Father Greg, you dog.

I read it, imagining my mom screaming the words.

I hate you. I hate you. I'm going to claw your eyes out, you fucking bastard. I will take my knife and cut you open. Does that make your cock hard? I'll kill you, all of you.

45

My skin humming from reading Father Greg's words, I drove fast. Did my mom really say those things?

I was driving to Cliff's house when my phone buzzed with a text. Desiree.

-Meet me at Shawnee's Roadhouse, southwest side of town.

-When?

-I'm there now.

When I got there, Desiree was drunk. Her spaghetti strap hanging off her shoulder, she slapped her hand down on the bar, and said in good humor, "Shut the fuck up, Gerry. That didn't happen."

The barman smiled at her, wiping the inside of a glass. It was standard dining dark, so you couldn't see the smudge on your glass or a cockroach scurrying along the ground. It smelled like onion rings and dirty dishrags.

I eased onto the stool beside her. "You OK?"

She turned to me and smiled, her eyes alert. Not so drunk after all. "Hea-ther," she sang. "I'm more than OK. How's M and M?"

A shiver ran up my back when she spoke of Emily in that familiar way. Like she could swoop in and take my daughter away, and Emily wouldn't know to hesitate.

"We're doing fine," I said.

"How's your *investigation*?"

I ignored her mocking tone. "Strange. Father Greg says my mom was possessed. Do you believe in that stuff?"

"Hell, yes," she said, eyes serious and round. "What else is there to explain the disgusting compulsions people have? How they can be split. How they can be two different people at once. It's the fucking devil, bitch," she said, belched, and laughed.

"What about a simpler explanation? Poor parenting."

She looked at me, her nostrils flared, and laughed. "You are adorable." She sipped her beer. "Hey, what does your hubby think about your investigation?"

I hesitated, entertaining the question. What would he think?

Her jaw dropped. She grabbed my shoulders with both hands. "You haven't told him. Wow, that is seriously fucked up, Heather," she said, a cozy smile in her voice. She liked me more for keeping secrets.

"It's not that fucked up." It wasn't. I wanted to uncover my family's past on my own. Once I offered him a loose string, Trevor would pull it until everything unraveled.

Besides, a relationship could be solid while secrets were kept. Trevor and I—our relationship wasn't based on heart-to-heart conversations. It wasn't austere. There were no drops of blood in lockets, no anniversary rules. There was no drama. Our relationship was based on shared jokes and a similar calm approach to life, politics, and religion. We shared the same taste in music and a commitment to our family. We both liked coffee and an occasional beer.

"You tell your boyfriend everything?" I said.

"You got me there, bitch. You got me by the balls." She elbowed me, friendly, tipsy. "Alright, my lovely Heather. I pushed my pops for more info on Dawn's murder. Thought I'd get more out of him than you. Dad said Dawn was too friendly, maybe someone thought she deserved punishment for being a tease, leading on a bunch of her customers at Marjory's."

That was along the lines of what Father Greg had said. *Perhaps she shouldn't have been so friendly with people.*

"He said your mom lived with her psychologist for a month or so. Signed the confession after she'd been there a few weeks. Her doctor was this rich, know-it-all asshole." *Cliff, the head doctor.* "My dad didn't like him. If you're thinking about visiting him, I wouldn't."

I tucked a strand of hair behind my ear.

"What's this?" Desiree said. She grabbed my wrist, pulled it toward her, and studied it. She brushed her thumb back and forth over the veins of my wrist, giving me a shiver. The faint outline of a bird drawn in blue pen remained, even though I'd scrubbed it.

Heat bloomed in my neck and cheeks. "Emily had us draw tattoos on each other. She's fond of you," I said. It wasn't all lie.

Desiree studied my face, her fairy-blue eyes gentle and welcoming. She laughed and dropped my wrist. It fell limp into my lap. She sipped her beer. Set it down and wiped her mouth with her wrist.

"When's your arraignment?" I said.

"Couple days from now, but don't worry about me. I've got friends in low and high places."

I figured. I considered pressing her about her attempted break-in—what had she been looking for and had she done it again? *She's not going to tell you shit.*

"You're gonna visit him, right?" she said. "The asshole head doctor?" She swung her head over her shoulder, gave me the sexiest smile.

"I was on my way there when you texted."

She sighed, and her smile changed. Less seductive, more whatcha gonna do? "Alright, sister. Don't say I didn't warn you."

"I was able to unearth one of my patients' repressed memories using hypnotherapy and medication. What they did to her was horrific. When she was a little girl, they had drugged her, placed three electrodes on her forehead, one in her vagina. They would tell her things they wanted her to believe, and if she didn't agree with their beliefs, they would shock her until they got compliance."

Doctor Clifford Paulson, PhD Psychology
Transcripts from the Sixth Annual Conference on
Adult Manifestations of Childhood Trauma
THE RADISSON PLAZA HOTEL, CINCINNATI, OHIO

46

An hour later when Emily and I walked through the door, Moldy Mildred smelled of orange chicken. White paper bags were strewn across the counter, wrinkled and spotted with grease. Trevor and Sawyer were sitting at the table, eating and laughing.

My strange day—my tense visit with Holly, my bizarre conversation with Father Greg, and meeting Desiree at the bar—fell away. Home, even if it was here in Hunther, felt warm and friendly.

It was a good family dinner. We didn't need the crutch of background music or TV, we had Trevor. He was the oil to our rusty gears. When he was present, the kids breathed easier and their eyes sparkled. They wanted to please him with their good spirit, their best joke.

Trevor asked good questions. How many kids vape *during* class, Sawyer? Do kids throw food in the lunchroom, Emily?

Trevor always had a story. Today it was a huge hawk that landed on the roof of the car beside him when he'd stopped at an intersection. Then, did you know that the bathroom in the Jewell grocery store is on the mysterious, not-talked-about upper level?

"Can you read my fortune, Sawyer?" Emily said.

Sawyer peered over her shoulder. "Your generosity will be rewarded," he said. "Oh, Emily, that's a good one."

She smiled at Sawyer. She liked his affection, couldn't care less for the fortune.

I was lucky, so lucky, to have these people.

Sawyer's cup was empty, so I stood to grab the milk. Trevor followed me. Swallowing his fortune cookie, holding his fortune in his hand, he pressed me against the refrigerator, inconspicuously pushing his pelvis against me. He locked eyes with me, and something peculiar and unreadable flashed behind his easy eyes—desperation or love—then it was gone. He smiled and leaned close. His breath tickling my neck, he whispered in my ear, "My fortune says I will soon sink my fingers into something warm and wet."

I put my lips against his ear and whispered, teasing, "Maybe your fortune is to do last night's dishes. I'll fill the sink with warm soapy water."

Pressing my lips to his neck, I caught a strange scent. Earthy. The odor of musty caves and tidal pools.

Hours later, pulling on my bedtime T-shirt, a threadbare Lollapalooza, one hole near my navel, one under my armpit, I said, sincerely, curiously, "Are you fucking Paulina?"

Trevor dropped his jaw and left it there.

"She's so motherly and generous," I said. "If you are, I'm not mad. I kind of wanted her to give *me* a blowjob."

"Heather," he said, appalled by my language. He was like

this sometimes. He had this difficulty putting the mother-me, the wife-me, and the pre-marriage fucktress-me in the same body. Like an old rickety stick shift, he had a bumpy time with the transition. He had the same difficulty transitioning within himself. If we were fucking, and Emily happened to knock on the door, he had to stop. His penis went as limp as cooked asparagus.

"What about DeeDee?"

"Seriously? Heather. No. How could you even ask me that?"

"Like this, I'm asking. I hear she's loose with rules."

"What do you mean loose with the rules?"

"Oh, nothing." I didn't want to take away Judy's cigarette stash under the toilet lid. She had negligible joy as is.

Plus, the cigarettes might speed along her death. Win-win.

Oh, come on. If she's gonna bite it, what's the difference between four more weeks or eight?

Trevor pushed me against the closet door. "Paulina," he whispered while thrusting against me comically. "Can I stick my penis in your pierogi?"

Laughing, I pushed him hard and he fell back onto the bed, tripping on a shoe midway. He rocked back, grabbing his foot and hamming it up. "Ow. There's so much crap everywhere."

Both of us laughing, when I moved close enough to him, he yanked me down and rolled me onto my back. "I *miss* you. And my toe *hurts*. And I have to leave at 5 a.m. tomorrow so I make my early morning meeting. I don't want to wake up that early. And I want someone to take care of *me*. And I'm not having sex with Paulina or DeeDee." He laid his head down on my clavicle and tried to burrow in against my bone. It hurt a little.

"I'm sorry you hate it here, but it could be worse. Em and Sawyer could be bitching and moaning as much as you are."

I pinched his nipple.

He howled, and his hand darted between my legs, the move less sexual, more of an ambush tickle. I swatted his hand and he moved it and jabbed me in the side. "At least you have caterpillar friends. You've turned into Snow White, talking to the animals."

Oh, how I loved this man who made me laugh, who made me not take myself so seriously.

Slowing down, breathing heavy, he slid his hand down my pants and parted me gently with the slow swipe of his finger.

His face went slack, his eyes blank. He rose onto his knees and unbuckled his belt, unzipped his pants. "Heather Bishop you tell me what you need." He yanked down my underwear with one rough tug. Pushed my knees open.

"I need to get out of this pissant town," I said, eyes wide, and burst into laughter.

He pinched my thigh gently, jokingly, but to the point. He needed me. He needed me to unburden him of his stress, his exhaustion and disappointment. All these things weighing on him, he needed to bury them inside me. He pulled my shirt off, dipped down, and bit my nipple. It was a good hurt. He slipped his finger inside me, and I twitched against his hand and wrist. He slid out, teasing me.

"Heather," he growled, his voice low and menacing. "Tell me what I earned."

Let me just say, I have never been a fan of dirty talk. Most guys got their sex ed from porn; they got so used to jacking off to bad sex lines, they got *conditioned* into using it.

Dirty talk was supposed to be the punch line of the conversation, the best part, but for me it actually pulled me out of the moment. If you mean to fuck me, skip the nonsense and fuck me. But, whatever, I'm a trooper.

Trevor's dirty talk had a twist that was less gimmicky, less grating on the brain. Trevor liked me to say things that, if written down instead of spoken in lusty moans, you could write on a child's best homework paper. He liked me to call him, *Good Boy* and *Big Man*. He liked me to tell him how *good* he was, which wasn't strange if it was taken to mean how good he was at sex, but his dirty talk requests rang of gold star charts and positive reinforcement.

"OK, big man," I said, slowing down, pushing his finger where I wanted it. "You're *so good* to me. You're such a good boy, you earned whatever you want."

I was in the midst of my after-sex pee when I heard Emily shout, "Momma? Momma? Momma?" She didn't even wait a full second between calls? Theoretically, how could I possibly scramble to her room that fast? I was annoyed, but being annoyed was OK as long as I played the role. I was a good mother if I showed up in my daughter's room when she cried in the middle of the night. It didn't matter if I hated doing it. If I showed up, I was the opposite of my mom. Sometimes, it's as simple as that.

I finished peeing and hustled into her room.

She was sitting in bed. The nightlight glow illuminated her face, eyes open but glazed. Tears shiny on her cheeks.

"I'm here, Em."

"I had a nightmare that a stranger broke my window and put his hand over my mouth and nose, and I died."

"It's only a bad dream. Momma's here." I tucked her teddy bear under her arm. I lay down beside her and wrapped my arm around her tummy. Her body was warm, her breathing was rhythmic.

I thought she'd fallen back asleep until she said, "Would you rather have me die or everyone in the whole world?"

I opened my eyes. She was staring at me. "Neither. I don't want anyone to die."

"But if you had to choose. Would you rather have me die or everyone?" She spoke calmly, but she was wide awake.

"Well, since I'm your momma, I never want you to die so I guess I'd pick you over everyone else."

"You'd want Dad and Sawyer to die."

"No. I'd want none of them to die. But it also doesn't make sense that I'd want everyone in the whole world to die. It's too tricky of a question."

"You'd pick me over Sawyer."

"I'm Sawyer's momma too. I'd pick him too. I'd pick both of you."

"But you're not really his momma."

"Well, he didn't grow in me. And he has another momma. But I'm his momma too."

"Do mommas always love their children?"

My heart ached. "Yes."

"Do mommas love them even if the children are bad? Even if they lie or steal?"

"Mommas love them anyway," I said, my eyes stinging. "Go to sleep."

She closed her eyes and, moments later, she was snoring the soft snore of children. Their noses are so small, they can't help but breathe noisily.

I walked into our room, my eyes quietly leaking because no, mommas didn't always love their children. I was ready to tell Trevor everything.

That a man I'd bludgeoned knew where we lived, that someone had sent me texts, luring me back to Hunther, that someone else left a dead opossum on the front porch as a warning, that I was scared for our family, that I was obsessed with a townie girl, that decades ago my mom had confessed to killing a girl, and that Rodney probably did it. And I was ready to tell him what happened to Becky too.

Trevor was on his back, our billowy comforter bunched under his chin, covering his body, but stopping short above his ankles. His bare feet stuck straight up. His socks only covered his toes and draped flaccid onto the bed. He struck me as wholesome and cartoonish. Everything about Trevor was sweet, funny, and for my amusement. Even his snore seemed comical, a loud, phony snore that would make the kids laugh.

I didn't want to wake him, not now, but I needed to tell him.

Things were happening. After all these years of being on my

own and thinking I'd left it all behind, I heard my past rev its engine once, twice, the deep tone resonating through cool, dry air. Across a wide field of tall grain, some hulky engine kick-started. Old pistons were sparking, and gears were beginning to turn, shaking off flecks of rust, finding their grooves. My old life, hidden by thick, dusty crops, was coming for me.

47

I had been six years old. I woke abruptly in the hallway closet. Something had woken me. Thinking it was morning, I pushed open the bifold doors and walked downstairs to watch early morning cartoons, the shag-carpet feeling of the stairs comfy and pushing between my toes.

A quiet struggling noise. I stopped on the stairs, listening. Someone sniffing, crying into their pillow. Sounded like it was coming from the boys' rooms. That couldn't be right. I'd never heard Rodney or Shane cry before.

Maybe the smothered crying was coming from Mom's room, in which case, I should get downstairs quickly. Mom was unpredictable. Sometimes a warm glowing ball of love coming down like Glinda the Good Witch; sometimes, the Wicked Witch, all bitterness and rage.

By the time I made it to the bottom stair, the small windows alongside the door caught my attention. Sunlight coming through was tinted a magical pink. The windows were streaked with paint. Holly must have been finger-painting. Oh, she's gonna get in trouble for that.

Walking toward the TV room, I felt a gust of cool morning air and shivered. The back door was wide open, which was strange. I had always been the first one awake.

The birds were noisy early in the morning. I couldn't name them, but I was familiar with their songs and with the woodpeckers' drilling. Pink, orange, and yellow leaves were everywhere in the grass, drawing me outdoors to collect them. Harsh morning rays of sun lit the yard, highlighting dew clinging to leaves and grass. I hated the feeling on my bare feet, the cold, wet, poking grass. The fallen leaves clinging to my skin. I reached down and picked one up. Yellow with red veins and an orange glow at the edges like a halo.

A branch creaked once, twice. The noise drew my attention across the yard.

Hanging from our gorgeous fiery maple, the source of all these stunning leaves, was Becky's body.

48

TREVOR

I drove in the dark along a two-lane road, my window down. I was sleepy, and the crisp predawn air was keeping me awake. I had an early meeting. My boss knew I was coming from Wisconsin—scheduling an early meeting was a dick move.

Ahead in the road, two glowing eyes. I slammed my brakes. Adrenaline burst through me as my tires squealed and tried to grip the road.

Deer.

My car stopped. Acrid smells of burnt rubber and hot brake pads infused air. I switched on my brights.

Not a deer.

A cow stood in the middle of the road, its eyes staring dumbly at me.

My pulse beat in my forehead, the beginning of an early morning headache. *Stupid cow.* Irritation prickled up my neck. I had a sudden urge, a rage, to clip its back legs.

I could do it too. There were no cars on the road now in either direction as far as the eye could see. My foot remained on the brake, but itched to shove the gas pedal.

As a teen, if I saw anything in the road—a duck, a turtle, a deer—I stepped on the gas and tried to smash it. That need to tear an animal apart, tear myself apart, had pulsed inside me. It had been primal. Like being in the throes of sex, nearing orgasm when the mind went offline. No thinking. Only need. A need for release.

Bloodlust.

That urge, bloodlust, had gripped me too many times during my teenage years. Now it dragged up a memory: the feeling of my knees in wet grass, a half-filled bucket before me, the weight of my grandfather's hunting knife sheathed in my belt, and the dark biting night around me. The bucket stinking of animal and iron and skin. Its warm liquid steaming in the cold.

I had plunged my hands into the bucket and loved the feeling. Blood.

My clothes had been filthy and damp. I'd stunk like a pig, my tongue stale and meaty in my mouth.

Bloodlust.

I blinked. The cow was walking slowly toward the side of the road. Still no cars on the road. I could hit it, but the urge had passed. I crept the car forward, honked. The cow made it safely into tall grass.

My dress shirt was damp at the back, clinging to my skin. Why had I been so out of control as a teenager? I'd had this desire to drive too fast with my headlights off; to run through the woods in full dark, no worry of tripping on a root or impaling my eye on a branch; to tear things apart.

What the fuck had been wrong with me?

49

HEATHER

With Emily and Sawyer at school, I backed out of the driveway. As I drove down Winding Way, a silver Infiniti passed me.

I stopped in the road and peered over my shoulder.

The Infiniti pulled to the curb in front of my house. Desiree's boyfriend's brother got out of his car. Brandon. He rang the bell. Stood on the curb with his hands in his pockets like he was just a nice guy.

What did he want?

As he walked back to his car, I drove away.

I told myself I was headed to the grocery store right up until I found myself parked in front of Holly's driveway.

The front door was open. The hallway beyond the screen was dark. I knocked, and her dog went wild, his nails scraping and sliding across the floor. He bumped his nose against the screen, and I startled when the screen door opened an inch before slamming shut on his nose.

"Diesel. Get back here, you big goddamn baby." Diesel was a rottweiler. Holly shuffled down the hall, said, "He's super sweet. Come on in."

When I hesitated, she opened the screen as if we were friends, as if we were family, *we were*, and let the dog go after me. I pushed the dog away and followed her into her kitchen.

Her house was dingy, but smelled good. Freshly brewed coffee, the rich, silky stuff.

"Your timing's perfect, for once," she said. "I just made coffee. I splurged and got Starbucks beans. Diesel, go lay down." He listened, curling up in an oversized bed.

"Take a load off," she said, nodding at the kitchen table and shoving aside a pile of envelopes, bills, magazines. She picked up a carafe and poured into mugs. "You said you just moved here, you had to be here for your dying mother-in-law. Where do you usually call home?"

"We live in Chicago."

She put a mini ceramic pitcher filled with cream on the table along with a two-pound bag of sugar. She sat across from me, spooned sugar into her coffee, and sighed like life was a huge pain in the ass. "So your husband's from here too? What are the odds of that?" she said, lifting her eyebrows.

Not that rare. We met in Chicago, which is only a couple hours from Hunther. I had to admit though, once I found out he was from Hunther, it made him seem a bit magical. I hadn't remembered my early childhood in Hunther—it had a fuzzy, fairytale quality in my mind, more of the Grimms' version, shadowy and gruesome—and I'd wondered if Trevor could shed light on it. If he'd heard of one of my sisters or brothers. No, he'd said he'd never known them. He was Rodney's age, but didn't remember Rodney. I wasn't surprised. Rodney was brooding and cruel in my memory. A loner. If Rodney had a crowd at all, it would have been the rough one. Trevor had said Rodney must have gone to the other high school, Hunther South.

Holly's implication was marinated in suspicion. Which was odd because how would that plot go? Trevor knew my parents were alcoholics, found me in Chicago so he could... love me and make me feel safe? Ooh, that's one devious motherfucker.

Then again, everything out of her mouth was whet with suspicion. Understandable. *You cut ties with the family, haven't seen her for twenty years, and now here you are, visiting her house for the second time in forty-eight hours.* She had twenty years of suspicion stored up inside, earning interest.

"Hunther's small, but it's not *that* small," I said. "And, the older I get, the more often I find myself saying 'small world.'"

"Hm," she said and sipped her coffee. "Do you work?"

I nodded. "I do blood draws at a testing center in Chicago. I'm not working while we're here. My manager, well, we get along, and my job is waiting for me. I miss it."

I did. I missed the routine of knowing exactly what I was supposed to do with my time. I missed the clean, harsh smell of isopropanol, the stretch of rubber band around flesh, touching a stranger's skin, and the precision and fine tip of a needle.

"Cream or sugar?" she said, pointing to the pitcher and sugar bag on the table.

"I'm good." I sipped. "The rumor about Mom killing Dawn Young, it was all news to me. But, you knew? When we lived here, you knew?"

"Vaguely. I mean, I was *eleven*. I guess I'd always assumed they were questioning her because she drove Dawn to work.

I assumed there'd been a misunderstanding."

"Did you know Dawn?" I wasn't sure why I was asking.

"No, but I watched her paint a few times during Mom's garage art classes. Remember those?"

"Sip and paint." I nodded.

"You're right," she said and laughed. "Too bad it wasn't a big money maker back then like it is now. She was good at that. She was funny and wild. She made those women laugh."

I'd heard laughter coming from the garage. I guess I'd never assumed my mom was the cause.

Holly's eyes grew misty. "Mom was generous with Dawn. Lent her scarfs, jewelry, shoes. Never had her pay for art class or her supplies."

I didn't remember Mom as generous. It was strange, these two versions of her. Having this conversation with my sister was strange too. It wasn't quite pleasant, but it was *comfortable*. Like that old pair of shabby, smelly slippers that you kind of wanted to throw out, but you couldn't bring yourself to pitch them because they were so cozy. I wasn't worried about annoying Holly or pissing her off, which was kind of nice. I could see myself lingering here, revisiting memories, our conversation chasing tails for hours. Brief laughs followed by stretches of casual disagreement. The thought exhausted me.

Say what's on your mind so you don't have to come back if you don't want to.

"I think Rodney killed Dawn, and Mom confessed to cover for him."

"What?" she said, flinching as if I'd slapped her. "No way, Heather." She shook her head. "Rodney couldn't hurt a fly. He was so gentle."

"Rodney was scary."

"What?" She laughed. "Rodney was sensitive."

"After we moved," I said, "Rodney went to the doctor for regular blood tests. Do you remember that?"

She nodded and said, tenderly, "He had migraines. Sometimes he'd have to go sit in a dark room."

"Don't you remember Rodney and those dead opossums?"

She flinched again. "What? No. I have no idea what you're talking about."

Everything was upside down here. I was losing patience, getting pissed off.

From the next room, a voice called, "Holly?"

"I'll be there in a minute, Bruce," she said loud enough for him to hear.

"You said you came here to help Mom," I said. "You wanted to show me something."

She sighed, annoyed as well. Stood and went to her refrigerator, grabbed an envelope stuck under a magnet, put it in front of me. The envelope had been torn open. It was addressed to our mom; the return address was Minnesota.

"After Mom's funeral, I brought all her boxes, all her crap, to my house. Well, I started going through her stuff and came across this."

I opened the envelope and flattened the paper. A letter. It was worn thin. It had been folded and handled many times.

Melinda,

Step 9 here. You're probably familiar. For you, it was AA. For me, NA.

I stopped reading and raised my eyes to Holly's. "What's NA?" She dropped her head an inch, stared at me, stone-eyed like I was stupid. "Narcotics Anonymous," she said.

"Oh," I said, and started the letter from the top.

Melinda,

Step 9 here. You're probably familiar. For you, it was AA. For me, NA. Potato potahto, addiction is fueled by the desperate need to escape emotional pain. Mostly bullshit, these steps. God this, God that, Ask Him to remove our character defects. Trust in God because you're pathetic and not capable like you've always suspected. Anyway, if God's steering the boat, why'd He sink my boat in the first place? And if He messed me up so bad that I had to get hooked on drugs, why would He help me now?

I'm guessing the religious stuff makes you cringe too. I go along with it though for the meetings, hearing other people's stories, what rituals help them. That has been useful.

Anyway, Step 9. Make amends to people we've harmed except when it would injure them or others. *I'm stuck on this. Me writing this letter pretty much guarantees someone will be injured. It might be you. But what I feel that's more important than even maybe putting you in danger is this: someone owes you an apology. I am sorry for what happened to you. There. The thing is, and here's the Pandora's box I'm leaving on your doorstep.*

Watch at your own risk. I've made copies of the videos.

I should have contacted you earlier, I know.

Basically, this is an apology and an invitation to more trouble.

Pretty shitty, I know. I've been told I'm cold more than once in my life.

-Sin

"I don't understand," I said, my heart feeling fluttery, fragile as a butterfly's wing. "I don't understand a single word. And why is it signed *Sin?*"

"I have no idea," she said. "This letter was dated a month before Mom was murdered. I didn't find any videos or flash drives in her apartment. Whatever was on these videos, someone killed her for it."

"That's just… *crazy.*"

"Is it?"

"Yes," I blurted. "*Very* crazy." Even after the texts I'd received, I wasn't completely sold on the idea that my mom was targeted, that it hadn't been a robbery gone wrong.

"Mom didn't live in the city," Holly said as if she'd read my mind. "She didn't have much, and whoever broke into her apartment had to know that. She had a damaging or scandalous video of something. Whoever broke in, they took it, and they killed her."

The recent break-ins came to mind.

Holly gulped her coffee. "The police responded like you did. They thought I was crazy." Her mouth twitched into a frown. "I just wish I'd asked Mom about what happened back then. I was little when we moved away from Hunther, and I never brought it up because it, well, it was such a painful time for Mom. It was like bam, bam, one thing after the next. Dawn died, Mom was gone for four or five weeks, she came back, then Becky died. I don't recall much about Mom being gone. Just that Dad farmed us all out. I stayed with Chrissy's family. Shane stayed with Kirk, his friend from baseball. Rodney stayed with Dad. You went to someone's house too, though I'm not sure where you went."

I was with Mom. And Claire and Donnie. At the head doctor's house.

Even if I didn't remember being with Mom, even if I barely remembered the girl and boy, I was happy to hold a puzzle piece.

Holly said, "Becky stayed with Gal and Gary Kender. You know, our next-door neighbors?"

I remembered their names and their presence next door. And their pool.

Holly said, "Mom was happy my entire childhood, until she went away for those four or five weeks. After she came back, she was different."

Because Mom had confessed to killing Dawn Young.

I studied the letter again. *Sin* was written easily, in carefree cursive, the same way you'd write your name. But who would name their kid Sin? I was aware people got creative with naming their children these days, but Sin was unpleasant. Like naming your kid Vlad the Impaler. It could be short for something. Sina. Sinead.

That was the logical explanation, but my conversation

with Father Greg wouldn't let me go. I kept thinking "Sin" as in an evil act.

"Holly?" her husband called, more desperately.

"Coming," she shouted. To me, she said, "Heather. You have to go ask Gal and Gary about Mom. I can't do it. I'm in a bind here. Ever since we got here." She whispered roughly, "The first week we were here, Bruce had his stroke. He can talk now, but hasn't got most of his vision back, and walking isn't easy. He has been saying, joking, 'If I die, then you'll be able to pay the bills.'" She stopped abruptly; eyes watery. "He loved being physically strong. It's superficial, strength, but he loved being able to fix things around the house. It kills him to be the weak one. It kills him that I have to help him stand so he can wipe his ass," she hissed at me, angry, as if something about this situation were my fault.

"Holly?" he said, whining.

"Here I come," she called.

She flipped the empty envelope, wrote something, and shoved it in my face.

It was an address.

"What's this?"

"The old house. Go there. Ask Gal and Gary. It's the least you could do." She pushed her chair out and left the room.

50

I drove straight there. Not because I owed Holly anything but because things should have been coming into focus, but they weren't.

I matched the address she gave me to the address on the mailbox. I pulled to the curb in front of our old house and stared at the narrow two-story. How had all of us fit in there?

The wood siding was painted yellow. Baskets sprouting lush ferns hung from the fascia. Two white Adirondack chairs angled toward each other on the porch beneath the baskets. The house seemed worn, but loved. The current occupants were yellow-happy, hanging-baskets-happy. A minivan sat in the driveway. A maple with lumpy roots was buckling the sidewalk.

I felt nothing. No longing. No anger. No nostalgia. I barely recognized it. If Holly hadn't given me the address, and I'd been on a walk in this neighborhood, I wouldn't have known this was the house where I'd spent my first six years. Who remembers their first six years anyway?

I found comfort in that. Whenever I yelled at Emily or gave poor advice, I took a deep breath and told myself, she's only six, she'll never remember you this way. By the time she's twelve though, you'd better have your act together.

Was our sugar maple, that peacock of a tree, still standing in the backyard?

The memory slid into focus: Becky hanging from the clothesline, one shoe on, one off, hands in tight fists, neck clawed, broken blood vessels webbing the skin around her eyes, the fall foliage a stunning backdrop of trembling yellow and peach. Branch creaking under her weight.

I didn't want to know if the tree was still there.

Which house belonged to Gal and Gary?

I was pretty sure it's the one to my left. I used to run out the back door of our house and swerve left to jump in their pool.

From the street, I had a view of where their pool had once been. They'd removed it and planted grass. Beyond the backyard, a stretch of thin forest.

This is the place where I once died. Drowned.

Based on a collage of my siblings' memories, the whole family was at the Kenders'. My brothers were playing horseshoes with Gary. Mom, Dad, and Gal were sitting in lawn chairs, smoking and drinking beer.

They had an above-ground circular pool. It was crappy, but to us kids, there was nothing more magical. Becky and the Kender girls played Marco Polo. I was excluded because I was too small. Too little to play water-tag, but not too little to swim unsupervised in a five-foot-deep swimming pool, go figure.

I circled the pool, hand-over-hand along the edge. Occasionally I dolphin-dove, trying to touch the mysterious, sky-blue, bubble-gum-plastic bottom of the pool.

There's probably a minute or two lapse in the story where

no one remembers how it happened, but the story picks up when McClane Kender, nineteen years old at the time, noticed me face-down, lying at the bottom of the pool. McClane had an intellectual disability. He'd been shuffling along the outside of the pool, saving struggling water-logged houseflies, and mumbling the word *Skyscraper* over and over.

When he saw me lifeless at the bottom, he'd shouted, "Fire, fire, fire!" and flopped over the hot metal edge, splashing clumsily into the water.

Always shout *Fire* when you need help, Gal had taught her son. "It's the only word that will always get people to come running. Help, for some reason," she'd said, "in this godforsaken world, doesn't work."

Gal Kender, who was as drunk as my parents, easily pulled my small body from McClane's hands. She laid me down in the grass and breathed and compressed me back to life. She wasn't a nurse—she worked at the post office—but knew CPR. It happened so quickly, no one bothered to call 911. Becky wrapped a towel around my shoulders and sat beside me in the grass.

What stood out most was my parents' reaction. My dad, buzzed and apathetic in his chair, eyes glazed and sleepy, took another sip from his beer can.

My mom, her face flush with alcohol and anger, stood. "Goddamn," she said, her teeth clenched, "it is always something." She marched back to our house and slammed the door behind her.

* * *

I rang the Kenders' doorbell, waited a half minute, and rang it again. I was getting good at being a pest.

A woman opened the door. She was dressed nicely, wearing flats, like she had just come home from lunch with her group of ladies. Her wrinkles were of the deep variety associated with years of smoking or terrible genetics. Her thin lips fell at the corners in a scowl.

I forced a salesman smile. "Mrs. Kender?"

"Yes." Curt. She didn't want to buy whatever I was selling.

"I'm not sure if you remember me. I'm Heather Hornne. My older sister Becky was friends with your daughters."

"Melinda Hornne had five children," she said, nodding, "Heather? Oh, you were the *baby*." She tried to make it sound cute, but her eyes squinted and distain seeped through. Like, *aw, I betcha you were spoiled*.

"Yep, I'm the baby." I shifted my weight. "Can you tell me anything about why my mom was a suspect in the murder of Dawn Young?" Before she could ask, I said, "My mom is dead so I can't ask her about it."

Gal looked past me, down toward the ground. "It was because your mom drove Dawn home that night. That's what you get for having a big heart in this town, you get accused of murder." The pissy way she said it made me wonder if Gal got accused of something as well.

"What about your pet opossums? People said my mom killed them."

"Phillis and Deeter? Nah," she said, and opened her screen. She walked past me, squatted down slowly at the edge of her grass, and pulled up a dandelion weed. Tossed it in her grass, brushed her hand against her pants. "McClane and Rodney saw the coyote going at one of them. They chased it away, but they were too late." She smiled, and it was sincere. "Your brother was so sweet. He held a memorial for those opossums. Tried to save Phillis's babies. He nursed them with a dropper for days before the last one of them died."

What?

I pictured Rodney standing beside my little kid self, his skin flush with heat. Flies hovering. Trinkets laid out around the opossums. Eight of spades. Marbles. Dream catcher with a brown feather. A cross bound with red yarn. It struck me as creepy and superstitious. I had never considered this was his version of a loving ceremony. When he ran away with the babies, I imagined he did something filthy and cruel with them.

"Father Greg said my mom was not herself. He said he performed an exorcism."

She laughed. "He loves that hokey pokey. Talks about possession once a month. Like menstruation." She pulled another weed. "During my time of the month, well, when I had a time of the month, I loaded up on salty chips. For Father Greg, it's exorcism."

Gal Kender was not a fan of this town and its people.

"What about my mom going away for a while?"

She tossed the weed in her grass, stared at our old house, and nodded. "Depression. She went to see a psychologist, but then, well, she was just gone, and I didn't hear anything about it. Your dad asked if Becky could stay with us. He said your mom was being treated for Multiple Personality Disorder."

"Multiple Personality Disorder? I-I never…" I trailed off.

No one had ever mentioned a disorder. I was hearing so many different things. My mind shifted through memories of my mom, searching.

"I didn't believe it either. Your mom, when she came back, did not want to talk about it. Not at all. So I didn't ask. And you guys moved shortly after."

I was going to mention my drowning incident, and thank her for saving my life, but it felt pathetic in the shadow of all the other tragedy. I said, "How is McClane?"

"McClane's in The Fairchild Home." She said it dryly, terminal. As if this one statement explained everything about him. I was guessing Fairchild was a place you put an adult who needed full-time care and safety when you decided that you, the parent, were no longer able to provide those things.

"Oh," I said awkwardly. I struck a blank with her daughters' names so I went for the husband. "How is Mr. Kender?"

"Gary is in Milwaukee County." Same monotone, dead-end answer. Gal had become a real downer.

"For business?"

"Milwaukee County Prison."

"Oh," I said, "I didn't know. I'm sorry."

"And my daughters?" she said, annoyed, assuming I was going to continue this nosey line of inquiry. "Cheryl's in California. Farah hung herself a couple years ago." She didn't say it with sadness, but with piss. As if Cheryl moved as far away as she could manage to ruin Gal's life. As if Farah killed herself to spite Gal.

Her words hit me like a sucker punch, unexpected and hard. In my mind, Becky's neck dropped against the clothesline, her hair cascading over half her face.

Gal walked past me, opened her screen, and stepped inside.

"Just like Becky," I said, my voice a rough whisper.

Without another word, Gal closed her door.

"Why do we study psychology for years and years, after all? We want to help people. The brain is a strange island, and some of us get stranded there all alone."

Doctor Clifford Paulson, PhD Psychology
Transcripts from the Sixth Annual Conference on
Adult Manifestations of Childhood Trauma
THE RADISSON PLAZA HOTEL, CINCINNATI, OHIO

51

I pulled into the garage and walked down the long driveway to get the mail. Like a needle skipping a vinyl record, my mind kept repeating snippets of my conversation with Gal. *Farah hung herself a couple years ago. Gary's in prison.*

I wanted to know why.

Rodney held a memorial for those opossums. Tried to save Phillis's babies. He nursed them with a dropper for days before the last one of them died.

Why had my child's mind twisted Rodney's kindness into something horrific and repulsive?

Because he *was* strange and secretive. He was. Even if he hadn't killed Gal's opossums, he could still have killed Dawn Young.

Multiple Personality Disorder. Your mom was being treated for Multiple Personality Disorder.

I knew the symptoms. Detachment. Blurred sense of identity. Notable changes in personality. Did it fit?

A utility van stopped in the middle of the street, the side door opened roughly, and Desiree stepped out. She wore a T-shirt cut off below her breasts, jeans, and her hair down. Smokey eyes, glossy lips.

"Hea-ther! So this is where you live?" The utility van and the two males in the front should have put me on edge, but

Desiree was thrilled to see me. Total serendipity.

"What are you doing here?" I said.

"We heard they got a *baby*. We wanted to peek at the menagerie. The new one is precious. Two harsh markings above her eyes like she's a killer, but she's the sweetest thing."

My nerves sighed, at ease that she wasn't here for me.

The male in the passenger seat laughed at something, his laugh like a series of slow hiccups. High. He's high. It was the skater-haircut who worked at Aldi's. Both males in the front seats were young, twenty, twenty-one.

"There was another break-in the other day," I said, my tone calm and sleepy. My nerves were shot from my conversation with Gal. I was zapped of energy. "Was that you?"

"What?" She was a good liar, but I already knew that.

"What were you looking for? I'm so curious."

She smiled and moved close to me. In my space. "Heather," she said, her lips glossy and sultry. "Come party with us. It will be fun." She placed her hand under my waistband at my hip. "I miss talking with you. You are so, so easy." Her voice was husky, but there was something childlike there too. Her hand skated around to my front. Her fingertips slid down below the waist of my pants, her nails touching my underwear. She took hold of my waistband and gave it a tug.

I could have pushed her away. I tipped my mouth near her ear and whispered, "Is it jewelry? What are you stealing?"

Her hand dropped away from my skin, her playfulness gone. She laughed a little. "You don't seem like you'd be, but you are persistent."

"Did my mom know your mom?"

"I don't think so. I don't know much about my mom." She glanced down at the tattoo on the inside of her wrist. "Other than she liked to draw. As a kid, I found all these sketches of hers."

Just like Dawn. "Did your mom know Dawn?"

"Probably not. My mom was five or six years older than Dawn, so they would have missed each other in high school. Also, Dawn was here in Hunther for only a few months before she was murdered. Transient. No roots. Almost like she never existed." She took a few steps back. She was done talking to me. "Your mom's dead. What's it matter?"

What did it matter? I'd picked at this scab over and over. I was familiar with its bumpy, snagged edges and with the blood oozing out from underneath.

"I never liked my mom," I said. "Didn't care much for my siblings either. I thought they were toxic." It was a popular term now—toxic. Trendy even. It wasn't then. "Now I hear they're involved in a murder, maybe satanic stuff." I shook my head. It still sounded crazy. "I need to know if I'm right. That they were toxic. That I wasn't imagining it."

She smiled, her eyes dreamy, as if I'd told her a love story. "I get that, I do." She took a few steps back toward the van. "But when you know people are bad, when you know for sure, it doesn't make things better. It's worse." She turned, stepped in, and slid the door closed.

52

TREVOR

There was a Prius in Mom's driveway, so I parked on the street behind Paulina's car. Who drove a Prius?

I pulled my keys out of the ignition and stepped out of my Toyota. I had worked an honest, productive day at J&B. Logos—white space with a spray of color and bold letters just off-center—lingered in my mind.

The front door opened, and an old man stepped out. He wore khaki pants and a tweed jacket. He held a book in his hand.

It took me a second. I forced a smile over clenched teeth. "Hey, Father Greg." I crossed the lawn. "What a surprise. What brings you here?"

"Oh, hello there, Trevor. Your mother's nurse, Paulina, called me, said your mother was asking after me. We had a lovely visit."

These women. These stupid women who adored their priests. They were like schoolgirls. They loved fussing over their clergy, loved that they could flirt with these men because it was one-sided and safe.

I shook Father Greg's hand. He had a firm grip, and his hand was warm and comfortable. He smiled and looked me in the eye, and let me go after a beat. Priests had perfected the handshake. No one did it better. "Nice to see you," I said. "I'd better get inside." I turned toward the house.

"It's good to have you back in town, even if it's for your mother's sickness." He pressed an index finger to his lips as if it would clear his mind. "You know, the funniest thing. Your mother told me you married one of the Hornne girls. Is it Heather?"

Chills pricked along my scalp. "Yes. Heather."

"She stopped by to visit me the other day. She had questions about her mom."

Rage blossomed in my chest. Hairs on the back of my neck stood on end. I had worked so hard to protect Heather. "Oh. OK," I said. "Good to talk, Father. I'd better get inside."

On the porch, I fished in my pocket for Mom's house key. My cell buzzed with a text.

-Tomorrow. 4 p.m. Parking lot of Paul Bunyan's Canteen.

53

Today had been draining, so it was especially uplifting that two of our monarchs hatched from their chrysalises.

Sawyer, Emily, and I sat on chairs on the back deck. Both kids had a butterfly latched to their pointer finger, hanging upside down and flapping its wings slowly.

The late afternoon sun warmed my cheeks. I was sleepy. Watching the butterflies dry their newly opened wings eased my tension. Those colors—fiery orange with precise black lines webbing in perfect symmetry, white dots like pearl-laced edging—were brilliant and creamy. The patterns on their wings, made from the finest silky powders, were a reminder that life had order. Sometimes you just had to look for it.

"Why is mine not flying away?" Emily said.

"He's still drying his wings. Patience."

"There he goes," Sawyer said, watching his butterfly fly away, wonder on his face.

"All the caterpillar poop was totally worth it, don't you think, Sawyer?" I said.

Ignoring me, he watched the caterpillar flit around, its path wild and jumpy. It seemed senseless, but it was a survivor's tactic. Unpredictable, erratic behavior kept you safe. It made me think of Desiree.

Eyes on his butterfly as it landed on a milkweed, he said softly, "My mom left me a message. Said she wanted me to visit her in, well, that place."

I bit my lip. *Say the correct thing.* "I can drive you if you want. Anytime you want."

He said nothing.

"Or your dad could take you," I said. "Whatever you think."

He nodded. Then, to give him space, I turned my attention to Emily. "How's your caterpillar doing?"

Emily shook her finger a little, maybe to give him motivation. The butterfly let go of her finger, looked like it was swooping down to take off, but then fell and landed on the deck beside her chair. She stood and turned to see where it went, but her sneaker stepped on it.

"Careful!" I yelled, out of my chair and pushing her to the side. Emily fell.

Sweaty and panicked, I scooped up the butterfly and walked quickly away from them and around to the side of the house toward the milkweed patch.

Behind me, Emily howled. "Why'd you push me, Momma?"

Sawyer, accusing, angry, "Did you step on it, Emily? Did she?"

Emily cried louder. The door slammed, and her crying quieted. She'd gone inside.

It was alive, but one of its wings was wrinkled.

Sawyer marched up behind me. I could smell him. I could feel his fury charging the air. His voice biting, he said, "Did she *kill* it?"

I wanted to tell him, *It probably wouldn't have survived as a baby caterpillar unless we'd brought it inside. We saved more than would have survived.* But now was not the time for logic.

I tucked it under a bush, out of sight. "It's OK, Sawyer. She stepped on the very edge of the wing. It was an accident, but it will be fine."

Pissed off, he went inside.

I stared into the depths of our backyard. Green. So many shades of green. Cicadas shrieked—*tick tick tick*—their song rising and falling. A single bird called out, telling her family it was dinnertime. Her call grew frantic and shrill. Then, in the distance, the raspy growl of a big cat.

I scurried inside, bolting the door behind me as if a cougar might figure out how to turn my door handle.

I found Emily crying in her room. "I'm sorry I pushed you. I panicked."

She hid under the covers of her bed. It was hard being small. I didn't want her to feel the shame that I had felt so deeply.

I sat on her bed and petted the curve of her back. "The butterfly is fine. He flew away," I lied. "I was just worried you were going to stumble on him, so I pushed you to the side, but I didn't mean to push you hard. I'm sorry." It felt good to say sorry. My parents never said sorry. Another word, another deed, by which to measure myself. "Will you eat some milk and cookies with me?"

"OK," she said, sniffling under the blanket.

"I'll bring the cookies up to your room and we can have a

tea party. Will you set a blanket on the floor and put out your picnic plates?"

She pushed the blanket off, springing up with a smile as if she'd popped out of a cake. "Sure!"

"I'll be up in a couple minutes."

She was humming and digging in her closet by the time I closed her door.

Sawyer's door was open a few inches. He was moving around in his room in that rough, impulsive way teenage boys moved. Closing drawers too hard. He wasn't striving for obnoxious; it was a combination of testosterone and not realizing his body was bigger than he'd remembered.

I know I'm not your biological mom, but I'm here for you...

Nudging his door, I said, "Sawyer, would you like to have cookies with—" but my words caught.

His back to me, he was tucking a handgun into his jeans. He turned and flinched, alarmed to see me. In a flash, that fear turned to anger. "Can't you knock?"

"I'm sorry."

I should have said, *Why do you have a gun?*

He grabbed his phone off his dresser and was moving fast. "I gotta go." He brushed past me in a whoosh of icy fresh deodorant, knocking me off balance, and rushed down the stairs.

I caught myself against the wall, broke out of my shock and followed him down. "Sawyer! What are you doing? Where did you get that?" By the time I got to the door, the screen slamming its frame, he was already sitting in the back of that same black pickup.

I hesitated, not wanting to be the crazy mother that ran after her son as he drove away, embarrassing him in front of his friends.

Who cares about embarrassing him? He has a gun. He's not old enough to buy a gun.

"Momma?" Emily's voice sang. "All ready for our picnic."

"I'll be up in a minute," I said, surprised by the calmness in my voice. I called Trevor.

"Hey," he said. "Everything OK?"

Your son, I almost said.

"Sawyer has a handgun. He left the house with friends, and he had a handgun tucked in the back of his pants. I don't know whose it is. I thought you talked to him about guns."

"I did. Relax. It will be OK. Probably it belongs to a friend, and they are going for target practice. Don't worry. He's a smart kid. He's a good kid. I'll call him." Trevor always knew what to say. Two gears. Not worried or not too worried.

I thought about sleeping in Em's room tonight, locking her door. Then, felt awful for it.

54

That night I dreamed Becky was walking in the grass, heading to our backyard. I trailed behind her, watching her long milky-white legs. She wore jean shorts that she'd cut off herself and washed a dozen times to unravel the cut edge. Long frays swung from her shorts as she walked.

"If we'd lived in a bigger town," she said, "that might have saved us. If she'd gotten help at a big hospital. Cleveland, Mayo, MD Anderson, one of those." She scratched behind her knee, and her long dark hair swayed.

Stopping in front of the shed, she reached up to undo the deadbolt. As she lifted onto her toes, the bulb of muscle in one of her shiny calves flexed. She wore cheap white sneakers that she'd dirtied up right home from the store, literally popped the tags off and rolled them in dry dirt so they wouldn't look new.

She got the bolt loose, the hinge creaked, and she disappeared into the shed's darkness. I held the door, but wouldn't go in. Two mice had run over my bare foot in there before.

"But how could those big hospitals make her better?" I said. "She was a witch."

Becky emerged from the dark shed with clothesline looped

in her hand, tilted her chin down, and smiled.

"We're *all* witches, Heather. Devil worshippers and murderers, all of us, you silly goose." She ruffled the top of my head, messed my hair.

"I'm not a witch," I said.

She lassoed my neck with clothesline, wrapping the slack around my neck once, twice…

Panic ratcheted in me with each wide swing of clothesline, the *swoosh*, my skin pinched tighter and tighter. I didn't fight her. My arms hung paralyzed at my sides.

"But you're the biggest witch of alllllll," she said, her mouth opening wide like a prehistoric fish, and something wiggled on her tongue. Squirming, the size and shape of kidney beans, all of them with translucent pink skin, the hint of dark organ-sized shapes beneath. Opossum fetuses.

I jerked awake, my clothes sweat-damp, the inside of my mouth dry. My eyelids felt tight and puffy.

Dead weight pinning my thighs.

Emily. Her legs flopped across mine, her soft skin warm and sweet. She thrived on skin-to-skin contact, even in her sleep. I eased her sticky legs away and rolled slowly off her bed, careful not to creak the mattress. I picked up my phone from her floor and closed her door quietly behind me.

Sawyer's door was closed. Trevor's door was open. Everyone still sleeping. A hint of light creeping into the dark sky.

I crept downstairs, wrapped myself in a light sweater, and sat in a chair out on the back deck. Fog shifted in the dark, cloaking the pines completely, masking half the lawn, and creeping up toward the house. The morning smelled damp and cold. It must have rained last night.

I hadn't been ready yesterday. I wasn't ready now either, but I googled Gary Kender on my phone.

Volleyball player comes forward with accusation, and other students' testimonies follow. Gary Kender taught Chemistry and coached girls' volleyball at Huston Middle School in the nearby town of Penbridge. In 2016, he was convicted of sexually abusing several students and sentenced to serve fifteen years.

I pulled my legs up and cried softly into my knees. I couldn't be sure, I'd never be sure, but it was the closest I'd come to answering the question of why Becky did it. Had my parents suspected back then? I bet they hadn't. They'd been friends with the Kenders up until the day we moved away.

Had they ever heard about Gary's conviction? Probably not. Holly would have mentioned it.

Was Gal Kender, the woman who saved my life when I was small, the woman who was sticking up for my mom, sticking up for Rodney, one of those horrible women? A mother who didn't believe her child when they finally and painfully confided that Dad's been coming in their room at night, who swears to God *My husband would never do that*, who didn't believe her child even when the skeptical court system found enough reason to lock the bastard up, who didn't believe her child even after her daughter killed herself. Even now.

The door opened behind me, startling me.

"Wow, it's so foggy." Sawyer. "That's so cool. You can't even see those pines."

Last night's panic over Sawyer running out of the house with a handgun came back to me, but it was muted. Already history. I worried about Sawyer, but my worry was more like a vague muscle ache instead of a bleeding wound.

"Good morning," I said, wiping my eyes.

"Oh. Are you OK?"

"Yeah, I'm OK."

"Is it because of yesterday?" His voice was a soft apology.

I gazed up at him and smiled sincerely. "No. Not at all about you. I was thinking about my sister, actually. The one who died young."

"Oh. Sorry about your sister." He moved his hand up the back of his hair. "Sorry about yesterday too. I will give the gun back. Dad. Well, Dad and I talked."

I nodded. "Thank you." I was, but I also didn't want to dig into this conversation twenty minutes before the bus came. I didn't imagine he wanted to either. "I can make you a sandwich if you're interested."

A low, almost imperceptible mumble, like the vibration of a distant train, grew into a guttural, big cat growl.

Sawyer's eyebrows went up. "What the fuck?"

I stood quickly, opened the door for him, and followed him inside.

He laughed softly, shaking his head. "I can't believe our neighbor has cougars. This place is fucked up."

"So incredibly fucked up," I said, laughing. And just like that, me and Sawyer, we had something between us and only us.

55

Trevor made me breakfast. Sawyer caught the bus. Emily played quietly in her room.

Trevor told me about his late-night conversation with Sawyer. Sawyer's friend loaned him the gun and was taking him for target practice.

"Sawyer's a city kid who's been dropped into a rural town," he said. "Makes sense that he'd be intrigued. I told him we'd go to the firing range next weekend. Hunting a few more times too. Sawyer's good. It's my fail."

"Don't be hard on yourself. You're juggling a lot," I said. "You want some?" I pointed to my plate.

He smiled. "Nope, it's all yours."

Sitting at the table with Trevor, sipping hot coffee, dipping my toast in eggs, talking about the kids, it felt good. But it didn't last.

"I've got to get going," he said, laying his palm on my hand.

"Trevor?"

His hand fell away as he stood and walked to the sink. Outside, the deck was wet. It was drizzling.

"Days ago, you said the name Dawn Young rang a bell?"

"Who?" Behind me, the faucet turned on.

"The first night we got here, when I asked you about her

murder, you said her name rang a bell. She was a girl your age. No, she was maybe a year older. She was murdered here when you were in high school. You would have been a junior, I think."

"I don't know, maybe. Although my memory isn't sharp right now and I'm tired. I've got to get going." He turned the water off. "Let me chew on it, and we'll talk later." I felt his presence behind me, the warmth coming off him. His lips pressed the top of my hair, and he left. The spot he kissed me felt breathy and moist.

Father Greg seemed to think visiting his brother, the head doctor, was a waste. But Cliff was the one my mom had confessed to. I was hoping he would help me puzzle it together.

After I dropped Emily at school, I drove to the wealthy nook of Hunther.

Harvest Road sloped upward, the street wide and curving and shaded by old oaks. Every five or ten acres, a long driveway trailed to a gorgeous house. Some of them massive with statues of lions or fountains and side coach houses and backyards that stretched high above the river. Some of them quaint and smaller, but with elaborate touches like a wrap-around porch or an inground pool framed by Spanish tile. Houses on the left had views overlooking Crooked River; houses on the right had backyards that led to private woods.

What did these wealthy folks think of the outdated town surrounding them? The Dress Barn, Marjory's Greasy Spoon and Donuts, the woman who had a cougar menagerie in her backyard. No fancy restaurants, no specialty delis, no salt spas or upscale massage in this town. Where did these people dine, shop, and satisfy their expensive tastes? Maybe they had their expensive tastes shipped to them and they rarely left their beautiful houses.

I parked in the street in front of Cliff's house. It wasn't opulent, but was large and brown brick. Father Greg was right. It looked like an elementary school. Made sense if Cliff had patients staying in the building. His driveway wrapped around to the back, which would also accommodate employees' cars. If he had patients living here, he'd need staff.

The front of the building was dark, unwelcoming, private. The porch was small, roofed, and hidden by hedges.

It was only drizzling, but I didn't want to get damp. I ran up the long driveway and rang the doorbell.

A woman's voice came through a speaker to my right. "Good afternoon. Who is it?"

"Hello. I'm looking for Cliff." I realized I didn't know his last name. "My name is Heather Hornne. My mother used to be one of his patients. Um, she is, she's no longer alive, but I had some questions for the doctor."

A pause. Then, "Alright, dear. Give me a few minutes."

Alright, dear implied she might know me. Maybe this was Cliff's wife, Claire and Donnie's mom. Or maybe she was the nanny or the housekeeper while I lived here.

I turned away from the house, gazed at the lawn, the ornamental trees, the wrap-around driveway. None of it jogged my memory.

The door opened to a simple foyer, the sharp, sweet smell of roses wafting on cooled air. She was in her sixties, stylish in white capris, a thin gray sweater, and ballerina flats. Jewelry on her ears, neck, wrists, and fingers.

"Heather." Smiling, she said my name the breathy way some people say, "Ocean," or "Vacation." Her blond hair was neat, her makeup was perfect. "You don't remember me," she said, her eyes kind.

"No, I'm sorry."

"I'm Alice. Come in, my dear. I had book club last night and I have so much leftover sushi. Cocktails too." She winked and headed down the hallway, peeking back once. "Please close the door. We've got a wasp's nest in our cherry tree."

I closed the door, followed her to a gorgeous kitchen remodel. Huge island. A white slab of quartz with asymmetrical gray streaks, glimmers of silver specks. Copper oven. Stone backsplash. Carved kitchen table. Old farmhouse style with a modern twist.

She pulled a silver tray out of the refrigerator. "Why don't you take this out to the sunporch. I'll grab us some drinks, and we can catch up. I'm so glad you are here, Heather."

I took the tray and did as I was told. The triple sliding door was already open so I walked to the screened porch, set the tray down, and gazed at the backyard that stretched a few acres before the woods fenced the property. Even though the day was gray and foggy, the drizzle made for a calming soundtrack—a hushed applause.

One hundred feet back, to the right, a white shed. Beyond it, an old, unmanicured mulberry tree twisted and grabbed at the back of the shed, like a claw. A trio of birds flurried under the tree, maybe to eat fallen berries. The image of the shed ensnared by the mulberry tree sent sparks up my spine, left me breathless. Beyond the mulberries, a narrow creak wound away.

"You remember the fort," she said.

"Yes."

"Iced tea," she said, handing me a glass, ice cubes clinking. "You remember Claire and Donnie?"

"A little. I didn't remember their names."

She tilted her head as if to convey, oh how sad that you don't remember all those good times. "Oh well. You were so young, five, six." She smiled and rested her chin in her palm. "Most of us don't remember being that small. We recollect stories that we've been told over and over. Or we think we remember events based on photos, but the mind is a funny thing."

She sighed, a peaceful smile upon her lips. "There's simply not enough room in our brain box. It prunes and makes way for stronger connections, more recent memories. Come sit and eat some sushi." Eyebrows raised, she said, "It cost me hundreds, but my ladies group last night barely touched it. Sushi is too exotic for them, I guess."

"Does Cliff live here?"

"He's here, but I'm afraid he can't help you. He's recently had a mental decline. Dementia usually doesn't come on so fast. Or perhaps we just didn't realize," she said and shrugged. She sat and pointed to the chair beside me. I sat. "He's sleeping now. He sleeps a lot. It's alright. We're retired." She laughed and reached out, brushing her hand against my arm. "When he's awake, he works on crosswords. He doesn't get but one or two words the whole day, but he likes the feel of the paper in one hand, the pencil in the other. He likes to preserve the ritual, I think."

She gazed past me. "He was a brilliant man once upon a time. He is owed dignity in his decline," she said, her voice resolute. "I'll keep him here as long as I'm able to. We had some good years, and I'm hanging on. In sickness and in health! I'm sorry, I'm rambling. So, tell me. How did you end up here at my house?"

She forked a veggie roll, dipped it in neon green wasabi, and set it on her plate, slicing it into smaller pieces with a knife.

"Father Greg told me where you lived. He told me Cliff was my mom's doctor."

"Wait. Wait. Let me guess." She lifted her palms and her eyebrows, a skeptical comedian. "He told you he did an exorcism on your mom."

I nodded.

"He's a bit..." she looked up, searching for a word, "eccentric." Forked a piece into her mouth. "Eat. Please."

I wasn't hungry, but it looked delicious. Colors brilliant as Play-Doh. So much more appealing than my macaroni and cheese dinners. I used my fingers, grabbing a spicy tuna roll, skipped my plate, and stuffed it into my mouth.

"Greg means well. He's a kind man. Oblivious, but so many men are. And priests can be..." She paused, sipping her tea, searching for the right words. "Greg saw what he wanted to see. We're all guilty of that sometimes."

I sipped my tea. Too sweet. "Why did he get involved then?"

"Oh, we had him stay for the weekend from time to time.

Some of our live-in patients were comforted by having a priest around. I'm sure he prayed over your mom, sprayed her with his emergency holy water." She sipped her tea and said, "I can't imagine him doing anything bad. Not because I can't imagine him doing anything bad ever, but because there was always someone around, my family, the nurses." She laughed, delighted by slandering her brother-in-law. "I mean, I don't think Greg's a bad guy. I trusted him around my children their whole lives. To be frank," Alice said, "I do not believe in demonic possession. And your mother? She had Multiple Personality Disorder."

So, Gal was right.

"You could see how MPD would get confused with possession, couldn't you?" she said, sighing, like an annoyed academic. "The disassociation is present in both cases, the confusion between the two was unavoidable."

"What do you think was my mom's involvement in the Dawn Young case?"

"She did it," she said, plainly. "She killed that girl."

"But she took back her confession," I argued. "Said she'd been drugged."

Alice thought about it. With hardly any emotion, she said, "Well, once she left the safety of this place, and police had her signed confession in hand, she was facing the reality of getting charged. I would have walked it back too, said anything to take it back. Wouldn't you?"

"Would your husband say the same thing?"

"If you were to ask my husband, he would tell you

Multiple Personality Disorder usually manifests after someone undergoes abuse during their childhood. That abuse, if it's traumatic enough, can make them violent and unpredictable."

My mom had a younger brother who died young, bone cancer, but she had great memories of him. He kept pet doves, he played the accordion, he always left chocolates in her shoes. Her mom, my grandma, died when I was a toddler, but my siblings cooed over her, said she was sweet, baked us angel cakes topped with whipped cream, and loved baseball. She was a hoot, shouting at the TV, belting "Take Me Out" during the seventh inning stretch. Grandpa died when I was in utero. He had been racist and grouchy, kept his car tidy, and cobbled wooden animals for his son and daughter. Mom grew up in an apartment in Chicago, they moved to a bungalow on the outskirts of the city when she was a teenager. Every tidbit I'd heard about her family, abuse and violence didn't fit.

Alice chewed the side of her lip and twisted one of her rings. It seemed like she was weighing whether she wanted to tell me something more.

"Please tell me what else you know," I said.

"Back in the '80s and '90s, there were a number of psychiatric journals documenting Multiple Personality Disorder being a manifestation of ritualistic abuse, sometimes satanic in nature." Chills crept through me. The dampness of my clothes from the rain was finally soaking into my skin. "That's what Cliff thought, that she was mixed up in devil worship."

"What would make him think that?"

"Well, she spoke of cutting Dawn Young with a knife," she said, matter-of-factly. "So did you."

"No," I said. "I couldn't."

She smiled sympathetically. "You blocked it out. Memory loss is common in Post-Traumatic Stress Disorder."

Coldness seeped deeper into me. I felt it in my bones. My teeth chattered.

She took another bite of a veggie roll from her plate. I glanced at the sushi platter, and my stomach twisted. I felt stirred up, turbid. Nothing was settling to the bottom. There was no clarity rising to the surface of my mind.

"How are your siblings, hon?" she said, keen to move the subject on, her eyes now kind.

"I don't keep in touch." Seemed like the easiest answer.

"Family is funny, isn't it? My children, when they were small, they were *everything* to me. My air, my food, my water. But then they grow up and they form their own opinions and they don't need you, and sometimes you wonder, who the heck are you, child, and how is it possible I raised you?" She laughed. What would it have been like if I'd had this woman for a mother, someone who drank tea instead of vodka? Someone who made the effort, with herself, with conversation.

"Do your kids live near?"

"My youngest, Pierce, he hadn't been born yet when you stayed with us, he's my loyal one, my helper. He's in Hunther. My oldest, Claire, she's gone and hates coming back. She's defiant. Bitter. Maybe because she hasn't found a man yet, I don't know. Maybe because I was too strict. You're always toughest on your first, no helping that. But you two girls, you were *such* a pair when you were little." She smiled, liquid memories in her eyes. "You were wonderful girls. Good girls. Now my middle child, Donnie, he's an entrepreneur. He's my wild child. My smart ass. He comes around here and there, but he's, well—we don't agree on much."

"Oh, I have a question," I said, as if I were a student. "How did I end up staying here in the first place?"

She tapped her finger on her chin. "Your father, well, he was overwhelmed. We offered, and he accepted. I think he thought that having another girl to play with would be good therapy for you. And it was." Her face lit up. "I don't mean to shove you out, Heather, but I have an appointment. Let me wrap this sushi for you. I hardly have an appetite as I get older, and I hate to toss it in the trash." She grabbed the platter and headed into the kitchen.

I brought both glasses to the kitchen, set them on the island. True to her word, she already had a foiled rectangle ready for me. "So nice to see you, Heather."

She followed me down the hallway. "Oh, these are my children. Photos in the room on your left. When they were teenagers." I peered in the study. Huge mahogany desk. Bookshelves. Tidy. Framed black-and-white photos on an evergreen-painted wall. One of their entire family, and one of each child. My breath caught as I recognized one.

"No grandchildren yet," she said. "Hopefully one day I'll have photos of some little ones up on the wall."

"Thanks again." I hurried out to my car, the gentle rain feeling cold and prickly. I was trembling with new anxiety, new confusion. One of her children was the man I'd hit with my flashlight. The man who parked in front of my house, threatened me.

Brandon.

Donnie.

Her middle child. The entrepreneur. Her wild child.

The toddler I'd played with when I'd lived here.

"What is the purpose of the brainwashing, the Satanism, you might ask? I think they want a population of people who will prostitute themselves, smuggle drugs, all sorts of lucrative and degrading acts. You know there are even ties to powerful people in government. I don't want to name organizations, for my own safety."

Doctor Clifford Paulson, PhD Psychology
Transcripts from the Sixth Annual Conference on
Adult Manifestations of Childhood Trauma
THE RADISSON PLAZA HOTEL, CINCINNATI, OHIO

56

I waited in my car in the parking lot of Paul Bunyan's bar. Drizzle had turned to rain. I squinted at my windshield, searching for his car.

All because of Dawn.

I had loved her like *crazy*. Man, that feeling, being sixteen and my heart thumping so hard for her, it was bursting. I had wanted to cover her mouth with mine and never let either of us come up for air. I wanted to bite her bottom lip because it was too soft, too irresistible, and when her blood mingled with my saliva, it would taste like communion.

That night, Dawn had told me to pick her up from work, that we'd make another fire by the river. It was a good night for a swim.

Heat hung low in the air, warming my neck as I stepped out of my truck and walked up to Marjory's. This was the first time she'd asked me to pick her up after her shift. If our relationship hadn't been official before, it was now.

Bells chimed as I opened the door to Marjory's.

It was slow, as usual for a Sunday evening. Two booths full with families, two tables outlined with kids from school. A waitress working the tables.

Dawn was at the counter, leaning over and drawing

something on a napkin for some guy. He had finished eating and was studying her as she drew. His plate was mostly empty. He had eaten his sandwich and left the crust. He was old to be watching her like that, watching her mouth, his eyes dipping down to her breasts. He was maybe twenty-five, thirty. My stomach burned and my jaw clenched.

She slid the napkin across the counter and smiled at him. He put it in his shirt pocket, stood, opened his wallet, and slid cash across the counter, said something that made her laugh. She went to grab the money, but he held onto it, teasing her. She laughed, yanked it away, and headed to the register.

The back of my neck burned.

The asshole headed to the restroom.

He's just some guy. She's being nice to a customer—nothing wrong with that.

On her way to the register, she met eyes with some other guy at the counter, patted his hand, and continued on. I felt a twitch deep in my head, like gears tripping. What the hell? Did she flirt with everybody? The guy touched the back of his hand to his mouth. Maybe wiping food away, maybe inhaling her scent. I wanted to knock him down too.

He looked around, kind of nervous, like he'd done something wrong.

It was Rodney Hornne. I knew him from school.

Dawn happened to glance up. "Trevor," she said, smiling around my name. No guilt. There had been no guilt on her face, no shame, no flash of embarrassment.

I swallowed, but my mouth felt dry.

Two days later, Dawn would be dead.

57

HEATHER

I put the wrapped sushi in my refrigerator. I peeled off my damp clothes and took a hot shower to counter the coldness I felt in my bones. I stood under the harsh spray too long, grateful to be alone, to not worry about using up all the hot water. I dried my hair even though it would get wet again, and was out the door again with my umbrella. Rain drummed, and the sky was the color of a filthy washrag. It was still summer, but there was a touch of cold to this September rain.

Walking up to my house was my friendly deer-jerky-gifting neighbor. His timing was beyond comparison. Seriously. Was Tracy always out walking?

"Hey, Tracy. I'm on my way to pick up my daughter from school." The rain splashed my shoes and pants. Tracy carried an umbrella and wore black rubber boots. He waved and smiled, lumbering diagonally up my lawn, a brown grocery bag in his hand. "I made iced sun tea today and mozzarella meatball subs. I've got too much."

Thanks to Alice and Tracy, I wouldn't have to throw anything together for dinner.

"Thank you. My husband loved your deer jerky. I didn't even get a chance to try it."

"I'll bring more by."

"Oh, no, that's—"

"Listen," he said. "I'll be quick, but there's one other thing. About your son."

My blood chilled. "What is it?"

"Last night I was out late, around 2 a.m. I was taking Rosy on a walk. I saw some teenagers screwing around by the Ollers property. The boys ran. I didn't get a good look at any faces, but I wanted to let you know in case he's sneaking out. I ran into Chrissy Ollers this morning and she told me her baby cougar is gone. Someone cut one of her wires so there was a hole small enough for Luna to get through."

"A cougar on the loose?" I gazed down the street at the large lawns, the oak trees, the unkempt hedges, the cars in driveways and parked on the street. A cougar could be hiding anywhere. "I didn't hear anything from the school. Wouldn't they send out an alert?"

"I think Chrissy wants to keep it quiet. She doesn't want anyone poking in her business."

"You mean, she didn't contact police or animal control?"

"I don't think so. People in this town, well, they don't like government in their business."

"How is a *cougar* on the loose a political issue? It could hurt someone."

"Nah. She's just a baby cub for now. She prolly won't survive on her own in that forest even. Still, never turn your back on a cat." He laughed.

"What?"

"It's a saying. Cats love to sneak up. Anyway, they're looking for her. I'm gonna join the search party."

"Please don't expect me to not contact the school."

Gazing down at the puddles, he said, "If they go digging around as to how it got loose and anyone's got cameras, your son might get dragged in." He was only sixteen, but I'm sure the system could screw him somehow. Put him in a juvie detention center. Like Mother, like son.

"Are you threatening my family?"

"Me? No," he said, and he wasn't. He was warm and breezy. "I'm not a fan of soap operas, is all."

Goddamn. Tracy Summers, of the glazed preacher eyes and barer of meat gifts, was calling me a dramatic pain in the ass. I had to give him credit though for warning me that Sawyer might be in with the wrong group of friends. I'd have to mention to Trevor that Sawyer might be sneaking out at night.

"I hate this place." I hadn't meant to say it aloud. "Thank you for the food. Thanks for telling me about the boys. I have to go."

He gave me a two-finger salute. "So long, Chicago."

I hustled to my car with my umbrella, clicked the unlock button, and turned back. "Tracy?"

He turned slowly, like an old man with a bad shoulder and a bad hip.

"What do you know about the Paulson kids? Like, quick summary."

"Sinclaire's a doctor. In Rochester, I think. Brandon's got his fingers in shady businesses. I told you that. He gambles, has debts." Tracy had told me that. It's just that he hadn't mentioned Brandon's last name. "Pierce is a pig," he said.

"Chauvinist or police officer?"

"Both. The type of guy who pushes people around, but his family's money and power keep him out of trouble."

"Right. Thanks." I closed my umbrella, tossed it in the car, took the thermos out of the bag, and backed out of the driveway.

The thermos was nice. Aluminum with a sturdy cap. So nice, I would have to return it. Tracy Summers was interested in some sort of back-and-forth relationship.

I jiggled the thermos to clink the ice inside, opened it, and sipped. It was ice cold, mostly tasteless, and refreshing. Far better than Alice Paulson's syrupy sweet tea. Tracy Summer's Sun Tea. He really did have a fabulously girlie name.

By the time I pulled up to Emily's school, sweat popped along my forehead and I felt chilled. Sickness was creeping in. My mind spun back to my conversation with Alice Paulson. She said her daughter Claire was bitter. That maybe she'd been too hard on Claire. *You're always hard on your first.*

Tracy called her Sinclaire. *Did she happen to go by Sin?*

58

No running out of the school doors through the grass to meet me. No skipping. No smile. Emily walked with her eyes cast down.

"Hi, Em. I'm happy to see you," I said. Sweat slipped down my sides, and my stomach cramped.

She ignored me, but slipped her hand in mine.

I tipped my umbrella over her head as we walked. "I'm sorry if you had a bad day, Emily. I'll listen if you want."

"I can't believe I have no cousins. I mean, you had four brothers and sisters. That's a lot." What brought this on? Likely one of her classmates had been describing a big family party.

"You have Sawyer," I said. "He's better than cousins."

"It's not the same. He doesn't play. I want kids my age." Seemed I might be in for another round of Emily and Trevor's tag-teaming, *jokingly* begging for a baby. They'd done it before.

"Sorry, kiddo." We walked through the lawn silently, water soaking through our shoes. My toes were cold and wet. I couldn't wait to get home, get in my pajamas and get in bed.

I opened the car door for her, and she climbed in. "I mean," she said, "how can all of your brothers and sisters be dead? That's crazy. It's like a curse or something."

I wasn't about to agree with her. Tell her how me and

Death, we'd been chummy. And I wasn't going to tell her Holly was alive either.

"Some people have bad luck, that's all," I said, closing my umbrella and tossing it onto the floor of the passenger seat. The smell of meat and tomato sauce from Tracy's sub made my stomach lurch. *You might have to pull over to throw up, you know?* I half collapsed into the driver's seat. Rain drilled my windshield, aggravating the headache beginning to clamp down. *It's a short drive. You can make it home.*

I flipped on my wipers and headlights and eased the car onto the road.

"I don't feel good, Em. Here's my phone." I passed it back, and without a word, she took it. Soft, electronic game noises ensued. The rain pelting my windshield was louder.

At a stop sign, I hit the brakes like a drunk. Too hard, too abruptly. The thermos fell from the cup holder and rolled in the footwell.

"Mommy, you need to drive better."

"I'm sorry. I don't feel good."

My stomach swimming, I turned onto the main street. I hadn't been sick like this for a while. Well, it's the start of the school year, the stomach bug usually makes its way around pretty quickly. Or maybe something I ate. That sushi. It was probably the sushi left over from Alice Paulson's book club. Can food poisoning come on that fast?

My question fell away as I passed the strangest scene in the parking lot of Paul Bunyan's bar. Two familiar cars. Two familiar faces. Two faces that should never be seen together.

A silver Infiniti and blue Toyota RAV were parked side by side. The men leaned against their cars, standing in the rain, facing each other.

Trevor and Brandon.

Brandon Paulson, the toddler I'd coddled, the man I'd bashed with my flashlight, the man who'd been stalking me.

There were too many cars on the road, their headlights on and windshield wipers batting the rain. I couldn't turn around quickly. *You can turn at the next stoplight.*

At the next stoplight, I put my car in park, threw open my door, and puked in the road.

59

"I can't do this anymore," I said, leaning against the passenger door of my car, the rain soaking me through.

When I was a kid, knee deep in the river, fishing in the rain—raindrops coalescing in my eyelashes, drops plinking everywhere around me, making that *shhhh* fizzle of a frying pan—I loved getting soaked through. This now, I hated it. The sky was gray and low, a thick wool blanket.

Brandon Paulson leaned against his driver's side door, smiling. "But what do you think Heather's gonna say when she hears about your little secrets?" He laughed and added, incredulous, "How do you go a whole marriage without mentioning that shit?"

It's not that hard. Seriously. Like when you forget someone's name, maybe it's someone you work with or a neighbor three houses down, and you keep running into them and thinking, well, their name will come to you next time or someone else will say it, only that never happens, and too much time elapses and it becomes way too late to ask their name. Your relationship without first names continues; you share funny stories, talk about their road trip to Disney and their terrible boss and even the nitty gritty of parenting (grounding and parental controls).

Not knowing their name sucks, it's cringey and embarrassing, but it's not important to the soul of the relationship.

It's exactly like that.

I should've told her earlier, told her parts of the truth at least, but here's the thing: I hadn't known she was a Hornne when I met her; Heather used a different last name. We were weeks into our relationship before she shared her birth name. I should have told her then, but I worried she would have ended it. I kept telling myself, in another week, I'll tell her next week. And then, well, it became too late.

I shook my head.

Brandon drummed his fingers against his car. "Pop your trunk, will ya?"

"What about when my mom dies, and I'm back in Chicago?" I said. "We done then?"

"We'll see, brother. We'll see," Brandon said, which meant I was his bitch as long as he wanted. "Pop your trunk, Bishop, and stay in your car."

I got in the driver's seat and popped the trunk. Gripped the steering wheel tight in both hands. Rain dripped from my hair, rolled down my cheeks.

Bad luck.

It was bad, bad luck running into Brandon Paulson weeks ago at Shawnee's Roadhouse. When you're middle-aged and married, nothing good happens in bars. We were both chatting with the bartender, and ended up talking to each other. Buzzed, I'd let too much slip. That I was back and forth taking care of my mom. That I'd married someone from Hunther. When I was leaving, he asked my name.

"I heard about you," he said slowly, nodding, cogs slipping into place. "I'm friends with a buddy of yours from high school," he said, serendipitously, like I'd offered to pay his tab. "That was some crazy shit you did. And then you married one of them." He slapped his hand on the bar, laughing.

My trunk slammed. Brandon came around to my window and knocked on the glass once with his knuckles. I rolled my window down, and rain splattered the leather interior, misted my face and arm. "We're all set, man," he said. "When we get there, I'll hang back and be your lookout. Keep your phone handy in case there's trouble."

My socks were wet and cold inside my shoes. My shirt clung to my chest. I turned my face away from him, toward my steering wheel, and nodded.

"Don't be such a pussy, OK?" he said. "We make a good team. The last guy I worked with was nowhere near as professional as you."

I laughed at the compliment—a single Ha! Getting called a "professional" by a guy like Brandon Paulson.

60

HEATHER

As if my sticky nausea and acidic nostrils were pixie dust, we made it home.

I made it to the bathroom on Jell-O legs, trembly and loose, and collapsed on the floor. I stared, glazy-eyed, at the inch of water-damaged and rotting wood around the toilet's base. I cleaned when we got here, but I'm not sure I ever got to scrubbing the germs from the last family off this wood floor.

That thought did it, and I puked again. Not much came up besides strings of bubbly spit, a few sesame seeds from the tuna roll, and a touch of bile. I'd puked several times at the stoplight and hardly had anything left. I flushed the toilet and stood, splashing water up my nose and into my mouth.

I lowered myself back down to the floor and laid my head upon a pillow. Emily must have grabbed it from my bed. Sweet Emily. Had I asked her for a pillow?

My small delivery person was nowhere in sight. Barbie's fluttering, enthusiastic voice drifted in from the TV room. Sounded a little like Barbie, a little like porn.

Had I really seen Trevor and Brandon talking or was that a sick fever dream glazed with a sheet of rain?

It was them.

I'd wanted to turn around and pull up beside them in the parking lot. I hadn't had the energy, and I just needed to get home. *Besides, what would you have said to them?*

61

I opened my eyes to deep, menstrual red.

I blinked a few times and rolled from my stomach onto my side. Like wiper fluid rubbing around a bit of oil on the windshield, my view was smeary, but readable.

Oh. The Red Room. The Murder Room.

If I had had the energy, I would have laughed.

Light typically came through the small front windows, but the room was shadowed and dim. Which meant I'd been sleeping for hours.

Voices in the kitchen spoke quietly, conspiratorially.

"Hello," I attempted.

The sharp scrape of chair legs against the wood floor. Then, Trevor and Sawyer stood over me. Trevor's hand moved across my forehead, brushing back my hair. His hand was cold and felt so good against my hot skin.

"Heather," he said. "Glad you're back from the dead." His voice rang phony and theatrical. I was so weak, if he wanted, he could put me in the trunk and toss me off Crooked Bridge.

Come on, Heather. He wouldn't.

"Do you remember what you ate today?" he said.

"I think it was the sushi."

"Where'd you get sushi?"

"A friend. Throw it away. It's in the fridge."

"We're not in the city, things aren't as fresh around here," Trevor said. "I don't think I'd even trust the Red Lobster in Yellow Valley." Even though there was a condescending tone to his voice, it felt good to hear Trevor criticize this town. I curled up in his criticism like a dog circling near its owner's feet and settling in nose-to-tail.

"Sawyer?" I said.

"I'm here," he said, his voice kind.

"The neighbor said he saw teenage boys let the baby cougar out."

"What? That's crazy. I didn't do that." His reaction was over the top. He totally did it.

"Sawyer, don't mess with those cougars. They could kill you. They could kill Emily."

"I'm not an idiot." He stomped into the kitchen, opened the refrigerator. The suction resisted and released. I yearned for the whoosh of cooled air, but the lunchmeat refrigerator smell would make me sick.

"Heather, what are you doing?" Trevor said, irritation hardening around his voice.

"There's a cougar loose in the woods."

"Are you sure?" Trevor said. Skeptical. I couldn't blame him. I was still feverish.

"Yes. The neighbor told me it's loose. Don't let Emily out." Panic struck me. "Where's Emily?"

"She's sleeping. It's almost midnight." His cool hand on my

forehead again. "Relax. Go back to sleep." His hand stroking my forehead felt so good, so kind.

I was done throwing up. I'd be back on my feet tomorrow, but now I was dead tired. My throat felt raw and scraped. My back muscles ached.

I didn't want to ask, I hated to ask my dear Trevor—my policy had always been to leave things be, to go to bed angry, let the argument fade until I could barely remember what it had been about—but I had to.

And I was expecting, *hoping*, convincing myself that Trevor would still turn out to be the good guy. Like maybe Brandon Paulson was threatening Trevor with a lawsuit because I'd bashed his head, and Trevor was paying hush money to save his dear wife from the horror of it all.

"Trevor?"

"What is it?"

I closed my eyes. That made it easier. "Why'd you meet Brandon Paulson in a parking lot?"

A pause so pregnant, the room could burst. *Please. Just don't lie.*

"What are you talking about?"

"I saw you. Paul Bunyan's bar. How do you know Brandon Paulson?"

"I don't know what you're talking about," he said, defensive, a hint of anger. "You're not feeling well. I'm going to get you some water." His footsteps moved away.

He should have said, *Heather, who is Brandon Paulson?*

It's OK. Let him think about it. Leave him to twist and come up with an excuse. And then, I thought, I'd accept his excuse, whatever it was, because Trevor was a good guy. I wouldn't divorce you even if you conspired with Brandon Paulson, the man I skull-fucked with a Maglite, the man who stood on my front lawn days ago and threatened me.

If I had energy, I would have laughed.

Conspired with Brandon Paulson.

Conspired to what?

Sawyer and Trevor whispered in the kitchen, but I couldn't make out what they were saying. Fatigue threaded through my muscles. My throat was dry. Good thing Trevor's bringing water.

Whispering was too much work for them, and their voices broke to quiet speaking. "Is she gonna be better by tomorrow so we can go?" Sawyer said.

Oh, that's right. His mom. Little Miss Sticky Fingers. Sawyer had a date with his mom in Cook County's Women's Correctional.

Be nice. He's just a kid, aching for life to make sense. It had to feel demeaning, like that stupid purse was worth more than staying straight for her only kid. My heart ached for him.

"We'll see, Sawyer," said Trevor, sounding distracted.

"What if she's not better?"

"Then we'll stay here. We can't leave her when she's this sick." My heart cheered for Trevor and shook its pom poms. I wanted him to be my perfect Trevor.

"She ruins everything," said Sawyer.

As weak and dazed as I was—I desperately needed a glass of water, but I think Trevor had forgotten—a small voice inside said, *Yes, that might be true.*

62

Twilight's soft blue glow seeped into the room where the curtains failed to meet. Predawn. My mouth tasted sour, and my skin was greasy. My stomach muscles pulled and ached.

Trevor snored obnoxiously beside me. When had I crawled into our bed? I had a pang of love for him, but it was shellacked in strangeness and distrust.

Liar.

I turned on the bath, plugged the drain, and aimed it for scalding.

I was wearing yesterday's clothes. I stripped them off and eased my sore body into the tub. The hot water dissolved the sickness from my skin and warmed me. Questions fluttered in my mind like a flock of small birds swarming to food, pecking, settling, and frightened away, fleeing back up to tree branches.

Who wanted me here? Who sent me those text messages? Who left a dead opossum on my doorstep? Who killed Dawn? Who stabbed my mom? Why had Gal said a coyote got her opossums but everyone else said it had been my mom?

The steamy air dissolved the sludge in my mind, and strings of conversation came to me.

Holly. *Whatever was on these videos, someone killed her for it.*

Father Greg. *Cliff called me in... because your mother had signs pointing to satanic indoctrination... Melinda agonized. Nurses had to tie her down. She'd screamed. . . I'm gonna cut you with my knife. Does that make your cock hard?*

Gal Kender. *He loves that hokey pokey. Talks about possession maybe once a month.*

Alice Paulson. *She had Multiple Personality Disorder... She killed that girl... She spoke of cutting Dawn Young with a knife... So did you... You blocked it out.*

The letter from Sin.

Basically, this is an apology and an invitation to more trouble... I've made copies of the videos.

Sinclaire's a doctor. In Rochester, I think, Tracy Summers had said.

Cleveland, Mayo, MD Anderson, Becky had said in my dream. *That might have saved us. If she'd gotten help at a big hospital.*

Claire, she's gone and hates coming back, Alice Paulson had said.

Each comment was nothing more than loose change, but add them up, they were enough to buy something.

I had assumed Tracy Summers meant Rochester, NY. But there's a Rochester, Minnesota, made famous by Mayo Clinic.

Sin was an awful self-given nickname for Sinclaire, but at this point, it seemed likely.

I pulled the drain plug.

Trevor was still sleeping, snoring.

I didn't want to talk to him. I didn't want to ask him again about Brandon Paulson and hear him lie again.

I had never been much of a talker.

317

Trevor and I working through a disagreement looked a lot like two beefy, flannel-wearing, bearded guys sitting side by side at the bar. Lots of grunts, sipping our beers, nodding. It was something Trevor liked about me, that I wasn't a talker. It was something I thought I liked about myself, but now that I thought about it, it was window dressing. Something I could brag about to myself, I'm low maintenance, I'm not a talker, but it didn't serve me.

Downstairs, the TV was on low volume. Emily was trying to not wake anyone on this glorious no-school Saturday morning.

I filled a cup at the sink. I was so thirsty, so dehydrated, my head pulsed along with my heart. I gulped. "Hey, Emily, how would you like McDonald's pancake sandwich for breakfast?" My stomach crawled into itself at the thought of a greasy sandwich, but if I bought one for myself and left it in the bag, my stomach might come around in a few hours.

"Whoohoo!" she screamed, jumping onto her feet on the couch.

"Shh. Dad's sleeping," I said, suddenly terrified I'd hear his lofty, clownish footsteps pound on the stairs. Who was this man?

63

I woke up from a nightmare, Dawn's face lingering in my mind. Her skin gray, her eyes lifeless and swollen. I wished I didn't know what she looked like dead.

I reached for Heather. The sheets on her side of the bed were cool and empty.

As my brain came online, guilt rushed in. Then, anger.

She'd seen me with Brandon Paulson.

The realization was awful, but it was there. This wasn't going away. She knew too much.

I stretched my neck, cracked it, flexed the muscles in my hands. I pulled on my pants and went looking for her.

She was gone. Emily too.

I searched for her location on my phone, but she'd turned off her location tracking.

Skin hot, palms sweaty, I called her.

No answer. I waited for voicemail. Controlling my frustration, I forced a gentle, kind tone.

"Heather. I'm taking Sawyer to see his mom today, but, well, we need to talk. I've done something terrible."

64

HEATHER

I parked my car on the street, left the windows half down, and gave Emily my iPad. I walked through the long stretch of grass toward Asher Moss's door. The cow lay in the grass, watching me. Even if she were standing, I wasn't worried about her anymore. I was becoming comfortable with the nuances of this town.

I was halfway up his lawn when Asher called, "Over here." He stood at the far corner of the house, almost out of sight. I walked around to meet him.

Leaning against a shovel, he wore loose jeans and a tank top, dark curly hairs escaping from the scoop neck. He held the shovel handle in one hand and finger-shot me with the other. "Heather Hornne, right?"

Beside him, three potted rose bushes sat in the grass, their blooms full and yellow, browning at their edges. A pair of gardening gloves lay in the grass as well. He had dug his first hole.

"Yes." I considered commenting on his beautiful rose bushes, asking why he wasn't waiting another month for the weather to cool before he planted them, but Emily was in the car. "Gal Kender said a coyote killed her opossums. She said her son saw it happen. Why would she tell you and me a different story?"

His gaze dropped to his rose bushes. "Huh. That's weird,"

he said. "Maybe her husband told me that." He looked at me, shook his head. "I don't know. I'll have to check my case notes. I dug them out a few days ago after you stopped by," he said, that aw-shucks smile spreading on his face. He raised an eyebrow. "Her husband's serving time, you know?"

"You think he was involved with Dawn's murder?"

He shrugged. "Could be. He molested a few kids."

I might have winced. My heart ached. It felt torn and pulpy. I pictured Becky, so slender, skin flawless, swimming in the Kenders' pool while Gary did yard work. All those weeks my mom and I were staying with the Paulsons, and Becky stayed with the Kenders.

"Someone put a dead opossum on my front porch the other day."

"Well, that's crummy." He rubbed the back of his neck and looked down at his pile of dirt. "Sounds like someone's trying to warn you to back off. Threaten you, your family, don't it?"

Sure did.

I didn't think the same person would be sending me texts, luring me to Hunther, then dumping a dead carcass on my doorstep. Had to be someone else.

"Thanks for your time," I said, and headed back to my car. I wasn't halfway there when he called my name.

"Your husband is Judy Bishop's son?"

I hesitated, alarm skating up my spine.

"When you stopped by before, you said your mother-in-law was Judy Bishop, right?"

"Yeah."

321

"Have you asked your husband about Dawn?" he said. "He was one of the boys who found her body. Those two, they were a thing."

Trevor was calling me. The circus theme ringtone, for the first time, sounded ominous. I let it go to voicemail.

I called Visha on my hands-free. While it rang, I peeked in my rearview mirror at Emily. She ate a breakfast sandwich while staring at the iPad screen in her lap. The car was smoggy with syrupy fast-food odors.

"Well it's about time," Visha said.

"I have a huge favor to ask."

"I'll do it."

I laughed even though I was falling apart. "Can I drop Emily with you for the day? And for a sleepover?"

"Of course, oh my God, Aradhya will be out of her mind excited, but why aren't you staying to visit?"

"I'll tell you when I get there. I've got to go." I ended the call. I'd tell her I was following some thread on my mom's death, and I was not ready to talk about it. She knew my family was a tender subject.

After I'd dropped off Emily, I pulled into a gas station. While the tank filled, I sat in the driver's seat and searched the Mayo Clinic's medical staff on my phone.

There she was, looking plain with her hair ash blond and

cut close, no smile. Sinclaire Paulson. Pathology. Not psychiatry like dear old dad.

I stared at her photo, searching for something, some vague characteristic, a fleshy mole, an arch of one eyebrow, that I might recognize. There was nothing.

I called and was transferred four times before a tired woman, someone who was borderline too laid back to work at a hospital, told me Claire was on shift till 3 p.m., but sometimes stayed late.

I checked my watch. I should be able to make it there by 3 p.m.

I returned the nozzle and screwed on my gas cap. I breathed in gasoline fumes. I loved the filthy smell. Always brought me back to the day I met Trevor.

Silly, relaxed Trevor, his lips wet and cherry red. A Slurpee in one hand, a jug of gasoline in the other. "Super Bass" blaring on the outdoor gas station speakers, him telling me that no one would beat him up while this song was playing. He'd tossed his Slurpee and written his phone number for me on the inside of his suit jacket.

He was one of the boys who found her body. Those two, they were a thing.

My stomach turned. It couldn't be true, could it?

Sliding behind the wheel, I was tempted to listen to his voicemail. Instead, I queued up a YouTube playlist and some podcasts about Multiple Personality Disorder to listen to during my drive (*Sybil, The Great Hysteric*; *Is MPD Real?*; *See My Alter Switch*; *MPD and Satanic Ritual Abuse*).

65

Multiple Personality Disorder had emerged and reemerged a number of times throughout history. First, in 1957, when *The Three Faces of Eve* hit theaters. Then came *Sybil*, a late-seventies box office success. In the decade following *Sybil*, cases of MPD diagnosis skyrocketed, going from barely a hundred cases to over 40,000. The American Psychiatric Association officially recognized Dissociative Disorders in the early 1980s and, within a few years, MPD emerged as the most common of the Dissociative Disorders, though MPD was mostly a US phenomenon.

When a mental health condition only occurs in one country, doctors and scientists should be skeptical. No skeptics emerged.

The doctors who seemed to be most familiar with MPD were selected to head the Advisory Committee for Dissociative Disorders. These men were the authority, the publishers, and the profiteers as they sold out weekend workshops in Chicago and Boston, telling tales of cases and detailing how to diagnose and treat.

Anyone could see the commonalities between MPD and Judeo-Christian *possession*, just like Alice Paulson had said. The dissociative similarities were blatant, waiting like a dirty Band-Aid, edges peeling away, begging for someone to rip it off.

One of those doctors finally tore it off, publishing an article linking the MPD epidemic to child abuse committed by devil-worshipping cults. He hosted conferences to spread the word. Satanic cults were everywhere, he revealed, internationally organized, with councils and hierarchies. The general public ate it up. No one could explain exactly *why* organizations were slitting babies' throats, drinking their blood, and worshipping the devil, but they also couldn't get enough of it. Individuals were outed and prosecuted, though most cases were eventually dismissed for lack of evidence.

I paused the podcast to take a bathroom break at a rest stop and buy a soda from the vending machine. My head hurt, and my skin crawled. Partly because yesterday's sickness lingered, and partly because this podcast was getting under my skin. How did people buy into these conspiracies? Pulling back onto the highway, I pressed play on my podcast and continued listening.

The expert psychiatrists revealed that satanic ritual abuse was often part of transgenerational family traditions, like quilting and tree-trimming. Some families had been holding meetings, committing child abuse, and sacrificing animals and babies for hundreds of years.

A terrifying and irresistible story, the media rolled with it. Skeptics looked down at their shoes, half-worried they hadn't realized Satan's followers had been here all along, brushing past them in the grocery store, and half-worried to speak up for fear of being labeled and witch-hunted by the crazed mob.

A half dozen years later, the FBI Behavioral Science Unit

at Quantico put in their two cents. They'd done a multi-year study and found no evidence of the existence of satanic cults engaged in criminal activity or the sacrificing of thousands of American babies.

It was like the emperor parading about in his new robes. At the parade's start, everyone assumed his robes could only be seen by the intelligent and the good Christians. Once the child had called him out as naked, people couldn't believe they'd gone along with it.

Psychiatrists distanced themselves from MPD and Satanic Ritual Abuse. They doubted the existence of MPD, claiming most cases were faked or therapist-induced, a by-product of manipulative psychiatrists. They cited MPD patients' excitement to share their stories, claiming real mental health issues don't typically seek attention and celebrity.

The Satanic Panic skeptics who'd stayed silent through the '80s felt safe to come out of the woodwork in the mid-1990s and vilify the psychiatric rock stars of the previous decade. The False Memory Syndrome Foundation sprung up as the legal clearinghouse, countering false claims of "recovered memories" of child abuse, satanic or not.

By 1994, MPD was removed from the manual, renamed and revised to Dissociative Identity Disorder—this new name less freakshow, less scandalous, but still defined as the presence of two or more distinct personality states or identities within one person's psyche. Some psychiatrists agreed DID indeed existed, but was rare and unsensational. If a person had different identities, you couldn't *see* a switch, and it wasn't a thrilling show; it was just another mundane and frustrating mental health challenge.

As I pulled into the parking garage at Mayo Clinic, I was dumbfounded at the damage these psychiatrists had caused. How had I never heard about this?

Desiree had said Cliff Paulson, my mom's psychologist, was a rich, know-it-all asshole. Had Cliff Paulson been one of these doctors who sensationalized MPD and Satanic Ritual Abuse? Is that what happened to my mother?

66

I spent thirty minutes being ping-ponged between receptionists and hospital wings that seemed miles apart. No one wanted to tell me where I could find Sinclaire Paulson. I should have worn nicer clothes, put on makeup. People don't trust middle-aged women that don't look moderately painted and primed. Our wrinkled, worn faces gave off an unstable vibe.

I quit the receptionists and asked employees in scrubs and lab coats. I finally found a man in a lab coat too young to worry about job security who said, "I know Claire. Follow me."

"Thank you." I told him my name, that I knew Claire from when I was a kid, and I followed him like a lost puppy. "Do you work with Claire?" I said only because I didn't like listening to our shoes click against linoleum.

"No, I'm in clinical path; she's in anatomic. She works in the tissue lab. I couldn't stand that. Too much microscope work, my eyes would bleed." He laughed. "Wait here." He used the lanyard around his neck to open a door and went inside.

"I will. Thank you," I called as the door whooshed shut. I felt like I was waiting to meet Oz.

The door opened a few minutes later. She was short with close-cut ash hair, like her photo. Her eyes were green, her face was pale, and she had dark circles under her eyes that she hadn't bothered lightening with makeup. Her expression was sharp. This was not a woman who smiled to make you feel comfortable. I immediately liked her.

"Heather?" she said, her voice flat, deep.

"Yes. Claire?"

"Wow, this is weird. I remember you. I mean, I don't recognize you now, we're really fucking old, but I remember you as a kid."

"I'm sorry, I don't remember much."

"No offense taken. Besides, I was a year older than you." She smiled. "I'm joking. Why, well, I mean, it's nice to see you, but why are you here?"

"You wrote a letter to my mom?"

She sighed. "Right. Yeah, yeah. I was getting over a drug thing, making peace, all that crap. How is your mom?"

"She was murdered. Robbery gone wrong." There was no point in sharing Holly's theory and making Claire feel like she shouldered some of the blame.

"Oh, man, that sucks. I'm sorry. That's awful." She dug her hands into her pockets, bit her lip, and glanced down the hall.

"I'm not here to, well, I don't want to stress you out. Your letter, I read it, it was kind."

She nodded, a worried look on her face, maybe scratching at her brain to connect her letter to my mom's murder. She'd said so herself in her letter, that her reaching out to my mom was an invitation to trouble.

"You mentioned videos?" I said, my voice rising because even though I drove five hours to get here, I was still questioning this.

329

"Yeah, yeah. I have copies of my dad's videotapes on a thumb drive. I stole them actually. I copied them when I was an undergrad, when I finally realized my dad had done bad things. My parents were out at this hospital thing, this black-tie event." She raised her eyebrows, getting a kick out of this story. "I rigged a setup, copied them to a hard drive. It was kind of hilarious." She shifted and puffed up her cheeks. "I should have given them to your mom earlier. I meant to, actually, but, I… well, I was unsure of myself, and then college was rough, and I had this on and off drug thing."

She looked down at her shoes, bit her lip again. "I haven't talked to my parents for over a decade. I'm not excusing what my dad did, but he would not do well outside his Hunther bubble. I didn't want him to go to prison, you know?"

Prison. Jesus. What did he do?

"No. I don't know. I didn't even know me and my mom lived with you until a few days ago."

"Oh, oh," she said, considering all the things she'd said, maybe regretting them. "Oh, God. I don't know where to even start."

"What about the videos. Can I see the videos?"

"Right. Why don't you give me your address, I'll mail you a drive."

"I am kind of anxious about this. I don't mind waiting until you've finished work, if that's OK with you."

"Oh, OK. I have something to wrap up. If you can wait thirty minutes, you can follow me to my place. Or, well, it might take an hour." A switch had flipped. She went from helpful and nostalgic to suspicious. She did not want to deal with this right now.

"I can wait. I'm gonna get a coffee while you finish up. Give me your number so we don't lose each other."

"Huh?"

"What's your number?"

She hesitated, then gave me her number. I called it right away. In her pocket, a bird tweeted.

I smiled. "Now you have my number, in case we lose each other."

"Great," she said flatly, doubting all her choices. Copying her dad's videos, cutting ties with her parents, writing a letter as part of her 12-Step therapy. "See you in a bit," she said and disappeared behind the employees-only door.

No way was I leaving for coffee. I sat on the cold, shiny hospital floor, my back against the wall.

67

Claire's apartment was small, ugly, and dated. Cheap carpet, cheap blinds, laminate. Her parents were filthy rich, and here was Claire, living in a crummy apartment.

Maybe she was frugal, lived cheaply, had a million dollars socked away, and was planning an early retirement in the Keys.

"So, you're a doctor?"

"Yeah. I'm a doctor and I drive a junky car and live here." At the sink, she poured two glasses of water and handed one to me. "Cheers to student debt." She clinked my glass. I wasn't ready for it, so I splashed a little. She sipped. "There's more to it than that, but there is serious student debt." She opened her mouth, closed it, and said, unable to contain her smile, "Do you remember our backyard circus?"

"No."

"Oh my gosh, that's such a shame. This one time we built a ramp from plywood. We built it right in the grass and I rode my bike up it and you were supposed to toss a ball in the air for me to catch mid-flight, I have no idea what we were thinking, and you beamed me in the head with the ball and I went tumbling and was crying and you came running to help me but you tripped on the hose that was filling Donnie's baby pool, and we were both lying on the ground, and Donnie stood from sitting in the pool and said, 'Good job. Good job.' He was only wearing a diaper and it sagged down to his knees. Oh my God, we laughed so hard."

Her smile hung in reverie, and she sighed. She unclasped her bracelet, dropped it into a shallow dish holding jewelry. "I was so confused how I had this best friend sister living with me one day and the next day you were gone. You don't remember living with us? Like, at all?"

"No. Shortly after living with you, my sister died. I think I have a bit of PTSD-memory loss."

"I'm sorry," she said.

"It was a long time ago." I shrugged, trying to lighten things. "Anyway, the suspense is killing me here."

She grabbed her laptop and brought it to the couch. "Listen, my parents, they—my dad—he stole drugs from the hospital where they're benefactors. He shouldn't be a doctor. I mean, I should have written a letter to APA or the FBI—"

"You obviously feel awful about what happened," I said. "I get it. Can you just show me?"

She set her laptop on the coffee table, and I sat on the couch in front of it. She said, "I'm going to change, and, well, you probably want to watch this alone."

"This is widespread, folks. It is systemic and organized. The brainwashing, the programming, the murders, it's no joke."

Doctor Clifford Paulson, PhD Psychology
Transcripts from the Sixth Annual Conference on
Adult Manifestations of Childhood Trauma
THE RADISSON PLAZA HOTEL, CINCINNATI, OHIO

68

The video was playing, the seconds scrolled by on the bottom right, but the camera was recording an empty room. A white faded line moved vertically into frame, then disappeared. She'd digitized the recording, but the deterioration of the original film had been preserved.

In the room, a white cloth bag, cinched closed, sat upon a floral rug. In the background, a low corner table, old fashioned with wire latticework.

My armpits were sweaty, and I was chilled from the inside out.

How bad could this be?

A slender black cat with brownish-yellow eyes, a witch's cat, walked out from Claire's kitchen, meowed, and jumped onto the opposite end of the couch. Curled up on the top ledge.

A male voice, off-camera, said, "Why don't you sit over there by that bag. Right there on the floor."

A little girl in blue jeans and a red and white gingham shirt came into view, sat on the floor, crisscross.

The girl wore her brown hair in a bob. I couldn't make out the expression on her face. The video's quality was fuzzy, colors were faded, and the picture frame speed was crummy.

The white line moved into frame and out again.

I'd been expecting a video of my mom. Had Claire put in the wrong video? A video of herself as a kid?

The male voice, off-camera, said, "Go ahead and open the bag."

The girl hesitated.

"Nothing to be afraid of. Open the bag." He was impatient and pushy.

Was I getting a look at Claire's bizarre childhood?

Be patient. My mom's clip was probably coming up next, taped over this home video.

On camera, the girl opened the bag. A few wooden blocks tumbled out onto the thin carpet. The video went fuzzy again. White vertical lines flashing, then clearing.

The girl placed one block on the carpet and placed another on top of that. She was going for a single tall tower. Terrible architect, no foresight.

"Yesterday you started to tell me about a knife you had at home in the kitchen," he said. "You said it was a long knife."

My stomach tightened, like a snake coiling defensively.

Wait. Wait.

"You were telling me about your mom's kitchen knife. That she had it with her."

No. Can't be.

The snake in my bowels coiled tighter.

Was that—

"Heather," he said. "I need you to pay attention." The girl, *me*, ignored him. She stacked one block on top of the next. She was on block five now. Any second, it would tip.

His fingers moved in front of the camera lens and he snapped them at her.

She—*I*—looked up.

"Heather, do you like smelly stickers?"

Little Heather nodded.

"Let's see what I have here," he said. "Oh, there's popcorn! Let's see if it really smells like popcorn." The sound of his nail scratching paper. "Oh, yes! It does. How about that."

My six-year-old self looked at him, straightened my back, full attention.

"I'll give it to you if you can tell me what your mom did with that knife, OK?"

The snake in my stomach, coiled tight, reared its head, ready to strike. *Don't you do it, you little bitch.* As if it wasn't already done. As if I could intervene.

I nodded, my words following. "Mm-hmm."

"Now, you said there was someone lying on the ground. Was it a woman?"

"No."

"Was it a man?"

"No."

"Well, come on now. It had to be one or the other, didn't it? I thought you were a smart little girl and I thought you wanted a sticker. It was a woman, wasn't it?"

"Yes."

Dumb little bitch.

"Here you go," he said. His hand moved in front of the

camera, handing my younger self a sticker. I took it with both hands and pressed it against my nose, my eyelids closing like it was ecstasy. "Good girl," he said.

I wanted to whack my little kid self across the face. What a sucker.

"Oh, now, here, I have another one. Pizza. Do you want to be the first one to scratch it?"

"Yes." I smiled.

"Perfect. Good girl. First tell me what your mom did with that long knife."

Energized now, my mind on the prize, I rose on my knees and slashed at the air with my make-believe knife. "She slashed at the belly."

On Claire's couch, I cringed, my shoulders shrinking. I wanted to become as small as possible. I wanted to disappear. My embarrassment so burdensome, it flattened me.

"Then what?" he said, still off-camera.

"The belly opened up and all these tubes came out. They were kind of white. They slipped out. There were a lot of tubes."

Déjà vu came on strong. Slashed belly. White tubes pouring out. The image was just out of reach, but it's close.

On Claire's couch, the cat rubbed its head against my leg. I patted it stiffly, my palm wet with sweat.

"And what was that like?" he said.

"It smelled. It smelled bad." My six-year-old self sniffed at the sticker in my hand again. "And I thought they smelled bad on the *outside*."

Suddenly I had it. Like capturing a fly. One second, you

didn't have it, the next second, it's buzzing and bouncing against your hot closed hands.

Star Wars. Luke is freezing to death, lying in the snow. Han Solo slashes the belly of his tauntaun, its bloodless innards spring out, dozens of white tubes the size of fingers. Han Solo, his expression fraught with nausea, says slowly, "And I thought they smelled bad on the outside."

I smiled at the eureka feel of it, at the absurdity of my little kid self retelling a scene from a movie. It's funny, it's creative. Maybe I wasn't as much of an idiot as I thought.

But the serendipity dropped, fast and hard, like kicking away a tree stump that someone was standing on.

I hadn't meant to, but I'd slipped a noose around my mother's neck and kicked the stump away.

"Very good. You are a smart girl. Here you go. Pizza! Tell me if it really smells like pizza."

Little Heather took the pizza sticker, placed it on her thigh and scratched at it, bending it. Stupid kid didn't even think to lay it against a hard surface. She smelled it and smiled.

"I have a grape one for you if you're really smart. This is a tricky question. Kind of like a question for grown-ups. Can you tell me why your mommy slashed at the belly? If you can tell me that, you get the grape sticker. The grape has eyes and a mouth, see?"

Little Heather's gaze shifted just left of the camera. "She did it for me. She was brave. I was cold and she wanted to save me."

"Did she say the word 'devil'?"

Little Heather said, "I don't think so."

"What about the word 'Satan'?"

"No."

"Oh, Heather," he sighed. "I thought you were a smart girl. I know it's not easy, but you can be a big girl, a brave girl. I have this sticker for you if you are brave and smart. I bet it smells so good, like grape bubble gum. Like grape jelly. I know you are a smart girl. Did Mommy say 'Satan'?"

Little Heather stared left of camera, enraptured by the sticker. "Yes."

"Did she cut that girl down the middle?"

"Yes."

"What a good girl. Here you—"

I hit pause, and my six-year-old self's hungry stare was fixed to the left, on that grape sticker. I couldn't bear to watch anymore, but I could imagine the rest of it playing out. He'd probably showed my mom clips of this interview, and in her devastated, hopeless, and drugged state, she'd confessed to a murder she hadn't committed.

My mom's alcoholism, her meanness: it began with me.

My mom ruined my life, but I had ruined hers first. It was a game of tag I'd mistakenly thought she'd started.

My phone was on the passenger seat. When it rang, I kept my eyes on the highway and answered without checking.

"Heather, it's Claire." I wasn't expecting it to be her. "You left."

"Claire. I'm not up for talking."

"Wait. Wait." She inhaled, sighed. "Give me a second,

OK? I probably should have given you a warning. But I wasn't thinking you'd leave, and you missed the other videos. You missed the good parts."

There couldn't possibly be good parts.

"What?"

"My dad recorded your dad as well. When your dad heard what you'd said, he realized you were talking about *Star Wars*. He threw an epic fit, threatened my dad, and got you and your mom out that day."

My head was hot. My eyes burned.

Why hadn't my dad raised hell in this town? Why hadn't he exposed Clifford Paulson? Maybe he tried, but it's hard to go up against money and power.

"Heather, if it weren't for you, who knows what would have happened to your mom? My dad was committed to the idea that your mom killed Dawn. He drugged and harassed her until she signed that confession. I mean, it's insane, right? She walked into my dad's office for depression and was tricked into committing herself. Heather, you got her out."

"I backstabbed my own mother."

You've done worse though, haven't you?

"You were so young." Claire was smiling; I could hear it in her voice.

I thought of my mom after Gal resuscitated me. My mom had said, jaw tight, her body stiff and hateful, "Goddamn. It is always something."

69

The sky looked like a bruise with deep purple and blue splotches, and a smattering of ugly yellow.

Crossing back into the city proper was bland. No landmarks. No welcome signs. Just that small rectangular sign framed in white, letting me know I was here. Prairie grass in all directions. There was windblown trash along the side of the road and, when the wind blew from the west, the smell of cow manure.

Up ahead, Shawnee's Roadhouse. The flat metal roof in the distance looked welcoming because my bladder had been strained for hours. I should have peed at the hospital, or at Claire's, but I'd been too anxious. Home was a twenty-minute drive, which was twenty minutes too long.

I pulled off the highway into a quarter-full gravel lot.

My phone rang again. I didn't recognize the number, and immediately worried about Emily. "Hello?"

"It's Dez. Where are you?"

"I'm driving. Well, I'm stopped now for the restroom." I grabbed my purse and headed toward the restaurant.

"Where?"

"Shawnee's."

"Oooh. Wait for me. I'll be there in ten." She ended the call. I immediately regretted telling her where I was.

After I used the restroom, I walked on crushed peanut shells to a barstool. Same place we'd sat before. Same dim lighting and lacquered wood bartop. I'd barely eaten today, and I was hungry. My stomach seemed to have no recollection of yesterday's sickness. I ordered a cheeseburger, fries, and a coke.

I texted Visha.

-How are the girls treating you?

-They are sweet. Glad you texted. A friend needs me to work for her in the morning. Can you or Trevor be here by 9 a.m.?

I hadn't thought of Trevor grabbing Emily. That would make sense since he was already in Chicago with Sawyer.

Did I trust him with Emily after seeing him with Brandon? *C'mon, Heather. It's Trevor.*

Asher Moss's words echoed in my head. *He was one of the boys who found her body. Those two, they were a thing.*

-I can be there early, Visha. I'll text before I leave, like at 6:30 a.m.

The bartender, who was washing glasses, gazed over my shoulder with a hungry look in his eye.

A beat later, "Hey, bitch." The words rolled of her tongue loosely and with joy.

She wore a tank top and frayed jean shorts, and had a strappy purse diagonal on her chest, dramatically separating her breasts. Heavy, smudged eyeliner. Of course.

She plopped down on the bench beside me. "Two whiskeys in shot glasses, a tall coke. Thanks, baby." She drummed the bar with her fingertips.

"I'll pass."

"Come on. Live a little," she said, loud and animated, as if she were talking to a big group of us gals, trying to get us all riled up for a girls' night out.

The bartender slid the shots and her coke in front of us, a smile aimed at Desiree.

"I'll pay," she said, turning toward me. "God knows I owe you." As if a shot canceled out what I'd spent for her bail.

"Why didn't you tell me you knew Cliff Paulson?" I said, hoping to catch her off guard.

"Drink first," she said, bossy.

"I'm not a drinker."

"What's gonna happen? You gonna turn into a pumpkin?"

I put the glass to my lips, got them wet with whiskey, put the glass down. "There."

"It's not lip gloss, Heather. It's not a dirty dick." She tipped her shot back, emptied it.

The image of that little girl, me, holding her sticker to her nose, crept into my mind and my heart. The shame was jagged.

I relaxed my throat and tossed it back. My throat burned, my skin prickled. My brain flexed, pissed and horrified. My lungs threw a fit.

She smacked me on the back, laughing. "You'd think that was your first shot of whiskey ever."

Something like that.

"So where's my baby? Where's Emmy?" She really did love Emily.

"With a friend."

"That's good. Two more, baby," she said to the bartender. Fast, like a car. A red sports car, so bright it was always out of place in every parking lot.

He slid two shots in front of us and walked away. I stared at the amber liquid, vibrating in its glass. "When I was at the Paulson house, I saw photos of your boyfriends," I said, exaggerating the plural. "Last time we talked, you acted like you didn't know Cliff Paulson. Why are you even here?"

"Me? I'm like—" She breathed deep and gazed up at the ceiling. "What am I like? I'm like the lighthouse, flashing its light, telling the ship it's getting to close to the rocky shore."

I sighed. "Did you know what was on the videos before you broke into those houses?"

"Nope, and I don't care. No offense, but it's like ancient history to me. Thirty years ago. I wasn't even born. It's like a ghost story."

"What's on those videos is pretty fucked up. Also, pretty damaging to Doctor Paulson."

"Duh. That's why the family wanted those videos back. I guess your mom contacted Paulson, said she'd seen the videos, and Paulson figured she'd gotten the videos from past employees, nurses or something."

After what those nurses had witnessed, why hadn't they ever come forward? Maybe their consciences never bothered them. They'd convinced themselves the doctor knew best. Maybe they feared the Paulson family's retribution. Maybe they feared culpability.

"Doctor Paulson killed my mom?"

"No idea, but he is a major douchebag. Always talking over me, loud, total know-it-all. Well, not recently. Recently, he's…" With her index finger, she circled her ear. *Crazy.*

"You broke into those houses for Brandon?"

"Something like that."

"Why would you risk so much for some guy?"

"Isn't that what you do for family, for Trevor, take risks? Let things slide? No better reason to take risks than for family. Or a *lover*." She sang the word lover like we were middle school girls at a sleepover.

The bartender popped a basket in front of me. Cheeseburger. Fries. Desiree moved my coke out of the way for me. "Besides," she said, "what's the risk? My swim instructor job? My shit apartment? They're not sending me to prison, believe me."

"Right. Friends in high places." I cut my burger in half. Took the napkin from under my coke, it had a wet ring from my glass, and placed it in front of Desiree, plopped the burger down. "It's never too late to reinvent yourself, go to school?"

"'Reinvent yourself.' Listen to you. Like you're some mentor." She laughed, tipping her head back. Her canines slipped out. Again, it reminded me of a woman pulling up her silky dress to flash her creamy thigh. "What if you don't want to reinvent yourself?"

"I guess you break into people's homes, looking for decades-old videos."

Her smile widened. "Food will ruin the whiskey. Now or never." She held her shot glass up, waited for me to do the same. I raised my glass to her and tossed it back before she did.

My throat burned. My body shivered with chills. My shame was a dark stain, something pesky like wine, and the whiskey was rubbing it out, fading the color.

Same reason my parents drank.

We ate in silence for a couple minutes, comfortably. When you know bad things about a person, it adds a luxurious layer of comfort. You can put your feet up on their couch without worrying about offending them.

"So, if you're the lighthouse, and I'm the ship, what's the rocky shore?"

She shrugged. "His reputation?"

"But the statute of limitations on medical malpractice is seven years," I said. "It's the same for psychiatry."

"I'm impressed. Statute of limitations? So dang smart."

"I couldn't even sue Clifford Paulson if I tried. So then, what is he trying to hide?"

"Beats me. I'm just the dumb girlfriend. You know, Alice does all this work with the hospital, her father helped build it, so maybe she worries about her reputation in the town. There is an upper class here, you know. It's teeny, but it exists. Old money that settled here near a pretty river. Rich people really like money and they really like pretty views of water from their castles. Ever notice that?" Desiree reached over my plate, grabbed a handful of fries.

"You should watch out for Dr. Cliff," I said. "He's manipulative."

"Maybe thirty years ago. Now, he's a teddy bear with buttons for eyes. He couldn't grab my ass if I walked by. Hey, give me a ride? A friend dropped me off." She dug in her purse and laid cash on the bar. She smiled at me. "Hey, you have crud in your teeth. Sip your drink and swish."

I sipped my coke, slid my tongue over my teeth, didn't feel anything sticking out.

We walked to my car. She moved like a child, swiftly and unselfconsciously. She slid her boots off in the passenger seat, propping her bare feet on the dashboard. The red polish on her toenails was chipped.

I backed out, gravel grinding under my tires, the sound loud and strange, like it was inside my head, like it was everywhere.

"I met your dad's cow," I said, and we both laughed.

"Yeah, my dad is really good to that cow. He treats her like a queen." She propped her elbow out the open window. "He's one of those who likes animals better than people."

The solid yellow line in the road was electric yellow, and the night sky glowed, mystic colors swimming. I blinked twice, hard. I'd only had two shots. Maybe it was a combination of whiskey and all that driving today. I gripped the wheel harder. Released my grip and tensed again. The sound of my tires clunking over the road was loud and pleasing, like listening to a heartbeat through a stethoscope.

"You feeling it?" she said.

"What?"

"Shrooms."

"No, you didn't," but my voice sounded like a record slowed way down, the pitch so low it was underground, two feet under with the dirt and worms.

I should have been mad at her, but I wasn't. I felt *good*. Everything smooth. The shame of watching my little kid self backstab my mom persisted, but it was light, only a balloon I was holding onto.

"You'll have a hot night with your hubby now," she said. I glanced over at her. Her lips were glossy and wet, and her blue eyes sparkled with fairy dust.

"He's not home," I said and laughed.

70

Sawyer and Trish, they'd had a good visit.

Sawyer had been relaxed, telling Trish about driver's education, about going hunting, about hearing a cougar growl yesterday morning, and Trish had listened. Her face was clean, her eyes were bright and alert. No drugs, no phone to distract her attention. Her hair had the stripped-down look of the poor. Without beauty products, fresh color, curling irons, it was merely hair, flat and dull.

My feelings for Trish were complicated. When I boiled it down, she had given me Sawyer, so I loved her for that. My love for her no longer buzzed, but it rested deep in the marrow of my bones.

But ever since Sawyer had visited his mom, he'd been quiet. We'd grabbed a pepperoni pizza from Lou Malnati's and headed to the condo.

It felt good to be back. The condo smelled good, like a new place somehow, like vacation, all clean linens and unbreathed air. We ate quietly, enjoying our home, enjoying the lack of Emily's chatter or Heather's reminders.

"It's weird how some little stupid thing can land you in prison," Sawyer said, staring at his pizza. "Steal a purse, months in prison. How's she gonna get a job when she gets out? I don't want to go to prison.'"

"Why would you go to prison?"

"I'm gonna make some mistake."

"You can make mistakes. Just not illegal ones."

Sawyer was quiet for a while, taking huge bites, chewing fast, swallowing painfully. "We let that baby cougar out. We cut two of the links, grabbed it. It got loose."

The urge to yell rose up, hot and acidic. *Sawyer, you idiot.* I kept quiet instead. The cougar was just a baby, it wouldn't kill anyone, and he's just a kid. I made worse choices. Way worse. "It's gonna be OK," I said. "We'll find it and solve it."

Sawyer shoved his plate away and put his head on the table. He was motionless for a half minute, then his back trembled.

"Sawyer," I said, rubbing his back. "You are such a good kid. You are a great kid. It's only a mistake. We'll go mend the fence, and it will be OK. I made way worse mistakes when I was your age."

"I feel this disgust under my skin," he said, his voice liquid and phlegmy. "I hate myself."

"Sawyer. I was like that too. You change. You won't always feel that. The things I did when I was younger, I would never ever do those things now."

Sawyer lifted his head. His eyes were wet. I hadn't seen him cry since he was six or seven. Jesus, ten years. Had I really not seen the kid cry in ten years? And when was the last time I'd embraced him?

"What did you do?" Sawyer said, curious, his voice childlike.

The shame I'd buried deep inside myself, so deep I'd forgotten it. That shame had been clawing its way out this past week, screaming so loud I couldn't ignore it.

Maybe if I told him, he wouldn't feel so bad about himself. Or maybe he'd never look at me the same.

"I hurt people," I said. "The kind of hurt that leaves scars on the skin."

Sawyer wiped his tears away. "Tell me." There was sorrow and desperation in his eyes. The kid was struggling. Of course he was. His mom's in prison, he's in a new place, a small town, living with his stepmom and stepsister full-time for the first time ever.

I closed my eyes, covered my face with my hands, and talked. About finding Dawn's body. About that morning, a month later, when my mom told me it had been Melinda Hornne who'd killed the girl I loved. Melinda, a witchy lady who'd had a litter of kids and drunken painting parties in her garage, had confessed. Mom told me the whole lot of them, the Hornnes, were Satan worshippers. When my mom worked in the church's food pantry, Father Greg had told her all sorts of disgusting things about Melinda Hornne.

At school that next morning, when I saw that soft-bellied, dirty-haired devil-worshipper, Rodney, the kid who'd been flirting with Dawn at Marjory's, I pictured Dawn's swollen corpse and her glazed, cloudy eyes, and I fucking lost it.

It was like gasoline had spilled inside my head. My eyes burned and my throat felt clawed. It was a head-throbbing blur, all of it. Grabbing the kid's hair, dragging him into the bathroom and smashing his head against the urinal. Not seeing the blood everywhere, not feeling the blood on my own lips, my hands, until Rodney lay unconscious on the floor.

Now I set my palms on the table and looked at Sawyer. He didn't hate me. His eyes were wet like mine. I pushed my plate away and kept talking.

Rodney hadn't been in school the rest of the week. Word was going round that I'd given him a concussion. Good. That devil-worshipping, murder family deserved what it got. Actually, no. They hadn't paid enough. Where was the justice for Dawn?

That weekend I got mean drunk at a party and hit a deer on my drive home. The deer bolted out onto the road so fast though, I probably would have hit her even if I'd been sober. I bumped my head, but it didn't split the skin. The pain in my head, the dent in my truck, the alcohol heating my blood, all of it fanned my anger.

I dragged the deer to the back of my truck and heaved her in. She wasn't big, barely one-hundred-fifteen pounds.

Her blood slick and warm on my hands, the meaty stink up my nose, I knew what I needed to do.

It was three in the morning by the time I'd finished. I slit the deer's throat, collected her blood in a bucket, and splashed that family's windows with blood. When relief didn't come, and my heart throbbed with rage, I'd walked around to the back of their house, laid down in the woods, and cried myself to sleep.

Enough. You can't tell him what happened next.

71

HEATHER

Desiree and I were out of the car and running through the grass. It was cold and wet against my ankles. We were on the gravel path that ran behind my house—it glowed and rolled like a curvy slide taking us up into the sky.

I'd left my car in the street, maybe in the grass, but it was fine. It was cool.

"Are we going to his house?" I said.

"Whose house?"

"My neighbor. He shot a deer and made me jerky."

"Shit, bitch, you are floaty. We're going on an adventure." And she grabbed my arm and pulled me off the glowing path into the grass. I tripped on something, dragging her down, and she fell onto me, laughing. Her body was soft and her smell was spicy menthol and eucalyptus lozenges. When she lifted off of me to roll onto her back, her hands were on my shoulder and under my breast, and it tickled. We giggled like kids.

"He made you deer jerky?" she said. "Maybe he likes you."

"And iced tea. He made me tea." We both found this hilarious. "Tracy Summer's Sun Tea," I said.

"That's what he calls his spooge? Come here, bitch, take some of my sun tea in your mouth."

We kept on laughing on our backs until we couldn't breathe. Had to stop. Our laughing slowed to big hefty smiling exhales.

The grass was luscious and damp against my neck. Settling into calm breathing, I stared up at the black sky sprinkled with radioactive salt. "You never see this many stars in the city." Stars pulsed closer, then away, sucking me in, and pulling away. The sky moved like a kaleidoscope, shifting in various shades of black.

"What is the worst thing you have ever done?" Desiree said, her voice's fast-car vibrato gone. It was sad and velvety, an old Cadillac. It would take my secrets and drive them far away.

"I killed my sister." The words came out easily. They didn't hurt. The grass, the sky, Desiree's warm skin touching mine: it was all forgiving.

"No, I don't believe it," she said softly.

"I watched her kick the stump away. I watched her hands claw her neck, trying to pry away the clothesline that was cutting into her neck, strangling her. I watched her legs kicking at the air. Her shoe fell off and her skin turned ashy blue. I could have put the tree stump back for her. I could have run to get help. There was time. It took a long time for her to die. They say it takes about two to four minutes. That's what I've read. I was six, and I didn't understand what she was doing. I thought my siblings were playing another joke on me—that they'd all jump out laughing any second—so I just stood there, barefoot, in the cold, wet grass, and watched her die."

Her suicide had a slow-motion mystical quality to it, like it wasn't real. Under the sugar maple where the wind rustled the glowing leaves, making them flicker like flames, in that early morning light, it felt theatrical and surreal. She's playing a joke on me. They are all playing a joke on me. Just like with Roxy.

Desiree's warm palms were on my wet cheeks, and she was pressing her soft lips to my forehead. "That wasn't your fault."

"I know." My heart and head felt light. I knew, but I didn't.

"Oh man, I wanted a sibling so bad. I hated living with just my dad." Her hands fell away from my face and she rolled onto her back. "He was decent. He made sure I had clothes and crayons and lunch for school. He took me fishing and hunting. Gave me presents and jewelry he got when he was away on fishing trips, unique stuff, cool trinkets, but after a while, that lost its magic. I really hated him for a while, for years. I'm over it now. I'm over hating him. I'm over wanting a brother or sister, but man, I wanted one so bad when I was a kid."

"What's the worst thing you've ever done?" I said.

"I've never done anything good."

"You're nice to Emily."

The grass felt like plush carpet, a cozy cool bed. Crickets were chirping, hundreds of them, haloing my head. Beyond the crickets, a raspy rumbling. A big cat purring. It rolled through my bones, feeling like a thunderstorm.

"When did you give me mushrooms?"

"When I moved your drink."

"Why'd you do that?"

"Because I like you and I want you to feel good," she said, her menthol breath warm in my ear. "I want to pet a kitty." She wiggled her hand into my pocket. My skin hypersensitive, the sensation was charged. I squirmed against her fingers and felt my keys pressing into my thigh. She said, "Do you want to pet a kitty?"

72

TREVOR

I woke up to my phone ringing. As I reached for it, the soft vibration of the 'L' train rumbled the walls of the condo. I missed this place. Our condo had an optimistic, airy vibe. It was only money and décor, but art and architecture affected our psyches, plain and simple.

When I saw who was calling, my peace shattered.

"Hi, Visha. Everything OK?"

"Not quite. I have Emily here. Heather said she'd call me when she was on her way because I have to drop Aary at daycare and head to work. Heather hasn't called, I can't reach her on her phone, and I need to leave soon."

"Emily's there?"

"Yes. She dropped her off yesterday. You didn't know?"

"I'm at the condo. I'll be there to get Em in ten minutes."

I quickly pulled on my pants and shoes, worry breaking through my skin in an anxious sweat. What had Hunther done to my family?

It's not Hunther, it's you. Things have always worked out for you. You've gotten away with everything. Now your past is coming to collect, asshole.

I called for Sawyer, telling him to get dressed, we had to hustle, I'd tell him why in the car. As I grabbed my keys and wallet, I thought about what I'd told Sawyer last night, and what I'd omitted…

I'd fallen asleep in the woods behind the Hornne's backyard late that night. Hours later I woke up to screaming. The sky was white with light. I smelled like blood and dirt. My neck itched with sweat.

A woman and a man were screaming and shouting, rushing frantically around the backyard.

"Get the ladder, get the clippers," the man screamed. He stood under this gorgeous maple tree, his knees bent and his back leaning awkwardly backward, his arms in front of him. The strangest stance. What was he doing?

A body. He was holding up a body, trying to lift it.

Someone hung themselves in the Hornne's maple tree.

The mother, hysterically crying and screaming, in her nightgown, fought with the ladder to set it down. The ground was bumpy with tree roots, and the ladder tipped and fell. She picked it up and set it straight, screaming, "Becky," her voice animal and screeching. She climbed the ladder, holding hedge clippers with the sharp end up.

Becky Hornne.

Seconds later the girl's body fell onto her father, both of them tumbling into a heap, a flash of dark hair, pale flesh, limbs. I looked away.

A little girl stood off to the side, holding yellow-orange leaves in her hands, silently watching her parents and her sister.

I'd turned away from it and walked deeper into the forest, suddenly sorry for all I'd done to their family.

73

HEATHER

I dreamed of cats licking my cheek, their rough tongues scraping and scraping until my skin peeled away. I dreamed of the cold dewy grass cradling me. Of a pulsing black sky. Of a handsome man leading me through the jungle, a machete in his hand. Of Desiree's sharp canines slipping out as she smiled and bit my hand hard. Instead of crying, it got me laughing. Her saying, *I love you. I do. You will barely feel it.*

Here came the cat again, purring, baritone vibration, tongue licking me. Hot breath. A bad smell. Fish and worms.

I opened my eyes to Tracy Summer's dog panting in my face, looking at me with those sweet, dumb eyes.

Low lighting and wood paneling. A scratchy wool blanket on me. Two small windows set above the couch, both offering picturesque views of grass. I was in his basement.

What the fuck?

The dog was so close, her hot breath was pulsing on my face. She licked my cheek. What was her name? Rhonda? Marley?

"Eww," I said, and sat up fast, my hand aching, my body tender. My hand was bandaged. I stared at it. What happened to my hand?

"Oh, good. Chicago's awake." Tracy Summers. Camo pants.

Something clinking. A spoon against a glass. A metallic smell.

My sleepiness switched to cold panic. "Why I am here? What are you doing?" And what was that smell? Dog breath was like a bouquet of gardenias compared to what I was inhaling now. Piss. Lots of piss. And shit.

"I am stirring some ice into tomato juice for you. Good for a hangover." He held out a glass of something red and creamy. His eyes were watery, slightly yellow, and his mouth was a straight line surrounded by patches of hair. He needed a shave.

"I'm not hungover," I said, without considering it. Was I? My mouth was dry. I felt fine, minus the thirst, panic, and my throbbing hand. No way was I drinking anything he offered. Not with how foul the room smelled. "Thanks for the offer, but I'll pass." The dog licked my pants at the knee, and I jerked away.

Tracy laughed. "Who doesn't like a golden retriever?"

"Me."

"Pardon me, but that's kind of creepy. Did you get attacked by a dog? Come here, Rosy." *Rosy*.

"My mom fed stray dogs and cats so they were always lurking in our yard. She fed them, pet them, nuzzled them, but neglected her own kids. My annoyance stuck." And, had *he* just called *me creepy*?

"Oh, I'm sorry about that." He sounded truly sorry, which made me feel even more awkward. He set the tomato concoction down on an end table to my left. It was crowded with a strange medley of items. Rubbing alcohol, cotton balls, a handheld centipede game, four plastic water bottles, a hunting knife, and a cylinder of what looked like… baby formula? Beyond the table, the floor was strewn with newspaper and empty water bottles. Jesus, it really did smell like shit in here.

"Well, Heather Bishop, you might not have gotten drunk, but you were on *something*." He stood in front of me, hands on hips.

Mushrooms. That's right. Desiree gave me mushrooms.

To my right, unfinished wood stairs led up. Bolt cutters lay on the floor near the bottom stair. I wanted to be home already, but he was blocking my way. "Your hand was bleeding so I cleaned it," he said.

"Oh, thanks. I was wondering." I glanced at my wrapped hand. "I'd like to go now," I said, and hated the weakness in my voice. I wasn't really scared of Tracy Summers, was I? Except he was blocking me. And also, why was I in his basement?

"Of course," he said, backing out of my way.

As if on cue, and as if this were a circus, a furry critter pranced clumsily down the stairs, its furry paws far too large for its body.

"Cougar," I said, but my voice failed. "Cougar." I was two years old again, stating a single word, but meaning so much more. I tensed my shoulders, sat, and pulled my feet onto the couch as if getting my feet off the floor would save me.

"You hungry, Looney Tunes?" Tracy said, tossing the cougar an empty water bottle. She pounced on it, sending it shooting against the wall. She crouched, suspicious of the bottle, then pounced again, this time catching it.

"You stole the baby?" I said. "You stole Luna?"

Tracy Summers grabbed a baby bottle from behind his chair, added a scoop of baby formula, and shook it. Liquid shot out of the hole in the nipple, caught him on the face.

"Naw, I didn't steal her. I was out for two days searching for her, worried a hawk would nab her. Chrissy wasn't out there searching; she was at home sulking," he said, a gossipy lilt to his voice. He held the bottle near the floor, wiggled it. "You were hungry, weren't you, my beautiful baby?" he cooed without self-awareness, his voice oscillating, like he was talking to his own baby. "Come here, Looney Tunes." The cougar perked its head up, spotted the bottle, and pranced over. Tracy aimed the nipple down. The cougar pawed at it, chewed on it, and started suckling. Tracy scooped the cougar into his arms and held it on its back, cradling it like a baby. If I wasn't so terrified, if I wasn't so morally bound against exotic animals as pets, I would have crept over to pet the cougar, rub my thumb over its furry paws.

"You can't keep a cougar in your house."

"I know, I know," he said. "I ain't giving her back to Chrissy though, you can bet on that. She had her how long before she lost her? Naw, I'll bring her over to the zoo in Milwaukee. Couple more days." The way he said it though, with such longing, days might stretch into weeks. He wanted to keep her.

"If you keep her, she will kill your dog. On purpose." I said it because he needed to hear it. Tracy might be a person who didn't care if a baby cougar killed him or another person, but he did care if it killed his dog.

"I know that's a risk, I do, but you should see how they cuddle." He looked at me and laughed. "I'm not keeping her. I'm not. Hey, where's your little one?" he said flatly, no judgment.

I panicked. Where *was* Emily? I had a daughter. Since the day she was born I was responsible for knowing where she was. My nerves settled. Visha. She's with Visha.

"With a friend." Oh, no. What time was it? I was supposed to pick up Emily early. "Where's my phone?" I stood.

"No clue, but those people you were with? I would stay away from them."

I turned. "What people?"

Rosy sniffed the cougar's head and licked its cheek.

"Some girl and a guy."

A guy? "I was with a girlfriend," I said, picturing me and Desiree lying in the grass, giggling like kids. "There was no guy."

"Well, all I can tell ya is that I was out walking on the trail around back, and you and this couple were messing with the cougar cage." He absentmindedly fondled the cougar's rear paw. Tracy Summers was a natural mother. "So I shined my flashlight on y'all, and the couple ran. I didn't get a good look at them. Your hand was bleeding pretty good so I brought you home and cleaned it. You zonked out. I rang your doorbell to tell your family, but no one answered." He was also a mother hen and the neighborhood's watchdog. "The guy left a pair of bolt cutters in the grass. Nice pair. Take them home with you. Then you'll find out who the guy was. I'd imagine he'd want them back."

I picked up the bolt cutters and stepped up the stairs. "Thank you for bandaging my hand."

He nodded. "I don't think a cougar bit you. I think it was the cage wire that got you."

Both statements were equally fucked up.

74

I walked down Winding Way toward our house, my limbs heavy, the bolt cutters in my hand. The sun was too bright. My phone was missing. I was pissed at myself for letting Visha down.

I typed in the keycode to the garage.

My car was parked inside.

Some parts of last night were a blur, others were colorful and psychedelic. I didn't remember parking the car in the garage, but Desiree's bare shoulder brushing against mine lingered. Her puff of warm cigarette-kissed breath across my face, as she whispered, "I wish you were my sister."

I dropped the bolt cutters near the garage door and went inside. The kitchen was dim and quiet. My heart ached for the kids. I missed Emily's constant touches. Sawyer's stingy grins and blazing eyes. We had our awkwardness, but I wanted that kid to feel peace and happiness. I wanted him to feel loved. And Trevor. Regardless of what he'd done, lied about, there had to be an explanation. He was the backbone of this family.

I grabbed a coffee mug from the cabinet. A photo collage mug made with family photos. The mug Trevor had declared my favorite. He was right. It was my favorite. I filled it with water and drank.

"You are such a weirdo." Spoken softly, from the other room. I dropped my mug, and it shattered. Ceramic shards with puzzle pieces of family photos scattered everywhere. Desiree in the doorway to the kitchen, looking at the mess. "Oh, I'm sorry, hon. I totally didn't mean to spook you. I was just," she thumbed backward, "looking at your caterpillars. Some fat sons of bitches. And there's these tiny balls of shit everywhere."

"It's called frass," I said, absentmindedly, and squatted to pick up shards.

"Frass. It's like French, right?"

"I don't know."

"Bitch, I was worried about you. Like where the fuck'd you go?"

"My neighbor said he found me passed out in the grass. Where'd you go?" I dropped a few shards in the garbage. I was sad about the broken mug, but I could order a new one.

"I came here."

"He said I was by that cougar cage." I looked at the line of scabs on my arm, the bandage on my hand. "He said you ran. He mentioned a guy. There wasn't a guy though, was there?"

"Did he say it was me?" she said. "Did he see my face?"

"No. He didn't see. It was dark. Was there a guy?" A shiver worked its way through me. What if it was Brandon Paulson?

There was a scuffle of a shoe against the floorboard.

A man appeared behind Desiree, and it wasn't Brandon Paulson. He was tall with long, muscled arms. Boots. His navy T-shirt tucked into his belted jeans. Young, like Desiree. He held his forearm up at eye level; a caterpillar crawled along it. His eyes on the caterpillar, he laughed. "I hope these aren't poisonous."

"Only if you eat them," I said, but alarms were ringing along my nerves. *Pierce. This is Pierce. Tracy Summers said he was a pig. Both a cop and a chauvinist. He, they, are in your house. They broke into your house. He is a stranger. Where's their car?*

"Heather, this is my boy Pierce," she said, her eyes and smile full of emotion, but I couldn't pin down which. Adoration, lust, reverence, maybe a little fear?

He gave a shiver, shook his arm, and flung the caterpillar to the ground. "Weird. I just got creeped out big-time." He smashed it with his boot. Greenish yellow snot squirted out from under his boot, hitting the side of the oak cabinet, sticking there.

Horrified, I stepped back. *They broke into your house. Get out.* I turned to run, but Pierce moved at me, fast. They tell you to fight like hell—do anything and everything to get away: run through a glass door; jump out of a moving car; fight even if someone's got a knife to your throat—because they're going to kill you anyway.

Here's what they don't tell you. The fight is sometimes over before it starts. Your adrenaline didn't get anywhere near climax, it's only taking off, wheels lifting off the tarmac, but the fight is over. Maybe because he is bigger and stronger, so much stronger than you.

He came at me fast and smashed his hand over my mouth. The inside of my lips banged against my teeth, and I tasted blood. His other hand twisted my arm behind my back. He moved fluidly and rotated me, his hand still on my mouth, and he was behind me, his groin jammed against the small of my back. "No screaming. People are going to church this morning." His voice rough, not even out of breath. I was pulling, pushing, flailing against his grip.

One punch to my right kidney, and the pain was so blinding, sharp as sunshine, I couldn't breathe. I fell forward onto the counter, my cheek hitting hard.

He pulled my arms tight behind my back and she was binding them with what felt like duct tape. He jammed a sock in my mouth, fastened it with duct tape, and she wrapped my ankles. Pain gripping my lower back, still so bad, my breath hadn't come back to me.

"I'm gonna make you *eat* one," he whispered, his breath hot and close to my face.

Why was he so mad at me? He'd never met me.

"Hell no, you're not gonna make her eat one," Desiree said. "I got to clean up that bug snot on the floor, I don't want to clean up her puke too. Besides, we don't have time for your games. Sun's up. Took you so fucking long, Heather. Jesus Christ. I fell asleep on your couch."

I glanced down at the shards. Trevor would know something happened.

Desiree must have followed my gaze because she said, "Don't worry, baby. I'll clean that up too. Trevor won't notice a thing."

Sock in my mouth, I couldn't respond, but I gave her an eyes-wide, angry look. Bitch. Back-stabbing bitch.

She held my gaze, her eyebrows softened. She said softly, as a statement, not a question, "You want to know why."

Fuck, yes, I wanted to know why.

"Enough," Pierce said. "Let's get her into the trunk."

75

On my side, ankles bound, wrists bound behind my back, I tried to calm my breathing so I wouldn't die vomiting and inhaling his sweaty sock. It kept triggering my gag reflex. I kicked at the sides and back of the trunk, but found no give anywhere. Didn't they say you could kick out the tail lights? This hollow advice was failing me, and I was bitter and doubtful of all those "What to do if" videos.

Panic distorted time. Maybe we drove for five minutes, maybe twenty. I took breaks from kicking, then would go at it again. It's because my ankles were bound, that's why I couldn't get a strong enough kick. But I did bust through a tail light, slicing my calf in the process. It stung for a moment before the pain faded. I pushed my feet out, hoping someone would see them.

The car slowed, turned pointedly, and bumped over a curb. Drove a minute more, and lumbered to a stop. The parking brake yawned and ended with a click. The engine died, but some belt continued to spin. The engine ticked. They spoke quietly near the front of the car, their voices muffled.

One set of footsteps neared. "That's just gonna piss him off more," Desiree said, smacking the bottom of my shoes. I pulled my feet back into the trunk. The trunk moaned as she leaned against it. The flick of a lighter, an inhale. Exhale. The smell of smoke leached in.

"I was a sneaky kid, a bored kid," Desiree said. "I went through drawers and shoeboxes and toolboxes and attics. Adults don't seem to know that about kids. How kids don't leave a goddamn thing unturned. Everything is a potential treasure." She laughed, but her laugh had a sullen quality.

What was she talking about? My ankles throbbed. Sweat dripped down my neck. I concentrated on my breathing and listened.

"So, I found things," she said. "Tokens, I guess. I thought they belonged to my mom or his girlfriends; he had girlfriends after mom died. I found the cocktail napkins with birds drawn on them when I was seven or eight and asked him about it. Did Mom like to draw birds? He was so pissed; I didn't understand why. By the time I got to high school, I was suspicious but I couldn't put my finger on what it was I suspected, you know?"

Wait. Cocktail napkins. Dawn used to draw on cocktail napkins for her customers. Is that what she's talking about?

"I'd found a plated bracelet engraved with the name 'Leah J.' I searched the name online, and one of my searches came up with this seventeen-year-old in Minnesota who went missing a few summers before. I tracked down every photo there was of this girl until I found the one where she wore the same bracelet."

Asher Moss? I pictured his smooth jaw, his aw-shucks smile, his lake blue eyes. He'd had that compulsive energy, but he seemed easygoing, smooth. And, he loved that cow. He'd hidden his psychopathy and redirected me impeccably. A shiver ran through me.

"I did the math. I was twelve when he killed Leah J.," she said, disappointment in her voice, but it was old and had lost its power. "There was Leah and Dawn and at least one more, as far as I know. It's funny, I went back and forth between denial and realization a bunch of times. When it sinks in slow like that, in that back-and-forth way, and when you're still a kid, and you're not sure what's real, you get used to the idea of it, comfortable with it. It's not so shocking somehow. And the thing is, he was a good dad. So even when I was sure he'd killed a few girls, when I was literally holding evidence, I was *still* doubting myself. Does that make sense?"

Yeah, it did. Kids' ideas of reality are so malleable, they can get used to anything. Dad might be a serial killer, but he's also a good dad, so it's fine.

Desiree sighed heavily. No tears though. This was nothing more than archeology to her, dry bones dug up in her backyard. Clinical and cold. "I didn't know about the purple ring. Obviously. I thought that one was my mom's. How could I know what was hers or theirs? If I had known, I never would have worn it while you were in town. Your mom must have given it to Dawn."

Had Asher taken it off Dawn's finger before or after he'd severed it?

Desiree moved the gravel around with her foot. "I got the bird tattoo when I was sixteen to piss him off, show him I knew who he was. You're not going to believe this, it's the craziest thing, I think he *forgot* about the cocktail napkins. I showed him my tattoo, and he wasn't fazed, said, 'cute tattoo.' Fuck." She kicked the gravel again.

The stink of my panic imbued this tight space. I kicked and writhed, made noise, but couldn't do much else. Not having to look me in the eyes, that I couldn't interrupt, had to make it easier for Desiree to reveal so much. I hated her for it because I was trapped and gagging on her boyfriend's filthy sock. If I weren't bound, if we were sitting on barstools at Shawnee's, I might feel for her.

"You wanted to know why Paulson would have your mom sign a confession? I think my dad saw what was going on with Doctor Paulson, either he saw him abusing patients or he realized Paulson was stealing drugs from the hospital, whatever it was, my dad saw an opportunity. I think he told Paulson he would keep quiet about the doctor's strange practice if Paulson got your mom to confess. That confession got my dad off the hook."

Asher Moss was probably the one who gifted me a dead opossum. *Sounds like someone's trying to warn you to back off, don't it?*

He was the one who wanted me to back off.

"I've never killed anyone," she said, lifting her hip off the trunk, and letting it fall again. "Seriously. I don't feel violence in me, but it's like, whatever, people die. I didn't want to hurt you, but this situation is fucked, you know? I mean, I don't want my dad to go to prison and you're digging things up and the Paulsons want you gone. So, I don't know."

I kicked the sides of the trunk as hard as I could until my breathing grew shallow and my vision dimmed. Footsteps approached quickly. "Shut the fuck up in there," Pierce said, and he popped the trunk. The sunshine was blinding, silhouetting their figures in bright white halos, shading their faces. "If you thrash, I'll throw you down, punch your other kidney."

He hauled me over his back, his shoulder cutting into my diaphragm, making it impossible to breathe again, especially with the sock in my mouth.

Just as dizziness took my vision away, I felt cool inside air. He tossed me onto a couch on my back. With my arms behind my back, muscles stretched and snapped. The pain near knocked me out.

"I need her arms," another female voice said.

Alice Paulson.

"Oh, for God's sake," Pierce said, tipping me on my side and walking out of my field of vision. In front of me, a pretty glass table. A vase with freshly cut yellow roses. A window with no curtains, showcasing a lush yard, the shed backing up to that knotted mulberry bush.

The Paulsons' house.

"I got to go back and fix that fence," Pierce said. "Did you see when we drove past, the cougars pushing where I started cutting?"

"I saw," Desiree said, drinking something, gulping, setting the can on the counter. "Where did you say Chrissy was?"

"No clue. I told her to be gone for twenty-four hours. We can't put her in there in broad daylight. Now that plans have changed, I got to go back and fix it."

Their *former* plan was suddenly clear. It was a psychotic plan, but it was also surprisingly clean. Autopsy reports would show I had alcohol and psilocybin in my blood. Evidence would indicate I'd been home alone for the night, broke into that cougar cage, and got mauled. Desiree and Pierce would not be suspected. Even if her fingerprints were on my car, even if someone saw us together. She didn't know I was going to throw myself to cougars. My mom's history would be brought out, a fresh coat of shiny paint, and people would nod, and say, *Oh, Melinda Hornne's child, of course she was troubled. She'd been asking around about her mother's case, and she'd probably been depressed.* Me sneaking into a cougar cage to get ripped apart would make perfect sense to them.

I stayed idle, trying to regain my energy for when I had a chance to fight. *If you get a chance.*

"Fix it later," Alice said, stern yet calm. The sound of a gentle pat on his hand. "Let's first take care of our guest, then you'll go fix the fence. And if a cougar gets out in the meantime, it will add distraction, which is a good thing. The family will be looking for her soon. So, change of plans. Here's what we're going to do. Go OxiClean her car, she's bleeding. Set plastic down in my trunk."

Panic shot through me again, and I twisted and yanked my wrists. The duct tape barely budged.

Alice said, "Desiree drives Heather's car out to the edge of town. You take my car and drop the body in the river. Pick up Desiree, then drive back here. First, go clean her car." Seconds later, a door closed.

The swish of her slacks, thighs brushing against each other. Alice kneeled on the ground, facing the glass table near my head. She set a makeup case on the table, unzipped it, took something out, set it on the table. A syringe.

I tried to twist, but I was bound too tightly. Tears dripped down my cheeks.

"You were a sweet little girl," she said. "Not very smart, but you made Claire and Donnie laugh." Her smile grew. She'd looked so lovely to me the other day with her stylish hair and her easy way. Now, she looked like a monster. Her straight white teeth, her stale dry lipstick. "I used to find you in Brandon's room at bedtime," she said. "You'd be holding his elephant stuffy, pretending to make it talk." She set a vial on the table. I tried to scream, but the sock gagged me. My vision blurred with tears. "And here you are now, out of nowhere," she said, irritation cutting through her fake calm. "I kept thinking you would stop digging. You forced my hand, dear, you have to know that." She pressed her hand against my cheek. It was cold.

"I'm not the asshole. That one up there," she pointed at the ceiling, "the one who acts all innocent now, he's the asshole," she said, amusing herself, as if we were two women sharing stories about our husbands' mess. "I'm just his clean-up crew. Always been that way."

She stood slowly, her knees and her back bothering her. Before she was up, I used my core muscles to lift my upper body and drop it on the glass. I'd hoped to shatter the table, make her lose her vial, but the table was solid. Muscles in my

375

arm tore, and the pain was extraordinary. My bottom half fell onto the wood floor, and my upper body followed. My head cracked against the floor.

"Oh, for Christ's sake, Heather," she said.

When my vision cleared, she was on the other side of the table, bending down to pick up her vial. At least she had to search for her vial and syringe.

"Alice?" A voice came through a speaker in the kitchen. "I think someone's here."

She rushed to the kitchen. "I dropped something. I'll be up in a minute," she said, out of breath.

"My husband," she said, sarcastic. "My excitable, brilliant, bossy, and arrogant husband, who stole dozens of medicines from the hospital my parents helped build." She went around the table, got on the ground, and peered under a chair. I struggled to a sitting position. "Oh, he'd come back from a satanic-abuse-causes-MPD conference and he'd talk for hours and wouldn't sleep for days. And I loved his manic phases, I really did." She was reaching under the chair. I tried to stand, but couldn't from this position. I fell back to the side and rolled my forehead onto the floor, and tried to use my forehead as leverage to stand. "But then your mother came to him for depression, and oh, did he do a number on her. It was obvious she hadn't killed Dawn Young, but my Clifford wanted it to be, he wanted his own case, just like the famous psychologists, and he poked and interrogated until he got his way. He duped his brother. He duped a lot of people."

What Father Greg heard my mom say—*I will take my knife*

and cut you open. Does that make your cock hard?—it made sense. Cliff abused her until she gave him the confession he wanted.

"Got it," Alice said, sitting up, a look of accomplishment in her crazed eyes. "What a goddamn twist of irony when it's the head doctors who are the crazy ones, eh?" She unwrapped the syringe, stuck it in the vial, and tipped it upside down. As she drew liquid into the syringe, I made it to my feet and threw my body at her awkwardly. We both went down. I was back on my side, and she scurried away to a safe distance.

I was on my forehead again, butt in the air, trying to rock into a standing position, but she pushed me over. We both spotted the syringe, and she grabbed it. She stood, came at me, and kicked me in the stomach. Knocked the wind out of me. "You and your idiot mother. I couldn't believe she had the nerve to call me and tell me she knew what he'd done." She kicked me in the stomach again. "Well, I couldn't have it." She came around behind me and kicked me in the back.

As I was trying to catch my breath, a jab got me in the arm. I rolled onto the syringe, cracked it, the needle snapping, tearing my skin.

"Alice?" from the kitchen speaker again.

"What a pain in the ass he is," she muttered, studying the syringe. "Good," she said, "enough to slow you down."

She was right. My arm felt warm, and it was spreading quickly. The pain in my stomach and back was dulling.

She walked away, but marched back. She stood over me and said, "Those *other* doctors with renowned names had a big city hospital to pay millions for their settlements. Those famous doctors, the ones who conned my husband into their make-believe notions of MPD and satanic cults, they are *still* practicing. My husband doesn't have a big city hospital to back him up. Our insurance would crush us. This house is not even paid off."

I laughed into the wet sock. It seemed so funny. Her house wasn't paid off, and they were going to dump me in the river. I got it though, it was a money thing. Even if your crimes are decades old, your life insurance policy could be voided. She couldn't have patients digging up their old cases.

"Alice? I think someone's here," from the top of the stairs.

"Don't come down. I'll come up," she yelled, out of breath. "He's fucking exhausting. Even if we were stripped of our money and reputation, he'd still think he did nothing wrong."

Her footsteps moved away quickly, her flats clicking on the floor. Like a cockroach.

My wrists felt fat and bloated but nothing hurt anymore. I felt good. I tried to roll onto my forehead, butt in the air, but I fell onto my side. *She got you good.*

I imagined Emily's wild smile, her teasing Trevor. He'd feign anger, say, "That's it," stomping toward her, and she'd squeal and run away, loving to be chased, knowing she was going to get a tickle. And Sawyer's laugh, it was the absolute best. You didn't get to hear it much, so it was such a treat.

I loved them so much. I felt light, and the room was curling sweetly around me like the softest blanket.

"I had this one patient, a woman, who came to me for depression. She was depressed for many reasons, including the murder of this girl, a friend of hers. Through intensive therapy involving medication and hypnotherapy, I drew out the truth of her situation. It was like pulling a thread and watching her whole life unravel. As a result of her childhood trauma from satanic ritual abuse, she had developed Multiple Personality Disorder. As you know, severe and chronic abuse can cause disassociation. More than that, she was actually the one who had murdered her friend. She had repressed those memories, shoved them down so deeply, she wasn't aware until I pulled them out."

Doctor Clifford Paulson, PhD Psychology
Transcripts from the Sixth Annual Conference on
Adult Manifestations of Childhood Trauma
November 14, 1991
THE RADISSON PLAZA HOTEL, CINCINNATI, OHIO

76

Gentle pressure under me, lifting me. I was being carried by an angel. God rays warmed my skin. I was dying again and it didn't hurt. Same as last time.

"Trust me," he said.

The smell of woodsy cologne.

My skin brushing against leather. A door closed. Acceleration. An abrupt stop, and my head hitting something, but everything felt wrapped in cotton. Tape ripped away from my cheek. The sock pulled from my mouth.

Acute stinging up my nose, and burning in my brain like dumping rubbing alcohol on a paper cut. I writhed, smashing my head against the window. That, I felt.

"Stop screaming," a voice said, "you're going to be OK."

I had been warm and floating one second, then falling hard and cold, into the passenger seat of a car, everything sharp and uncomfortable. My arm muscles were on fire, and blood dripped into my eye. I turned to see who was driving and screamed.

Scab along his forehead. Those sly eyes. Brandon Paulson.

He pressed a button on his side door, and the locks clicked. With my hands bound behind my back, I couldn't have opened it anyway.

"I'm not going to hurt you," he said, driving away from the house. "I gave you Narcan to counter the overdose. You're going to feel a little crazy, your teeth will chatter, but that will fade. Trevor called me. I am bringing you to him, swear to God."

"Untie my wrists," I yelled.

"I will. I will. I want to get away from them first."

"Untie my wrists," I shouted. "Untie my wrists. Untie my fucking wrists." Over and over until he slammed on the brakes and swerved. He turned to me, fury in his eyes, his jaw coiled. Like he wanted to kill me. He punched the glove compartment. It popped open, and its contents spilled onto the floor.

"You're being a fucking bitch." He went to reach down between my legs, stopped, and said, "If you kick me, I swear to God I will drive you back and drop you on their doorstep. I'm reaching for scissors."

He grabbed the scissors. "Lean forward."

He cut my wrist, and I hollered, but then my hands were free.

He dropped the scissors and shoved his foot on the gas. He drove fast, checking his rearview.

"Why did you threaten me?" I said.

"What are you talking about?"

"You came to my house—"

"Looking for Trevor," he said as if I were overreacting.

I grabbed the scissors and cut through the duct tape holding my ankles. "Why? Why did you meet Trevor?" I kept the scissors on my lap.

He grabbed a pair of sunglasses from the dashboard and

slipped them on. He checked his rearview. "I got into some financial trouble with, well, I had a few debts. Milwaukee meatheads hassling me. I can't stand to ask my mom." He exhaled. "Trevor saved my ass, so you know, timing-wise, I got lucky. I ran into him about a month ago at Shawnee's. I knew if I could get you here, I could force his hand."

If I could get you here...

It clicked.

"That was you? You sent me those texts?"

He said nothing.

Force his hand? "What did you force him to do?"

"Nothing bad. He was running animals for me. It's easier with two people, and I'd just lost my last guy to—"

"Running animals?"

"Mostly venomous snakes, some birds, tiny turtles. He'd transport them in plastic containers. You know, like Tupperware?"

"What are you talking about?"

"Underground exotic pet trade."

"You're fucking crazy," I said. "Let me out."

"I'm saving your ass, aren't I?" he shouted and brought his fist down on the steering wheel. The horn honked. I'd wrecked his notion that he was the hero in this situation.

"You *knew* your mother murdered my mom and you let it go? Let me out, right now. You're insane, all of you."

"You need to shut up," he said, his jaw tight.

His phone rang and he answered it. "I got her. We're a couple streets over, but call firefighters out for a fire, then call the cops. Don't mention my name. We are being tailed by my brother, who's a cop." Holding the phone to his ear, he turned onto Winding Way, but took the turn too wide and clipped a mailbox.

"Is that Trevor?"

He ignored me and said into the phone, "Fuck that, actually, I'm gonna keep driving right past your house. I'm gonna drive her to the fire station on 85th. Meet me there." He dropped his phone in the side door.

He checked his rearview again. "They're coming fast and they're dead set on throwing you in the river. Still want me to let you out?"

I looked over my shoulder. Pierce's car swerved around another corner, and was closing in fast. "You can't get to the fire station. This street, it's a dead end."

"Shit. Put your hands out."

Just as I dropped the scissors and braced myself, he braked hard and shifted fast to reverse and turn. Four houses away, Trevor, Sawyer, and Em stood on the porch. Sawyer went back inside. Forgot something. Probably his cell phone.

I turned to Brandon. Outside his window was the strangest scene. Several hundred feet from where my family stood on the porch, a cougar lay in the grass, front and back paws stretched out—an endearing look for any four-legged animal. Eyes closed and aimed up to the sun. Basking. Another cougar approached from behind him, maybe ready to play.

"Go back, Trevor. Go back in," my voice a whisper of a prayer, of telepathy, as I stared hard over my shoulder at

Trevor and Emily on the front porch. Trevor was staring at his phone, dialing.

As if he'd heard my telepathic prayer, Trevor stepped inside. But Emily lingered on the walkway. Her arms spread for balance, she hopped on one foot.

"Call them back," I screamed. "Tell them to go back ins—"

The sound of crunching metal, and an explosion in my face. The feeling of my body pitching forward and back.

Smoke shifted before my eyes; the sun shot through it. No, it wasn't smoke. Yellow dust. A burnt powder smell. White pillowcase on the dashboard.

It took me a second. Oh, the deflated airbag.

Brandon moaned beside me. His head leaned back onto the headrest. There were brown shards embedded in his forehead, and blood leaked into his eyes. The airbag had shattered his sunglasses, sinking the sharp pieces into his forehead. A white deflated bag lay in his lap too, yellow dust hanging in the air in front of his face. As he breathed in, he pulled a current of dust, and coughed it out. His wrists lay in his lap, burnt and weeping blood.

Nothing life-threatening, but the pain was probably bad. "I'll get help," I said.

I reached for my door handle, but it was already rattling.

In my passenger side window, Pierce was hunched over, knocking on the window with his gun, smiling.

As long as Trevor got Emily inside the house.

"I'll open the door. I'm coming." I rattled the door handle, but it was locked. "Please. Just don't hurt my—"

His face crashed against my window. His cheek flattened and spread, his face slid down, leaving a smear of blood.

I screamed.

The cougar walked backward, its mouth gripping Pierce by the back of his neck. His legs were like hoses being dragged through the grass, his hands trying to get at the cat's head. *Never turn your back on a big cat.* This big cat dragged Pierce toward where the other cougar was minutes ago. But it wasn't there anymore.

I reached over Brandon, drawing a louder moan from him, and unlocked my door. I stumbled out and ran toward Emily. Several hundred feet away, she stood outside our house, mouth open and staring in my direction. She'd witnessed a cougar attack a man. She was probably wondering if she'd imagined it.

"Emily!" my voice cracking. "Go inside!"

"Momma?" Her voice was quiet, barely audible. She ran toward me.

I ran harder, waving her away. "Go inside! Go get Dad!"

She'd already made it to the next-door neighbor's yard when I saw the cougar crawling slowly toward Emily, on its belly, almost lazily. *Stalking.* It made a hissing noise, sounded like a snake.

"Emily, go inside!" I veered toward the cougar. No idea what I would do when I reached it—tackle it, kick it—but I needed to get in between that animal and Emily. My screaming didn't lure its attention. It was honed in on Emily. It stood and crept toward her.

"Emily. Go back!"

Emily, *thank God*, saw the cougar, and stopped dead in her tracks.

"Back away, Emily. Don't turn around." *It can't resist your turned back.*

She took a few steps back, fell, then turned and ran.

Oh my God.

The cougar sprung to its feet and took off after her, sprinting effortlessly.

I ran harder, leaning forward, too far forward, and fell as an explosion rang out. My ears ringing, I got back to my feet.

The cougar was backing up, tail between its legs. Its body dropped to the grass. It stood again, turned, and limped away.

Trevor had Emily in his arms. Sawyer was holding something in his hand, his arm extended and aimed above the ground. A gun. Trevor put Emily inside, and he was outside again, running toward me.

Another explosion from behind me. I dropped again and searched for the source.

Tracy Summers stood over a cougar. Its beige fur bloomed red. Tracy's chest trembled. His rifle in one hand, his other hand covering his eyes. Under the cat's paws, Pierce's body lay static, shaped awkwardly, limbs pointing in the wrong directions.

My ears buzzing, I turned back toward our house. Trevor was halfway to me. Emily darted outside, but Sawyer set down his gun and grabbed her. He pulled her into his arms, pushing her face into his shoulder, and carried her back inside.

77

They saved Molly, the cougar Sawyer had shot.

An EMT on scene had a brother who managed the Milwaukee Zoo and a sister who was a vet. Calls were made on the scene, and the vet arrived within twelve minutes. She tranquilized the cougar, and the staff arrived soon after to transport the cougar for surgery. The bullet went through the cougar's chest above its left side, just missing the pulmonary artery, and exited cleanly. We weren't outside to watch the animal fixers descend on our neighbor's lawn, but heard it was quite the scene of professionalism and efficiency Hunther had not experienced in some time.

Buttercup, the cougar Tracy Summers shot, could not be saved.

Molly, Asia, Winnie, and Luna were transferred to the zoo. When Tracy Summers handed over Luna, they didn't ask him a single question. They assumed the baby cougar had escaped from Chrissy's house that day.

The headlines read: ONE COUGAR SHOT DEAD. ONE MAN MAULED TO DEATH.

Off the record people said Hunther had gotten lucky. Only one dead. Could've been more.

I cried for that cougar and strangely, I cried for Pierce Paulson. Grieved his death like the brothers and sister I'd never properly grieved. Grieved my mother. All of them.

Grief would hit me at strange times. When I was dumping Sawyer's dirty laundry into the washing machine. When I would find one of Trevor's bunched up socks under the bed. When I was walking on the preserve path, and a red maple leaf riding a soft breeze landed on the chalky white gravel.

Emily cried too, several times a day for a few weeks. "Life's not fair, Mommy. Poor Buttercup. It wasn't her fault."

Sawyer had nightmares. He'd wake up and stand in our doorway like a zombie, half asleep. Sometimes he'd sleepwalk back to bed, sometimes he'd stand there until he woke up, or until I woke up to pee and found him there. I'd say, "Sawyer, get in. Between us."

His face shiny with sweat, his hair sticking in all directions, he'd lie on his back and stare at the ceiling in between Trevor and me. Once he'd said, "I dreamed I was in prison."

I turned to him, petting his hair as tears rolled down my cheeks. "No. You are the very best boy, Sawyer. You are a hero. You are my hero, Dad's hero, Emily's hero, your mom's hero. We love you," I said, until he fell back asleep.

Three weeks later we were headed to Marjory's for donuts. Sawyer was driving. Donuts had become our after-school ritual. Weekend ritual too. When you are working through a tough time, donuts are as good an answer as any.

Trevor was with his mom. She didn't have long. We'd be back in Chicago before Christmas.

At the corner where Sawyer turned into the parking lot, two young boys sat in lawn chairs on the side of the road beside a sign and a cardboard box. After Sawyer parked, I said, "Let's go see what they've got."

Kittens. Curled up into each other for comfort, itty-bitty cries and meows. Three left. "Which one should we get?" I said to Sawyer and Emily.

78

Trevor told me everything, and I did the same. It felt good to talk. Talking about shame took away some of its gravity.

"Your mother would want you to forgive yourself and so would Becky," Trevor said. "You were so little. Think about it. There's nothing Emily could do as a six-year-old that you wouldn't forgive. You were only six. Forgive yourself like you'd forgive Emily. Like you forgave me."

It was easy to forgive Trevor. Who we are as adults often has no resemblance of who we were at sixteen.

Asher Moss was awaiting trial for the murder of Dawn Young and three other girls. Dawn had been his first. Jewelry found in his house and Desiree's apartment linked him to at least four murders across Wisconsin, Michigan, and Minnesota. Even with me stirring up the past, he never worried enough to dispose of the jewelry he'd collected from his victims. The people who should worry most about their tendencies and behaviors usually have the most self-confidence.

When Alice Paulson was in custody for my mom's murder, her husband's health improved. It turned out she'd been feeding him high doses of Valium to keep him out of her way, so she could clean up his mess like she always had. Cliff

Paulson was in the thick of lawyers, trouble, and bankruptcy. It looked like Brandon Paulson might be able to walk away clean.

I wondered about the texts Brandon had sent me. He lured me to Hunther so he could blackmail Trevor, but had he also wanted his parents to face justice? He set this in motion; he had to know I would expose his parents.

Desiree got probation. All of her crimes, she claimed, she'd done because Pierce had threatened her. She was still working at Aldi's. Her attempted breaking and entering charge had been dropped too, like she'd predicted.

Sinclaire mailed me a flash drive, and I passed it along to Holly. She worked with a journalist to tell the Paulson story. Two more of Dr. Paulson's patients came forward and claimed they'd been manipulated and mistreated.

I wasn't sure Holly and I would keep in touch once I moved back to Chicago, but I was OK with that and I thought she was too.

My goals were meager. Forgive myself for the trouble I'd caused. Forgive myself for lacking self-identity. *Change your narrative*. Forgive and forgive.

We have three kittens. Mildy, Ninja, and Jellybean.

"Now that we have pets, you can't leave me," Trevor said.

"I never would."

I wouldn't divorce you even if your sixteen-year-old self thought my mother murdered your first love and you beat up my brother and painted our house's windows with deer blood and your current self got blackmailed into smuggling venomous reptiles.

I wouldn't say this aloud because Trevor was struggling to forgive himself too. But damn, that's a creative one, isn't it? Truth was always stranger than fiction.

79

After Christmas, Holly mailed me a box. She'd finally finished going through Mom's stuff. When it arrived, I locked myself in the bathroom with a pair of scissors, sat on the floor, took a deep breath, and opened it.

There were a few ribbons from art contests I'd won, a photo of my soccer team, a few pictures I'd drawn for my mom. A still life of fruit. A curled-up cat. They weren't bad. Lots of photos. I studied them, brushed my thumb over their glossy surface. There were pieces of torn notebook paper. Maybe pages out of my mom's journal. Honestly, she didn't seem like the type. Maybe these were letters she'd written. I started with the paper on top.

Oh, Heather. I was tired. Sad. Worn to the point of not caring. Depressed. I was depressed. I have depression. That's why I went to see him. I was tired and sad all the time and then I couldn't stop thinking of Dawn Young. Poor Dawn with her own weak mother, poor Dawn, another girl who would be chewed up and spit out, a girl who had so much potential, so much talent—oh, Jesus, Mary, Joseph, you should have seen her paintings of Crooked Bridge over the river, sunset like a gorgeous cocktail.

I'm sorry I let you down, my littlest one. I didn't do enough for you. I didn't teach you how to stand up for yourself. I didn't give you enough attention, make you feel as special as you were, are.

I hope when you grow up you can forgive me my anger, my drinking. My stupid vodka. I'm drinking it now, can you believe it? Ha. Of course you can. It polishes the sharp edges, dims my blaring failures. I was the one who went to him. I got myself into that mess.

I hope you find love and you have children of your own and you do better than I did. You are better than me. You have that wide-open mind, that running-wild, blurred-lines imagination. I love that about you. I have always loved that about you.

AUTHOR'S NOTE

Fair warning—if you happen to read authors' notes before you read their novels—this note is a bit of a spoiler to my book!

My novels come from a mingling of ideas, usually three or four, that my mind has been kneading separately for some time. These ideas touch edges, and then, what do you know, they are suddenly inseparable. Like making dough.

The primary inspiration for this novel was the PBS Frontline documentary, *The Search For Satan* (1995). I stumbled upon this particular Frontline episode years ago, and the women's horror stories stuck with me. I am in awe of medical doctors, nurses, psychiatrists, and psychologists for their dedication to helping people's bodies and minds. Even so, it's crucial to remember the individual stories of medical ignorance and cruelty that stain human history because they continue to reoccur. If your interest is sparked by this documentary, as mine was, tuck yourself in with your laptop and get cozy—there is a rabbit hole waiting for you online. I've slid down a few of those dark tunnels, and they are filled with conspiracy, manipulation, and dangerous personalities. Truth is typically stranger than fiction. Using a true story as inspiration oddly carries the risk of going too far and making the novel unbelievable. I hope I pulled this off.

And no, my cats didn't come from *Tiger King*. You were wondering, right? My first draft was nearly complete when that show released. A decade ago, I watched *The Elephant in the Room* (2010), another documentary, this one about exotic pets in Ohio. This documentary is something special and, if you have the time, I highly recommend it. I knew the topic would rear its furry head (and sharp teeth) in one of my books, and this was the one. In my first draft, they were tigers. I changed them to cougars in a later draft. Tigers are more deadly, but cougars have killed their fair share of humans. Especially cougars that live in unnatural conditions with unknowledgeable owners. Another interesting thing about cougars: they don't roar like other big cats. Instead, they purr, chirp, and scream. My dog and I had a good time listening to cougar vocalizations on YouTube. I set the story in Wisconsin because the exotic pet laws remain looser there.

There were a few other ideas that went into the dough of this story, but they were merely questions I wanted to explore. Things like autobiographical memory loss, birth order, and using the word "toxic" to describe people and families.

I didn't include an author's note in my first book. I wish I had. I love hearing where authors get their ideas, so I decided to pull back the curtain for this one. Anyway, I hope you enjoyed the show.

ACKNOWLEDGEMENTS

Insane gratitude to my patient editor, Sophie Robinson, who saw enough drafts of this book to make her head spin. No doubt she grew weary of my emails, declaring, "Just a few more edits!" Thank you for your fabulous ideas and for steering me in the right direction. And for letting me be stubborn on occasion.

Thank you to Natasha Qureshi for your editorial insights, and to Hayley Shepherd and Saskia Dunn for catching my mistakes.

To my entire Titan team, along with the team at Penguin Random House, thank you for your enthusiasm and tireless effort to get my books in front of readers. Special appreciation to Polly Grice, Sarah Mather, and Katharine Carroll in publicity. And to Julia Lloyd, for nailing the cover! And, I loved the creative Christmas cards, Polly and Hannah.

Barbara Poelle, agent extraordinaire, comedian, and friend, thank you for championing my books. Gratitude to Heather Baror-Shapiro and Danny Baror for foreign rights.

The most delightful part of my publishing journey has been becoming part of this phenomenal author community. It is a friendly and nurturing environment full of comic relief, humility, reassurance, and cheerleading. For all the friends I've made here – I love you people from the bottom of my heart. Special appreciation to the authors who've said cool things about my books: Samantha M. Bailey, Mary Kubica, P.J. Vernon, Hank Phillippi Ryan, Samantha Downing, Jeneva Rose, D.J. Palmer, Vanessa Lillie, Megan Collins, Wendy Walker, Sherri Smith, Alice Blanchard, Jamie Freveletti, Joanna Schaffhausen, Sophie Littlefield, E.G. Scott, and Lisa Unger.

To the librarians, booksellers, bloggers, and bookstagrammers, you are treasured. I have enjoyed spending time with the inspiring Bookstagram community this past year, loving your clever videos, beautiful photos, and thoughtful posts. Much appreciation to all who have reached out to me. So many of you have become friends.

To all of my friends who have been shouting out my book to everyone they know, I owe you.

To my mom and mother-in-law, sisters, in-laws, nieces, and nephews, your unconditional support means the world. I've got my vaccine appointments scheduled, and hopefully, by the time this book is in bookstores, I'll have hugged all of you.

I began *Confess to Me* before the pandemic but finished the first draft (along with countless drafts and edits) during the pandemic, with my three kids doing school from home. Woodworking earmuffs became part of my writing costume and working routine. Occasionally I escaped to the car to meet deadlines. Thank you to Marc, Ed, Jon, and Sam for picking up my slack, helping with the cooking, dishes, cleaning the flooded basement, fixing the broken refrigerator, and with everything else that went sideways this year. I know you older kids are sick of your parents. I am sick of us too. Thank you for sticking it out and keeping your heads screwed on. Little One, thank you for the cuddles and Dog-Man comedy. Marc, thank you for your enduring love and support. My books are dark, but my life with you four is all light.

Love to Indy, the glue of this household, everybody's best furry friend, hug-partner, and confidant. Good dog.

Lastly, immense gratitude to the readers. You make the book-world go round.

Sharon Doering lives in the Chicago area with her husband, Marc, their three kids, and a peculiarly civilized dog, Indy. In her other life, she was a science professor, a biotech stock analyst, and a xenotransplantation researcher. She has also been a good waitress, a mediocre bartender, and a terrible maid. Sharon is working on her next novel.

@DoeringSharon